THE OATHBOUND WIZARD

Christopher Stasheff

$\ggg\ggg\ggg\ggg\ggg\ggg\ggg\ggg\ggg$

THE
OATHBOUND
WIZARD

$\ggg\ggg\ggg\ggg\ggg\ggg\ggg\ggg\ggg$

A DEL REY BOOK · BALLANTINE BOOKS
New York

A Del Rey Book
Published by Ballantine Books

ISBN 0-345-34713-7

TEXT DESIGN BY DEBBY JAY

Manufactured in the United States of America

First Edition: March 1993

CONTENTS

THE OATHBOUND WIZARD

CHAPTER 1

Lovers' Quarrel

The horse was steaming, and Matt was fuming. They clattered in over the drawbridge and past the guards with nothing but a perfunctory grunt. They exchanged a glance and shook their heads.

Matt pulled up by the stables and tossed the reins to the first groom who came running, then turned away on his heel, stalking toward the towering bulk of the keep. The groom stared after him, shocked—the Lord Wizard was unfailing in his politeness, with always time for a cheerful word or two.

But Her Majesty's Wizard was anything but cheerful, and in no mood to be polite to anyone, least of all Her Majesty. The fact that he had to ride a mere horse only made things worse. Of course, he had had to be content with ordinary mounts since his dragon friend Stegoman had gone gallivanting off with his other friend Sir Guy on an errand of errantry, a gallant mission to save the kingdom of Ibile from the wretched stew of sorcery it had simmered into over the last two hundred years—and, at the moment, Matt wished most ardently that he had gone with them. The danger seemed of relatively little importance compared to the simple fact of a mission worth undertaking. Not like this last little fracas, which . . . !

He stormed up to the doors of the royal apartments, but as he laid hold of the handle, a sentry leaped forward, albeit with trepidation. "Nay, my Lord Wizard! Her Majesty hath not given leave!"

"Too right she hasn't!" Matt snarled. Alisande seemed to have developed an aversion to Matt's company lately, probably because every time he saw her, he pressed her to set a date for their wedding. But they had been engaged for three years now, so it wasn't surprising that Matt was getting a little impatient. It was time to have it out with her. He yanked the door open and stormed into the corridor, trailing a howling wake of horrified sentries and servants.

The queen looked up from her writing, blue eyes wide in surprise, then in outrage.

It almost stopped Matt—not her rage, but her beauty. The oval face was framed in a cascade of blond hair, unbound here in her private apartments, and set off perfectly by the mauve of her casual gown.

Almost.

"Why don't you just *say* you don't want me around anymore?" Matt slapped his gloves down on the table. "That last trip was something any village magician could have taken care of. No, strike that—he would have sent his apprentice!"

"I did not deem a plague of locusts a trivial matter, Lord Wizard!" Alisande said in a voice that would have frozen penguins. "It may be of little moment to you, but the poor peasant folk thereabout thought it disastrous!"

"Sure, because *their* village magician had dropped dead two years ago, and their baron was too cheap to hire a replacement! And don't tell me you didn't know that!"

"Assuredly, I did—and thought it your office to see to it! What, must I undertake every smallest matter myself? Have I none to aid me?"

"Oh, come off it with the wounded violet routine! You could have told me why the baron didn't have a magician, and I would have sent one out."

Alisande's gaze faltered. "Mayhap, yet still 'twas thy duty to see to his installation."

"And just conveniently put myself out of your way for a fortnight, so you didn't have to worry about my importuning you!"

Alisande tried to bring her gaze back up to his, but didn't quite manage it. "Wherefore ought I find concern . . ."

"Because I keep pressing you to set the date! Which is scarcely surprising, considering how long we've been engaged! But every time I bring up the subject of marriage, you keep putting me off—and off, and off. Meanwhile, I hang around here like your tame poodle—just another ornament for your palace, never getting to do anything I really want to do!"

"Not what you wish! Pray Heaven any of us could do what we wished! And what is it you wish to do?"

"Marry you!"

Alisande took a deep breath, fighting for patience and trying to still her beating heart. "It shall come some day, Lord Wizard."

"Yes, I understand it will. I seem to remember some sort of promise to that effect . . ."

"Promise?" Alisande's gaze sharpened. "I made no promise!"

"Oh?" Matt cocked his head to the side. "Then what would you call those words we exchanged on Breden Plain?"

"My appeal, and your response. As I mind me, 'twas yourself who did give promise that day, not I—and somewhat unwillingly at that."

"Well, I'm more than willing now!" Matt swallowed down outrage. "And you may not have actually given me a promise, but there certainly seemed to be something implied."

Alisande tossed her head impatiently. "In a moment of weakness, I gave you a kiss, naught more—and, Lord Wizard, a kiss is not a promise."

Matt held his face impassive while he absorbed the hurt. Alisande saw, and quailed within, but met wooden face with flint.

Finally, Matt said, "If that kiss happened in a moment of weakness, then you have a weakness for me—which means that, underneath your mask of duty, you're really in love with me, and hopefully, want to spend your life with me."

Alisande bridled, the more so because it was true. "You overreach yourself, Lord Wizard. Yet whether I love you or not, I may not act upon it."

Matt just stared at her.

Then he said, "Let me get this straight. You love me, but you can't do anything about it?"

Alisande kept her face hard. "You must needs know that a queen cannot marry for love—but only for the good of the kingdom, using her marriage as a way of forming an alliance, or in other ways benefiting her people."

Matt felt his stomach sink—he did indeed know. So, of course, he tried to fend off the vision of a lifetime of hanging around the court as the bachelor least likely to succeed, by going on the offensive. "That means that if I were the king of some other country, you'd marry me?"

"Aye, if the goodwill of that land were of need to my own."

"Okay—so I'll go win a kingdom." Matt started to turn away.

"Speak not so foolishly, Lord Wizard!" Alisande snapped, with her first hint of real temper. "Kingdoms are not to be had for the asking! To say such is nigh to sacrilege!"

"Oh, come on!" Matt turned back. "There has to be a kingdom somewhere near that has a rotten king, and needs a new one."

"Aye, both Ibile and Allustria—yet I do well but to ward against them, with all my horses and all my men! How should we conquer them?"

"I'll find a way."

"You cannot!"

"I swear to God I will!" Matt shouted. "I'll kick that Ibilian monster-monarch off his throne or die trying!"

Alisande blanched, and the throne room was suddenly as silent as a tomb, even the guards staring in scandalized shock. Matt glanced at them out of the corners of his eyes, and something inside him said, in a very tiny voice, *Oh. I should not have said that, should I?*

Then Alisande caught her breath and shouted, "Guards! Seize that man! Bind and gag him! Chain him to the thickest wall in my deepest dungeon!"

Matt stared, unbelieving. His one true love? Sending him into solitary?

Then the guards hit, and he believed. Two men hugged his arms and two more his legs, picking him up bodily, ignoring his struggles. He opened his mouth to shout a spell, but somebody's glove jammed in between his teeth. Enraged, he tried to spit it out, but someone else was already wrapping a sash around his face and tying it tight. He couldn't speak, he couldn't gesture!

"Well done," Alisande said, discreetly disregarding the guards' ashen faces. "Now bear him to the dungeons, and chain him to the wall. Then mount guard over him, inside the cell and out—and if he should even attempt to speak, give him so shrewd a knock alongside the head that he loses consciousness again. Oh, be sure, he must not speak! Or he will cast a spell!"

Matt felt his stomach sink, as the guards turned him about and headed for the stairway. Alisande was right, unfortunately—and the guards had hit too fast for him to get his mouth working. He was well and truly trussed this time—and not liable to get out of it.

But his one true love! How could she *do* such a thing to him? Humiliate him so? Not to mention the discomfort!

Easy—she didn't love him. He'd just been a valuable asset. A heavy mass seemed to weigh down upon his spirits, as the guards hauled him down, down through the keep and into the dark of the dungeon. Dark, yes, but no darker than the mood that descended over his soul.

CHAPTER 2

Free Thinker

The blacksmith finished riveting the manacles chaining Matt's wrists behind him and stepped back with a look of trepidation. "You know we wouldn't have done this on our own, Your Lordship."

Matt glowered at him, but he couldn't keep it up. Reluctantly, he nodded. It wasn't just fear of his magic—the common folk all liked him too well to do anything against him. Most of them, anyway. He gargled something that sounded like grudging acceptance.

Relief washed the smith's face. "Godspeed you, Lord Wizard. Heaven knows, you have served her Majesty too well to deserve such as this!"

"'Tis not for you to say, Smith!" the captain of the guard snapped. "Out with you, now. 'Tis enough for you to know the Lord Wizard will not seek revenge."

Matt muttered and nodded. He couldn't really blame a man for doing his job properly. He shrugged.

The smith broke into a grateful smile, hoisted his portable anvil, and went out the door.

"We shall leave you now, milord," the captain of the guard said. "Yet I, too, would have you know, 'tis not by my wish you are here."

Matt didn't know whether he was trying to mend his fences, or give support—but again he shrugged the apology away. The man was just doing as he was bound to do, by his oath of service. Alisande was his queen, after all.

The captain seemed faintly relieved. Had he understood Matt's thought so well as that? But no, Matt hadn't recited a telepathy spell. How could he, bound and gagged?

"Even so, I mislike coming between a man and his leman," the other guard growled.

Matt understood—domestic disputes were always rough on the cops. *But don't worry, boys, I won't hold it against you,* he thought as hard as he could.

Again, the look of relief. "Is there aught to make you comfortable, milord, ere we go?"

Matt nodded, working his mouth around his gag, then miming the act of drinking water.

"Aye." The captain hefted a wineskin. "There must be two of us for when you wish to drink henceforth, must there not? Unstop his mouth, soldier—and stand ready to smite him if he should speak a single word."

The guard nodded as he untied the sash, face hard. "I would I did not have to, Lord Wizard, yet such is the queen's command."

The gag came out, and Matt drew a long breath of clean air with relief. The captain held out the wineskin, and Matt leaned back and drew a long draught. Eyeing his jailers warily, he decided not to try speaking even to thank them, and opened his mouth with a sigh.

It was a new and more comfortable gag they put in—no doubt the captain wanted his glove back—but to say a gag is "more comfortable" is to say a torture is "less painful." Matt resigned himself and slumped back against the wall with a sigh. It was going to be a long existence, with a very dry mouth and aching jaws.

The guard finished tying the gag back in place, Matt sat down with a groan, and the captain nodded, turning to go. "May all be as well for you as it may, Lord Wizard."

The door slammed shut, but there was still a torch, since the remaining guard needed light. After all, there wasn't much point stationing him there with his short cudgel, if he couldn't see whether or not Matt had worked his gag loose.

And Matt was certainly in a mood to try, feeling angry, vengeful, betrayed, rejected, and bewildered. Where had he gone wrong? How had he lost Alisande's love? Or had he ever had it in the first place? Was it class paranoia, the nobleman's antipathy toward the social climber? Or was it just friction between man and mate, telling her what she wanted to hear but in the wrong way?

No, it couldn't be that. He had told her he loved her in fifty different ways, fifty times at least in the last three years, some of them as ardent and romantic as any woman could want—and she had certainly responded; he could have sworn she was burning to answer his fervor with her own. But something had held her back . . .

> Alas, my love, you do me wrong,
> To treat me so discourteously,
> When I have loved you oh, so long,
> Delighting in your company!

She had even worn green sleeves when they were questing together!

The guard shifted nervously and glanced down at Matt, commiserating. Matt felt an irrational flash of gratitude toward the man, and tried to smile reassuringly. But his mind strayed back to Alisande—didn't it always? He tried to pull himself out of the slough of despond, but the betrayal weighed on his spirits too heavily.

> What ails thee, captive Knight at arms,
> Compelled to enforced loitering;
> Where niter gathers on stone walls,
> And no birds sing.
>
> I saw pale kings, and princes too,
> Pale warriors, death-pale were they all,
> Who cried—"La Belle Dame Sans Merci
> Hath thee in thrall!"

Again, the guard turned to him, and this time his expression would have done credit to a bloodhound. Matt tried to smile bravely, but he wasn't really up to it.

This was ridiculous! Here he was, just making the guard and himself both miserable. He had to jolt himself out of this self-pity and get back in action! It was a time to be doing, not moping!

Do what?

Good question. In Merovence, magic worked by chanting poetry, sometimes reinforced by gestures—and he couldn't chant very well if his mouth was stuffed with a gag. Gesturing was possible with chains on his wrists, but somewhat limited. Besides, gestures couldn't do anything alone.

> For a life to dwell
> In a dungeon cell
> Growing thin and wizened
> In a solitary prison . . .

He broke off with a shudder. He had a momentary vision of his future . . .

My hair is gray, but not with years,
Nor grew it white
In a single night
As men's have grown from sudden fears.

The guard sniffed and wiped a tear as he glanced at Matt out of the corner of his eye. Matt plucked up his spirits to wink, and take a playful kick at the man's knee with the ankle that was not fastened to the wall. The guard looked surprised, then grinned down. "Eh, your Lordship! I should ha' known naught would keep 'ee down for long!"

Matt winked again, though he felt like crying, before his attention strayed back to his dilemma. Finally, he began to feel indignant, a very healthy sign. Definitely better than moping. The ignominy of it! He, the topmost wizard in the land—thanks to all the verses he knew that this land had never heard of—chained in dungeon vile and not able to do a thing about it! And all because Alisande had been quick enough to think of a gag before he did! She may have tired of him, but she wasn't about to let him go—oh, no! Salt him away in storage in case he suited her whim again! How like a woman, always to want a new beau for her string!

For a moment, his resentment submerged in admiration of her. What a woman! Such presence of mind, such quickness of wit, to realize in a split second that, gagged, he couldn't work magic, and so couldn't escape. Such determination, such tenacity, such selfishness!

Well, that wasn't really fair. Her kingdom came before herself, in her own mind—that's why she was a good monarch. But could he really manage having a wife who thought her kingdom was more important than her husband?

She appeared again before his mind's eye, and he knew in a moment that he could. After all, that devotion to duty was part of what made her admirable.

But did she always have to be so damned right?

Yes, she did—at least, in public matters. The "Divine Right of Kings" really worked, in this universe. Nice to know he ranked as a public issue. On the other hand, it might have been nice if, to her, he'd been more than a national asset.

Or was he? Come to think of it, if she was in love with him, it was a personal matter—and, in personal matters, her judgment could be flawed.

The old scientific instinct stirred in him. How about the empirical test? After all, who knew for sure that he couldn't escape?

Everyone, that's who. In this universe, magic worked—and it worked by poetry. But a spell had to be recited aloud in order for it to work—everyone knew that!

His spirits slumped again and, for the first time in three years, he found himself wishing ardently that he was back in the old, familiar, dead-end college-campus life he'd known before.

> I am a man of constant sorrow,
> I've seen trouble all my days.
> I'm going back to East Virginia,
> The place where I was born and raised.

The guard turned to him, startled, alarmed. Matt frowned up at him. What was there to be alarmed about?

Matt's going.

Excitement spun through him. The guard had picked up his sadness before—that's why he'd been looking sympathetic. And he was resonating Matt's feelings of longing to go, now!

And why not? Matt had been thinking in verses!

Then why didn't all his thoughts make spells happen?

Because they usually weren't in verse—and when they were, they were fleeting verses like these, all emotion with no action, no imperative!

So if he did silently say a verse with an imperative . . .

But everyone knew a spell had to be recited aloud.

Sure—but just because everyone knew it, didn't always mean it was true.

Matt set himself and tried to think of the verse that he had used to free himself and Alisande from imprisonment in this very castle, those long three years ago.

> I know a bank whereon the wild thyme blows,
> Where oxlips and the nodding violet grows,
> Quite over-canopied with luscious woodbine,
> With sweet musk-roses, and with eglantine.
> There shall I fly, to celebrate the light,
> Freed in these flowers with dances of delight.

He waited expectantly for the disorientation of physical projection, waiting, waiting . . .

Disappointed.

He glowered up at the guard, feeling an irrational resentment of the man for still being there. Apparently verses *did* have to be spoken out loud.

Then a still, small voice seemed to speak within him, encouraging, but with a suspicion that some other power was operating here, that his spells would have to be in harmony with that other power before they could work.

It made sense. He knew very well that he would have gone down in defeat more than once, if his magic hadn't been supported by the spiritual guidance of Saint Moncaire, the patron of Merovence. And if Saint Moncaire had other plans for him right now than just breaking free to go wandering around feeling sorry for himself . . .

On the other hand, did he really want to do Saint Moncaire's work for him again?

Well, he could at least find out what the contract said before he signed it. He threw himself on the figurative mercies of the angels, asking where they wanted him to go.

The answer welled up in him, feeling uncomfortably like a compulsion. But about all you can do for a geas is go where it tells you, so Matt shrugged in surrender and recited an old folk hymn:

"Servant, go where I send thee!"
"How shall I send me, Lord?"
"Well, I'm going to send thee one by one,
    One for a little bitty baby,
    Was born, born, born in Bethle—"

Light glared, and he found himself somewhere else entirely. This time *he* stayed still, but his stomach flipped over. He staggered, taking a deep breath against nausea, and put out a still-manacled hand to steady himself.

He felt rough bark beneath his palm. He turned, surprised, to see a tree behind him, and decided he wasn't in the dungeon anymore! He was free, in the sunshine and the open air! He took a deep breath of breeze, grinned wide, and looked about him.

Then he saw his surroundings, and his stomach felt a little queasy again.

CHAPTER 3

Forward, Lady!

"Yet there must be some way in which a vow may be revoked, my Lord Archbishop! Can Heaven truly wish a man to act upon words spoken in rash passion?"

"It can," the Archbishop said, with a sad smile. "'Tis therefore we must be chary of our words, Majesty, and not swear oaths in vain."

They were still in the great hall, the sunlight striking through the stained glass of the western windows in tints of rose and blue, making the flagstones glow—but those colors seemed, to Alisande, to be the embers of her hopes. "But to court death and damnation, Lord Archbishop! Surely Heaven cannot wish a man to do so!"

"As to the danger of death . . ." The Archbishop turned thoughtful, then slowly nodded. "I can see that Heaven might wish it so—if our good Lord thought the man had some sure chance of succeeding in his holy purpose. We must all do God's work on earth, Majesty, as much as he does want of us, in such fashion as we may. The stronger must do greater tasks—and mayhap this is Lord Matthew's." The "Lord Matthew" stuck in his throat, but he forced it out. "And as to the danger of damnation, why! Does not each of us walk in that danger every moment of our lives, Majesty? And each of us is tempted, but none beyond his strength to resist. Be assured, if God has sent . . . *Lord* Matthew into a place of such temptation, He will give your wizard strength enough to resist."

"That is cold comfort," Alisande said, morose—but the Archbishop could see she was at least a little reassured. Then she looked up at him with a scowl. "Yet you have no need to be so cheered at the thought of his absence!"

The anger of a monarch stabbed like a sword; the Archbishop's heart skipped a beat in fright. Nevertheless, he spoke up bravely. "Pardon, Majesty—yet this self-exile is the most hopeful news that I have heard since you came once again to this throne."

"Hopeful!" Alisande spat.

"Hopeful," the Archbishop said firmly, drawing himself up. "That the man who so strongly aided you in casting out the forces of evil from this your kingdom should now be sworn to a quest to overthrow the vile sorcerer-king of Ibile? Aye, 'tis cause for great hope! Nay, I cannot truly be sorrowful to hear such news."

"Nor to think that this candidate for royal consort may soon be dead," Alisande said, acid in her tone.

"Your Majesty truly must make some provision for the succession," the Archbishop answered. "I entreat you! For what should hap to us all an you were to die before your time, without an heir?"

He thought he had done a rather good job of avoiding the question.

The guard heard the boom of imploding air, and turned to stare at the place where Matt had been. The manacles jangled, empty, against the stone. He gazed wide-eyed for a moment, then pushed his jaw back into place, heaved a sigh, and turned away to knock on the wicket and call for the captain of the guard, shaking his head.

The captain of the guard duly reported to the seneschal, who wasn't having any and told him it was his job, so the captain settled his sword belt, squared his shoulders, and turned to face the throne room with a heavy heart, reflecting that he hadn't really thought he was going to get out of it anyway.

"The brightest hope for my providing a succession, has just been cast into my dungeon, Lord Archbishop," Alisande retorted. "An you do wish me to bear an heir, you had best bethink you of ways to assure his return!"

The Archbishop seemed dubious. "Misunderstand me not, Majesty—Matthew Mantrell is a good man and noble. Natheless, he is not of royal blood."

"And is therefore unfit to be consort to a queen," Alisande finished for him. "Yet it is ironic, milord, that though that doubt has lingered in my heart these three years, I find it banished of a sudden—but only by the knowledge that Lord Matthew may be taken from me!"

The Archbishop felt his heart sink.

"Nay," the queen said, "be assured, I'll marry no one else—and surely, his service to the crown, and his finding favor in the eyes of Saint Moncaire, should have made me see his worthiness! He is the hope of Merovence, now and in the future." And of herself, she added silently. "I prithee, Lord Archbishop, tell me this understanding I have gained is the accomplishment God wished, by this vow of Lord Matthew's. There must be some way to negate his oath—for surely, he did not truly intend to take arms against Ibile, alone!"

The Archbishop sighed, with a sad shake of his head. "Majesty, I cannot—for why else would a wizard, one who knows the nature of geasa and compulsions, have so bound himself?"

"He had forgot the power of words, here in Merovence," Alisande replied, "for they have no such strength in that other world he hails as home. In the heat of his passion and his anger, he thought words to be idle, only an expression of his feelings."

"Would you have me believe that the highest wizard in the land had forgot that what he swore to, in this land of Merovence, he was bound to?"

"Aye." Alisande's smile curdled. "If we had told him so, he would have protested that we did take his words too literally."

The Archbishop nodded, understanding. "Yet on reflection, Majesty, he would know that was the precise nature of the problem."

"Problem!" Alisande looked up, the color coming back into her face. "Why, 'tis but a riddle after all, is't not? And has a solution like to any other!"

"Majesty?" The Archbishop definitely didn't like the sound of what he was hearing.

"He cannot be bound by that oath! For three years ago, he did swear to serve me! How then can he leave my presence, if I do require his service here? For I most earnestly do!"

The Archbishop pursed his lips. "You mean that, at the worst, his two oaths might counter one another?"

"Nay, better—I mean that the second can have no effect, for it cannot displace the first!" Alisande actually smiled. "He cannot undertake a quest unless I command it—and I do not."

But the Archbishop was giving her the sad smile again, and shaking his head. "I regret, but I must inform you, Majesty, that the vow cannot be broken, unless Heaven and the saints really do not wish

Lord Matthew to attempt the purification of Ibile. In truth, if God did wish, this later vow would overbear the first—yet I think the occasion does not arise."

Alisande's scowl was enough to make his heart quail. "How so?"

"Why," the Archbishop said, "Ibile has ever been a threat to the welfare of Merovence, to her borders and her people, since ever the first sorcerer Grosso overthrew the rightful king of Ibile and brought the reign of evil down upon the whole kingdom. Nay, Majesty, by seeking to fulfill this oath, Lord Matthew does not only God's work, but yours also!"

"Yet it is not my will!" she cried, as if it were torn out of her.

"It is Heaven's, though." The firmness of authority came back into his voice. "And you are sworn to uphold the will of Heaven, Majesty, so far as God reveals it to you."

Alisande slumped, a moment's despair evident in every line of her body.

The Archbishop acted almost automatically, reaching out to the aid of a soul in need. "Be of good cheer, Majesty. Lord Matthew goes not alone into this kingdom of wickedness—he goes with the might of Heaven to strengthen him. I doubt not that Heaven will give him all the aid it can, of saints and angels, for they must surely want him to erase from Ibile this foul blot of a king, yea, Gordogrosso and all his minions."

"Yet will he prevail?" she moaned. "For Heaven works through us, Lord Archbishop, in this world—but so can Hell, if we wish it to. Has Matthew enough goodness to stand against the sorcerers? For he was never a saint!"

"He may become so, in this striving," the Archbishop pointed out, "or come much closer to Heaven, at least. Besides, Majesty, be mindful—if Matthew Mantrell can topple Gordogrosso and purge the wickedness from Ibile, he will most surely have proved his worthiness to be a lord—and your consort."

Alisande lifted her head, a strange light coming into her eyes. "True," she said, "if he still will love me."

The captain of the guard stepped through the archway, caught her eye, and bowed.

Alisande's mouth went dry; somehow, she knew he had bad news. "Approach, Captain!"

The young knight strode forward, trying not to look for a place to hide.

"What news have you for me?" she demanded.

The Captain bowed, and reported, wooden-faced, "Your Majesty, the Lord Wizard is not in his cell."

Alisande took it well, you had to say that for her—she sat still as a statue for a minute, then asked, "Was he bound?"

"Aye, Majesty."

"And gagged?"

"Aye, Majesty!"

Then Matthew had managed the impossible again, working a spell without speaking it aloud. Admiration for the man welled up within her, with an almost covetous longing for him—but too late, too late. Still, she managed to push the thought aside while she nodded crisply and said, "Thank you, my captain. You may go—and the rest of your guardsmen with you."

"I thank Your Majesty." And the captain meant it, nodding to his soldiers with relief and turning to march out. They followed unhappily, feeling that they should have done something more—but who could have, against the Lord Wizard?

Alisande turned to the Archbishop and inclined her head. "I thank you for your words of comfort, milord. And I will entreat you to pray for Lord Matthew."

"With every Mass." The Archbishop bowed and turned to go—he knew a dismissal when he heard one.

The great doors closed behind him, and Alisande let herself collapse, with the fleeting, vagrant thought that Matthew could at least have waited until after she had dined, so that he wouldn't have spoiled her appetite.

Then the fact of his absence really hit her, and she felt the anger mount. Good, good! It would help her through this, might almost drown the feelings of desertion and remorse . . .

But what else could she have done? Really? As queen, she was blessed—cursed?—with Divine Right, always knowing which course of action was best for the welfare of her people, and never hesitating to take it—even if any action would prove useless. It was just her bad luck that what had been the best decision for the monarch had been the worst for the woman.

Or was it the other way around?

CHAPTER 4

No Refund, No Return

Matt stared at the unfamiliar landscape around him, stumbled, then caught his balance and managed to right himself. Still agog, he decided he could see why magicians said their spells aloud. It definitely gave better results!

Then it hit him—well or poorly, the spell had worked! Even without reciting it aloud—the gag was still in his mouth. It had worked!

Why?

No time to figure it out now; he filed it away for analysis when there would be a moment of leisure—i.e., one not filled with trying to stay alive—and got down to the serious business of getting that gag out of his mouth.

His hands were chained behind his back, and his mouth was filled with dry cloth. Free his hands, and he could untie the gag—or free his mouth, and he could make up a spell to get rid of the chains. Which to do first?

Make sure there were no enemies about to pounce on him—that did kind of take first priority. "Enemies" included mountain lions, wolves, and other mountain dwellers that might consider him to be just the right snack. He turned around slowly and saw that he was alone on a hillside. He relaxed a little—then realized that he hadn't had any trouble turning. His ankle had been manacled to the wall, but apparently the manacle hadn't come with him.

That made sense—the end of it being attached to the wall, it counted as part of the castle he had been trying to get away from.

Therefore, it had stayed behind—but his wrist chains, being attached only to him, had come along.

Well, he was grateful for every little bit of progress. Free feet were better than nothing. Then a light bulb turned on inside his head, showing him a scene of himself as a child playing the old game of trying to step through the circle of his own arms, with his hands clasped together. As he remembered, he'd managed it—but he'd been considerably more agile at ten than he was at twenty-seven.

Or was he? His first few weeks in Merovence had put him back into very good shape, and he hadn't lost much of his muscle tone in the last three years—Alisande had kept him very busy going from place to place in the kingdom, troubleshooting and wiping out left-over pockets of sorcery. Most of it, he had to admit, had been necessary, at least for the first two years. The third year, though, had been full of make-work errands. The memory galled him, especially since he was pretty sure what had instigated them—Alisande's need to be away from him.

The thought scored his heart, so he thrust it aside and got down to experimenting. Carefully, trying not to lose his balance, he bent his knees, getting his wrists as low as he could and stretching the chain as far as it would go. Then, slowly, he lifted his left foot and tried to push it over the links.

His toe caught.

For a second, he teetered, madly trying to keep his balance, then fell crashing to the ground. He lay still for a second, trying to contain the burst of anger—it wouldn't do any good to let it out at the moment, anyway.

Why not just make up a spell? If he could get out of a prison, he could get out of a chain.

Two reasons. The first was that the transportation spell had worked well enough, but not perfectly. In fact, Matt's spells frequently tended not to have quite the effects he had planned, anyway, and the imperfections that came from reciting the verse silently might have very painful results. The second was that magic had a way of attracting the attention of other magic-workers, and Matt would just as soon have his hands and mouth free before having to try to deal with any wizardly tracers Alisande might manage to have her second-class magicians try on him.

Or any hostile locals, for that matter . . .

On the other hand, now that he was on the ground, he had no balance to lose. The idea made sense—so much so that he thought he should have tried lying down in the first place. Well, now that he had, voluntarily or not, he could try stepping through the chain with a bit more leisure. He pulled his left foot up, jamming his knee against his chest, and very carefully moved his toes past the chain. Then he straightened the leg—with a feeling of victory. Now, if he could just do it with his right . . . He rolled over onto his left side and slowly, carefully, raised his knee and pulled his right foot through. Then he sat up, smiling around his gag as he looked down at his hands, there in front of him. He felt an immense sense of accomplishment.

He stretched the chain tight again and lifted it over and down behind his head. His fingers pulled at the knot in the cloth. It wasn't easy—the guard had tied it to stay, as tightly as he could. A fingernail snapped, but Matt had needed to trim it, anyway—and, finally, the gag was off! He pulled the wad of cloth out of his mouth, spitting out lint, then working his mouth to bring saliva, moistening his tongue and lips. Finally, he opened his mouth again, to sigh with relief—and to recite a quick verse that made his manacles spring open and fall to the ground. Then, at last, he could stand up again, and really look about him.

Matt took a breath of cool air as he gazed at the high slope before him. Then he stilled—that air *had* been cool, hadn't it? Funny—it was high summer, in Merovence.

Therefore, he wasn't in Merovence.

The thought sent prickles along his scalp. The first spell—the one that *hadn't* worked—had been the same one he'd used when he'd spelled Alisande out of prison, three years before, and he'd still expected to wind up next to a little brook, under a canopy of musk roses, eglantine, and woodbine. This place, though, looked to be at a much higher altitude, and the evergreens certainly didn't resemble the deciduous bower he'd had in mind.

Well, you couldn't expect a spell that had only been thought, to be as effective as one that had been recited aloud, could you?

Or had somebody wanted him someplace else?

He went back to looking at the scenery, trying to ignore the hollowness in his stomach, and decided that the landscape was definitely uneven—not in quality, as pine forests and alpine meadows are always beautiful, but in terrain. He was hard put to find a horizontal line anywhere, and the ground rose up toward the edge of the sky like the back of a giant stegosaurus, shadowing half the little valley in which he stood.

Behind that back stood the sun.

He hauled his stomach back up from the gulf it was trying to sink into and reflected that it *could* be much later in the day—he could have traveled *really* far. But somehow, he doubted that he'd moved more than a few degrees in longitude—one time zone, at the most. He'd arrived at Alisande's castle right after dawn, and would have escaped no later than mid-morning. That meant the sun had still been in the east—so if it was on the far side of those peaks, he was on the western side of the mountains.

In Ibile. The kingdom of black magic.

He put the qualms behind him—he was the one who had said he was going to invade Ibile and capture its throne. In fact, he'd sworn it—and he couldn't blame the Powers That Be if they had taken him at his word. He should have been more careful with his language—in his anger, he'd fallen back into lifelong habits and used expressions that were a trifle more emphatic than they should have been. By the rules of this nutty universe, that meant he was bound to do what he'd said. Totally unfair, he decided, but not all that unjust. It was a great way to break a man of swearing, but it seemed a trifle extreme.

He put the issue aside and forced himself to smile, enjoying the simple pleasures of the moment, drinking in the wild beauty of the place, and he allowed himself to feel a bit of guilt over having left Alisande so suddenly. But only a little—he had to admit it had begun to pall on him, having a girlfriend who could handily order his head chopped off if she wanted to. The notion was decidedly intimidating, even though he knew Alisande would never do such a thing.

Unless it was in the best interests of her people, of course.

He grinned, his spirit feeling as though it had wings. These mountains were so free! He hadn't realized how confined he'd felt.

And soiled. Alisande might have been good and a force for right, but the forces of corruption were always at work, and the backbiting at court had been growing nastier lately. After only three years, too.

Well, he was out of it, now. He started walking up the valley.

The land rose up, and the woods opened out, until he could see that the path led up to a notch between peaks. At a guess, he was in the mountains that formed the border between Ibile and Merovence—the Pyrenees, in his own universe. Probably called that here, too. He stopped, looking about him, and saw a few fallen trees lying by the path. He went over to them and picked up a likely-looking one, held it up, and thumped it on the ground. It bent too easily for inch-and-a-half thick wood, even though it looked sound. He frowned and cracked it over his knee. It crumbled, and he nodded in vindication—rotten inside. He tossed it away, picked up another, and thumped its butt hard on the ground as he looked up at its twisted top. It was hooked and gnarled, but it held. Matt smiled in satisfaction and turned back to the path, then attacked the slope with his new staff in hand.

The problem, he reflected as he panted to the top, was that he hadn't had time to magic a horse away with him. He could conjure one to him, of course, but that would be just as good as putting up a sign that read "wizard here," if any of the magical brethren were looking—which they were bound to be; Alisande would surely waste no time hunting up a minor magus for a bloodhound. And, of course, not to mention the sorcerers of Ibile . . .

He wished he hadn't; the thought gave him a chill.

Of course, he didn't *have* to stay here.

Certainly the Powers of Right wouldn't hold him to an oath he'd made in anger, on the spur of the moment! Especially now that he'd had a chance to realize what he'd really gotten himself into.

Would they?

Surely not! So he could go back to Merovence easily, just by reciting the right spell! He thought one up, started to speak it—then paused, with the words on the tip of his tongue, remembering about Alisande's journeyman wizards being able to detect his use of magic—and Ibile's sorcerers as well.

Well, it wouldn't matter if he was out of there. He took a deep breath and chanted,

> "Send me back to Merovence,
> Where the flying songbirds dance,
> And the dawn comes up serenely,
> Giving sinners one more chance!"

He held himself braced, waiting for the momentary disorientation, for the sudden jolt of ground against his feet . . .

Nothing happened.

He swallowed against a sudden thickness in his throat and tried again. After all, maybe the Powers just didn't like his choice of destination.

> "Take me back to Bordestang,
> Where the swinging church bells rang.
> Let me stand by the cathedral
> Where the outdoor choir sang!"

He held himself braced and ready, knees flexed, breath held . . . Nothing, again.

He let his breath out in a sigh, relaxing and reluctantly admitting to himself that he wasn't going to get out of this one that easily. He'd been dumb enough to swear to unseat Ibile's evil tyrant, and Heaven had taken him at his word. He couldn't really complain.

Actually, he didn't dare. What might happen, if he let loose a stream of profanity about the situation? He was going to have to be very careful what he said from now on.

Well, if Heaven wouldn't help him get back to Merovence, he'd have to do it on his own. He turned toward the sun, noticed a trail that seemed to go more or less in the right direction, and set out toward the east—and Merovence.

He'd been hiking for an hour, and he could have sworn the mountainside hadn't come any closer. Optical illusion, no doubt—the roadside brush had been passing at a steady rate, and when he looked back, he saw a long trail of footprints.

Then he heard the shouting. And screaming. And the clash of arms.

He was sprinting before he knew it, lurching over the uneven ground, just barely avoiding the occasional pothole. The sound was coming from the other side of a hillock, off to the right of the path.

He darted up the side of the rise and saw the outcrop of scrub at the top. Discretion put the brakes on valor, and he dropped to his belly, wriggling up under the bushes, pushing them carefully aside till he could make out the scene below.

It was a little village of round huts walled with wattle and daub and roofed with flame. Every thatch burned, and the flames were starting down the walls. Two soldiers were still running from house to house with torches, laughing and touching the flame to anything that would start a blaze. Four other soldiers were catching women and girls as they ran out of the houses, herding them toward the village common, while a dozen more cut down the old men and big boys who were valiantly trying to hold off the soldiers with clubs— but sticks against swords stood no chance, and several grandfathers and a boy were down in pools of their own blood, while the others were on their knees, or staggering back, clutching wounds that spread red stains over their tunics. They had delayed the soldiers long enough, though—the men of the village were coming in from the fields at a run, their scythes waving.

The soldiers turned, their halberds flashing, and the men fell, bellowing in anguish, clutching at stumps of arms or welling gouges in their chests.

The four men on the round-up squad herded the women and girls into a circle.

Only four of the husbands still stood, so three soldiers turned away from the carnage to start sorting through the pile of pitiful possessions ransacked from the houses. The sergeant turned away, too, and started sorting through the women.

He pulled the younger women out, tossing them to his men. He seemed to have an unerring instinct for the unmarried. One young farmer saw, howled, "Dolores!" and turned, plunging toward her. A halberd flashed, and he rolled on the ground, his eyes glazing.

"Corin!" his sweetheart screamed, and ran toward him, but a soldier caught her and swung her about, catching the back of her head and planting his mouth over hers. She gave a muffled scream, writhing and striking at him. He lifted his head to laugh and ran a hand over her body.

The last farmer fell.

The soldiers had three of the women down, their skirts above their waists; they fumbled with the fastenings of their pants.

"You cannot!" a mother screamed, wrenching herself loose and dropping to her knees to try to shield her daughter. "She is too young!"

"Never too young!" The sergeant shoved her aside; she fell, sprawling. He guffawed, then bellowed, "We have been too long besieging your lord's castle, woman, and my men have grown bored. I mean to find them some diversion—and what could be better than raping virgins?"

"We are no virgins!" a terrified girl shrieked from the ground. "None of us in this village!"

"Why! Do ye hear that, Sergeant?" cried one of the men, with a gap-toothed grin. "Seems like we're invited."

"Aye. Never turn down hospitality, says I," the sergeant answered.

The girl screamed.

"She lied!" the mother cried, pale-faced. "All these lasses are virgins!"

"Why, the greater pleasure for us, then," the sergeant retorted. "No woman is ever too young for this sort of game."

The mother scrambled up, but the sergeant stopped her with a hand under her chin. "And perhaps not too old, neither. Nay, you've looks enough left." He shoved her back; she fell sprawling, and two of his men caught her ankles, tossing her skirt up. The sergeant fell to his knees, unbuckling his belt.

Matt had had enough. The spells he'd tried should have already attracted any pursuit that was coming—and if he brought down any more, he'd just have to deal with it when it came. He pulled a leather thong loose from his shirt and began to tie knots in it, chanting,

> "Let there be no blade in your scabbard,
> Let your lust become much the laggard,
> And that which should stand to attention,
> Lie low, like a coward's intention!"

Below him, the soldiers stilled. Then one of them began to fumble frantically, but another quickly tied himself back up. One or two men howled, and the sergeant bellowed, "Witchcraft! Which of you old hags has done this?"

"Done what?" one of the oldest women asked, her face blank.

"You know well what!" the sergeant snarled, and whirled to backhand her across the face. "But it won't work, granny! If we can't hurt you one way, we'll hurt you another! Have at 'em, men!"

His soldiers turned to with a bellow of loosed frustration.

Matt realized, all over again, that rape really was a crime of violence more than of sex. Without even thinking, he chanted,

> "Seek out—less often sought than found—
> A soldier's grave, for thee the best;
> Then look around, and choose thy ground,
> And take thy rest!"

The soldiers froze. Then, one by one, they toppled over, eyes glazed.

The women stared, uncomprehending.

Matt didn't stay to watch the sequel. They'd figure it out, fast enough—and for himself, he didn't know whether the soldiers' rest was temporary or permanent. Not that it mattered—those women had a score to settle, and no one could blame them if they did it. Especially because, if they didn't, and the soldiers revived, *they* would take the revenge they had just now intended. No, Matt couldn't blame the ladies for self-defense—and he didn't think anyone else would, either.

He was about a hundred feet away on the other side of the hill, and going fast, when he heard the huge, massed scream of rage behind him. He went faster.

Half an hour later, he figured he was clear, no matter who came— even if it was a sorcerer homing in on the location of a spell. Matt didn't dare rest long, but he sat down by a stream to take a deep breath and let the shakes hit, then pass. After his insides had almost quit quivering, he began taking slow, deep breaths, striving for calmness, but shaken to realize just how evil the land had become.

He was filled with remorse—which, he told himself, wasn't merited. But he should have stopped the soldiers sooner—and found a way to do it without killing them. Oh, sure, he might have only stunned them as it was—or he might have killed them. And if he hadn't, he had no doubt the women of the village had finished what he'd begun. No, for either side, he'd botched it.

He wondered at his own hesitation, but was afraid he knew the reason. It was, quite simply, that he hadn't really taken sides till it was too late.

After what felt like half an hour but was more likely only ten minutes, Matt pulled himself to his feet again and set off down the road. The walking helped him regain his composure. He didn't dare stay too long in one place, especially not near a site where he had worked a spell. He trudged on down the trail.

Or up. Finally, the path began to rise. He labored upward, wiping the sweat from his brow and wondering how he could possibly have thought the day was cool—but that had been a while ago, now. He glanced at the sun, figuring it was a little after noon—but was surprised to see that it was halfway down the sky. Of course—an hour of hiking, a few minutes to interfere and take sides in a local quarrel, and another couple of hours on the road again—it did add up, didn't it?

He couldn't help but think he was a fool. On top of not doing a good job of interfering, he'd put his own neck in the noose. It hadn't been his fight, and it did increase his chances of trouble with the local authorities—those men had been uniformed, and well armed; they were no mere bandits.

Bandits! The thought left him uneasy; he scanned the steep sides of the trail and the hillside above. He found himself beginning to evaluate every upcoming landform as an ambush site—not a bad precaution.

So, with his hackles raised, Matt marched east, feeling as though every man's hand was turned against him.

Finally, his shadow was so long that its top was high above him, and the dried grass on the hillside before him was gilded by the setting sun. He plowed to a halt, dog-tired but satisfied—he'd made it almost to the top of the mountain pass. It was a good place to stop for the night—there was just enough daylight to hunt out a spring and a cave. He looked around, saw a glitter off to his left that might be water, took a step toward it—

And the world suddenly swam about him. Giddy and nauseous, he dropped to his knees, putting a hand down to stabilize himself, thinking, *Heatstroke. Exhaustion.* Then the world steadied; he straightened up with relief that the spell was over . . .

And saw the hillside. Miles away.

He looked around in a panic and saw the pine groves bordering the alpine meadow.

He was back where he'd started.

And it was dusk—down in the bottom of this little valley, night had fallen.

Somebody didn't want him going back to Merovence.

He had a notion Who, and for a moment was on the verge of saying some very nasty things about that Somebody. Then he remembered what had gotten him into this mess in the first place, choked back his anger, and heaved a sigh. Then he turned to begin looking for berries. Or maybe a rabbit.

He woke with the sun, glowering at the embers of the tiny fire. He'd had a lousy night, waking at every tiny sound, worried about enemy sorcerers—but apparently they didn't have a fix on him. Probably because he'd been bound away from this location when last he'd worked magic. Or because they didn't think he was anything to worry about.

You'll change their minds about that, something said inside him.

Matt almost laughed. Right now, he didn't feel as though he could be a threat to anyone. An uneasy night's sleep, the chill of the morning, and a handful of berries just didn't make for high morale. He rolled up to his knees, scooped some dirt onto his burned-out campfire just in case, then pushed himself to his feet and started out toward the rising sun again. This time, though, he angled away from the path, heading toward what looked to be the nearest hillside.

As he went, he wondered about that "siege" the soldiers had mentioned yesterday. It could mean that there were a lot more of their kind about. He'd have to be careful.

So he was—and the day passed without incident. Also without food. If there was small game on this mountainside, it was very good at hiding. Either that, or the siege had cleaned out everything edible. So what with one thing and another, he was in a very glum mood as he toiled up the hillside, glowering at the golden glow of sunset behind him, his tall, stetched-out shadow looming before him . . .

And the world went crazy again.

This time he didn't even manage to keep to his knees; he just fell, tucking in his chin and rolling. He lay on his back, waiting for the dizziness to pass. It did, and the evening sky became clear—roseate at the edges, and with the first dim stars beginning to show. Pine boughs fringed the edge of his field of vision. He didn't need to get up and look around—he knew he'd see the alpine meadow again.

Hunger gnawed his belly, but he had managed to find some berries during the day, and even a hoard of nuts that last year's squirrels had disdained—so, what with one thing and another, he was even more exhausted than hungry. He just closed his eyes and let sleep take him.

He woke in the false dawn, cold and wet with dew. He sat up, stiff in every joint, and braced himself on an elbow as he regarded the beautiful mountain meadow with glum certainty. Yes, he was back where he had begun, and two days' hiking had been wasted.

Well, not entirely wasted—he had established that Somebody definitely did not want him going back to Merovence. That Somebody would probably be very happy to let him go farther west, though, into Ibile. He just hoped that Somebody didn't regard him as being completely replaceable.

He shoved himself to his feet with a sigh, stumbled to the stream for a drink, then set off into the forest to see if there were any more obliging squirrels who hadn't come back for last year's nuts. He was sure he'd be drawn to them, if they were there—he was beginning to feel like one of their kind.

He did find a handful of nuts, and a few more berries. Dizzy and weak with hunger, he struck off again—but parallel to the mountains, this time. He wasn't about to go any farther into Ibile than he had to—but maybe he could find a village with an inn somewhere in this valley, or at least a farmhouse willing to part with a bowl of porridge. It did cross his mind to go back to the little village and ask for a handout, but it occurred to him that the surviving women there might not have a very high opinion of strange men, just at the moment—so he stayed in the valley, and away from the trail. Hopefully, he'd find a new village—or maybe even a road.

Half an hour later, Providence finally smiled on him—he bumped into an apple tree. Literally. In fact, it took him a moment to realize what had hit him—he was that far gone. He looked up, saw the red fruit, and plucked one with a howl of joy. Eight bites and two apples later, it finally occurred to him to wonder what a lowland tree was doing in the evergreen zone. He decided to take it as a sign that Heaven wasn't completely abandoning him, and took another apple. Then he remembered what overeating could do after a long fast, and pulled off his cloak to wrap up a dozen apples. He set off southward again, resolutely resisting the temptation of the weight on his back.

He didn't have to resist very long—all of a sudden, the weight was gone.

He stopped, appalled, then swung the cape in front of him, opened it, and looked in—at its lining. That was all. It was completely empty—not a stem, not a pit. He sighed and threw the cloak over his shoulders again, remembering the Hebrews in the desert, and the manna—how they were to take only as much as they needed for a day. Apparently, he was only supposed to take enough for one meal. The Lord would provide, it seemed. He set off again, resigned to his fate.

But he did feel much better.

CHAPTER 5

A Rare and Surly Monster

The sun was almost directly overhead, and those apples had been a long time ago. Matt was beginning to feel weak again and was getting into a pretty nasty mood. Once again, he thought of cursing his misfortune, and the Powers that had enforced it on him—even if it had been his own dumb fault for making a vow he hadn't meant—but he caught himself with the words on the tip of his tongue. He didn't quite dare let them out.

And didn't need to, for that matter. He frowned, listening to a distant sound that suddenly became audible, then died away again. He could have *sworn* that had been the sound of someone using foul language . . .

No. Not "sworn." Not again. Ever. Not without thinking it over very carefully first.

But what *was* that sound? Of course, it could have been the wind; he could hear it moaning in the crevices of the pass ahead.

Then he frowned, tilting his head to one side and listening more closely. That was no wind, that was a creature—and it was moaning as much in anger as in pain. Matt stepped forward carefully, moving quietly, ready to jump off the path at a moment's notice.

The voice rose again, and Matt froze. He couldn't make out the words, but the tone was definitely angry and outraged. Then the voice slackened off into growling again, and Matt began stalking.

There was nothing in sight, but the trail angled sharply at a big rock a little way ahead, and the moaning was growing louder. Matt sidled up to the rock and, very quickly, ducked out for a peek.

The moan blasted into a roar, and Matt ducked back in a panic, sure he had been seen.

But the roar was followed by words. Matt frowned; he couldn't quite understand them, though they seemed to be in the hybrid language of Merovence that he understood as well as English. He concentrated, trying to allow for accent—and it clicked; he was just able to make out the words.

"That motherless monster of a sorcerer who set this hellish trap! I'll bite him into twenty pieces! I'll pluck him naked! I'll drop him from a mountaintop!"

Whoever it was, it certainly didn't sound like a courtier. Matt stepped out from hiding and stalked forward carefully—if it was a soul in distress, of course he wanted to help. Though come to think of it, that voice didn't exactly sound human.

The words did, though—it ranted on through a series of curses that would have done credit to the most creative sailor ever to work his way down to the brig. Matt stepped around another outcrop and saw—a very singular creature. In fact, he doubted there could be two of them, and if there were, the other one certainly didn't have a huge boulder holding it down by its wing.

The other wing was beating furiously as the beast tried to pull away. They were eagle's wings, though on the grand scale—a thirty-foot wingspan, at least. But it had the head, neck, and tail of a dragon, and its body was that of a huge lion.

Matt couldn't help himself. "What in the name of heaven are *you*?"

The beast turned his way with a surly growl. "A dracogriff, of course!" it answered. "What're *you*?"

"A wizard," Matt said automatically, then leaped for cover as the monster lunged at him with a huge roar.

"Thought you were gonna sneak up on me, huh?" it bawled from somewhere on the other side of the boulder Matt had ducked behind. "Thought you were gonna drug me and drain me, huh? Couldn't get any nestlings' blood, so you thought you'd settle for one as young as you could get, huh?"

"No!" Matt ducked up long enough to shout the syllable. He dropped down again and called out, "You've got the wrong wizard!"

"Wrong wizard? They're *all* wrong wizards! How could there ever be a right one?"

"Look," Matt said, trying for patience, "you've got the definitions reversed. Wizards are good guys—their power comes from research and right living. The sorcerers are the ones who get their power from evil."

"The Devil you say!"

"That's right. Only I don't—I swear by the saints. And I'm trying to break the habit."

"I'll bet. And you didn't make this rock fall on me while I was sleeping, to make sure I'd still be here when you caught up, huh?"

"That's right—I didn't."

"Sure you didn't! Just like you haven't been chasing me all across Merovence and through these mountains for the last four years!"

"No, now that you mention it. I spent the last three at the queen's castle."

"Oh, yeah? Then how'd you just happen to be coming this way right when I was anchored down, huh?"

"Well . . ." Matt swallowed. "You remember that 'swearing by the saints' I told you about?"

"Yeah . . ." The monster was beginning to sound puzzled.

"I, uh, kinda got carried away the last time I did it."

"Carried away where?"

"To Ibile. I mean, I swore to kick the king of Ibile off his throne, or die trying."

There was a sudden and total silence. Then the other side of the boulder erupted into a coughing, cawing sound. It was a minute before Matt realized it was laughter.

Scowling, he stepped around the boulder. "All right, it's not funny!"

"Not to you, maybe! But from here? It's a hoot and a holler! *Eeee!*" The monster blinked away tears. "Boy, you sure wanna die young!"

"Yeah." Matt swallowed heavily. "I, uh, wasn't thinking too clearly."

"I'll say you weren't! Didn't it kinda sink in that the saints wouldn't let you off?"

"Well, not at the time . . ."

"Not much of a wizard, are you?"

That stung. Matt drew himself up to his full height. "I'll have you know I'm the Lord Wizard of Merovence!"

"No fooling?" The dracogriff stared, impressed. "Hey, if you're so high and mighty, how come you made a dumb mistake like that?"

"Reflexes," Matt mumbled, deflating. "I didn't grow up here, see. I was born in another universe."

"Universe?" The dracogriff frowned. "How can there be more than one?"

"Search me." Matt spread his hands. "I only know that there is. I grew up there, where we don't quite believe in religion as strongly as you do."

"Believe?" The dracogriff reared its head back, eyeing Matt strangely. "What's to believe? There's a good One, and a bad one, and they each give off magic power. Everybody knows that."

"I know." Matt sighed. "It's like saying you 'believe' that when you throw something up in the air, sooner or later, it'll come down again."

"Yeah." The dracogriff growled, looking uncomfortable for some reason. "Or like saying you 'believe' in the wind—or in ghosts."

"Right. Anyway, I started trying to translate a booby-trapped poem . . ."

" 'Booby trapped'?" The dracogriff frowned.

"Yeah—it was a spell in disguise. But we don't believe in spells, either . . ."

"Kinda dumb, aren't you?"

Matt flushed. "You could put it a little more delicately. Anyway, when I managed to translate the poem well enough to recite it, I looked up and found myself in the middle of Bordestang."

The dracogriff just stared. Then its mouth lolled open, and it began to make the noise again.

"Please." Matt held up a hand, looking pained. "I feel dumb enough as it is."

"Awright, awright," the dracogriff grunted, throttling down its amusement. "So how'd you turn out to be such a big-shot wizard, if you didn't believe in magic?"

"Maybe that's why. Because I wasn't raised with it, see, I could look at it from the outside—and I had to try to figure out how it worked."

"So you could dope it out better than any of the locals." The dracogriff nodded. "That's so stupid, it almost makes sense."

Matt eyed the boulder. "You might say you're not in any position to throw stones."

The monster's good humor vanished on the instant. "Oh, shut up," it growled, turning to glare at the rock. "A guy's got to sleep some time, don't he?"

"Yeah, sure he does. You're just lucky it didn't hit you on the head."

"Not lucky at all," the dracogriff growled. "He wants my blood fresh when he gets it." Suddenly, it lunged at its own wing, jaws gaping.

"Stop!" Matt shouted.

The dracogriff jolted to a halt, wincing. "Not so *loud* . . ."

"Eschew such behavior!"

"That's what I'm doing!" The monster opened its jaws again.

"But you *can't*," Matt cried in a panic. "How will you fly on just one wing?"

"Better a hiker than a corpse," the dracogriff grunted.

"Why not just push it off?"

"What do you think I've been trying to do all morning?" it growled.

"Maybe you just can't get a good angle." Matt came over to the beast's trapped wing. "Here, let me try."

"No *way!*" the monster bellowed. "It was one of you guys who got me into this fix in the first place! Let you near me? You'd just put a whammy on me that'd make me turn belly-up! Stay back there, buster!"

"But I just want to help . . ."

"Yeah, help me into an early grave! Got a thing about blood, don't you? By the bucketful, sure! Come within five feet of me, and you're lunch, boyo!"

"Now, wait a minute." Matt took a step forward. "I don't mean any harm. Probably your enemies are my enemies."

"Or you're one of 'em! Get *gone!*" The dracogriff bared its teeth and lunged. Matt leaped back—and the dracogriff slammed out against the weight on its wing with a bellow of pain. "*Now* look what you did!"

"Absolutely nothing." Matt frowned around the monster's head at the rock. "It didn't budge an inch, with your full weight against it. Funny . . ."

"Oh, yeah! It's a bundle o' laughs!"

"No, no." Matt waved the sarcasm away with irritation. "I mean the boulder itself. It's only a foot-thick chunk of granite, and it's more or less spherical. It ought to have at least *started* to roll."

"Well, it didn't."

Matt looked up, eyes widening. "Did you say it was a sorcerer who was hunting you?"

"It wasn't the little boy who looks after the sheep, bucko."

"It's enchanted!"

"Great," the dracogriff snorted. "Just great. You finally got the idea. Give the big-shot wizard a crest for his coat of arms."

Matt scowled. "I told you this stuff didn't come naturally to me. Okay, so it's magic. *Now* let me see what I can do."

The dracogriff stared. "What're you talking about?"

"Getting that boulder off your wing," Matt said impatiently.

"With a *spell*?" the dracogriff bawled. "A fumble-fingered filigree like you would probably take off the whole *wing*!"

Matt held up a palm. "A little patience, please."

"Patience, my tail fin! You just get the hell away from my wing, y' hear me?"

"I hear you." Matt's eyes never left the boulder. "I've got your measure, too."

"Measure, nothing! You just get outa here!" When Matt didn't respond, the dracogriff screamed, "Out! I said *now*! I won't take any favors from your kind! I don't want anything to do with you! Just get outa here, you hear me?"

"No way," Matt muttered. "I think I see how to do it."

"Get out, or I'll *gnaw* you out!" the dracogriff raged. "I won't owe you!"

"Well, it's your life—but that doesn't mean I have to let you throw it away."

"It's not your lookout!" the dracogriff bawled, and lunged at Matt, jaws gaping.

The wizard leaped back, and the dracogriff jolted up short against the tether of its own wing again. It roared with pain, and Matt said calmly, "You see? One way or another, it's got to come off."

"The rock?" the dracogriff howled. "Or the wing?"

"Well, I *was* thinking of the rock—but you seemed pretty willing to take off the wing just a few minutes ago."

"That would have been *my* doing," the griff growled. "Get your greedy eyes offa me!"

But Matt frowned down at the boulder, pacing around the monster so he could see the rock from all sides—and carefully staying out of range. So he didn't see the faint glint of hope that came into the dracogriff's eye.

"I've got the spell," he said slowly, "but I'm reluctant to use it."

"Then don't," the dracogriff grunted. "Just get outa here and leave me alone."

"Not so fast. I don't want to use the spell because as soon as the rock's off your wing, you might charge out and chew me up."

The dracogriff snorted. "Not a bad idea. Better get while the getting's good."

"Well, I wasn't asking for anything major—just a solemn promise that you wouldn't try to hurt me."

The dracogriff narrowed his eyes. "How come you don't want an oath?"

"I'm allergic to oaths just now," Matt answered. "Also, I've seen too many people break their most solemn vows—especially the ones they make at the altar. If you won't keep a promise, you won't keep a vow."

"Funny place you come from," the monster growled. "How can a guy break an oath? You do whatever it wants you to."

Matt just stared at him for a moment. Then he said, "Interesting point."

He turned back to the superheavy rock. "I don't suppose there's any way to get you to cooperate, then, is there?"

"Help you get me? No way, bucko!"

"That's what I was afraid of." Matt sighed. "Okay, I guess we have to go on faith." He didn't say in what.

The dracogriff tracked him with its gaze. "Whaddaya think you're doing?"

"Just having a look." Matt began pacing around the dracogriff's pinioned wing, just out of biting range. Satisfied, he nodded, stepped back, raised his hands, and chanted,

> "It's going to rock right off the wing today,
> It's going to rock and a-rock till it rolls away,
> This rock'll roll, it'll roll away today!"

And it did—but very slowly. At first, the rock barely quivered. Matt frowned and recited the verse again, more slowly, concentrating so fiercely on the boulder that everything else seemed to grow dim. He felt the gathering of forces that always accompanied a spell—but they seemed lesser now, weaker, compared to the huge inertia that he felt all about him. He focused his mind on moving that rock, reciting the verse even more slowly—and the boulder tipped, ever so slightly, to the left, then rocked back down a little faster, then up to the right, then back down. Back and forth it rocked, harder and harder, until finally, as Matt intoned "roll" again, it poised, was still for a moment, then tipped on over and rolled, slowly at first, but gathering speed, right off the dracogriff's wing.

"At last!" the monster cried, its wing slamming up with a whoosh. "It's free—just from chanting a verse! Awright, I'll admit it—you really *are* a wizard!"

Matt relaxed, perspiring. "Nice to hear. For a minute, I had my doubts."

The dracogriff stared. "You didn't *know* you were a wizard?"

"No, I knew that, all right. It was just much harder to make that spell work than it should have been." And even harder than it had been two days ago at the village. Matt wondered about that.

The dracogriff shrugged. "Maybe it's just because . . . What's the matter?"

Matt was staring after the rock, appalled. "The rock! It's still rolling!"

"So what? It'll stop."

"No it won't—'cause I didn't tell it to."

"So let it roll." The dracogriff gazed up proudly at its wing. "I don't think anything's broken."

"No, but it will be! That runaway rolling boulder could hurt somebody!"

"Oh, don't be such a gloomy Gus," the dracogriff huffed. "Who could it hurt?"

"Anybody it runs into—it's building up a lot of momentum! And we're in the mountains—it could start an avalanche!"

The boulder rolled over the lip of the pass and out of sight.

"Well, stop it. You're a wizard."

"I took too long thinking up the spell! I could stop it now, but it's out of sight." Matt took off running, tripped on a cobble, and fell flat on his face.

"Hey, there! Easy, easy, little guy!" the dracogriff called. "You can't go running around on a rocky road!"

"But I've got to catch up!" Matt scrambled to his feet and winced at a bruise in his thigh. "If it starts an avalanche, it could wipe out a whole village!" And he limped away.

"Awright, awright!" the dracogriff exploded. "Enough is enough!" He caught up to Matt in two leaps and swerved to cut him off. "Here—left foot on my knee, right foot up and over."

Matt skidded to a halt. "What're you talking about?"

"A ride of course! Boy, for a wizard, you really are slow. Up on my back! You'll never catch that boulder on foot!"

"It's not your problem . . ."

"It was my wing it was on, it was me you made the spell for! Up on the back, bucko! You don't think I'm going to settle for owing you, do you?"

"You don't owe me anything," Matt snapped.

"No, just my freedom and my life! Don't you tell me that's 'nothing'! Now climb aboard!"

Matt eyed the lion back warily, thinking that what had happened to she who rode the tiger might also very well happen to he who was lionized—but there wasn't really much choice. "All right, and thanks." He stepped up on the dracogriff's knee and swung his bruised leg over its back with a wince. "But this settles our account."

"The hell it does," the dracogriff snorted. "Hold tight, bucko."

"Like a leech," Matt promised.

"I *hate* flying," the dracogriff grumbled, but its huge wings beat once, twice, and they were airborne.

"I know what you mean." Matt's stomach was trying to stay behind on the ground. "I'd rather take the train, myself."

"Don't think for a second that you're gonna train me!"

"Wouldn't think of it." Matt looked down and swallowed heavily against a rising stomach. "Uh—long way, isn't it?"

"Only to the bottom of the mountain—and the lump you want is just a hundred feet under us."

"Just" a hundred feet still looked like an awfully long way to Matt. He tried to remember that he had ridden dragon-back before, but it wasn't much reassurance. "Circle lower, will you? I need to stay near it."

"Awright, but don't blame me if I run into a downdraft." The dracogriff spiraled down.

Matt saw the rock bouncing and skipping from ledge to ledge. A huge boulder stood smack in its path, and Matt could have sworn his rock would smash itself to flinders on its big cousin—but it bounced off with scarcely a chip and went rolling merrily on its way. "Can't *anything* stop it?"

"Course not," the dracogriff huffed. "It's enchanted."

He was right, of course. Matt's spell had told it to roll, but hadn't said anything about stopping.

And it was heading right toward a huge slab, a virtual menhir, that was leaning at an angle so steep it couldn't possibly hold itself up! "Go around!" Matt shouted.

> "Take a turn,
> And go around, round, round,
> As you go o'er the ground
> With a crunching sound!"

He said it carefully, and with great concentration. But the focusing of his attention seemed to come a little more easily this time—and, slowly but obediently, the rock swerved in a half circle, around the menhir, over the edge of the shelf it perched on, and plunged on down the slope.

"You *can* make it mind!" the dracogriff cried in amazement.

"Yeah," Matt muttered, "as long as I say the verse in time."

"Just tell it to stop, why don'cha?"

"Good idea." And Matt intoned,

> "Stop!
> 'Cause I'm thinking of you,
> Stop!
> 'Cause you know I moved you.
> Stop!
> And never go rolling awa-uh-ay-ay-ay!"

The concentration was almost automatic—but Matt could feel himself weakening. Why was magic requiring so much more effort, all of a sudden?

The boulder jerked to a stop so suddenly that it had Matt wondering about inertia.

"I can't believe it!" The dracogriff dipped low, circling just over the stone—and sheered off with a yelp of surprise. "Hey! It's hot!"

"Of course!" Matt cried. "*That's* what happened to all that kinetic energy! It converted to heat!"

The boulder was glowing a dull red.

"Hot enough to make an updraft," the dracogriff grumbled. "Next time warn a guy, okay?"

"Sorry. I didn't realize—I've never done this spell before."

"Look, could you stop making it up as you go along?"

"Not for a while yet." Matt sighed. "I haven't worked out a spell for every occasion."

"Lord High Amateur," the dracogriff grunted. "Hey, can I get down now? Heights make me nervous."

"Oh, yeah, sure! But not right here, okay? It'd be a rough haul back up."

"Funny man," the dracogriff snorted as it banked and started climbing. "Just for the record, I need at least a hundred feet to take off or land—unless I wanna come straight down, and that's not too healthy."

"I believe you." Matt frowned, trying to decide whether or not to be indelicate, but curiosity won out, as it usually did. "Say, uh—doesn't flying come naturally to you?"

"A lot more naturally than magic comes to *you*." But the dracogriff's voice had an edge to it. "I mean, climbing trees comes easy to you overgrown monkeys—but does that mean you like it?"

"Yes, most of us . . ."

"Spare me the news about the ones who don't," the beast answered. "At least you're part of a 'kind'!"

Matt sensed sensitive territory and tried to be careful. "Oh, come on! There have to be others of your species!"

"It ain't a species, whatever that is!" The dracogriff could vent a little anger over Matt's attitude, which helped. "We're crossbreeds!"

And getting crosser, Matt noticed. "There've got to be some others of your kind."

"If there are, I haven't met 'em!"

Well, that explained a lot.

"Dracogriffs don't come from mommy dracogriffs and daddy dracogriffs," the beast explained with sullen resentment. "Little dracogriffs happen when some tin-horned, back-stabbing, motherless, son-of-a-worm of a dragon, with more lust than conscience, finds a female griffin alone during her season—and it does happen, 'cause there're a lot more female griffins than males."

"Female griffins find dragons attractive?"

"Bucko, during her season, a lady griffin would find a stone slab attractive, if it were male—the poor little things are so frantic they'll go after anything. It's enough to make you wonder if Mother Nature knows what it's like to be female!"

"There're some females of my species who wonder about that, too. But doesn't the lady griffin try to fight off the dragon?"

"Maybe. What good can it do? A griffin has about as much chance against a dragon as a minnow has against a shark. Result? Me—whether she liked it or not."

"So that's where you get the lion body and the eagle wings?"

The dracogriff nodded. "The head and tail I get from my sire, may he shed his skin every hour. And if I ever meet him, I just might do it for him!"

"Meet him?" Matt frowned. "He didn't stick around?"

"Why should he? He'd gotten what *he* wanted. No, up and away he went—you don't think he'd bring a griffin girl home to Mama, do you? Oh, no, good enough for fun, that's how dragons see 'em—but forever? No way! Those arrogant, high-and-mighty, holier-than-thou hypocrites!"

Matt found himself trying to remember that his dragon friend Stegoman was really a very nice guy—had saved his life a few times, in fact—but he didn't think it would be politic to mention that just now. "But your mother stood by you?"

"A saint! She was a saint! Yeah, she stood by me, even though she had to spend her life in exile from her own kind—they thought I was an abomination. Said she didn't mind, though—I made it all worthwhile for her. No, she raised me out in the wild wood. Couldn't live on a mountaintop—the griffins have staked out all the ones the dragons didn't."

"Sounds kind of lonely . . ."

"You bet it was! Soon as I was grown, I dreamed up an excuse to go wandering, so she could go back to live with the other griffins. I'll look for her when I get back that way, though."

"No, no! I meant lonely for *you*!"

The dracogriff shrugged, almost unseating Matt. "You don't miss what you never had. I got to hang out around your kind, a little—woodcutters and foresters and such. Their hatchlings had fun playing with me, till they got big enough so they thought it was kid stuff."

"That's where you learned to speak our language?"

"From the forest kids? Yeah, that's where." The dracogriff sounded surprised. "How'd you guess?"

"Oh, just something about your accent." Matt didn't want to be more specific while he was still riding, and fifty feet up—getting thrown from the saddle could be pretty serious, especially since he didn't have a saddle.

The thought reminded him that he could be considerably more comfortable someplace else—almost anyplace else, in fact. "Uh, I see we're back to the top of the pass now."

"Yeah. Where'd you say you wanted to go?"

"Down! Look, it's been very good of you to give me a lift, but I really don't want to put you out any further."

"Look, bucko, I told you—I won't be owing to anybody."

"You don't owe me! You just paid me back!"

"For my life? Don't be a donkey! It's gonna take a lot more than one ride to make up for it. Now where'd you say you wanted to go?"

"Hey, look, really . . ."

"Much as I hate it, I could stay up here all day," the dracogriff said, with a note of menace. "You got a love affair with hiking?"

"No, riding is faster," Matt said with a sigh. "All right, and thanks—I'd be delighted to travel with you."

"That's better." The dracogriff angled downward.

"Uh—where'd you say you were going?"

"I didn't. Where're *you* going?"

"Into Ibile."

The dive leveled off into a glide very abruptly. Then, after a few seconds, the dragon head said, "You were serious about that quest stuff, huh?"

"Unfortunately—" Matt sighed. "—I was. Still want to go through with it?"

"Yeah." The dracogriff nodded. "If you're game, I'm game."

"Only if that sorcerer catches you."

"Won't do him much good, now," the dracogriff said, grinning. "*I'm* traveling with the Lord Wizard!"

Why, Matt wondered, did he have the feeling he had just been conned?

CHAPTER 6

On Being a Dracogriff

Even walking, the dracogriff made good time—those lion legs were long, and resilient. Matt wondered what it would be like when the beast decided to run, but he wasn't about to ask while they were on a mountainside.

He also wasn't about to ask without some kind of cushioning. Finally, he couldn't take it anymore. "Uh, could we try for a rest break now?"

The dracogriff pulled to a stop, turning its head back to frown. "After only half an hour? We're never gonna get anywhere if you can't last any longer than that!"

"I'm just out of shape."

"Awright, awright," the dracogriff groused, and crouched so Matt could climb down.

The wizard dismounted, feeling the ache in every limb. He set his palms against his buttocks and leaned back. "*Nnngah!* Uh, hope you don't mind my saying it . . ."

"Of course not," the dracogriff answered with an ominous glare. "What?"

"Well, you have, shall we say, a very strong backbone."

The dracogriff stared at him while it figured out what Matt was talking about. Then its mouth lolled open, and it made the coughing, cawing sound again.

"Please." Matt squeezed his eyes shut. "Please don't laugh. You don't know what it feels like."

"And can't, either, I'll be bound. You mean my lumps are hitting you right where you live."

"I wouldn't put it *that* way . . ."

"Of course you wouldn't—that's why it takes me so long to figure out what you mean. So whatcha gonna do about it?"

Matt eyed him warily. "Would you object to a saddle?"

"Saddle?" The beast frowned. "You mean one of those things that horses wear?"

"Kinda like that, yeah."

"Yeah, I'd mind," the griff growled, "but I guess I can stand it. I want some kind of fastening I can undo myself, though, in case you decide to go take a hike."

"That shouldn't be too hard to arrange." Matt felt a surge of relief.

"I don't think they come in my size, though."

That gave Matt pause. He eyed the dracogriff's back, frowning. "Well—it'll need a bit of tailoring . . ."

"Where're you gonna find a tailor for saddle leather?"

"Right here." Matt grinned. "Verses to any size or length, that's me. If I can cut the words right, the saddle should come out just as we want it."

The dracogriff eyed him narrowly. "Ever conjure up a saddle before?"

"No," Matt confessed, "but it shouldn't be too tough."

"Sure," the dracogriff muttered.

"Oh, come on! Have a little faith. Now, let me see . . ." Matt looked up at the sky, frowning in concentration. "A horse, a horse, my kingdom for a horse" wouldn't do—he was after the accessories, not the appliance itself. Besides, he didn't want to spend it before he'd ever earned it. "Horse and hattock! Ho, and away!" was a little better—but who wanted to ride sitting on a hattock? Come to think of it, what *was* a hattock?

Finally, he settled for:

> "Oh, Stewball had a saddle,
> And I wish it were mine,
> Scaled up for a draco
> In a size ninety-nine.
>
> With buckles of silver,
> And chasings of gold,
> And the worth of this saddle
> Has never been told!"

The air glimmered before them, building into a hazy something that clarified and solidified—into a huge coil of leather that broadened out into a contoured top at least four feet across.

They just stood there staring at it for a while. Then Matt turned away. "Confound and blast it! When will I remember to check the fine print!"

"Well, it's pretty . . ."

"It ought to be, with all that precious metal—but it's, shall we say, a little too generous? I mean, I know I've gained weight these last three years, but not *that* much."

"What happened?"

"I called for a saddle for a dracogriff—so I got one big enough for you to ride in."

The dracogriff stared. Then its mouth lolled open again.

"Please!" Matt squeezed his eyes shut. "Not the laughter. Please, no. I can change it easily enough."

"Oh, yeah?" The draco chuckled. "This, I want to see!"

"All right," Matt said. "Here we go." He glared at the saddle, thinking furiously, then chanted,

> "From a size for a griff to a size for a man,
>   Great saddle, shrink down till my hands' double span
>   Will encompass your breadth, while your cinch holds its
>   length.
>   Great saddle, dwindle, but retain your full strength."

"Doesn't seem to be working too well," the dracogriff remarked with some relish.

"Well, what can you expect from homemade verse?" Matt snapped. "I mean, it's not as though I had a master's poem to butch—uh, adapt, this time. None of the great ones ever went into rhapsodic detail about his saddle."

The saddle's form began to blur.

"On the other hand," Matt said quickly, "it could just be a delayed reaction."

The saddle turned into a tan cloud, but the great pile of leather under it held its form and clarity. Then the saddle coalesced again, looking just as it had before, only of no more than standard size.

"Hey, that's pretty good!" the dracogriff said, startled.

But Matt stared at the diminished saddle, appalled.

Then he turned away. "Confound it! Remind me to do my research next time."

The dracogriff frowned. "I don't see anything wrong with it."

"It's an English saddle," Matt explained. "I ride Western—or try to."

"What's the difference?"

"The Western saddle is a *lot* more comfortable—especially if you're going a long distance. Besides, it has a handle to hold on to."

"Picky, picky!" The dracogriff snorted. "Awright—I suppose we gotta wait while you change *this* one around, right?"

"Oh, I can live with it," Matt grumped.

"Spare me!" The dracogriff rolled its eyes up. "All I need is a martyr for a rider! Go ahead, go ahead! It's not as though we're in a race or anything."

Somehow, those words sent an eerie prickle up Matt's spine—but he turned back to the saddle, determined to ignore the premonition. "All right, let's see, now . . .

> "Back in the saddle aligned!
> With that good old Western design—
> A cantle so restful, a pommel so high,
> To grab and hang on to, if we're in the sky!
> Translate from English to wild Western style,
> So I'll ride in comfort, for many a mile!"

The saddle's form fuzzed again, becoming almost as nebulous as smoke for a minute, then coalesced and firmed once more, into a saddle that would have done credit to the best Hollywood horse opera.

"Are we done yet?" the dracogriff said hopefully.

"Yeah." Matt grinned down at his new word work. "How do you like it?"

"It's beautiful! It's lovely! It's you! Can we go now?"

"Oh, all right, all right." Matt hefted the saddle and turned to his mount. "Care to try on your new wardrobe?"

"Not really," the griff grumped, "but I made you an offer, and I'm stuck with it."

Matt paused, the saddle in his arms. "No, you're not. I don't want to impose . . ."

"Awright, so you're welcome, you're wanted!" the griff bawled. "Can't a guy gripe a little now and then?"

"Oh! Oh, sure!" Matt reached up to settle the saddle between the beast's shoulder blades. "Just didn't realize that was your normal operating mode. Sorry." And he ducked down to buckle the cinch.

There wasn't a whole lot to spare.

A few minutes later, Matt was back in the saddle again, and the dracogriff was prowling on down the slope. For a while, Matt just enjoyed the scenery, letting his spirits lift with the cool mountain air, feeling cleansed and almost whole again.

He stiffened, alarmed by the thought. "Almost whole"? When had he started feeling shredded? And why?

He nibbled at the thought for a few minutes, then put it aside for his subconscious to work on while he went back to enjoying the view. It was very relaxing, having a companion who didn't insist on talking a lot. Grumpy as he might be, the dracogriff promised to be a good traveling companion.

On the other hand, how much of a conversationalist would he be if Matt *were* feeling talkative? Just to try it out, he said, "I don't see how flying could possibly be more enjoyable than this."

"You're in the mountains," the dracogriff growled. "Wait till you see what it's like on the plains."

"Oh, I've ridden there before, too, and I'll have to agree—down there, a hike isn't anywhere nearly as much fun as up here. There, I'd rather fly."

"I'd *never* rather fly," the dracogriff snapped. "Let's just get that straight up front, okay? I don't fly if I can help it."

Matt frowned down at him. "It's just as safe as walking."

"Oh, yeah, that's easy for *you* to say! *You* didn't try to fly into the dragons' territory!"

Matt scowled. "What were you doing there?"

"Do *you* know what it's like to grow up without any of your own kind around?" the dracogriff demanded. "It's mighty lonely, let me tell you! Especially since I knew crisped well the griffins wouldn't have anything to do with me—they felt sorry for Mama, but they weren't about to have anything to do with her as long as I was there. So of *course* I dreamed about the other side of me! Of *course* I dreamed about growing up to join the dragons! After all, the cussed things are so ugly, my looks shouldn't have made any difference, no matter how grotesque I am! So when I grew up and left home, where *else* would I go?"

"You're not grotesque," Matt said softly.

"Oh, sure!" But the dracogriff said it with a little less conviction. "Besides, it's what's inside that counts."

"Oh, yeah? *You* didn't have one of their sentries catch you in the air! *You* didn't have him chasing you over half the sky with his flame turned up high and reaching out twenty feet for you! *You* didn't get singed and crisped and burned so bad you fell a hundred feet into a treetop!"

"My lord, you poor beast!" Matt whispered.

"But he didn't let up then, oh, no! The blasting monster stooped like a hawk and dove toward me, screaming the foulest names you ever heard in a blast of fire—and he was *enjoying* it! So I ran on the ground, but he kept coming back and coming back, and the more I ran, the more angry he got and the more vicious he got, until I finally found a little cave just barely big enough to crawl into, where he couldn't follow—and even *then* he prowled outside for the whole rest of the day, blasting the doorway and roaring at me that I was a . . . 'loathsome gargoyle,' he called me, whatever *that* was!"

"Couldn't you breathe fire back at him?"

"Not enough to matter," the dracogriff answered impatiently. "On a good day, I can light a fire. I just got all the *bad* things about being a dragon, see—all the good things, I got from my griffin mother! But maybe that's just the natures of the beasts."

"You ran into one of the worst of the dragons," Matt said softly. "There *are* good ones among 'em."

"Oh, yeah, sure, the way there are good sorcerers and good vultures! How the hell would *you* know, anyway?"

"Because I have one for a friend."

The dracogriff spun about with a roar.

Matt held on for dear life.

"Off!" the dracogriff bellowed. "Get off, this second! No friend of a dragon can be a friend of mine!"

He stilled just long enough for Matt to jump down—and to back away, fast. "Sure—it's your back. And after what that louse did to you . . ."

"Not me!" the dracogriff howled. "Mama! What would *you* think of the kind of creature who could do a thing like that to a poor helpless female?"

"I'd want to draw and quarter him," Matt said promptly, "but I wouldn't blame the whole barrel for what one rotten apple did."

"Easy enough to say," the dracogriff spat, a small blue flame issuing from his jaws. "Easy enough to say, when it wasn't you it happened to!"

"There were a few men who went after the woman I love," Matt said evenly. "I fought them off, and I would cheerfully have given them permanent jobs in the middle of a cornfield, as an alternative for the crows—but I don't blame *all* men for it. And my dragon friend *is* a good being—loyal, fair, and courageous. Stegoman *never* would have stood by and watched a bully burn you up that way!"

"I don't believe it—but if he was that good, how come he wasn't there to call off that monster?"

"Probably because he was off with me, helping save Merovence. I wish he *had* been there—he might not have welcomed you with open arms, but he sure would have kept that bully off!"

"I don't believe it," the dracogriff said again, but his mood was turning down from rage into surliness. "I can't complain about *you*, though."

"Look, if you don't want me along for the ride, I'll—"

"No, no, come on!" The dracogriff turned broadside and crouched. "Up and at 'em! Just don't let's talk about dragons again, okay?"

"Yeah . . . sure." Slowly, Matt climbed back into the saddle. He was silent as the dracogriff turned away and started back down the slope again, but soon he said, "Is that why you're having trouble getting home?"

The dracogriff gave a short nod. "Yeah. Mind you, it took me awhile to get going again—by the time that oversize worm roared off and left me, those burns were beginning to hurt—and I mean *hurt!* Not to mention the stink of burning feathers. Took me two months just to grow my skin back, and I couldn't catch much to eat the whole time—just the odd rabbit that came too near. So after I could walk again, it took another month just building up my strength—and all thanks to a brainless brute, a flaming idiot!"

"Then you began to walk home?"

"No *way* I was going to fly! And let me tell you, you don't know what distance is till you've tried to hike it! I came across Ibile in three days, flying—and I scarcely made a hundred miles in three days, running! Then I came to that blagstabbering thing with the fake smile and the red neck and the loud voice, and it chased me back twenty miles! I just barely got away from him, and that sorcerer popped up with his wineskin and funnel—and didn't *we* have a jolly dance before I figured I'd better run faster than he could spell!"

"And that's how it's been ever since?"

"Right. I gain thirty miles, and I run into some new kind of monster I've never seen before—what do they do in Ibile, hold contests to see who can breed up the worst new fright?"

Matt shrugged. "I dunno. Wouldn't surprise me, though, from what I've heard about this place. How've you managed to stay away from the sorcerer?"

"Well, I think he's not too good," the dracogriff confided, "for which, praise Heaven. But every time he comes up with a spell to hold me, I manage to find a hole in it. Like, the first time, he drew a pentacle with a one-foot gap in one of the lines, and crouched there in hiding waiting for me to step in, so he could jump out, finishing drawing the line, and shout the last phrase of the spell."

"But you saw it coming and turned away?"

"Of course not! I wasn't expecting anything, remember? But I flew. Just in the nick of time, I felt this thrill of danger, and I flew up fifteen feet and over two yards—then I lit out for the tall timber. First time I'd flown since I met that motherless dragon. Nice to find out I could do it if I had to."

He lapsed into a brooding silence. Matt had to jolt him out of it. "And the second time?"

"Huh? Second time?" The dracogriff turned his head around, frowning. "What do you care?"

"That black-magic-worker is still following you, according to what you've told me—so I might have to match spells with him. What'd he do the second time?"

"Oh." The dracogriff turned its head frontward again. "Well, the second time, he conjured up a fake lady griffin to give me the 'come-hither.' Dumb fool didn't know I would *never* do a thing like that to a lady, most *especially* not a griffin!"

Matt heard overtones of Oedipus, vowing to outwit the gods, and wondered how long "never" was. "So you just turned away from it?"

"Damn straight away, you bet your bodkin! Idiot sorcerer didn't know that I'd grown up with griffins avoiding me like a plague-carrier, either!"

Matt wondered if an "idiot sorcerer" might be anything like an "idiot savant." If so, he might have trouble ahead, regardless of the man's lack of judgment. "How'd you know it was him?"

"Oh, I checked. I went over a few hundred yards, snuck past, then snuck back in—and sure enough, there he was, hiding behind a boulder, waiting for his lure to do its job on me. But I gave him a royal hot seat, and he ran away yipping."

The guy definitely did not sound like much of a threat, but Matt planned to be loaded for bear anyway. "So he hasn't been able to catch you, just slow you down a lot?"

"Right—but he keeps getting better. The trap after that was a chunk of road that he'd created a bog under. I was just about to step on it when some churl of a rider shouted, "King's courier! Stand aside!" and slammed past me and right into the mud. Well, sir, you never saw a sorcerer hightail it out so fast—but the messenger shouted a spell to get himself out, then turned around and chased *me* back for ten miles, 'cause he thought I'd done it!"

"But you did see the sorcerer twice." Matt frowned. "How come you thought I was him? Do we look alike?"

"How should I know? I only saw him from the back! And you might have taken off your sorcerer's robe to fool me. All I know is, he's a sorcerer, and he's still after me."

Matt nodded. "And now he's chased you all the way back into the mountains. Want to tell me about the last try?"

"Maybe it was him, and maybe it wasn't," the dracogriff muttered. "But it was a huge snake, ten feet thick and, I swear, a hundred feet long if it was an inch, with breath that could shrivel the bark off a tree—I saw it do that; there's a whole woodlot, fifty miles in front of us, with naked trunks. And boy, could it move! When I tried to go around, it struck way ahead of me—and when I tried to circle around its tail, it whipped about and struck even farther than its back tip! So I pulled all my nerve together and tried to fly over, but it reared up and snapped at me—I just barely dodged aside in time! So I flew back a mile, then dropped and ran—but it kept coming, faster and faster. Wouldn't come up past the foothills, though."

"Trouble hauling all that mass upward?"

"No, trouble with the rocks I kept throwing down at it; sometimes it pays to be taloned. It went away when the sun set, and I figured I was safe—you know how snakes are about nighttime and cold. But I still got as high up as I could before I settled down for the night, and I made sure I slept where there was a lot of loose rock, so I'd hear it if it came."

"And where it would be really easy for the sorcerer to make a small boulder roll down and pin you."

"Awright! I can't think of everything!" the dracogriff bawled.

"No, and you do have to sleep some time," Matt said, "or you'll drop from sheer exhaustion."

"Yeah." The dracogriff sounded surprised. "Yeah, that's the way of it. You see a little more than your own side, don't you?"

"Well, thanks. I like to think so." Matt hoped he wasn't blushing. He went for a quick change of subject. "You know, I really appreciate the lift."

"I was going that way anyway," the dracogriff growled. "Hey, since it looks as though we're going to be together awhile, you might as well have a name for me. Call me Narlh."

"Narlh," Matt repeated, trying very hard to get the final aspiration correct, feeling honored, and knowing he was right. He suddenly realized he'd made a new friend, and had just added to his load of responsibilities—but it was worth it, worth it. "My name's Matthew; call me Matt."

"Matt," the dracogriff repeated, as though the name had a strange taste. "Boy, you people have funny names."

"They go back a way," Matt said, careful not to say anything about the dracogriff's name. "Hey, you know a good place to have breakfast?"

Narlh's pace was a lot quicker than Matt's; they went downhill rapidly and passed into a pine forest by midafternoon. The dark trees made Matt nervous, clustering so closely about the roadway—ideal conditions for an ambush, every foot of the way, and there was still the problem of that sorcerer Narlh claimed was chasing him. Not to mention the possibility of more powerful sorcerers, who might have been attracted by Matt's rock-moving spells; but they were a long way away from where the spells had been worked now. Still, the trail was pretty clear . . .

The gloom deepened toward dusk; the sun was going down, and so was Narlh's mood. He was starting to mutter to himself, and Matt wasn't all that enthusiastic about riding on a resentful monster. "Uh, it looks as though the trees are thinning out over there. How about pitching camp?"

"Fine!" Narlh angled toward the trees so rapidly that Matt lurched and clutched at the saddle. "Look," he said, "I don't mean to be a pain in the neck . . ."

"It was my idea, wasn't it?" Narlh snapped. He broke through a screen of branches, and Matt saw a clearing spread out about him, fifty feet across.

"Say, now! This is even better than I thought!" He hopped off Narlh's back, then stopped. "Maybe it's a little too convenient."

But Narlh wasn't listening. He was pacing away from Matt, following the curve of the trees, rolling his shoulders, spreading and folding his wings, and muttering to himself. Matt could only catch the occasional phrase, such as "Monkey on my back . . . confounded shrimp . . . muscles I didn't even know I had . . . being obligated to one o' those filthy humans . . ."

Matt decided he didn't want to know the rest. He shivered, pulling his cloak about him—they were still in the mountains, and the air was developing a real chill with the approach of night. He turned, scouting for fallen branches, and collected an armful. He dumped them in the center of the clearing, then hunted up a dozen large rocks, set them in a ring, and built a campfire in the middle. He glanced up at Narlh, thinking of asking for a light, but the beast was still pacing, and his grumbling had deepened. Matt shrugged, turning away, and fished in his belt pouch for flint and steel. Sure, he could have used a quick spell, but he was still leery of attracting attention, and he did kind of want to stay around for a while. He shaved a stick with his knife, laid it in a bed of dry grass, and struck the flint against the small file. Sparks jumped on the third try, setting the grass a-smolder. Matt breathed on the tiny coal, coaxing it into life; it grew bigger and bigger, then set up a flame—which ignited the shavings, and a real fire danced up. Matt sat back on his heels, feeling a glow of accomplishment just as big as anything he'd had from working magic—and bumped into something behind his back. Warily, he looked up, and saw Narlh's dragon snout over his head. The beast was looking at the fire.

"Not bad," the dracogriff grudged. "So your magic makes fires, too, huh?"

"Yes, but this wasn't magic," Matt explained. "Just flint and steel."

The dracogriff looked down at him with a glint of respect in its eye. "For real, huh? Hey, I guess you *are* a fire-maker."

"Well, sure, but so are most people."

The dragon head turned back to the fire. "That's right. I'd forgotten that, about your kind. Maybe you can't breathe fire, but at least you can make the stuff." He looked down at Matt again. "And you can make bigger fires with magic, huh?"

"Sizeable," Matt said carefully. It was reassuring to see Narlh coming out of his dark mood.

"How about food?" The dracogriff turned away without giving Matt time to answer. "Miserable way to travel . . . nothing to eat, all the game's been killed off . . ."

Matt frowned. "That's right, there is a siege going on in the neighborhood, isn't there?"

"You betcha, boyo! And those greedy soldiers have hunted down everything larger than a mouse already. Gotta be something, though . . ." And he shouldered away through the brush, still muttering.

Matt sighed and pushed himself to his feet. Time for him to forage, too—though from what Narlh had said, he wasn't going to find much. He poked around among the trees, not wanting to go too far from the camp fire, and did come up with a few fallen nuts and a bush with a scanty supply of berries. He came back to the fire, hunger gnawing at his belly, picked up a stone, and cracked one of the nuts. He pulled the shell open—and saw a shriveled, mangled bit of meat. "Worms have been here before I have," he muttered. "Well, a *real* warrior wouldn't need to eat, would he?" He picked up the next nut, set it against the rock, and picked up the stone . . .

Something slammed down on the ground right next to him. Matt found himself staring at a haunch of venison, unskinned.

"I didn't need it all," Narlh's voice explained. "Figured you might be able to use some. I was full, anyway."

Matt looked up at the gruff, scaly snout above him, amazed. "I thought I was the magician, here! How did you find game where there was none?"

"It was good at hiding," Narlh snorted. "I'm better at finding. Eat."

Matt smiled, oddly touched. "Well, thank you, Narlh! But are you sure . . ."

"A dracogriff can't afford to be logy," Narlh snapped. "I heard your kind needs to scorch it before you eat it."

"Yes, it is nicer that way." Matt started skinning the haunch. "Thanks, Narlh—a lot."

A few minutes later, the venison was roasting on an improvised spit. As soon as the outside was brown, Matt started cutting off slivers. It tasted good, very good—it had been a long time since those breakfast apples.

When the edge was taken off his appetite, he remembered his manners and looked up at Narlh. "Want to try a slice?"

"Don't mind if I do," the dracogriff allowed. "Must be something to be said for it, the way you're wolfing it down."

Matt held out the chunk of meat, which took a fair amount of courage as the huge dragon's head reached down to take it from his fingers. Narlh chewed once, then turned to spit the meat out. "Yuck! Ugh! How can you *stand* the stuff!"

"Sorry," Matt said, feeling sheepish.

"I guess it smells better than it looks," Narlh growled.

"Must be." Matt kept on trimming until he was full. Then he kept the core of the haunch roasting until it was almost charred on the outside. Well-done, it should keep for a day or two—and, though

Narlh seemed to be able to find game where there was none, there was no guarantee. Waste not, want not.

While it roasted, Matt raked some charcoal from the fire, let it cool, then started drawing—long, straight lines. He still didn't trust the forest.

"It is certain, then?" The queen sat tight-lipped, fingers pressed deep into the plush covering the arms of her throne. "He has crossed into Ibile?"

"Not so much 'crossed,' Majesty, as having appeared on the other side of the border." The messenger clenched his hat in his fists, worried about how the queen would react to her fiancé's defection. "The sentry on the topmost crag of Mount Damocles looked away, toward the other side of the range, then looked back—and saw him there. He says he will swear 'twas the Lord Wizard, an you wish him to, for he was in your army at Breden Plain, and stood near to his Lordship in the battle."

"He must have extraordinarily keen eyesight, to be sure of him at such a distance."

"Such clearness of sight he has, Majesty—'tis the cause of his being stationed at the mountain border." The messenger didn't mention the sentry's montagnard grandfather, who assured his descendent a warm welcome in the local villages, as well as keen eyesight.

He didn't have to; Alisande had chosen the mountain sentries herself, and for exactly those reasons. "There is no need to swear; I credit his report."

"He says also that he knew the Lord Wizard by his colors—his golden doublet and azure hose, and by the glinting symbols on his cape."

Symbols in a wizard's cloak, one might expect—though why Matthew had chosen to have a block-capital *M* embroidered in place of the usual stars and crescents mystified Alisande. Monograms she could understand, but Matthew did not strike her as swollen with his own self-importance in any other way.

It did, however, make him unmistakable. "I thank you, good courier." She sighed. "Now leave me, and take your refreshment in the kitchens."

The messenger stared in surprise, then bowed and backed away the proper distance before turning on his heel and nearly sprinting out of the throne room. He knew the propensity of royalty to take out their vexation with bad news on him who bore it, and was amazed and tenfold more loyal to the queen who showed such self-restraint as to thank him instead!

"He has done it," Alisande murmured to herself, wishing for the hundredth time for a chancellor with whom she could discuss such weighty matters—but that chancellor himself was now the subject of the discussion, and she would have to talk to herself in his absence. "You have done it, my love—you have stridden into the den of lions without care, and may shortly be without head." She shivered, feeling dread hollow her at the thought. "And what choice have I but to follow, and that with all my army, in some faint hope that I may bring you back alive." She shuddered and shook her head. "Ah, my Matthew! Wherefore could you not have thought before you swore?"

But she knew the answer—in fact, she *was* the answer. She rose to call up her heralds and set the war in train.

CHAPTER 7

Servant, Go Where I Send Thee

The night darkened around the camp fire, and the wind tore at its flames. Matt shivered as he sprinkled the white powder, closing the twenty-foot circle he'd drawn in the dust.

"And just what good is *that* going to do, I'd like to know?" Narlh humphed.

"A lot, if anything magical tries to get at us tonight." Matt stood up, dusting off his hands. "Or anything not-so-magical, for that matter."

"What's the powder? Lime? Chalk?"

"Talcum," Matt said, embarrassed. "It's the only verse I could think of offhand."

"How's it go?"

"I'd like to tell you, but I hate singing commercials. Besides, I don't want another bottle of the stuff right now."

Narlh frowned. "Doesn't seem like much, to keep out a sorcerer."

"Remind me to tell you how to keep elephants away."

"What's an elephant?"

Matt started to answer, then thought better of it. "A mythical beast." He glanced up at the moon, then turned back to inscribing the pair of concentric circles, hurrying now.

"Whatcha scared of?" Narlh demanded. "Something I oughta know about?"

"I should think you would already. The closer we come to mid-
night, the greater the danger from sorcery."

"Oh, yeah?" Narlh lifted his head, glaring. "So *that's* why the bum
could always sneak up on me! Why didn'tcha tell me this before?"

"Because I only met you today."

"Oh." Narlh frowned, looking away. "Yeah, there is that. Right
now, though, I don't see anything to worry about." He lay down, his
front legs walking around in a circle as he did, ending curled up with
his head on his toes.

"Nothing dangerous because of claws and teeth out there?"

"Naw, and nothing dangerous because of sharp, pointy sticks and
big ideas, neither. In fact, not a soul in sight."

Matt nodded. "It's the things without souls that worry me—and
the ones who have sold them."

Narlh lifted his head, eyes narrowed, growling low in his throat.
"They bother me, too." He eyed the double ring that now surrounded
their camp fire, about twenty feet out. "So that's all you have to do
to keep sorcerers away? Just sprinkle a powder?"

"No, I have to chant a verse, too." Matt paced around the inside of
the circle slowly, intoning,

> "Weave a circle round us twice,
> And close the ends with fiery thread,
> That we may sleep in peaceful beds,
> Flames guarding us from ill and vice."

Again, Matt could feel the magical forces thickening about him—
and thickening, and thickening. It felt as if he were wading through
molasses—but he kept at it, until the final rhyme.

"Sounds pretty," Narlh acknowledged.

"That was a spell, not a concert," Matt growled, not wanting to
admit he'd adapted it from Coleridge. But he was feeling stretched
taut—he should have seen something by now.

Suddenly, fire erupted all around them, between the two chalk
lines.

Narlh stared, transfixed.

Matt relaxed with a smile of satisfaction and tried not to worry
about what would happen if he needed a spell to act instantly. Whatever was wrong with magic here in Ibile, it slowed down the response
time horribly.

How could he counteract that?

Narlh interrupted his musing, turning to Matt with new respect, almost awe, in his eyes. "You don't do anything by half measures, do you?"

"On the contrary," Matt said. "I try to keep a sense of balance."

"If this is your idea of the middle, I'd hate to see you really let yourself go!"

"It's an interesting idea," Matt admitted. He wondered if he'd have the courage to do it—or the foolishness.

He turned to Narlh, pushing the topic aside. "Glad to see you're all tucked in."

"Why? Should I stay up and pace?"

"Not at all—I meant it. I'll take first watch."

"First watch?" The dracogriff frowned. "What's that?"

"Just what it says—staying awake and watching for enemies," Matt explained. "I'll wake you when the moon is at its highest—then *you* can guard *me*."

Narlh nodded slowly. "Smart. Very smart."

"Inspired," Matt said witheringly. "Evolution took care of the ones who didn't think of it. Shall I sing a lullaby?"

"Oh, no, that's all right," Narlh said quickly. He put his head back on his paws and closed his eyes.

"Already heard me sing," Matt muttered. Still, everything was under as much control as he could manage; he sat down cross-legged by the fire, keeping his back straight and looking over the flames toward the darkness. He patrolled with his eyes, letting his gaze move slowly over the clearing from left to right, then turning to look back over each shoulder, then front again. The trees were the things to worry about—there was no telling what might come from them. Or how; he memorized the position of each bush and rock, in case an enemy might try to sneak up under camouflage. He didn't really expect to see anything—the only enemies who wouldn't be frightened by his wall of flame were the ones who would be attracted by its magic; and they were more apt to appear in a burst of thunder than to sneak up. No way to see them ahead of time, of course—but at least he could be awake to do something about it.

He settled into the vigil, letting himself sink into a reverie, his eyes still watchful for anything unusual, keeping their patrolling pattern, while a part of his mind mulled over the day's events and problems.

Alisande came first to mind, of course. Now that there was a moment of stillness, he was surprised how much he missed her—her laughter . . . the glint of her eye . . . the occasional, very restrained, flirtation . . . her sudden bursts of anger, quickly controlled . . . her iron-hard resolve when she was crossed . . . her insistence on propriety . . . her avoidance of a wedding . . .

He took a deep breath, realizing he was growing angry again. Too much of a distraction; he was supposed to be on guard. Oddly, though, even his pique couldn't quite cover up the hollowness within him when he thought of her. Even if he had to be caught and shipped back to her, he decided, he did want to get back.

How could he arrange to get caught? Without being executed shortly afterward, that is.

Light flared.

A huge ball of light, too bright and too clear to be flame, so vivid that the blaze of his camp fire seemed to pale beside it.

Matt was on his feet, a dozen verses rushing through his mind, hoping that he'd be able to see what kind of creature this was who had invaded his circle in time to choose a spell and cast it. The bright, clear light made it unlikely to be a sorcerer, but what else was there in Ibile?

Then the core of the flare seemed to coalesce, and a form became discernible within it—something humanoid, with a suggestion of huge wings, and a face that shone so brightly that its features couldn't be seen. Matt raised a hand to shield his eyes from the sight, but a voice echoed inside his head: "Wherefore mockest thou the Lord, vowing aye and doing nay?"

Matt stared, taken aback. Then, slowly, he lowered his hand and said, "I beg your pardon?"

"Even now, thou didst seek a means to evade thy vow." The light-form's tones deepened, with the beginnings of anger.

"Hey, now, wait a minute!" Matt held up a hand—and was surprised to see the little hairs on the back standing straight up. Now that he thought of it, his whole scalp was prickling. Whatever this being was, it packed a lot of voltage. "I think you were taking me too literally!"

"Literally!" The form's voice was a whiplash. "Aye, to the letter! Dost thou care naught for the words thou dost use?"

"Of course not! I was an English major . . ."

"Then thou art bound by them—to the word, if not the letter, and most assuredly to the spirit!"

"No! I didn't mean . . ."

"Thou hadst warning. Did not our Lord tell thee to say 'yes' when thou didst mean 'yes,' and 'no' when thou didst mean 'no'?"

"Not that I remember, no. In fact, I'm not aware of ever having had a chat with Him . . ."

"Hast thou never prayed?" the light thundered. "Then didst thou converse with thy God! Hast thou never bided in silence long enough to feel the impulse toward good within thee? Then didst thou hear His answer! And when thou hast read the Gospel, thou hast heard His word!"

With a sinking heart, Matt remembered hearing the passage about prayer being read at Mass one Sunday. Stalling, he said, "Hold on a minute! You might be a devil, sent to tempt me to my doom! How do I know you come from God?"

"Canst thou truly doubt it?" The anger was approaching righteous wrath—and, in truth, Matt felt a growing certainty inside him. But the form of light went on. "Canst thou doubt that I am an emissary from the God of Abraham and Isaac, and His Son Jesus Christ?"

At the mention of the Holy Name, Matt's fear stilled. He was, after all, on the same side as the form of light; he needn't fear it. "He said we would know one another in the breaking of bread."

The center of the form of light grew out, separated into two hands holding a glowing loaf. They broke the bread in half and held out one piece. "Take, then, and eat—if thou dost think thyself worthy."

Matt paused in midgrab. "There was some talk about my actions, wasn't there?"

"Thy words, say rather."

"All right, my words." Matt eyed the glowing form narrowly. "Are you an angel, then?"

"I am."

Somehow, Matt couldn't doubt it. "Your pardon—and God's. My intention did not accord with my words."

The form was still; a high-pitched humming emanated from it for a moment. Then it said, "It is true—thou didst grow to manhood on an impious world, whose folk have long forgot the Third Commandment."

"Forgotten it, yes. Even people who claim to be religious use the word *god* as an expletive."

" 'Tis even as thou sayest." There was as much sadness as anger now in the angel's tone. "Yet surely thou, who wast trained to know the power of words and hast seen such power made clear in Merovence these three years past, should have known the impiety of that foul usage!"

"Yes." Matt's heart grew heavy. "Yes, I should have. But I was very upset, you see, and in my anger I spoke foolishly, without thinking."

The angel stood in silence; Matt heard only the humming which, he suspected, came from physical causes—molecules impacting an electromagnetic field about it?

The thought made him suddenly aware of a feeling that had been growing all along—a feeling of having been steered, manipulated. He narrowed his eyes. "Is not the Lord a little quick about taking my vow literally? Does He not consider my intentions in it? I sinned, in taking His name in vain—but would He not forgive, and release me from my geas?"

"He will forgive any human sin, as thou knowest! Yet what audacity hast thou, to ask Him to release thee!"

"I know." Matt bowed his head. "But the fact of the matter is that I didn't mean what I said—and when I realized what I was taking on, I definitely wanted to be free of it! Will the Lord really compel me to so suicidal a course?"

"What matters the life, 'gainst the soul's eternity?"

Matt's anger flared. "Easy for *you* to say—you've never had a body!" The surge passed, and Matt lowered his eyes again. "Sorry. But it's not so easy to face death and torture when you're corporeal. I thought the Lord only wanted willing volunteers."

"'Tis even so." The angel's voice was grim. "Thou art forgiven thy sin—and He will not compel thee. Turn, and return to thy place."

Matt sagged with relief. "Blessed be the name of the Lord!"

"Yet bethink thee," the angel said sternly, "thou didst swear—and this task thou hast sworn to do is greatly needed—not by God, but by thy fellow mortals. Dost thou not love Him?"

"Well, yes, but . . ."

"Then love also them! For hath He not said, 'So long as thou hast done this for these, my little ones, thou has done it for Me'?"

"Well, yes, I do seem to remember the passage, but . . ."

"Dost thou not wish to serve the Lord thy God?"

"But it's impossible!"

"All is possible, to God."

"But I'm not God! Not even a close relative! Besides, whenever I say the Lord's Prayer, I ask Him to lead me not into temptation! Isn't there greater danger in Ibile for my soul than there is for my body?"

"There is great peril, aye, for in Ibile a magic-worker may become a sorcerer and gain great worldly power indeed! Yet thy soul was in greater peril when thou didst take the Name of God in vain! Aye, thou art hereby forgiven, since thou didst come from a world far removed in time from this and had not gained full awareness of truth—as thou *shouldst* have had! For the God of thy universe is the God of this, and thou hadst the Scriptures and the Law! No more didst thou need! Thou hadst but to cleave to them, and thou wouldst have kept thy soul free from sin! Oh, beware, Wizard! For the next such sin will put thee into the hands of the enemy! And if thou dost pass from the state of Grace, he shall use thine own powers of magic to tempt thee and damn thee!"

Matt stood, frozen, feeling the horror that the angel felt. Then, very softly, he said, "How can I, then, have the audacity to confront the powers of Satan in a land whose rulers, and many of whose people, are dedicated to him?"

"Through the power of God, Wizard! For be assured, He will not forsake thee! He will be thy staff, he will fill thee with all strength thou dost need! So long as thou art within the state of Grace, thou hast but to call on Him, and He will give thee all the fortitude thou couldst wish, to defend thee against temptation! God will not allow that thou be tried beyond thy strength!"

"That is very reassuring." It really was; Matt began to feel a bit of courage returning. "But say, angel—how shall I stand against the power of sorcery? Can the Lord give me . . . No, of course He can, what's the matter with me? But will He? Will He give me the power to defeat a sorcerous king? And all the hierarchy of sorcery at his command? For surely, only a saint could channel so much of God's power!"

"Hast thou no wish to be a saint?"

"Well, of course. I mean, I do intend to be one, someday—but I had just naturally assumed it was going to take a long time in Purgatory, and . . ."

"No saint can intervene in the affairs of that benighted land of Ibile," the angel said sternly. "God will not send one of Heaven's host bodily against mortal humans, no matter how great their evil. He will not so strongly upset the balance here on earth; His saints work through the agency of human beings who open themselves to God and all His blessed ones."

"Well, I mean, I try . . ."

"That sufficeth—if thou dost try with all thy might to be good."

"But I've got such a temper! Such lust! Such confounded, overweening pride! I mean, here I was, about to take on all the evil of

Ibile, just so I could become a king, and . . ." Matt ran down. "That wasn't exactly the most worthy of motives, was it?"

"Thou hast given thyself answer. Yet be assured, thou art perfectible. God does not ask that you never fail—He asks only that you persevere."

"But that's what I've *been* doing! All my life! *Trying* to be good, even if I did develop doubts about what good was, and virtue and sin . . ."

He ran down again. The angel only stood there, humming.

After a while, Matt said, "I did find some answers."

"Not all."

"No—though I've just found one more." Matt frowned. "Of course, I should have realized. I know the power of symbols over the human soul; I should have realized that the Name of God was one of the most potent symbols that exists."

"Say, rather, *the* most powerful."

"The single one?" Matt lifted his head, then realized what that surge of questioning within him meant. "I still haven't learned, have I?"

"Nay. Ask thy self what the name of God comprises, and what that name doth constitute—and thou shalt be some little ways wiser."

Matt remembered the legend of the golem, and the Hindu catalog of names of God, and began to wonder again.

Then he realized that he was wondering, and broke down. "This is ridiculous! I can't possibly be a hero! I'm not sure of anything!"

"*Any* thing?" the angel intoned.

"Well—not enough, anyway."

"It *is* enough. It will increase, in its testing. Wilt thou, then, do the Lord's will?"

"Look," Matt said in desperation, "I don't even have enough magical *knowledge* to do this job! Whenever I try to work a spell, it's like swimming through glue! When I do finally manage to finish a verse, it takes longer and longer each time before it takes effect! I just don't have the magical clout!"

"Indeed," the angel agreed. "Ibile hath been so long steeped in sin that it is now saturated with sorcery. Therefore the spells of good wizards seem weakened, for they have so much greater a weight of evil to work against."

Matt caught the concept instantly—a sort of magical inertia, varying directly with the evil confronted. "Can . . . No, strike that. *Will*

God give me the extra strength I need to contend against magic like that?"

"He will give thee the strength, through the sorrowing patron of Ibile, who will ever stand ready to thine aid, if thou dost call upon him. Saint Iago is he named."

Not, Matt thought, the most auspicious of designations.

"Yet be not deceived," the angel said sternly. "If thou dost undertake this task for love of the Lord, He will give thee the strength—yet 'tis for thee to use that strength in such fashion as to banish these sorcerers of Ibile!"

"One against a thousand," Matt muttered. "Or five, or ten. I'm just not that smart."

"God will direct thee through His Grace—if thou art open to Him."

Matt thought of all the times that he had given in to anger, or the other temptations of the flesh, and shuddered. But he sensed, somehow, that if he turned back from this challenge, he would never be all that he could be. "I didn't ask for this."

"Nay," the angel said, "thou didst—not in the foolish haste of thy words alone, yet in a movement within thy spirit that led to them."

And that, Matt realized, was true. He had always been convinced of his own lack of worth—but his victory in Merovence had make him begin to think that he might be a better man than he had thought. In his cleanup campaign, each minor victory against a sorcerer had increased his longing for a bigger challenge, a stronger opponent to measure himself against . . .

But not *this* strong! "I just can't do it! Not alone!"

"Thou wilt not be alone," the angel assured him. "One already hath come to thine aid." It gestured toward Narlh's sleeping form. "There will be others—for many groan under the yoke of this sorcery."

Matt stared at the light, cowardice warring within him against courage and the need to prove himself. The moment stretched out . . .

Matt sagged. "I just can't do it."

The angel stood, humming, a moment longer . . .

Then, with a sound like a sigh, it disappeared.

Matt knelt, feeling the chill night air that somehow reached him through his guarding circle, then realized that it was a chill of the soul, a feeling of forlorn abandonment, removed from the messenger of God, from that partial contact with the Source of All . . .

He started to speak, then bit back the words, thought them over carefully, then swallowed, hoped he wasn't being as great a fool as he thought he was, and said, "Of course, I could *try* . . ."

The chill was gone; a warmth seemed to wrap him, and the thought sprang unbidden into his mind, that he had just reestablished contact with the valiant souls who had gone before him, whether to victory or martyrdom—and that thought made him realize that his refusal had been, in no matter how small a measure, his own cutting off of that contact.

If you wanted to belong to the club, you had to pay your dues. "Saint Iago," he breathed, "help me now, for I feel like the world's greatest coward!"

And the help was instant, the warm, consoling, comforting presence within him, reassuring, bracing, and filling the void of his fear with courage.

Staggering, Matt pushed himself to his feet, smiling up at the sky, his emotions a silent prayer of thanks, realizing that he was bound by his oath again, though he hadn't spoken it aloud—as much bound as he ever had been through foolish and hasty words.

He stood that way a moment, becoming aware of his surroundings again, noticing that the moon was near the zenith of its night's path.

Then he turned away and went to wake Narlh for his watch.

CHAPTER 8

The Sophisticated
Cyclops

Matt didn't remember sleeping that night, and certainly didn't go any-where, but his mind made a major expedition. It roved here and there from one thought to another, touching on idea after idea but never con-sidering any one for very long. All in all, he should have waked ex-hausted, but when he finally saw the sky lightening with dawn and gave up, he was surprised to find himself feeling fully rested and crav-ing action. He put it down to one of the many minor miracles that are continually happening and never really noticed much.

On the other hand, maybe the episode with the angel had been a dream. Or was the distinction academic?

Over a breakfast of very well-done venison, he told Narlh, "I've changed my mind."

"Keeps it clean." The dracogriff took another bite of haunch and asked chewing, "Whatcha got in mind?"

"Going into the heart of Ibile," Matt answered. "Eventually to the castle of the sorcerer-king, I suppose."

Narlh nearly choked on his venison. Then he started coughing, and Matt jumped up, pounding between the beast's shoulder blades. Narlh took a long gasp, then bellowed, *"Are you crazy?"*

"Probably," Matt conceded.

Narlh swallowed the offending venison and demanded, "Just what the hell do you think you can do in Orlequedrille?"

"Haven't the foggiest," Matt admitted. "But I'll know by the time I get there."

"Yeah, 'cause you'll get there in pieces! Or trussed up and ready for the torture chamber, if you're lucky! King Gordogrosso doesn't waste perfectly good captives by chopping their heads off, y' know—he kills them as slowly as he can, and with every last ounce of pain, 'cause he loves watching it!"

Matt shuddered and had second thoughts. Then he had thirds, and shook his head with adamantine resolve. "I'll have to chance it. There are too many people who'll go on suffering if I don't."

"And too many monsters who'll *start* suffering if you *do*!" Narlh scrambled to his feet. "Not me, Wizard! That's too dangerous for any decent man or beast!"

"I won't try to talk you into it." Matt worked at keeping his tone level. "I can't ask anybody to commit suicide with me—especially if it's going to be slow."

"Good! 'Cause I know a nice little valley, no men, no dragons, no ugly little sorcerers looking for monster blood! You go your way, and I'll go mine! Good-bye!"

"Good luck," Matt called after Narlh's retreating tail. He watched the dracogriff waddle away for a few minutes, then sighed and knelt to throw dirt on the flames. When the camp fire was dead out, he turned, wishing he had a pack to shoulder, took up his staff, and started away downhill, with the sun at his back.

It would have been nice to have company, he mused—especially since he was beginning to get a very cold feeling inside. He sent up a quick plea to Saint Iago, to lend him some strength—and was surprised to feel warmth spreading through him, and confidence, and serenity. He was even more surprised to realize that he was beginning to think that if he died, he died—but at least he'd know he had tried his best. And this life didn't really matter much, measured against the next. Here in this world, he might not have become all he could, but at least he would have died trying.

Which meant, of course, that he'd enter the afterlife still trying to become greater of heart and soul. It began to make sense, that martyrs became automatic saints . . .

"On the other hand, that's probably where the bad men are that made my hatchling-hood hellish."

Matt nearly jumped ten feet in the air. "*Yiiiii!* What in the name of . . ." Then he realized that Narlh's huge nose was just beneath his elbow and heaved a sigh of relief. "Did anybody ever tell you that you move very quietly?"

"Not so mousy as that," the dracogriff returned. "If you can't pay any better attention, boy, you're going to be fried."

"Lesson noted." Matt glanced at the monster. "I thought you were going to a nice, quiet valley."

"Yeah—until I remembered I've still got a sorcerer on my tail. For a while, at least, I just might be safer with you than without you."

"Besides, you might find the men who made you miserable?"

"I was kinda thinking about that. If I do, see, they're bound to be trying to destroy you, 'cause they're evil, and you're not—so I'd have a great excuse to fry them."

Matt frowned. "Don't plan on revenge, Narlh. It's just as likely to destroy you as them."

"What're you, a preacher all of a sudden? Besides, I know that! Anybody in Ibile knows that! Try for revenge, and you put yourself into the hands of the Evil One—and the king and all his henchmen are the Devil's agents! No, revenge in Ibile just sets you up as a victim—unless you're one of the top sorcerers."

Matt frowned. "Then, why . . ."

"'Cause if I'm defending you, I'm not trying for revenge." The huge dragon head grinned at him. "But just sort of along the way, I bump off the ones I've got a grudge against. Neat, huh?"

"Very," Matt said slowly, "except that your real motives might weaken your case a little."

"Not if I'm acting as an agent of Good. Look, what changed your mind all of a sudden, huh?"

Matt took a deep breath and said, "An angel."

"See what I mean?" Narlh started making the weird sound that passed for his laughter again. "I got 'em knocked!"

"I see." Matt sighed. "And I have to admit I'm glad of your company. You realize, of course, that we stand a very good chance of going down in flames."

"As long as it's not hellfire." Narlh shrugged. "With that sorcerer on my tail, I'm likely to be drained, anyway. But with a wizard to help, the odds are a little better."

"Yes, except that I'm leading you into greater danger," Matt said. "Still, look on the bright side—I might have strong enough magic to make them kill us quickly, in self-defense."

"There you go!" Narlh agreed. "Of course, if you decided to turn back, I wouldn't object."

"Be a little disappointed in me, though?"

"No, not really." The dragon head turned toward him, frowning. "Why do you say that?"

"Because *I* would be." Matt turned his face downhill. "Well, let's march. Looks like it's going to be a long day."

They'd only been on the road an hour or two before Narlh grew impatient with the slow pace and flew back to the campsite to pick up the saddle. Matt climbed aboard, and the dracogriff set off at what was, for him, a comfortable pace. Actually, it wasn't bad for Matt, either, once he got used to the notion of leaning forward in the saddle, to prevent the whiplashing that came from the monster's long, lazy leaps, and caught the rhythm of the slight posting he needed. Not much, though—Narlh's gait was like a horse with innersprings.

"I take it flying wouldn't be much faster than this?"

"Oh, some," Narlh allowed, "but I *hate* flying. Still, if you insist . . ."

A suspicion formed in Matt's mind; he remembered how close to the ground the dracogriff had stayed when last they'd flown. It hadn't been all that obvious, on a mountain hillside when they were chasing a rolling rock—but now, on a road with a much gentler slope . . . "If you would. Just for a little way—I want to stay used to the rhythm of it, in case we need to take off in an emergency."

"Oh, *all* right," Narlh grumped, and lit out in a long, flat run, faster and faster, wings spreading wide to the sides . . .

Then they were airborne. Matt looked down and saw the ground sinking away . . .

But not very far.

"Uh—you *can* go higher than this if you have to, can't you?"

"Don't worry," Narlh snapped. "If I see a tree, I'll loft over it." He took a quick glance at the sky behind him, then turned back to face front.

It gave Matt a chill. What would have happened if that tree had shown up while Narlh hadn't had his eyes on the road? "I . . . take it you'd prefer not to go higher if you can help it."

"Oh, I can help it! You can be sure of that." Narlh turned back to scowl at Matt. "What're you getting so nervous about? Who's doing the flying, anyway?"

"Me! So would you mind keeping your eyes on the road?"

Narlh snatched a quick glance at the sky, then turned back front, muttering something about the people in back always having to have things their own way.

Matt gave up. "Okay, that's enough for an air drill. You can go down now."

"Thank heaven!" Narlh huffed, and slowed down to a long gallop as he hit the ground. Matt was reminded of an albatross, with that need for a long runway—only this time, *he* was hanging on to its neck. It was a rough landing, but all in all, Matt decided it was safer than flying with Narlh.

It was afternoon when they spotted the refugee family. The father was pulling a handcart, slogging away, keeping the cart going mostly by throwing the weight of his body against it. The mother was carrying a baby, and the children were fussing, protesting with every step.

Matt's heart went out to them.

Then the mother saw Narlh. She gave a cry of alarm, and suddenly the cart was standing in the roadway by itself, as the family headed for the roadside brush.

"Hey! Hold on, there! Doggone it, I'm a nice guy!" Narlh roared, and leaped after them.

Matt just barely managed to hold on. "Uh—it might help if you didn't charge them, Narlh."

"What's this *charge* business? I'm just trying to catch up with them!"

"Yes, but to the uninformed, it might look as though you were chasing them. And you did sound kind of angry."

"Angry? Of *course* I'm angry! How would *you* feel if people ran whenever they saw you?"

"I wouldn't like it. And I didn't, either." Matt was thinking about a couple of girls he'd been attracted to in high school. "But believe me—it works better if you sit and wait for them to come to you."

Narlh dug his claws in and jammed to a halt by the cart. "Says *you*! Me, I'll try the old-fashioned method." He jammed his snout into the brush. "Yoo-hoo! Where are you? Come out, come out, wherever you are!"

There was a scrabbling noise, moving away from them.

"Aw, come on now!" Narlh said, exasperated. "I'm not gonna *eat* you, for crying out loud!"

"I think that might be just what they were worrying about." Matt slid off his back and stepped into the center of the roadway, calling, "Really, folks! He's got a nasty temper, but he's got a heart of gold . . . plate," he added, in case any sorcerers were listening. "And I'm a wizard, from Merovence. We really don't mean any harm. Why don't you come on out and chat awhile?"

Narlh frowned at him as though he were crazy, but kept quiet.

Finally, a man's voice answered, with a strong peasant burr, "If ye truly mean us no harm, strangers, ride on, I beg of ye."

"But you look really tired," Matt protested. "I was kind of thinking we could guard you while you take a good rest."

There was a pause, then a quick, whispered consultation. It ended, and the father waded out of the brush—but not very far. "Good day to you, then."

"God be with you," Matt answered.

There were multiple gasps and a quick flurry of whispers from the brush.

"If you speak the name of God," the father said, "you must be a good-magic-worker, if you are one at all."

"I am." Matt didn't mention that the man himself had spoken the name, with no apparent ill effects. "But what brings you onto the road, goodman?"

The man heaved a sigh, and what little starch was left in him seeped out. "Soldiers, sir. They were ransacking other cots not distant from ours, so we took what we could and left on the road."

Sobbing sounded from behind him, and he looked up, then turned away. He brought his wife out a moment later, drying her eyes and forcing a smile. "'Tis naught of your care, sirs."

"I know." Matt tried to look sympathetic. "It's hard to leave a home."

"'Twas well we did." She bit her lip. "From the hilltop, we looked back and saw the soldiers firing our cot." She turned back to weep quietly on her husband's shoulder.

Someone small peeked out from behind her skirts, and a larger edition stepped up boldly to inform Matt, "They drove off our pig and our sheep! And set fire to it all!"

The wife let out a wail.

"*Shhh*, silly!" A sister added herself to the tribe. "You'll only make Mama cry!"

The boy looked startled, then abashed.

Narlh snorted.

They all turned—to see the smaller boy whirling to flee, bawling. His sister caught him and made soothing noises.

Matt frowned. "Don't pick on the kid!"

"I didn't," Narlh snapped. "I was trying to be friendly."

The tears cut off, and the tyke turned to look back, wide-eyed.

"That's 'friendly,' for him," Matt explained. "Not quite the same as it is for you."

"Hey! Watch whose reputation you're slurring!"

"I thought I was improving it."

The bigger boy took a daring step toward the monster, then another, and another.

Narlh looked down his nose at him, then deliberately turned away.

The boy reached out and touched his flank.

Narlh ignored him.

The boy began to stroke the leathery hide, tiptoeing closer and closer to the front, a step at a time.

Narlh looked back, one beady eye transfixing the boy.

The lad froze.

Narlh snorted and turned away again.

The five-year-old shrilled with delight.

Big brother sneaked another step or two forward.

Matt turned away from the game of peekaboo. "I didn't know he had it in him."

"He is very big," the wife said nervously.

"Yes, that's why I thought we might do well on guard duty. Why don't you folks just sit down and have a bite while we watch for you?"

"Bless you, kind sir!" The wife tottered toward the cart and sank to the road beside it, cradling the baby in her lap.

"Uh, I had in mind *off* the road," Matt said, eyeing the dirt strip as though he expected a Sherman tank to come clanking up. "Just in case, you know."

"Aye, aye." The husband reached down to help his wife up. "Just a few more steps now, Judy, there's my lass. Some open grass there, off the road a pace, aye."

Judy sighed, managed to rise, and tottered off toward the shade of a tree, leaning on her husband's arm.

There was an explosive snort followed by a trio of delighted shrieks behind him. Matt swung about, alarmed, but saw Narlh turned back frontward, nose in the air, too lofty to be concerned about what was going on around his tail. Matt smiled and turned to the cart.

From the tongue he had to lift and pull, he gathered the soldiers had gotten the family donkey, too.

He pulled the cart off the road and near the tree, where the wife was nursing the baby. Narlh ambled along, nose in the air. Matt wondered if he was really watching for an aerial attack.

"Bless ye, kind sir!" The wife had a real smile on.

"My pleasure, I'm sure." Matt folded up cross-legged, facing the husband. "So you're bound for Merovence?"

"Aye, if I can come to those mountains!" the man said, exasperated. "They seem so close, yet ever do they retreat from me!"

"It's the clear air—it magnifies them so that they seem closer. I'd say you're still about two days from the pass at the top."

"You have come from there?" the man said, wide-eyed.

Matt nodded. "And I'd plan on lightening your load, if you can— some of that road is very steep, and it's all uphill."

The wife bit her lip again, and the husband said quickly, "We have brought little enough. What we have are things too dear to part with."

Matt just couldn't understand why married people seemed to acquire so many things that they couldn't bear to part with. Maybe it was because there were so many more of them.

He pushed himself to his feet. "Rest while you can. I'll send the kids over." He turned away to shoo the children from Narlh back to Mama. As they ran for the picnic, he muttered to the monster, "Never knew you were soft on kids."

"Hey, I think they look yummy!"

"Come off it. You were having as much fun as they were."

Narlh shrugged, with a rattle of wings. "Look, I missed out on it when I was a fledgling. A guy can try to make up for lost time, can't he?"

"I couldn't agree more." Matt glanced back over his shoulder—and saw the father carving a ham. His mouth watered. "They, uh—came well provided."

"Huh?" Narlh looked over, then turned away with a snort.

"Well, I thought it looked pretty good!"

"Each to his own," the monster said.

"Just what's wrong with it, anyway, huh?"

"It's not bleeding."

As he paced the circle on sentry duty, Matt reflected that Narlh must prefer his food still moving. When he said he liked fresh meat, he meant it. He gave the family about an hour, by the sun, then turned back to nudge the father. "Sun's past noon. You might want to get back on the road."

"Aye." The man sighed and forced himself to his feet. He reached down to help his wife up and called out, "Jorge! Cecile! Rampout!" The children left off playing hide-and-seek and came pelting back.

"Bless you for your kindness," the wife said, smiling, then suddenly dewy-eyed. "'Tis good to know a few souls still act with charity."

"More and more where you're going," Matt assured her.

"I must trust in that." The father sighed. "We have no money and will have no farm. We must depend on kindness, now."

"No money?" Matt lifted his head. "Say . . . maybe we could strike a deal."

"Deal?" The father was instantly wary.

"Yes. I'm living off the land, see, and it's not exactly fat here."

"Aye." The wife blinked away tears again. "The soldiers . . ." Then she suddenly realized what Matt was saying. "You must take some food! We have more than we'll need to come into Merovence!"

"Judy," her husband said, uncomfortably, "we shall not find food in plenty, just for crossing the mountains . . ."

"Right," Matt agreed. "I couldn't let myself just *take* food from you—you're too apt to need it. But I could give you some Merovencian coins, and you can buy fresh food with that. Lightens the load going over the mountains, that way, you see—and cuts down on spoilage."

The husband looked interested, but Judy protested, "We could not take money from one who has done us kindness . . ."

"I assure you, you'll be doing *me* a kindness, just by selling me some supplies! Here, now . . ." Matt reached into his purse.

A few minutes later, he and Narlh headed downhill as the family toiled away uphill again, their cart lighter by two hams, half a bushel of grapes, a bottle of homemade wine, half a wheel of cheese, and a loaf of bread.

"Sure you don't mind carrying all that?" Matt asked.

"So what are you going to do, get squashed by lunch?" Narlh snorted. "Be real, okay?"

"I keep trying . . ."

"As you will." The dracogriff snorted. "But don't you think two gold pieces was a little much for these provisions?"

"Well, maybe . . ."

"You could have bought it all for two coppers."

"True." Matt shrugged. "But how much good are coins with Alisande's picture going to do here in Ibile?"

"There's some truth in that . . ."

"Besides, that family can put them to good use. Basic supplies—"

"Supplies! For two gold pieces, they can buy a small *farm*!"

Matt nodded. "You know, I suppose they could . . ."

•   •   •

They hadn't made much progress by sunset. Narlh could travel by leaps and bounds when he had to—but not for very long at a stretch; it was tiring. Besides, Matt was in continual danger of whiplash, and traveling braced against Narlh's bounding was tiring for *him*. So they went at Narlh's normal pace, which was about as fast as a tired man could walk.

The good side was that, when evening came, Matt wasn't tired—at least, not terribly. He still had plenty of energy to set up camp and do whatever magic might prove necessary.

Preferably as little as possible; he felt as if he were lighting a beacon any time he worked a spell. No, if he could set up camp without magic, so much the better. Matt found a tree with a fork and wedged the butt of a fallen limb into it.

"What's *that* supposed to be?" Narlh demanded. "A bear trap?"

"No, a people shelter." Matt pointed at the sky. "We might have rain tonight."

"Good; I could use a bath."

"True, true . . ."

Narlh reared his head back. "Well! If you're going to be *that* way about it, I'm going to find some dinner!"

"You'll be amazed at the improvement when you get back," Matt called.

"You mean you're going to have a bath, too?" Narlh humphed, and waddled on out of sight.

Matt smiled, shaking his head, and turned to pick up the sack with the food in it. The comment about the bear trap had reminded him about the problems of night visitors—the natural kind. He wished he had some rope, but wasn't about to risk a spell for such a small item. Instead, he found a broken branch dangling from a nearby tree and hooked the sack onto a twig. Not as good as it could be—any passing bear could knock it down, and a wolf might even be able to jump up to it—but at least it would protect the provisions from raccoons, or whatever the local equivalent was. Badgers, probably.

Then Matt went back to cutting branches. He draped them angling between the ground and the limb, to make a serviceable imitation of a pup tent. He stepped back to admire his handiwork, thought of starting a fire and fixing dinner, then decided to check out the neighborhood while there was still a little twilight left. He'd noticed a small hill when they'd been surveying for a good campsite; in fact, he would have set up there if there had been any cover. But it was just a grassy knob on top, and he was a little shy about being overexposed.

Still, it would do nicely as a lookout. He climbed up, then stood looking around at the landscape, feeling an oddly pleasant glow. The countryside lay quiet in the gloaming. It still sloped, overall, but they were down into deciduous trees, and every so often, the trees opened out into farmsteads.

But the farmhouses were burned out, the byres and sties were empty, and the fields lay in stubble—or churned to baked mud by horses' hooves. Kipling's lines came unbidden to Matt's mind:

> They shall feed their horse on the standing crop,
> Their men on the garnered grain.
> The thatch of the byres shall serve for their fires
> When all the cattle are slain.

Kipling had been talking about soldiers putting down bandits, of course—but here, the soldiers *were* the bandits. Matt turned away downhill, trying to keep his good mood from evaporating completely.

"I say! Fell beast! Put me down!"

Matt looked up, jolted out of his reverie.

"I am innocent! I am a poor wayfarer, seeking survival! Release me this instant!"

A furious growling answered him.

Matt started running. He recognized that growl—it was Narlh.

And there the monster came, plodding toward him—with something big in his mouth. Big, and squirming. Matt peered through the gloaming, and could just make out a human form. Not very large, percentage-wise, but still human.

"This is completely outrageous! I meant no harm—therefore, neither should . . . Oh!" The stranger looked up and saw Matt. "Greetings, kind sir! Could you persuade this beast to let me go?"

Matt had a bit of a shock—the man had only one eye. Not that he'd lost one—he'd been born that way. It was right smack dab in the middle of his forehead.

Poise above all. Matt tried a half smile and said, "That depends on why he picked you up in the first place."

"Absolutely no justifiable reason! There was simply . . ."

Narlh drowned him out with a muffled roar.

"My friend seems to disagree," Matt pointed out. "How about a solemn promise not to run away, if he puts you down? Until we sort out exactly what you've done, at least."

"I've done nothing! I . . . Oh, very well. I give you my solemn promise."

"Ptooey!" Narlh put the little man down with an exhalation that sounded more like spitting. The cyclops rolled and came to his feet, while Narlh was still working his jaws and exclaiming, "Phew! What a flavor!"

"Well, no one asked you to have a bite," the cyclops said indignantly. "Always thought myself a man of good taste, actually."

"Yeah, with a taste for our foodstuffs!"

"You caught him stealing?" Matt asked.

"Not a bit! I haven't touched your food!"

"No, but he was sure trying!" Narlh said. "Had a big long stick, and he was gonna knock your food bag down!"

"That's not exactly friendly," Matt pointed out.

The cyclops sighed. "I know, and I'm quite sorry. But really, I haven't had a bite to eat for two days—the birds fly at the slightest sign of me, and the rabbits won't let me come near. I haven't even found any berries! I would have asked, of course, but there was no one by, and I was so *very* hungry . . ."

Actually, Matt didn't think the cyclops looked all *that* lean. Pretty bulky, in fact, though none of it was fat. It was easy to see, because all he wore was a sort of fur kilt. He was very muscular, particularly in the arms, shoulders, and chest—though his legs looked to be borrowed from a rhinoceros. In fact, he was a pretty good picture of what Matt had always thought a Neanderthal would look like, from the neck down.

From the neck up, of course, he was quite well formed, if you could overlook the ocular arrangement. Handsome, in fact—if Matt imagined him with two eyes. Also, of course, he wore a pretty heavy beard. That could hide a lot.

All in all, he looked pretty trustworthy.

"You're softening," Narlh pointed out.

"Why not?" Matt sighed. "I've been hungry enough to steal, myself—though I never had the opportunity. We'll stand you to a good meal, stranger. Or trade, rather." He smiled at a sudden idea. "Maybe you can tell me a bit about the countryside."

"Why, gladly, sir! By the by, whom have I the pleasure of addressing? As for myself, I'm called Fadecourt."

Matt caught the use of the phrase "I'm called." Apparently, the cyclops wasn't about to tell his real name. Wise, in a world where magic worked by words. "Pleased to meet you, Fadecourt. I'm Matthew Mantrell."

The cyclops' eyebrow rose. "The Lord Wizard of Merovence?"

"The same." This guy was a bit too quick for Matt's liking.

"Well! I *am* honored!"

"You don't say." Matt wasn't sure he wanted allies who were impressed with him—but a little kindness never hurt. "We were just about to start supper. Know anything about camping?"

"A smattering," the cyclops said, with a touch of irony. "I've done a great deal of it in the recent past."

"And not entirely willingly?" Matt led the way back to the campsite. "Any particular reason?"

"Oh, a few minor things taken from me, such as my station and my home." Fadecourt was trying to sound casual. "And a small matter of soldiers all over the kingdom apparently having been told to be on watch for me. I've only to step into a village before there's a hue and cry—and from some of the missiles coming my way, I gather I'm outside the protection of the law."

"Oh?" Matt looked up, interested. "There's law in Ibile?"

"To be sure—the king's will. Or whim, I should perhaps say. Still, Gordogrosso does seem to regard the taking of human life as his prerogative; it's forbidden to most other people. From the zeal with which I'm pursued, I gather he's decided to exercise that privilege, in my case—but at second hand."

Matt winced at hearing the king's name spoken aloud, and waited for an answering stir of the magical field—but none came. He relaxed. "I'm enough of a marked man as it is, Fadecourt. I'm not sure it's all that much in my interest to have a companion with a price on his head." Then another aspect of the issue hit him. He cocked his head to the side. "Just what did you do to get the king down on your case, anyway?"

"Oh, just the usual sorts of crimes—you know."

"Not in Ibile, I don't. Enlighten me."

"Well, the common run of things—saving virgins from evil lechers, slaying hideous giant snakes that were preying on villagers, protecting the weak from the strong—that sort of thing."

It made sense, Matt decided. Actions that were good deeds in Merovence would naturally be crimes here—especially if the lechers were in good with the king, and the snakes had been sent to punish the villages that had somehow offended him or his nobles. Matt made a decision and called back over his shoulder, "You might as well go hunt, Narlh. I think we'll be okay here."

The dracogriff mumbled something along the lines of sneaking back-stabbers, but he prowled off into the night.

Fadecourt looked after him in surprise, then turned back to Matt. "I appreciate your confidence."

"You've got the right enemies." They'd come into the campsite. Matt reached down the sack of provisions. "What's your preference—ham, or venison?"

"Anything!"

Matt pulled out the half haunch of game and handed it to him. The cyclops all but fell on it, slavering.

"Easy, easy!" Matt called, alarmed. "You'll give yourself a bellyache!"

Fadecourt froze. Then he said, "My apologies. Hunger is no excuse for bad manners. If you don't mind, though, I will have a few more bites."

"Sure, sure! Just don't overdo it, okay?" Matt turned away and began prowling around the clearing.

Fadecourt swallowed and called, "What do you seek?"

"Stones," Matt called back, "for the fire pit."

Fadecourt put the deer leg down—a major act of will—and came to join Matt. "This much, at least, I can do! There's one that would be good." He bent down and picked up a two-foot boulder. Then he saw another one, a little larger, so he shifted the first one into the crook of his elbow and scooped up the second boulder with his other hand. "Where did you want them?"

"In—in the center of the clearing." Matt pointed.

"Right-o." Fadecourt stepped lithely over to center and set the first stone down gently, then the second. "Leave this to me, old chap. You scout up the kindling, eh?"

"Yeah . . . sure." Matt just stared. Each of those boulders had to weigh a hundred pounds, at least—and they weren't exactly carved for ease of carrying. Matt might, just might, have been able to carry one of them with both hands, if he'd absolutely had to. More likely, he'd have rolled it—with the aid of a lever.

He turned away to hunt up kindling, wondering if he should maybe have asked Narlh to put off the hunting a little longer.

He laid the kindling, shaved a fuzz stick, and struck a spark with flint and steel, then breathed it alight.

"Will you not light your blaze with magic, Wizard?"

Matt shook his head. "Spells are like money—you shouldn't spend them unless you have to." For some reason, he was a little reluctant to tell this stranger about the problem of attracting sorcerous attention by using magic.

He pulled out a ham, drew his knife, and started to cut a slice—then stopped, amazed. It was like cutting wood. He struck it with his knuckles, and heard a definite knock.

"You might want to boil it," Fadecourt suggested. "It's dried, you see—and quite salty."

"I suppose I'll have to use a spell, then." Matt sighed. "I don't happen to have any pots with me."

"Come, sir! Have you never made a bark bucket?"

Matt looked up, surprised. "No, can't say that I have."

"Only the work of a few minutes! I'll be back in a jiff." The cyclops uncoiled, ending up standing, and prowled off into the night, slipping a flint knife from his belt.

Matt watched him go, pleasantly surprised—he'd expected the stranger to be panting with eagerness to see Matt work a spell. Apparently, he didn't have too many doubts about Matt's powers.

Or didn't it matter to him?

Matt shrugged, and rummaged around among the firewood he'd collected to start lashing together a tripod.

A long throat cleared itself off to his left.

Matt looked up, surprised, then smiled. "Thanks for the warning, Narlh."

The dracogriff came up and dropped a wild boar by the fire. "Why you humans can't hear a guy making a racket coming through the brush, I'll never know."

"Small ears," Matt answered. "How come you can find game when nobody else can?"

"They don't seem to want to stay hid when they see me coming." Narlh walked around a half circle, letting his hindquarters lie down and ending with his front section recumbent, too. "You might want to turn your back a little—I'm not big on table manners."

"Might help if you had a table." But Matt did hike himself a little way away.

"Where's the uninvited guest?"

"Oh, I took care of that—I invited him. He's off making a bark bucket for me, so I can boil some life back into this ham."

"Trying to butter you up, huh? Look, if you want some pig meat with the juice still in it, hack off a slice!"

Matt turned back, overcoming revulsion, and took out his knife. "Don't mind if I do, thanks." He skinned a hindquarter and cut off several foot-long wedges of meat. Then he skewered them on green sticks and hung them over the fire. "I appreciate it."

"I'll never miss 'em."

"Oh! I see you've managed!" Fadecourt came up to the fire, hauling a bucket.

"Yes, but we can fry the ham for breakfast—if we can make it chewable." Matt reached up, took down the bucket, and hung it from the tripod. "Thanks for filling it."

"Don't mention it." The cyclops folded himself and eyed the pork hungrily. He took up the hindquarter of venison, cut a strip, and munched.

The fact that he made some try at table manners impressed Matt more than the bucket.

"If you'll excuse me." He got up, went to rummage in the provisions sack.

"Certainly." Fadecourt's gaze followed Matt as he lifted out the can of talcum powder and went to the limit of the firelight, shaking out a white stream as he went backward around the camp fire, completing the circle, then making a second one. When he finished, he put away the powder and came to sit down by the fire again. "Just like to have it ready if we need it, you see."

"But of course." Fadecourt looked a little puzzled.

Trees whipped in a sudden wind.

Matt shivered and pulled his cloak over his shoulders. "Looks as though we may be in for a wet night."

"Ah, yes. The advantage to my sort of raiment is that it dries out rather quickly."

"Why not keep it from getting wet in the first place? A brush hut isn't that hard to cobble."

"So I see." Fadecourt eyed Matt's shelter. "I just may imitate you in that."

"Be my guest. I take it you were heading for Merovence, to get away from being chased?"

"Yes, but only until I had gathered the wherewithal to return."

"And what would that be?"

The cyclops' shoulders sagged. "I haven't the foggiest, really. I'm not in a position to hire an army—and I don't really imagine too many citizens of Merovence would be ready to march against the sorcery of Ibile. I suppose the best I could find would have been a wizard, who might have been willing to teach me some spells."

Matt definitely didn't like the sound of that. "It takes time to learn enough magic to protect yourself in this kind of country, you know."

Fadecourt heaved a sigh. "Well, if years it takes, then years I must

give to it—but I'll not forsake my fellow citizens in their extremity!"
He looked up at Matt. "And how do *you* come to be in the middle of
a tearing wilderness on such an ugly-seeming night?"

"I'm questing. You know—it's really in fashion."

"No, I don't." The cyclops frowned. "Certainly not in so hazardous
a place as a mountainside in Ibile, in the company of a dracogriff—
deuced prickly, the beasts are."

A snort answered him from behind Matt.

"No offense," the cyclops said easily. "I'm in something of the
same position myself, d' you see."

"Being very prickly?"

"No—being engaged in a search. It's a quest, in its way. A lost article, you might say."

"Oh." Matt frowned. "Where was it lost?"

"At the king's court," the cyclops said. "I had word of it from a
friend who has some acquaintance there."

Matt remembered that he might be the target of an effort to im-
press, and automatically demoted the "acquaintance" from a courtier
to a servant. "I gather the party who lost it will reward you hand-
somely for its return?"

"Oh, quite! Or, rather, he'll reward me rather unpleasantly if I return with no chance of retrieving it." Fadecourt gave him a toothy
smile. He had very large, very even, very white teeth.

"I see," Matt said with great originality, trying not to think about
those teeth. "Is it intrinsic, sentimental, or aesthetic value?"

"Oh, of only sentimental and practical value, I assure you." The
cyclops' eye took on the gleam of delight that comes from recogniz-
ing a kindred soul—and, just possibly, a good conversation. "At least,
I don't believe anyone would pay more than a few coppers for it."

"I take it," Matt said, "that if you discover its whereabouts, it
might be rather dangerous to go after it."

"It might that, yes. You see, I've little magic and less sorcery."

"Is that all?" Matt stared, frankly amazed. He recovered quickly
and managed a smile. "I'd think you might have a problem with, um,
guards, if there are any."

"Oh no, not a lick! I mean, yes, there probably will be men-at-
arms, but I'm not at all concerned about them. Strength of arms,
don't you know."

"No," Matt said, taking in the nearly naked form before him, "I
don't know. You don't have a weapon on you, except for that little
flint knife."

"No, I meant my actual arms—limbs, do you see."

"Oh, yes." Matt remembered how Fadecourt had collected boulders for the fire ring. "But don't overestimate your strength. Sheer lifting power won't help you against armed guards."

"There's a bit more to it than you've seen. Have a look." The cyclops rose and turned in one lithe, fluid motion, then stepped away to a four-foot boulder that must have weighed half a ton. He didn't even set himself, just took hold under the curve on both sides, hefted it up over his head (Matt ducked aside, panicked by the backswing), and tossed it off into the night.

Matt just stared, gaping.

There was a long hiss behind him—Narlh, with eyes glittering.

Somewhere out in the darkness, there was a faint crash.

The cyclops turned back to them with a shrug. "That's the way of it."

"Very impressive," Matt murmured, eyes glazed.

A little too impressive, in fact—not the kind of display calculated to win you a welcome to a stranger's fireside. From the sound of him, the cyclops must have been able to realize that; did he really think he was so engaging that Matt would chum up to him when he'd just proved he could probably tie Matt's guardian dracogriff in knots?

Or did he think Matt needed his strength badly enough to strike an alliance?

He just might have been right on that one.

"But that's all." The cyclops sat down again. "I can knock down any army, if need be. Of course, I'd rather not hurt the poor chaps, but I can if I have to. Or knock a hole in a castle wall, for that matter. But if they send the most junior of apprentice sorcerers after me, I'm lost."

"And," Matt said slowly, "you've taken the notion that I can counter a sorcerer."

"Quite. You do have something of a reputation in wizardry."

"But I could be lying—you don't *know* that I'm really the Lord Wizard." Matt frowned. "What gave you the idea I might really know something about magic?"

"Partly the fact that you're riding a dracogriff, a beast so scarce that any sorcerer would quite willingly kill for its blood—kill not just it, but anyone nearby."

Matt heard the long hiss behind him again, and a rustle of wings. "This makes you want to get near it?"

The cyclops shrugged. "I'm not afraid to, if that's what you mean."

Because he knew there was a wizard along? Or because he was too stupid to be scared?

Matt had a notion Fadecourt was anything but stupid. "Anything else that might make you think I'm a wizard?"

"Well, apart from the fact that you're sitting inside a magical guarding circle on a hillside in a country devoted to sorcery—no, not really."

"Just a few little simple facts." Matt nodded.

He straightened up and cleared his throat. "Ever do any painting?"

"Eh?" The cyclops stared, startled. "Why, yes, actually—quite a bit. What made you think so?"

"Just a wild guess. What instruments do you play?"

"The double flute and bassoon." The cyclops frowned. "How could you know that?"

"Just going by your general ambiance. What's your favorite book?"

"I would have to say *The Odyssey*," Fadecourt said slowly, "though I know it would be more politic to refer to the lays of Hardishane, in this part of the world."

Matt tried not to show his surprise. "Where did you find a translation?"

"Oh, I couldn't, of course. I had to learn Greek in order to read it."

That, Matt noted silently, was more than he had done. "How about the *Necronomicon*?"

"Never heard of it." The cyclops frowned. "Is it good?"

"Sheer madness—evil, too, I hear. Never read it myself, of course. Have you heard about the *Cabala*?"

The cyclops shook his head. "Not my cup of mead. Only interested in tales and histories, I blush to say." He wasn't reddening noticeably, but then, Matt was only seeing him by firelight.

"Histories? Say, I've always wondered—when was Hardishane crowned?"

"In the year of our Lord 862, and he died in 925, rich in virtue and still mighty in arms. While he lived, he drove the forces of Evil back from all these lands of the middle realm, and they basked in the light of goodness and order."

"Even Ibile?"

"Even here," Fadecourt confirmed. "Before his coming, the land was held by a people made brutish by sorcery—but he, and the good emperors of his line, held the land so clearly in the light of goodness that, within two generations, the folk of Ibile were courteous, peaceful, and cultured."

"While Hardishane's heirs ruled over the Empire." Matt frowned. "But the last Emperor fell, and the kings came again."

"Quite so—in 1084."

Matt looked up in surprise. "They held Europe united that long?" In his own universe, Charlemagne's empire hadn't really lasted more than a generation after his death, though it had continued in name down to the eighteenth century.

"They did, but Lornhane, the last reigning Emperor, was foolish and weak."

Matt noticed the qualifier. "The last *reigning* emperor?"

"Indeed. Tradition has it that Hardishane's line endures, and that his descendants still wander Europe, awaiting the time when Empire must be reestablished, or all the lands fall to evil and sorcery."

Matt nodded slowly—he had heard the legend. In fact, he had met the current heir. He traveled under the name of Sir Guy Losobal, and he was spectacularly reluctant to seek dominion. "So Lornhane did not die childless."

"No, but his heir was carried away to be reared in secrecy—which was well, for he doubtless would have been haled down and slain when his father died—for Lornhane's last years were made miserable by the chaos that reigned within his empire. However, he did have the wisdom to appoint kings to Ibile, Merovence, Allustria, and all the Northern Lands and Isles, to quench the feuding of the barons and establish some echo of Hardishane's order within their domains, by the time Lornhane died."

"And that line of kings endures in Merovence," Matt said slowly.

"Yes, though the forces of Evil nearly toppled them. I understand the queen's return to her throne was largely your own doing."

Matt waved away the flattery. "That's a bit of an exaggeration. I just did what I had to do. Not given much choice, in fact."

"Enough to have betrayed her and devoted yourself to Evil, had you wished." Fadecourt's eye glittered. "A worker of magic always has that opportunity, ever-present before him."

"Yes." Matt's voice hardened. "It's a constant temptation—and it must be constantly resisted."

"Of course," the cyclops said quietly, but Matt had the eerie feeling that he had just passed some sort of test.

He shifted uneasily. "How long did the line of kings endure in Ibile?"

"Oh, the *line* endures to this day, though none know where the rightful heir may be," Fadecourt answered, "and I assure you that the strongest sorcerers have exerted their greatest efforts to find him."

Matt lifted his head. "That must be *some* spell that's guarding him!"

"It must indeed. For myself, I fancy it was the doing of Saint Moncaire—that he crafted the spell to protect all of Hardishane's descendants, no matter how tenuous their relationship."

"But if he's hiding, he's not ruling." Matt frowned.

"Quite so. The reigning king was betrayed and slain some two hundred years ago, and a foul usurper seized the crown."

"And his grandson rules now?"

Fadecourt shook his head. "Such orderly succession is not the way of sorcery. The usurper Yzrprz was in his own turn assassinated, and the throne seized by the more-evil sorcerer Dredplen. His reign was long, though filled with terror—yet he died at the hands of a sorcerer more foul than he: the tyrant Gordogrosso, whose descendant reigns in the city of Orlequedrille still."

Matt winced. "Do me a favor, okay? Don't say the king's name aloud—it might attract his attention."

Fadecourt shrugged. "He cares naught—I am too insignificant."

"I might not be, though."

Fadecourt stiffened. "Quite true! My apologies, Wizard. Yet be assured, he knows not that I am with you."

"Yet," Matt said.

"Aye." The cyclops seemed unnerved. "Even the land may report your presence to him! Daily, his corruption widens, and may some day include even plants and rocks."

"It just gets worse as it goes along," Matt said, feeling numb.

"It does, and it will—until some man of good heart arises to overthrow this vile king." Fadecourt gave Matt a singularly penetrating glance.

Matt returned it, trying to reach a decision. He couldn't trust a total stranger, could he? For all he knew, Fadecourt might be a spy, just trying to get him to trick himself into saying he was planning to overthrow the king, so that some true testimony could be used at his trial. The cyclops might yell for reinforcements as soon as Matt said it, and he could find himself on his way to a hanging court before he knew it. Not that King Gordogrosso needed actual evidence, really, though it did tend to make things neater.

But the doggone stranger practically *knew* . . .

Then it occurred to Matt to relax and listen for guidance within him. Divine guidance, hopefully, though he'd settle for a good word from Saint Iago. He relaxed suddenly, smiling, and tried to feel some kind of nudge within his mind. In his own universe, some might think that such a method of decision-making would be the height of stupidity; but here, it should be foolproof . . .

He felt the impulse. Desperately, he hoped it was right. "Well, now that you mention it, that just happens to be my quest."

"What?" Fadecourt looked up with glowing eye. "The freeing of Ibile?"

"Good way to phrase it." Matt nodded. "Yes, I like your words better. Can you give me any idea what I'm up against?"

"Gladly, good Wizard! There will be some that you will rejoice to hear, but much that you will deplore."

"You're so encouraging," Matt murmured. "Tell me something good."

"Well, the best part of it is that Gordogrosso has not left his castle since he took power."

"Agoraphobia?" Matt looked up, interested. "Or is he just too paranoid to trust his advisers?"

"I cannot say—but he has not come out these fifteen years. You shall not, therefore, need to concern yourself about meeting the sorcerer in person."

"Until we come to his castle." Matt raised a finger. "I'm afraid that's part of the plan."

Narlh growled.

"Brave man!" Fadecourt cried. "And what will you do when you've come there?"

"Think fast," Matt said. "Actually, I hope to have come up with some sort of strategy by then. But you don't think we'll have any trouble getting there?"

"Oh, I did not say that! For look you, Gordogrosso's evil has so deeply taken hold of the land that only a few attempt any degree of goodness, and they must hide it."

"So. Every man's hand is turned against me, huh?"

"And every woman's. Each day, such few good folk as are left seek to flee the land—and are more often than not cut down in their flight."

Matt thought of the family he'd met earlier in the day, and was glad he'd found an excuse to give them a little help. "I suppose he's got a pretty good spy network."

"He has no need of it—for 'tis as though the very ground, the leaves of the trees, are so permeated with his corruption that he can see where any person is at any time. If some event is to happen, he can view it."

Matt felt his scalp prickling. "What? The land has become an extension of his nervous system? He just *knows*?"

"Well, not so bad as that," Fadecourt allowed. "'Tis said he spies by means of a magical mirror—so he must look ere he can see. Moreover, he must know that a person exists, ere he can spy upon him. Indeed, 'tis certain there are places even Gordogrosso cannot peer into—though no one is sure where they may be."

Matt's skin crawled as though he could feel someone peering down his back. "This isn't exactly building an overwhelming enthusiasm in me for this job."

"Oh, you must not give it over!" The cyclops leaned forward, reaching out toward Matt. "You are the best hope Ibile has had in a generation! Nay, valiant Wizard, I beseech you! Leave not the people of Ibile to toil in misery and sorrow! Come, and come quickly, to their aid! Defeat Gordogrosso and his evil sycophants!"

"Well . . . I . . . I'd be glad to," Matt managed, "but I'm only one man. Conceited though I may be, even *I* don't think I can take on the magic and might of a whole country, and win!"

"You shall have aid, every iota that we folk of Ibile can bring you! I myself will stand at your right hand and do all that I can to cast down your enemies! Only do what you must to save our land from corruption and Hell—even if you must take the crown yourself, to do it!"

Well! Matt couldn't have asked for a better invitation. Not that he had given up on the idea of winning a kingdom for himself, mind you, and thereby winning Alisande—but it certainly helped to be invited. Politics being what it is, it strengthened his position to have *some* shred of legitimacy to his claim. Probably helped his position magically, too, since magic here was based on right and wrong. "All right," he said magnanimously, "I'll give it a try."

After all, the angel hadn't said he couldn't, had it?

CHAPTER 9

The Siege Parlous

The soldiers had burned out the village and left the bodies to rot. Most of them had been so thoroughly charred that there wasn't much left to decay, but the positions of the blackened bones, and of the few intact but putrefying bodies, made clear what the soldiers' idea of fun had been.

It sent Narlh into a towering rage. "Where did they go? Evil! Corrupted! Back-stabbing, treacherous, wanton lumps of decay! Show me their trail! I'll hunt 'em down! I'll fry 'em all! I'll tear 'em apart and roast the pieces!"

"Easy, Narlh, easy!" The dracogriff's sudden rage had Matt more than a little frightened. "They did this a week ago, or more. They're far away now. It wouldn't do any good to ..."

"It would do me a lot of good!"

"Revenge will not aid these poor souls now," Fadecourt said.

"Killing those two-legged monsters would keep them from doing this to any other women! They did that to females of their own kind! It's bad enough when males do it to females from another species—but their *own*?"

Now Matt understood—the evidence of rape reminded Narlh too strongly of his own begetting. "Well, then, don't stop with killing off one band, Narlh. Kill off their king, the one who allows his soldiers to do this in the first place."

"Allows?" Fadecourt scoffed. "Nay, encourages! Exhorts! That none will dare turn their hands against him. Save your anger for the one who sets the example that these vicious underlings follow!"

"Vicious isn't the word for them! Look at those bodies! Even the men! Rape wasn't enough for them—they had to torture these poor people, too! And what'd they do to deserve it, huh?"

"Served a lord that the king disliked," Fadecourt answered, "whether they would or no. Nay, the long and the short of it is, there was none to defend them from the soldiers' decaying taste in amusements."

Narlh turned a baleful glare on them. "Your kind is twisted! Warped! Vile!"

"No argument," Matt muttered. "Come on, let's get out of here while I'm still more angry than sick." He picked up the pace, trying not to look either right or left until they had passed out of the village.

"Men can be good, dracogriff," Fadecourt was saying as they emerged. "What you have seen is what men can become, when they let their baser desires free."

"And when someone encourages them to be cruel and decadent," Matt growled. "When someone starts telling them that hurting other people is fun, and it's okay to have fun at somebody else's expense. The worse they get, the worse they find themselves wanting to be."

"Aye," Fadecourt rumbled. "'Tis when someone tells them that good is bad, and wrong is right."

"I'll flay him!" Narlh growled. "I'll tear him apart!"

"People can be twisted so badly that they enjoy hurting other people, Narlh," Matt said. "It's called 'sadism.'"

"Sad? It's horrible! Do they *have* to do it?"

"No. It's a strong drive, but it only gets to be a compulsion in the worst of them. Most people can keep it in bounds, because by the time they've grown up, they've learned it's wrong. But these people have grown up with a king who tells them cruelty is right, as long as there's a good chance they can get away with it."

"So if you show 'em they *won't* get away with it, then they'll stop! And the best way to show 'em that is to kill off the ones who do it!"

"Maybe—but there's no point in trying, as long as someone's protecting them from justice. You have to start with the one at the top."

"Let me at him!"

"I'll try," Matt said. "But first, we have to get to him."

Their first view of the village had been bad enough—Matt would have avoided it, if he'd been able to see it far enough ahead. But no, the trees had suddenly opened out, and they had found themselves in the middle of the char and soot. Matt wondered how many more like it he'd pass, before they reached Orlequedrille. There couldn't be *too* many, he told himself frantically—the noblemen had to have *some* taxpayers left. What good was owning the land, if you didn't have anyone to farm it? It made Matt edgy. Gordogrosso's forces were obviously in the vicinity, and if Fadecourt was right, the king could see everything that was going on in Ibile—so how come Matt and his friends hadn't been attacked by an army?

Finally, he tried the idea out loud—but with as much casualness as he could manage. "Any idea why the king hasn't sent an army after us yet?"

"Why," Fadecourt said in surprise, "he may not know that we are here. He must look in his magic mirror before he can see, you know."

Matt shook his head. "I've tried to hold down on the magic, but I have used a few spells in the last few days, and most of them have been to fight evil deeds. That kind of thing is bound to draw his attention."

"How so?" Fadecourt asked, frowning.

"Because a magician can tell whenever another one is working magic nearby," Matt explained. "At least, that's what happened to me in Merovence. I should think it would work just as well here."

"It may be as you say," Fadecourt said slowly, "but you did say 'nearby.' Would the king be able to feel your magic, all the way across the land in Orlequedrille?"

"Good point," Matt said slowly. "But I'd think the local baron could, and that he would pass the word on to Gordogrosso. I'd *also* expect him to come charging out with an army of his own."

"The local lord is penned within his own castle," Fadecourt explained, "and the king's soldiers besiege him. What you say may be true, but the lord cannot come out against you—nor is he likely to, if you oppose the king. The more confusion among his attackers, the better for him."

"Good point," Matt said slowly, "but wouldn't there be a sorcerer among the besiegers?"

"Aye, but he cannot move without Gordogrosso's command. He may tell the king of your presence, but His Corruption is not apt to weaken the siege by sending more than a handful of soldiers after you."

"Okay," Matt said. "Where's the handful?"

Fadecourt shrugged. "Mayhap they think you too small to bother with."

"These boys don't seem the kind to let anything pass, no matter how small." Matt remembered the village.

Fadecourt shrugged. "For myself, I would attribute your safety to the intervention of the saints. They have not completely abandoned Ibile, you know."

"Even though Ibile may have completely abandoned them. Yes."

"Would not the saints favor you, and wish to aid you in your quest?"

"You could say that," Matt said with a sardonic smile, remembering the angel. "Yes, you could say so." And he let it go at that—temporarily.

They were riding down the mountain trail when Matt suddenly reined in. "Hold on! What am I thinking of?"

"I'll bite," Narlh grunted. Fadecourt and Matt shot him looks of horror, and he said quickly, "No, no! I mean, *I'll* ask the question. 'All right, Wizard—what *are* you thinking of?' "

Matt relaxed. "It's what I'm *not* thinking of that matters. The siege! Here I've had it made plain every day to me, time and again, that there's a siege going on, with besiegers who have all the virtue of piranhas in heat, and all I can think of is, 'That's interesting. Good place to stay away from.' But if I'm really meaning to fight evil in this country, I ought to be going toward that siege, to see if I can help out any! Fadecourt, you've just come through that stretch of country. Can you lead us to the castle?"

Fadecourt exchanged a glance with Narlh. "I can, aye—yet whether or not 'twould be prudent, I must debate."

"Oh, it's anything but prudent! This whole quest is anything but prudent. I mean, if I'd been prudent, I never would have sworn to go kick Gordogrosso off his throne in the first place, would I?"

"Even allowing that," the cyclops said, "it may be that you should bypass this conflict. Is not the greater villain the more vital target? And should you risk your safety, let alone your anonymity, in attacking a lesser?"

"Oh, come on! That's the kind of thinking that's gotten this country into this mess! Of *course* we should attack evil wherever we find it! Trying to be smart, and becoming callous in the process, is playing into the sorcerer's hands!"

"I s'pose," Narlh grumped. "But it could be you're going after bait, you know."

"Bait?" Matt frowned. "You don't really think the king would mount a siege just to sucker me in, do you?"

"If he knew you were coming? Sure! From what I've heard of him, he's done a lot bigger setups for a lot smaller reasons!"

"Why hit a fly with a swatter when you could use a shotgun, huh?" Matt nodded. "Doesn't sound like a smart ruler, though."

"Nay, but think of it as a cat playing with a mouse," Fadecourt explained. "He derives such miserable pleasure as he may, from allowing his victims a maze in which to wander."

Matt frowned. "You're beginning to sound convincing."

"Yeah, well, it *could* also be that *neither* side is worth fighting for," Narlh pointed out. "You know how a man gets to be nobility here?"

"Why . . . he gets born. Doesn't he?"

"Sure, and he gets killed off fast, if he doesn't show any sign of being just as cruel as his papa is," Narlh snorted. " 'Nobility' in Gordogrosso's Ibile means being more brutal than the brutes and more merciless than the mercenaries."

"He speaks truth," Fadecourt said, his voice low. "Only those who delight in cruelty, and are swift to strike and slow to repent, become knights of Gordogrosso's liege men. And to become a baron, one must be also harsh and ruthless, and skilled in treachery."

Matt frowned. "Then how can Gordogrosso trust his vassals?"

"He cannot. He trusts them to seek their own advantage, and leads them by the force of their own greed."

"So he can trust them to do what's best for themselves," Matt said, glowering, "and he makes sure following his orders is in their greatest self-interest."

"Aye," Fadecourt said. "So if you would help a lord who is besieged, you would be aiding one villain against another who besets him."

"Choosing the lesser of two evils, is that it? Gordogrosso just lets his barons slug it out with each other whenever they want to?"

"Oh, nay! They must have his leave—or be sure he'll turn a blind eye."

"Which is to say, the pocket war has to be in *his* interest," Matt interpreted. "But doesn't that mean *one* of the two barons is less evil than the other? At least enough to get Gordogrosso mad at him?"

Narlh and Fadecourt exchanged a startled glance.

"It may be," the cyclops said slowly, "though it may more easily be that the one of them has angered Gordogrosso in some way, mayhap by insolence or by overreaching himself."

"Possible," Matt agreed, "but it's also possible that he won Gordogrosso's anger by trying to be good."

"Yeah, well, that could be," Narlh argued, "but even if it was, how could you tell which baron was the good guy?"

"By which side Gordogrosso has lent troops to." Matt lifted a hand to forestall Narlh's protest. "I know, I know, he might not have troops with *either* side. But we'll never know if we don't go look, will we?"

"I can think of safer ways to gather information," Narlh growled.

"Even if 'tis so, Lord Wizard, what advantage is there for you or your goal in aiding the one of them?" Fadecourt asked.

"That kind of thinking leads to capitulating to the forces of evil," Matt said, pointing the finger at him. "Or, more concisely, selling out. But now that you raise the question, any enemy of Gordogrosso's is an ally of ours. And you'll pardon me for saying it, but we could use a few allies. Look, it really won't take that long just to go check it out, will it?"

Narlh and Fadecourt exchanged one final glance. Then the cyclops sighed and turned off the road. "As you will have it, Lord Wizard. Follow—'tis off to the north, this way."

Four siege towers were set against one wall of the castle, and the crossbowmen on their tops were firing from behind thick leather shields. As Matt watched, one of them fell to the ground—probably screaming, but their hilltop blind was too far away to hear anything but a steady roar, punctuated by metallic clashings. In spite of their few losses, the arbalesters had swept the ramparts almost clear— certainly clear enough so that the attacker's knights were streaming onto the walls, followed by their soldiers. A few defenders rose up to obstruct them, but the invaders clustered around them and chopped them to bits. As Matt and his friends watched, the drawbridge came thundering down.

"The porter is dead," Fadecourt interpreted, "and they have cut the stays of the windlass. No matter how good your intentions, Lord Wizard, we have come too late."

"Too bad." Matt scowled at the distant scene, mentally berating himself for not having come sooner. "I'd like to know if it matters, though." Which translated as wanting to know just how guilty he should feel. "Can you see if any of them are king's men?"

"I can," Narlh grunted. "I was hatched for high sight, remember?"

"Eyes like an eagle?" Matt looked up, startled.

"*Those* shortsighted pests? Don't make me laugh. And, uh—yeah, the crossbowmen on top are all wearing the same colors. Same as the first troops in over the battlements, too."

"What hues are they?" Fadecourt asked.

"Red and black."

"Blood and mourning." Fadecourt's face settled into grim lines. "They are Gordogrosso's troops, indeed."

"Could it be the lord of this castle was less evil than most of his breed?" Matt asked.

"More likely overly ambitious—but even then, he could have proved a useful foil for us, to keep the king's attention whiles we came up behind. I do now regret that we came late."

"Maybe not completely." Matt tried to close his ears to the cries of dismay. "There's a chance the master of the house is staging a getaway."

"And leaving his men to bear the brunt of the assault." Fadecourt nodded, tight-lipped. "Aye; it hath the stamp of Gordogrosso's nobles. Would you help such a one, then?"

"Long enough to ask him a few questions. If he's as bad as you think, we can always leave him to his fate—but if he could be useful, we might help him get clear. Think we can find the postern?"

"Aye, if we must." Fadecourt sighed. "And after seeing that we may have missed a worthy chance, I'm not inclined to argue. Follow, then—we'll make the circuit of the walls. But from the ridge-top, an it please you."

"Sure." Matt looked back anxiously as they turned away. "I—don't suppose there's anything I can do to stop what's going on?"

"Sure," Narlh grunted. "You're the wizard, aren't you? But you can bet your bonnet there's a whole coven of sorcerers in there, on the king's side. In this country, that's probably why they won—out-magicked. Do you really think you'd do any good by taking 'em all on?"

"Not much, I'm afraid." Matt sighed. "Not that I wouldn't try, if I were sure it was worth it. Come on, let's find out."

They circled the castle, staying in the hills about half a mile distant, with the clash of battle ringing in the distance. It made Matt uneasy—he was still feeling guilty about not having intervened in time to save the farmers at the first village; that old attitude of "It's not my fight" so naturally took over. He felt he should intervene here, instead of skulking about. But his friends were right, there was no point in helping one villain against another, especially when he didn't know which was worse—or of jeopardizing his main mission by trying to help the underdog, as an automatic reflex.

Finally, he woke to the fact that they had come an awfully long way and were taking an even longer time trying to find that postern gate. "Uh—Fadecourt?"

"Aye, Wizard?"

"You do know where this back door is, don't you?"

Fadecourt shook his head. "I do not know this castle itself. I know only where the postern *should* be, not where it *is*."

"Which is?" Matt frowned.

"Toward the rear of the castle, or at least far from the gatehouse— wherefore have two doors side by side? And it should be near a watercourse, or a rocky defile that would hide those who flee."

"Both of which make it a good place for an attack," Matt noted. "So it would be pretty well guarded."

"Aye, or quite secret—in which case, it will be hidden."

Matt frowned. "So how are we to . . . Hey!"

"What'sa matter?" Narlh snapped.

"I see them." Fadecourt pointed.

Two knights were galloping uphill toward them, with a score of pikemen behind.

"What're *they* after?"

"Fugitives, at a guess."

"*Them?* They've got the royal livery!"

"No, no! They're *chasing* fugitives!"

"So I would conjecture," Fadecourt agreed. "Therefore, let *us* find them first, that we may learn—"

Three horses broke out of the scrub growth a hundred feet away, charging hell-bent for leather right at them. The first was a lady, the two behind her knights.

"Aside!" Fadecourt suited the action to the word. "Let them pass; we know not what they be."

But the two knights weren't of so generous a turn of mind. They saw the companions and turned their mounts, veering toward Matt and Fadecourt. Undeterred by the sight of Narlh, they leveled their lances and charged. The woman sped by Matt—he had an impression of chestnut hair whipping about behind a drawn and wide-eyed face, and a figure as graceful as the gazelle she was now imitating in her flight—then she was gone, sped past him, still fleeing.

"What're they after *us* for?" Matt wailed.

"Our large friend, and my poor self, are not the least threatening of beings, in appearance," Fadecourt grated. "Let us disarm them gently."

"Disarm them? I'm getting out of their way!" Matt leaped aside.

"That is the first step," Fadecourt agreed, but he stayed standing in the roadway.

"Jump!" Matt cried. "Or your name will be shashlik!"

Still Fadecourt stood his ground, glaring up along the lances at the knights, and Matt tried to think up a quick swerving spell. Of course, he didn't need to; at the last minute, Fadecourt cried, "Now!" and leaped aside, and Narlh spun off the path in a surprisingly graceful double turn. The knights shouted in anger, but thundered on by; they were going too fast to stop or turn.

"This time, we will unseat them," Fadecourt said calmly, as he stepped back onto the path.

"Are you *crazy*?" Matt shouted. "Those guys are medieval steam-rollers!"

"What kinda beasts are those?" Narlh looked up, interested.

"They'll not come so quickly now," Fadecourt pointed out.

But he was wrong. The knights reined in their mounts at the end of the meadow, turned, and came thundering back, lances leveled, building up more and more speed.

Fadecourt frowned. "That is not as they should do."

Matt looked up and shouted, "It's not you! They've got bigger game to worry about!"

Fadecourt looked up, indignant and offended—then looked where Matt was pointing and saw the two pursuing knights charging straight for him, with their pack of pikes in full voice behind them.

The cyclops took the better part of valor and leaped for Narlh, crying, "Away!"

Matt dashed to join them, calling, "Is it time to help the good guys yet?"

"We ken not who they may be! Wizard, away!"

Whatever the merits of the two lone knights, they weren't short on courage. They galloped full out toward the pursuers, blind to the mob. But their enemies were just as doughty, and their lances just as long. They slammed into the fugitives with a crash like an iron foundry going broke. Lances splintered; someone screamed; a body slammed down to the ground; and Matt squeezed his eyes shut. When he looked again, the two fugitives were down, along with one horse; the other was galloping away. The knights rode on over their bodies, unheeding, galloping toward the woods. The pikemen paused long enough to make sure the knights were dead, stabbing through the joints with their pikes, then ran after their leaders.

Matt winced. "Not long on mercy, are they?" Then he suddenly realized the knights were chasing nothing—at least, as far as he could see. "Hey! Where'd the lady go?"

"Into the woods," Fadecourt answered, tight-lipped. "If you wouldst save her, Wizard, 'tis now you must cast your spell."

Matt frowned. "Wait a minute, no. All along, you've been telling me not to pitch in until I know which side is good and which is evil. How come all of a sudden you know?"

"Why, because she is a woman."

Matt stared.

Then he sighed and said, "One of these days, I'll figure out the logic of that—or else I'll have to admit that chivalry can become a knee-jerk reflex. Okay, I'll try to give her a little help.

> "Overcast the day!
> The sunny welkin cover thou anon
> With drooping fog, as black as Acheron!
> And lead these pursuers so astray,
> That the damsel come not within their way,
> And speed and turn her pathway in her flight
> That she come never near within their sight!"

Huge forces seemed to bend about him, and he actually felt his words slowing as he spoke—but he plowed ahead, finishing the verse with sweat starting from his brow. He drew a ragged breath and shrugged. "That's about all I can do."

"Mayhap not." Fadecourt ran toward the fallen knights, chivalry personified.

"Right," Matt muttered, following at an uninspired jog. "What's it matter if they were just trying to carve your brisket? They're down and helpless, that's all that matters." Nonetheless, he came up behind the kneeling cyclops to see what he could do.

"Naught here—he is dead." Fadecourt turned to the second knight, his face grim. "Ha! He lives!"

"No . . . torture," the knight grated. "Quick . . . death."

"Doesn't he have any chance?" Narlh came up behind Matt.

Fadecourt pointed to the blood welling out of the knight's armor in a widening pool and shook his head.

Narlh nodded, his beaked face unreadable. "Nothing I can do here, then. I better go check up on the woman." He turned away and loped off down the trail.

"Good." The dying man had pushed the girl out of Matt's mind for the moment—but Narlh was right, she might need protection. Or reassurance, anyway—though Matt could think of much more reassuring sights than the dracogriff. She was likely to hide at the slightest glimpse of him, especially since the knights had been chasing her.

Of course, that was assuming she was innocent, and not a major villainess herself. In this country, though, Matt couldn't imagine that the knights could have had any moral reason for chasing her.

But moral or not, the man was dying. Matt understood why Fadecourt was so sure the knight had no chance of survival. If the pikemen hadn't been so zealous, the knight might have lived. What kind of medieval society was this, anyway? In *his* Europe, a peasant soldier would have been hanged for killing one of his betters, even if by accident.

"We are wanderers," Fadecourt told the knight, "not foemen. Can we ease you?"

"Aye. Shrive . . . me."

Matt stared. "Listen to your confession, and give you forgiveness?"

Suddenly, Fadecourt looked helpless. "We cannot; we are not priests."

"Repentance is enough." Matt knelt beside Fadecourt. "If you're sorry for your sins, you won't be damned."

"I . . . repent . . ." The knight's body convulsed. *"Aieeee!"*

"His master listens," Fadecourt said, thin-lipped, "and punishes him for his repentance."

"Repentance." Anger boiled—the sorcerers could at least let the man die in peace. But of course, that would have been the reverse of their main purpose, wouldn't it? Damning as many souls as possible. Matt lifted his head with grim resolve. He'd already worked one spell here, and if hanged for the kid, be hanged for the goat.

> "Let no evil force surround thee,
> But all saving grace be round thee.
> Let hateful powers fall and cease,
> And all kindly powers bring thee peace."

Matt felt the force of magic moving outward from himself, against very heavy resistance—but as long as it held, it was accomplishing its purpose: keeping the evil magic away from the dying man, so that he could pass in grace. "Gramercy," he panted. "I must . . . recompense . . ."

"You must die well." Matt set a hand on his arm. "Think of Heaven."

"Nay . . . of earth. No . . . debt."

"He will not die beholden," Fadecourt interpreted. "Give him some small assurance that his last charge is fulfilled."

"What, the maiden he was riding with?" Matt asked. "Be of good cheer, Sir Knight—she made it into the forest well ahead of her pursuers, and they're going to have tough going among those branches, so she'll probably be safe."

"Gramercy . . ." The knight's face twisted with sudden pain. "I have . . . discharged . . ." Then his face froze, eyes staring, and his whole body went rigid—then limp, and a last breath hissed out.

"Discharged your duty," Fadecourt finished, and reached over to close the man's eyes. "Good rest to you, Sir Knight—and may your toils in Purgatory be light." He stood, face grim, then turned to look down at Matt. "Come. Let us do what we can to fulfill his last charge."

"Right." Matt stood up and followed Fadecourt toward the trees.

As they came in under the leaves, they heard several voices shouting, with a lot of slashing and crashing. Fadecourt pressed Matt back behind a trunk, and three pikemen came barreling past them toward the meadow, shouting with anger and outrage. Fadecourt looked up at Matt in inquiry. "What did they see?"

"Heaven only knows," Matt said, "and I don't think I want to. Any idea which way the lady went?"

Fadecourt did, as it turned out—among his other skills, he was an excellent tracker. Not that it needed much skill, to tell that a horse had blundered through where there wasn't any trail—but how the cyclops could tell which horse had been ridden by a woman, Matt couldn't begin to guess. Still, Fadecourt followed the trail unerringly—until they came to a small clearing and discovered the horse contentedly cropping the grass. Fadecourt looked grim, but he simply searched the perimeter of the clearing . . . then kept on searching, until he'd come back to Matt. He frowned, puzzled. "I had found her trace—then realized it could not be hers. I searched on, found it again—and knew it for a false trail. Then I came upon the true trail . . . yet was suddenly uncertain that . . ."

Something was making an awful lot of crashing in the brush, was coming nearer. The horse lifted its head, staring in the direction of the sound, sniffed the breeze, then gave a whinnying scream and ran off the other way.

"Beware!" Fadecourt held up a hand. "What moves . . ."

The crashing exploded into a roar, and the roar resolved itself into words. "*Fershlugginer* unprintable *mirandible* hobgoblin! How in a harpy's hasp did the trail get trounced?"

Matt relaxed. "I don't think it's anything to worry about."

A huge body burst through the screen of brush and let out a roar of exasperation that ended in a two-foot tongue of flame. "How can a body expect a poor dracogriff to find a fool slip of a girl if the unprintable trail keeps changing on him!"

"We're having the same problem, too, Narlh." Matt stepped away from the trees out into the clearing. "At least, Fadecourt is—I couldn't have found enough trail to get confused about in the first place."

"Oh. You guys, huh?" Narlh paced up to them, still steaming. "A fine, thankless job you gave me, Wizard!"

Things suddenly connected, and Matt admitted, "Sorry. The more so because the confusion's my doing, I guess."

"Your what?" Narlh bleated, and Fadecourt looked up, startled. "How could it be so, Wizard?"

"Because I cast a confusion spell on anyone following her," Matt explained, with a sheepish try at a smile. "I forgot we might want to find her ourselves."

"Oh, real smart, Wizard! Real smart!" Narlh fumed. "I mean, you coulda thought of that *before* you sent me off chasing wild geese, y' know?"

Fadecourt wasn't looking too happy, either, but he said, "Aye. I heard the spell, too. I should ha' thought of it also."

"Nice of you to say so." Matt sighed. "But I'm afraid it's really no one's doing but mine."

"Can you not disperse the spell you've cast?"

"Sure—but the men who're chasing her might find her, too, then. And I can't be any more specific, waiving the spell just for us and not for them, without knowing her name or something else to identify her by."

"How come?" Narlh demanded, but Fadecourt held up a hand. "Do not ask, or he might answer—at more length than we wish."

Matt's mouth tightened in chagrin. He'd felt the old college instructor's juices starting to flow again and had been all ready to launch into a lecture.

"Right." He sighed. "Well, I guess the best we can do now is to set up camp and hope we hear her yell if she needs help."

"Well thought," Fadecourt agreed, "but not in midwood, with enemies thrashing about it, an it please you. Let us go seek some more defensible site."

"Not a bad idea," Matt agreed. "Maybe some high ground, anyway, even if we can't get out of the trees."

"I will be glad that our enemies must toil uphill to come upon us," Fadecourt answered. "Come, gentles—let us seek a slope."

He turned away, and Narlh fell into step beside Matt. " 'Gentles'? Who's he calling 'gentles'?"

"You and me," Matt assured him.

"Is that a compliment, or an insult?"

"A compliment, coming from him—so it shouldn't be an insult, going to you."

Narlh looked at him sharply. "You saying that what I'm hearing might not be what he's saying?"

"I've known it to happen." Matt sighed. "Let's just find a campsite, Narlh."

CHAPTER 10

The Chased Damsel

"How's dinner coming?"

Narlh looked down at the roasting pheasants and blew a little more flame on them. "Not bad. What'm *I* going to eat?"

"Hold on." Matt frowned. "How come you didn't figure they're for you?"

"Because the two of them together might, just might, make one very small appetizer. Can I go out to hunt now?"

"No, hang it—unless I'm going to chant the whole spell all over again."

Narlh looked upward and said, with clear reluctance, "I suppose I *could* try a vertical takeoff."

"No, don't bother." Matt was frowning. "The force field—uh, magical shield—closes over the top about twenty feet up, like a dome. Guess I'll just have to let you out." He turned and rubbed a patch in the talcum with one foot. "Next time let me know before I lock up, huh?"

The dracogriff stared. "That's all it takes?"

"That's all." Matt looked up, frowning. "What are you waiting for? Happy hunting."

"Be not apprehensive, Lord Wizard," Fadecourt said, by way of reassurance. "He will return alive and well. 'Tis not quite dark."

"No, not quite." Matt stood beside the warding circle, scanning the open meadow anxiously. The grass rose above him to a ridge, a long, natural avenue between ranks of trees.

"Would you not know if a sorcerer had cast a spell at him near us?"

"Well, I *think* so . . . *There!*"

Narlh was still licking his chops as he came back to the circle. "Hurry up!" Matt called impatiently.

"It was worth the trip." Narlh looked back at Matt. "What's got *you* all of a sudden?"

"That sorcerer who's been chasing you—I was beginning to wonder if he'd caught you." Matt tapped more powder over the break in the circle.

"I noticed that last night you laid the circle but did not enchant it," Fadecourt said. "Are you expecting greater trouble tonight?"

"Not really," Matt said, "and I'm not *expecting* trouble tonight, any more than last night."

"Ah." Fadecourt lifted his head. "Then you *did* expect attack last night."

"Let's say I was aware of the possibility," Matt hedged. "But since Narlh and I were keeping watch, I could have recited the words of the spell at the last minute, if there *had* been any sign of attack."

"Not trusting me to take my turn on watch, of course."

"Well, you are a little new to the party." Matt shifted uncomfortably. "But if there wasn't any trouble, I preferred not to cast a spell that might tip off the enemy to the presence of a wizard from the opposing side."

"I shall have to take your word for that." Fadecourt sighed. "I've no experience with the feelings of magic—only with its results. Still, I do wish you would trust me well enough to let me take my turn."

"I'm sure we will, after a few days. Now, how about those pheasants?"

After making quick work of dinner, they lay down, Matt bundled in his cloak, Fadecourt sleeping with his soles toward the fire, head pillowed on one arm. Matt eyed Narlh, pacing the circle, and he smiled at the feeling of security the sight of the dracogriff gave him, then closed his eyes and let sleep claim him.

A high, wavering scream slashed through his dream and jolted him wide awake. "Narlh! What the deuce—"

"Not me." The dracogriff stood rigid, facing off into the darkness. "From over there, toward the east. But it might be bait."

"Bait?"

"A ruse, to persuade you to charge out blindly into the night, where you'll have no warding circle." Fadecourt had risen, too. "By your leave, Lord Wizard, allow me to investigate."

"But what if you don't come back?"

"Let us discuss that when it happens, shall we?" The cyclops stepped over the circle and was gone into the darkness before Matt could say anything. He was back a second later—trying to catch up with the maiden who fled past him, screams of raw terror tearing her throat. So Fadecourt's back was to the forest, and he didn't see what was chasing her—a gauzy white shape, drifting after the woman against the night breeze.

"Hey! Over here!" Narlh called. The woman looked up, saw Narlh, and stopped dead in her tracks.

"He's friendly!" Matt called. "Over here! We're the good guys!"

The woman cast a glance back and up at the ghost, turned toward them—and stood, trembling with indecision, and screaming, screaming . . .

Fadecourt caught her up like a baby and pounded toward Matt and Narlh, leaping the circle and setting the young woman down by Matt. She threw her arms around the wizard, clutching him as though he were a tree limb above a hundred-foot drop. Her screams instantly dissolved into sobs.

The ghost drifted closer, seeming to flicker, its eyes hollow, its mouth wide in a silent call, waving both arms. As it saw Matt, it began to gesticulate frantically. Matt hardened with alarm—those gestures could be the accompaniment to a spell-casting! Quickly, scarcely thinking, he rattled off:

> "If charnel houses and our graves must send
> Those that we bury back, our monuments
> Shall be the maws of kites. Therefore,
> Be gone!"

The ghost's eyes widened in horror; it shook its head, and even Matt could see that the silent mouthings were saying, "No! No!" Then an unfelt wind seemed to hit the ghost like a jet plane, tearing its substance to tatters that faded and blew away.

"It's all right, now. He's gone." Matt couldn't help noticing how nice the young woman felt in his arms, the little hands clutched about his neck, the contours of her body molding into his, their movements as she sobbed . . . He pulled his mind off the subject abruptly. "There, now, the ghost is gone, and no one's going to hurt you. We're nice guys, here, really, if you don't mind how we look . . ."

"What's a matter with how we look?" Narlh demanded.

"I haven't shaved in three days," Matt improvised, "and I haven't seen a pool large enough to bathe in for a week. You'll have to pardon us, young woman . . ."

"Oh, nay!" Finally, she pushed herself away from him and began to wipe at her cheeks with a sleeve.

Matt hauled out a handkerchief. "Here, now, you'll soil your gown." He finally took a quick look at her by firelight and decided that might have been the wrong thing to say; her gown hadn't had a good afternoon, what with the forest brambles and a few stumbles in the dirt. "That must have been horrifying, a thing like that happening when you were alone . . . you *were* alone, weren't you?"

She burst into tears again. "Oh, aye, so very alone, since Lord Bruitfort took my father's castle! I escaped by the postern, but I've been wandering alone all this day and night! Bless you, kind sirs—but know that I'm pursued!"

At a guess, Matt decided the siege was over—not that its ending boded any improvement for the peasantry. "We saw—but the ghost's gone. Take a look, if you don't believe me."

"Oh, not the specter only—the soldiers! And a sorcerer, I doubt not. They'll not let me flee in peace, I assure you! Nay, good sirs, I must away from you, ere you share in my misfortune."

"'Tis they shall have misfortune," Fadecourt growled, "if they seek to take you from us! Fear not, fair maid—we shall not let them seize you!"

Narlh opened his mouth to disagree, but Matt said quickly, "Right! We couldn't abandon a maiden in distress, to pursuers who're trying to ravish her!"

The dracogriff shut his jaws with a snap. "Right. No way. Couldn't think of letting a lady go out alone."

Especially not one who looked like that, Matt thought. He finally had a chance to take a good look—and what he saw was riveting. The "creature" had a heart-shaped face amid long chestnut hair held by a hennin. She wore a bliaut of blue and a kirtle of buff wrapped around a figure worth killing for. Matt locked his eyeballs onto her face and held them there by pure willpower—he was an engaged man.

Fadecourt, however, didn't seem to suffer from that problem, though this certainly must have been a moment when he'd wished he'd had two eyes. The one he had was riveted on the young woman, wide open. Matt elbowed him in the shoulder, and the cyclops shook himself out of his hormonal trance to bow gallantly. "Where we can aid, maiden, we shall delight. What is your plight?"

"And, if you wouldn't mind," Matt added, "would you tell

us who we're protecting, milady?" Privately, he wondered just how Fadecourt could be so sure the lady wasn't just bait for another trap. But she was explaining her danger, which did sound plausible—and Fadecourt's instincts did seem to have proved accurate.

So far.

"I am hight Yverne, sirs," the maiden said. "I am the only child of the Duke of Toumarre. The Duke of Bruitfort, whose estates adjoin ours on the north—in truth, a vile neighbor!—did war upon my father. Through treachery of our garrison, he did defeat him and capture him, locking him in his deepest dungeon." The reminder of the day's horrors caught up with her, and she bowed her head, trying to stifle the sobs.

Fadecourt stepped up to clasp her shoulders, murmuring, "There, now, lass, 'twas terrifying, aye, but you are safe now . . ."

When her sobs had slackened, Matt asked gently, "That mention of treachery reminds me—can we trust anybody, in this country?"

"The Duke of Toumarre is a good man, by Ibile's lights," Fadecourt said slowly. "He kept troth so long as his seigneur kept troth with him, and maintained order within his demesne, albeit with cruelty and ruthlessness."

Yverne looked up sharply and stepped away from Fadecourt, face tear-streaked but outraged. "He was harsh, mayhap, but did no cruelty for its own sake!"

"Which is not entirely avoidable, in this country?" Matt asked.

"Even so," Fadecourt said. "And it may be that, like many fathers, he wished his daughter to grow into a woman devoid of the vices common to his fellows."

"Which would reveal an inner yearning for virtue." Matt studied Yverne so closely that the maiden blushed and looked away—which could have indicated her being a becoming innocent, or an accomplished dissembler.

A hunch led him to choose innocence. "So what it comes down to is that her father's enemies thought he was weak, because he wasn't depraved enough."

"Aye—and seem to have judged well, by Ibile's lights. Only the wicked are counted strong here."

"Well, let's see if we can't change that notion, shall we?" Matt turned back to Yverne. "I take it this Duke of Bruitfort is trying to catch you for his dungeons, too."

"He seeks to apprehend me," Yverne agreed, "but not for his dungeons. He wishes to take me to wife, whether I will or no."

Fadecourt spat an oath, and Matt felt his blood run cold at the thought of this pure maiden in the hands of a depraved sadist. Even Narlh gave a squawk of outrage. "Go tie him in a knot, Lord Matthew!"

"Well, we can put a hitch in his plans, anyway. How close is this duke, Lady Yverne?"

"I know not—though 'tis but this day since I've escaped from his men." She advanced, hands outstretched in pleading. "Oh, sirs, I beg of you, turn not away from me—for without your kind protection, I am lost!"

"Oh, you're coming with us, there's no question about that," Matt said quickly. "What kind of troops did the duke send looking for you? We confused a couple of knights, but that might not be all that are on your trail."

She spread her hands. "I know not."

"She did not stay to see him command pursuit," Fadecourt rumbled. "Natheless, I would think he has sent at least a dozen knights, and perchance even his sorcerer."

Then the horn sounded behind them.

Matt looked up in alarm and saw a man in a robe standing at the edge of the clearing, gesticulating and, presumably, chanting—but his gestures were lengthened by a three-foot, glowing wand. Matt frowned—this was new. Fear chilled him, but he tried to remember everything he'd heard about magic wands—why they were magical; what they could do.

To either side of the sorcerer stood men in plate armor, seeming inhuman and certainly impersonal behind their iron helms. As Matt watched, they kicked their horses into motion and started down the slope.

"Move!" Matt shouted. "Here come the bloodhounds!"

His friends started forward out of sheer astonishment. Then Fadecourt looked back. "Lord Matthew! You, too, must flee!"

"Be right along," Matt assured him. "I just have to counter whatever our friend in the robe is doing back there."

He found out as his voice slowed, taking several seconds for the last two syllables, and his voice slid down an octave. The sorcerer had thickened the air about them, somehow; his friends could scarcely move through the molasses! And to make it worse, Matt could scarcely get out a single word, let alone a whole poem!

Meanwhile, here came the Knights of Evil, hurtling toward them like express trains . . .

And grinding down to near immobility, as they hit the the perimeter of the spell, where time slowed down to a treacle.

Matt's spirits soared—the sorcerer had almost paralyzed his quarry, but his buddies couldn't get to Matt and his friends any faster than the fugitives could get away! And it might take Matt a long time to get a spell out, but it would take the knights even longer to reach him.

Matt took a deep breath, or at least a very slow one. Now there was time to think up a counterspell.

> "Fly, envious Time, till thou
>   run out thy race!
> Call on the lazy-stepping hours,
>   and let them limp in place!
> Let minutes blossom, seconds stem,
> Let time flow on at normal pace,
> But for us only, not for them!"

His friends began to move faster, but the enemy knights were still fighting their way through treacle. All well and good—but the duke's sorcerer would catch on and call off his own spell any minute. He was already staring—at a guess, no one had ever countered that enchantment before.

"Vile thing, I think I hate you!" the sorcerer screamed.

> "Evil king, now hark and hear!
> Make these rebels quake with fear!
> Hear me, mark us, circumspect!
> Lend me your aid, your power direct!"

"Beware!" Yverne clutched at Matt's arm. "He calls on his master, dread Gordogrosso! 'Tis the power of the sorcerer-king you now must face!"

"Maybe, but it will be wielded by a journeyman." Matt spoke up bravely, in spite of the shot of dread that trickled through him.

Fadecourt gently disengaged Yverne from Matt's arm. "Let him be, milady. He must think of naught but countering the sorcerer's power."

The sorcerer lifted his wand and shouted a spell in the unknown language, then cut the air with his wand overhand, ending pointing it at Matt.

"Angels and ministers of grace defend us!" Matt shouted.

A gout of light sped from the tip of the wand, widening as it neared

Matt, breaking into a pack of hyena heads, gibbering with insane laughter as they reached for him with bloody fangs.

Matt realized he hadn't made a rhyme. He added, "From those who with ill charm would rend us!"

Light seared, and a troop of spectral monks was suddenly there between the two forces—a whole choir, lifting its voices in a hymn. Behind it, the arches and frescoes of a church could be seen dimly.

The hyenas screamed and went tumbling back toward the wand, biting and chewing at each other in their haste. But through the monks, Matt could see the knights and men-at-arms, charging full out. His heart leaped into his throat—he couldn't do anything to stop them! For even as the hyenas hit the wand, the sorcerer banished them with a couplet and a riposte, then shouted another rhyme as he moved the wand slowly back and forth from side to side—and the choir began to waver and thin.

"Stay and sing!" Matt cried. "Thy blessings bring!"

Suddenly, he understood that the choir of monks wasn't really here—it was only intervening, lending the power of the hymns it was chanting; it was really in a monastery somewhere in Merovence, and his appeal for help had only sent the defending power of its prayers. But the soldiers charged right through the vision with a howl of blasphemous curses.

Fadecourt stood ready, with Narlh beside him, mouthing bad names. But the cries of blasphemy suddenly turned to cries of alarm, and knights and footmen alike plowed up the ground in their haste to stop, gibbering with fear at the sight they beheld. For all of a sudden, the ghost was there again, the same one who had been chasing Yverne, three times as large as he had been—but he was facing away from her now, reaching up and snatching off his head. With one hand, he thrust it out at the soldiers, eyes and mouth filled with fire, the other hand swelling monstrously, fingers flickering out into tentacles as it reached for the soldiers.

They screamed and ran, like the proverbial bats. Only their captain actually changed form, though—and he was flying away as fast as his leathery wings could take him. The choir disappeared, its heavenly song eclipsed by the howls of fear. The soldiers barreled back up to the top of the rise, knocking the sorcerer spinning in their flight. He wailed, flailing about for support, and caromed into a tree, clutching the bark with both hands. Then he looked up at the ghost again—and saw it shooting straight toward him. His mouth widened in an unheard scream, and he turned tail and ran, tripping and stumbling over his robe.

"Amazing!" Fadecourt stared after them. "You are indeed a doughty wizard, Lord Matthew!"

Matt shook his head. "Not that much. Oh, I called up the choir, sure—but the ghost came entirely on his own!"

"I had feared he had come to seize me!" Yverne shuddered.

"Nay, not a bit, lady!" Fadecourt protested, reaching up to clasp her hand with both of his. "He did protect us, not prey upon us! Ne'ertheless, an he did chase you, I doubt not the Lord Wizard would banish him."

"Looks as if he already did," Narlh growled.

"Huh?" Matt looked up. "Hey, wait a minute! I didn't mean . . ."

But the ghost was gone. Completely.

"Well, that's a puzzle." Matt scratched his head, frowning. "Whose side is he on, anyhow?"

"Ours, at the moment," Fadecourt answered.

"Yeah, but don't be too quick to think he's a good guy," Narlh growled. "Could be he just wants the sweet and tender thing all to himself."

Yverne shrank back at the gleam in the dracogriff's eye.

"Oh, don't worry, I don't eat your kind," Narlh snorted. "You don't even smell good."

Yverne stilled, conflicting emotions warring in her face. Matt could sympathize—after a line like that, he wouldn't know whether to feel reassured or insulted himself.

Then a nasty suspicion seized him. He stepped out over the talcum circle, carefully, prowling into the night.

"Hey!" Narlh leaped to catch up with him. "Where you goin'?"

"To make sure that scouting party really did run," Matt snapped. "They could just be hiding over the top of the rise, waiting for us to follow."

"Yeah, sure, and you're walking right into their hands if they are! No way, human! Wait for your guardian monster, y' hear?"

Matt slowed and waited, smiling. "Very reassuring, y' know?"

"Don't get mushy," Narlh warned. "Okay, up to the top, now—but only the top! Right?"

"Only the top," Matt agreed. Together, they stomped up to the top of the rise and looked down the other side. The moonlight glinted on an empty glade.

"I didn't think they looked as though they were about to stop," Narlh grunted.

"I'm delighted they didn't," Matt assured him. "That was the first taste I've had of Ibile's sorcerers—and I don't like the flavor."

"Oh?" Narlh looked down at him. "Different from the bad guys in Merovence?"

Matt nodded. "There's a—slimy feeling about this one, somehow. As if he'd been soaked in evil for a few years."

"Try a few centuries."

"I think he did. Besides, he used a wand."

"You don't?" Narlh stared, shocked. "That's right, you don't! Better get one fast, bucko. They all use 'em, here."

"They do? What for?"

Narlh just stared at him. Then he said, "If you don't know, then we're all in trouble. Do me a favor, huh? See if you can take a few lessons."

"I don't think they'll be in any mood to teach me," Matt said slowly. "Besides, if they were, I'm not sure I'd want to learn. C'mon, I saw a knife one of those soldiers dropped. That'll do me more good, I bet."

The queen called down her nobles all, being careful to leave the ones who had suffered while the usurper ruled her Merovence.

"But, Majesty!" protested the Duke of Montmartre, "what reward is this, for the loyalty of our service? Are we to have no share in the glory of this campaign?"

"You shall have the greatest share, esteemed Duke," Alisande answered, "for you and your fellow lords must bide, and ward this land of Merovence from the evil raptors who must surely pounce as soon as I am gone to the war, with the lords whom I trust only to follow their own self-interest."

"How shall you be safe, with such beasts at your back!"

"Such men as the Earl of Norville cannot be beasts, milord," Alisande explained, "or they would have been elevated, and given power, by the false King Astaulf."

"And would have died with him, I doubt not, as the Duke of Lachaise and Count Ennudid," Montmartre muttered. "Yet most of the others were numbered in Astaulf's army, Majesty, and fought against you at Breden Plain."

"As they were constrained to do," Alisande replied. "Only yourself, and the handful of lords who accompanied you in your dungeon cell, did refuse to march."

"Whereupon Astaulf took our armies and marched with them, in spite of us."

"Aye, but thereby did I know you for my most staunch adherents."

"Yet we should therefore guard your back in battle!"

"As you shall, my lord—for my royal city of Bordestang is my back, and Merovence is the rest of my body. My arm will be weakened, if you ward me not."

The duke capitulated with a sigh. "As you will have it, Majesty. Yet who will guard your person? For God forfend that a hair of your head should be touched!"

"I thank you, Lord Duke," Alisande said, smiling, "though I have hairs a-plenty. Yet be of good cheer—I will take your erstwhile cell mate, Baron D'Art, to command my bodyguard."

"Take also my eldest son, Sauvignon!"

Now it was the queen's turn to capitulate. "As you will have it, my lord," she sighed. "Though I think his fiancée will thank me not."

CHAPTER 11

Technical Wizardry

It was a problem, Matt had to admit; in fact, it gnawed at him, hollowing him out with an ache he hadn't realized was there, as he gazed at Yverne's blanket-shrouded but shapely form glowing in the light of the camp fire. Was he really a heel to find Yverne attractive? Or was that just a normal, and unpreventable, reaction?

He was engaged to an equally beautiful woman—but the "engaged" part was what made him feel like a monster. *Though you have to admit,* his amoral self insisted stubbornly, *that your beloved can be a little intimidating.*

Which was true—especially since, being his sovereign, she could have his head chopped off any time she wanted, and he couldn't ethically do anything about it.

So the hell with ethics?

Not quite—that had led him into more than one bind, in this world where magic came from either Good or Evil. He had a notion, though, that if it came to disobedience or execution, he wouldn't stick around to find out how sharp the headsman's axe was. Not that he would strike back at Alisande—he felt a stab of alarm at the mere thought. But he could go off on his own.

Come to think of it, that was just what he had done.

Stubbornly, his maverick side asserted itself again. He was enjoying this, blast it—except for the dangerous parts; and only Gordogrosso had really been a threat, so far. All in all, he liked the feeling of being back in control of his own life again. Alisande was, when you got right down to it, a very domineering sort of female.

But wasn't that what you would expect in a queen?

A strange, sick gargling noise sounded.

Matt sat up, frowning, looking about him into the night. What kind of creature was in trouble? And what kind of trouble? He glanced at Yverne again, to make sure she was all right—and she wasn't.

Fire?

Yes, she looked as if she were too close to the fire. Matt sat bolt upright. It couldn't really be!

It was. Her form had begun to soften and grow lumpy, like wax left too close to a flame. Her outline began to flow, and Matt watched, shocked into inaction, while the cold realization diffused through him that a sorcerer was trying to destroy Yverne. Was he determined that, if he could not have her, no one would?

Or was the lady a more important figure in the power struggles of this kingdom than Matt knew?

He was frozen, appalled, sitting in mute impotence as her form grew more and more fluid, slowing sinking as if it were a jelly figure on top of a radiator. Her substance was being sucked away; she was being taken from him, just as his friends and his world had been . . .

The thought jolted him out of paralysis. This, he could do something about; he wasn't being held by dependence. He rolled upright onto his knees, chanting,

> "A-roving, a-roving,
> Roving will be your ru-aye-in!
> Oh, go no more a-roving,
> Will you, fair maid?"

Yverne's form didn't grow any stronger—but it didn't melt any more, either. A strange sensation seemed to emanate from her, like waves from a pebble; Matt felt it, and more—he sensed it with every nerve his body had. It was like a touch of slime all over him, a reek in his nostrils, a discord in his ears.

He had to pull her loose from it. That last one hadn't been much of a verse, anyway—and it *was* progress, at least. Matt drew a breath, wiping sweat from his forehead, and intoned:

> "But come ye back, for summer's in the meadow,
> And all the land is green, and bright with morn;

It's I'll be here, in sunlight or in shadow,
Oh maiden, do not leave me all forlorn."

Yverne's form grew a little stronger, feminine contours coalescing from the flowing wax—but only a little. Matt gasped for breath and wiped his forehead; he could feel an ominous pressure all about him, two opposed magical "fields" gathering about him and Yverne, and they were growing stronger. The chill ran through him once more, at the thought that one misspoken word might trigger some huge release of energy—and what would happen then?

He looked about him wildly. If only he could see the enemy sorcerer, he might be able to make the magic field recoil on him. But all he could see were tree branches moving in the moonlight, up the slope on the other side of their camp, away from the stream . . .

There! On the side of the slope. A dark figure, silhouetted against the lighter gray of the sky, blocking the stars—and waving a glowing baton. Matt caught his breath—it was another wand-wielder! And as he watched, a ball of fire seemed to blossom from the tip of the wand and shot rolling down the hill, straight toward Yverne!

No doubt the wicked one thought that a visual symbol would strengthen his melting spell—and he was probably right, too. Matt had to think quickly.

"Thou the stream and I the willow,
Thou the current, I the wave;
Thou the ocean, I the billow,
Thou the fountain . . ."

It worked! A jet of water shot up from the soil, just at the edge of the ring. The fireball bounced into it, then on through it—but only a sopping cinder rolled up near the half-melted figure by the fire.

Narlh lifted his head, growling and blinking sleep out of his eyes—and Fadecourt sat bolt upright, staring about him.

He saw the half-melted form and bellowed anger. But Matt couldn't spare him any attention; he was too busy working on his counterattack. He called out,

"Bend and turn, and form a curve,
Be a circle, quickly swerve.
Turn yourself into a coil—
Then hiss and strike, his spell to spoil!"

The wand suddenly began to flex, coming alive, sprouting a head, and turning back on its owner. He dropped it, waving his hands—and Matt took advantage of the lull to ready another spell.

> "The fire seven times tried this,
> Seven times tried that effort is,
> That once more goes amiss . . ."

Almost at the end, Matt wondered why the enemy sorcerer didn't run—until he saw the man bend down and pick up a straight wand again.

Matt didn't delay. He chanted the last line: "Earth may quake, and so will this!"

The earth beneath the sorcerer's feet trembled and caved in. He fell sprawling. Matt grinned and started on another verse.

> "There be fools alive, I wis,
> Silvered o'er, and so was this.
> Take what wife you will to bed,
> I will ever . . ."

Suddenly, he couldn't say another word. He just stood there, mouth open, staring at the enemy sorcerer, who had picked himself up and was pointing his wand straight at Matt—and Matt couldn't lift a finger. He strained, trying to move his tongue, wiggle a little toe, move his . . . foot, anything—but that glowing wand tip held his gaze, seeming to grow and grow like an expanding ball, swelling, filling all Matt's vision . . .

He heard an angry roar beside him and saw a small boulder sailing toward the glowing ball . . .

Then, suddenly, the ball was gone, somebody was howling from where it had been, Narlh was racing past him and hurdling the guarding circle, out into the darkness—and Matt could move again. "What . . . how . . . ?"

"A rock from the fire ring," Fadecourt said, gloating. "Betimes, Wizard, you workers of magic cease to be mindful that good, old-fashioned physical violence can take out an enemy as well as a spell. I caught him in the midriff, even as I'd aimed. He'll be meat for our monster ere he can do more."

Apparently, the sorcerer thought so, too. He saw Narlh coming, gave a howl of horror, leaped to his feet, and went limping away.

"Well, the hip," Fadecourt amended. "I missed not by much, at least."

"Hardly at all." Even as Matt watched, the running sorcerer suddenly erupted into flame. Narlh put on the brakes, just managing to skid to a stop before he was singed. The flames died down as abruptly as they'd flared up, and the night was dark again.

"What . . ." Matt stared. "They sure do make spectacular exits around here, don't they?"

"Aye." Fadecourt frowned. "If he did go."

Matt turned. "Why, what else could he have done?"

"Naught—but his master might have done it for him," Fadecourt explained, "in punishment for his having failed."

Matt stared, horrified.

Then Narlh came panting up beside him. "Nothing . . . left of him. Not even an ash."

Somehow, Matt felt better about it, though he knew that didn't prove anything.

Then he remembered what the fight had been about. "The maiden— quick! We'd better get her back together, before it's too late!"

"Aye!" Fadecourt spun about, to kneel by the half-melted form. "Quickly, Wizard!"

What did you say to a half-melted lady? That it was just supposed to be a metaphor? Matt collected his wits and chanted,

> "Pygmalion, Pygmalion,
> Who turned cold marble into flesh,
> Let your hand and eye now mesh!
> A sculptor's art you must employ,
> For a thing of beauty's a lasting joy!"

The wax softened, then remolded itself, pulling back into the contours of Yverne's body, separating its colors into those of her gown and her face and hair. Her chest began to rise and fall again.

Fadecourt knelt by her, touching her hand, almost shyly, and murmuring, "Maiden, wake!"

He, Matt thought, had a very bad case.

Yverne rolled onto her back, eyelids fluttering, then opening. She looked up at the three males gathered about her, then sat up, staring in alarm. "Is aught amiss?"

They just stood there, staring.

"Nay, tell me!" she demanded. "Are enemies nigh upon us?"

Narlh looked away, expelling a long breath, and Fadecourt said gently, "'Tis past now, milady. We only waked you to be sure you were well."

"Wherefore ought I not be?"

Fadecourt gazed into her eyes before he said, "You remember naught?"

Yverne shook her head. "I lay me down, and prayed, and thought upon the day's events—and slept. What chanced whiles I dreamed?"

Fadecourt exchanged a glance with Matt, who shook his head. The cyclops turned back to the lady. "The sorcerer who pursued you came again, milady—but the wizard drove him off."

"No, be fair!" Matt turned to Yverne. "I just distracted the villain, lady. It was Fadecourt who knocked him out with a rock."

"Oh, you have saved me!" She looked from one to the other of them—but it was Fadecourt's hand she squeezed.

Matt turned away, seething. Here he'd fought for her, risked being frozen and having his mind blasted, saved her from being melted into a puddle—and she hadn't even known about it! He'd been the hero who had saved the maiden—and she couldn't remember a bit of it! There was, he decided, no justice in matters heroic.

Narlh nudged his shoulder.

Matt looked up, hauling himself out of a nice, soothing wallow of self-pity. "What's up?"

The dracogriff pulled something from under his wing, biting it by the end, then opened his mouth and let it fall at Matt's feet. "Found this out there, where the sorcerer was. He left in too much of a hurry, forgot to take it with him. Thought you might want it."

Matt stared down at the sorcerer's magic wand.

"Go on, go on!" Narlh urged. "You got to have a wand around here, Wizard, or we're all done for!"

Remembering how the wand had held his eyes and been on its way to burning out his mind, Matt was tempted to agree—but he felt reluctant. "It's a dead man's tool, Narlh. Besides, it's been used for witchcraft."

"Mayhap," Fadecourt said, tearing his gaze away from Yverne, "but when all is said and done, Wizard, 'tis only a stick of wood. I pray you, take it up and learn the use of it."

"Well—okay." Matt bent down and picked up the stick, alert for the slightest feeling of wrongness—but there was only a lingering sensation of faint unpleasantness, like the musty odor of a shut-up room. "I don't promise to be able to learn how to use it, though."

"Oh, you shall," Fadecourt said, with full confidence.

Much more confidence than Matt felt. "To tell you the truth, Fadecourt, I'm not exactly eager to use a thing of evil."

"'Tis neither good nor evil in its own right," Fadecourt assured him.

"I think I've heard that argument before—that no object is good or evil in itself, just in how we use it."

"Oh, no, friend Matthew! In this world, at least, there are some things that are evil in themselves, such as demons and lamias, and things that are good in themselves, such as churches and bells. A good thing can be profaned and turned to evil uses, it is true, yet a wand of holly branch is not among these, though it is a tree of power, like the rowan and the hazel."

"And the oak, and ash, and thorn? Not to mention the mistletoe, and the ivy, and the brier rose and . . ."

"I take your point; it may be that each wood has its own certain power. I would not know of such things—I am not a magic-worker," Fadecourt said, aggrieved.

Matt felt instantly contrite; a friend did not deserve that of him. "Sorry, Fadecourt. I just get nervous with things I don't understand."

"You shall come to understand it presently, friend Matthew, I am sure."

Matt looked down at the wand. It was almost certainly a powerful gadget, to be used for good or ill. He hefted it, making slow, experimental passes toward the darkness as the night murmured about him.

He was careful not to say anything, though—not yet.

CHAPTER 12

Work in Progress

Fortunately, the one wand spell Matt finally decided to try that night was putting people to sleep. He pointed it at each of his friends in turn and recited,

> "Golden slumbers kiss your eyes,
> Wake with smiles when you arise!"

And in each case, the friend in question promptly grew heavy-lidded, started yawning, and was asleep in minutes. Matt didn't sleep himself, though—he wasn't too sanguine about pointing the wand at himself. He had a notion it might set up a feedback cycle, and that was one magical equivalent to physics that he didn't want to find out about—at least, not from the inside. Besides, somebody had to stand watch.

It was a good excuse. The reality of the matter, of course, was that after that attack, he didn't feel much like sleeping. Neither had his friends, he supposed, but he hadn't been about to give them much choice. They had to be fresh and alert for tomorrow. So did he, but he'd cross that bridge when he came to it—though not until after he'd checked under the boards.

It was a good thing Matt had specified that they wake with smiles on their faces, for as soon as they remembered the night's events, they began to feel nervous again. By joking and forcing laughter, they managed to keep each other halfway cheerful; but as soon as they set out, they began to sag. Everybody was eyeing the low grass and scrub around them suspiciously. Matt made a few tries at light conversation, but they sank without a trace.

When Fadecourt figured out that they weren't having much luck trying to bolster their spirits, he began telling them the tale of Worlane, greatest of Hardishane's paladins—of his unrequited love for the eastern princess Lalage, and how that love drove him mad when he learned she had married. He turned out to be an excellent storyteller, so the tale caught them up and out of their own predicament very quickly.

They had hiked perhaps an hour when they topped a rise and saw a dark line shadowing the western horizon, with flashes of green where leaves tossed.

Matt halted. "What's this—a major forest on our line of march?"

"It would appear so." Fadecourt frowned, perplexed. "I came this way not five days ago, and there was naught but meadow and thickets."

"Your thickets have thickened." Matt felt his scalp prickle. "I think I smell sorcery at work."

Yverne looked up, startled. "Can you smell it, then?"

"Well, not literally," Matt admitted, "though there is a sort of . . . Well, no, it's not a feeling either, it's . . ." He ran out of words and threw his hands up in exasperation. "What can I tell you? There isn't any word for it! It's a sixth sense, I guess—the one I use to do magic with." He frowned down at Yverne. "Does that explain anything?"

"Enough," she answered, but her eyes were glazing.

Matt turned away. "Come on. I want a closer look at that forest."

Narlh and Fadecourt exchanged looks of misgiving, but they all went forward.

Matt stopped a few hundred feet from the forest. He didn't like what he saw. It was a dark, somber place of gnarled oak trees and bristling thorns, set against the backdrop of huge old evergreens. Matt mistrusted it on sight—any forest that was halfway between conifers and deciduous trees would have had relatively young oaks and elms. Whatever kind of forest it was, it wasn't natural.

In fact, it fairly reeked of sorcery, filled with menacing shadows and gnarled, evil-looking trees. Fadecourt could only scowl, shaking his head. "I could have sworn this forest was not here, Lord Matthew."

"And you would have been right, too." Matt pointed at a huge old trunk. A vine was writhing up through the underbrush at its base,

moving even as they watched, rising and thickening as it wrapped itself around the huge old bole. It wasn't the only one—other vines
were twining up around other trunks and sagging down from the
branches.

"Work in progress," Matt explained. "This forest is still under con-
struction."

Fadecourt said slowly, "It is true, by all the stars! The wood is not
quite finished yet; it is still a-building!"

Yverne tore her gaze away and turned to Matt. "Yet how can it be
new-made, and still be aged?"

"It just looks that way," Matt explained. "I suspect that, in reality,
if the term applies, it only came into existence last night, after I managed to win that little clash with the local wand-waver and pull
Yverne back together."

"Wherefore?" Fadecourt asked.

"To stop us, of course." Matt frowned. "My only question is, what
to stop us for?"

"To kill us," Narlh growled, half opening his wings.

"How?" Matt asked, feeling very practical. "They could have sent
an army against us back uphill—they could have caught us in any of
those gullies."

"Yes," Fadecourt said, "but the armies could not have come to us
in time."

Matt absorbed that for a minute before he answered, "Then this
forest is ;ust here to hold us up while they mobilize the militia."

Fadecourt nodded.

"So the last thing we want to do is stand still."

"Well said." Fadecourt strode resolutely toward the forest wall.

"Uh, maybe not." Matt held out an arm to bar the way. "I don't
know if I'm eager to go into a place when I'm being invited."

Fadecourt turned back to frown. "What do you mean? I see no one
who gives us invitation."

But Yverne gasped, and Matt just nodded toward the trees.
Fadecourt turned back to look.

A faint trail had appeared, not much more than a deer run. By its
side stood an old man in a robe that must have been at least two hundred years out of date. Matt squinted, but he couldn't make out the
details of its decoration—nor of the oldster's face, though he could
see a long, gray beard.

Fadecourt frowned. "Odd."

"Yes, isn't he?" Matt joined him in his frown. "You don't suppose he grew up in there, and hasn't heard that fashions have changed, do you?"

"Nay, I spoke not of his garb, but of his face. I have seen him somewhere—or his portrait, at least. I could swear to it."

"Don't." Matt laid a hand on his shoulder. "Strange things happen when people swear things around here. Believe me, I know. Don't do it if you can possibly avoid it."

"But what of this fellow in gray?"

"He shouldn't, either." Matt stepped past the cyclops. "But I think I'll see what he wants."

The old man held up a hand, palm out, arm straight toward them. Matt paused. "I don't think he wants me to come on."

"Mayhap we should heed him," Yverne said nervously.

"Maybe." Matt frowned. "I think I'll try to get a more complete picture from him. If you'll excuse me, folks?"

He stepped past Fadecourt's jaundiced gaze and went up toward the old man.

He had only taken five steps before the oldster quite calmly reached up and took off his head.

Matt froze, staring, waiting for the wash of horror to finish running through him.

While he was waiting, the old man tucked his head under his arm, turning into a ghost of his former self—not the old man, but the self they had seen chasing Yverne.

The damsel gave a little scream before she managed to clap a hand over her own mouth. Fadecourt was back and by her side in an instant, patting the other hand and murmuring reassurances.

Matt was wondering why the ghost could be seen in the daytime, until he realized the apparition was standing so far under the leaves that the gloom was almost nightlike. He set his jaw with determination and pressed onward.

The ghost began to make excited gestures. Matt stopped again, frowning, and called out, "Fadecourt—do your people have a system of sign language?"

"Nay," the cyclops snapped, and went back to comforting Yverne.

Matt frowned, remembering every bout of charades he'd ever played—not that it would have done any good to ask, "What category?" or "How many words?" But some of the ghost's gestures did seem to be on the verge of making sense, if you understood them as pantomime—the curled hand with two fingers extended downward scissoring could indicate somebody walking. But why was it walking in a U turn? And why that diagonal cut of hand across chest? Was he threatening to cut their heads off, too?

Then something almost clicked. Matt squinted, on the verge of understanding . . .

A brisk breeze stirred the leaves; a ray of sunlight lanced into the ghost's shelter. With a moan, he faded out, disappeared.

Matt stood, listening to the breeze and the summer insects, letting normality fill him again.

"What's it mean, Wizard?"

Matt looked up at Narlh. "I was just beginning to make sense of it."

"But you didn't quite get there?"

Matt shook his head.

"Shall we go, Lord Matthew?" Fadecourt came up with Yverne.

"Into the forest, or away from it?" Matt asked.

"Was not the ghost indicating that we should go in?" the damsel asked, glance flicking nervously toward the leaves.

Matt shook his head. "I couldn't even make out that much. That upraised arm could have just meant that we should stop because he wanted to talk to us—or it could have meant that we should stop and not go into the forest."

"He did afright the damsel and make her run before him." Fadecourt's jaw hardened as he glowered at the forest. "Are we to let him bar us now? I say nay!" And he stepped off toward the trees. "Let us dare this forest to do its worst!"

Matt made a long arm and caught his shoulder. "Hold it, friend. Its worst could be very bad indeed. Notice all the little yellow eyes in the shadows, giving us the evil look? And I don't like the way that tree is staring at me."

"Nonsense, Lord Matthew! A tree cannot . . ." Then Fadecourt caught sight of the oak Matt was pointing at. He gazed at it for a moment, then said, "I catch your meaning. It does look at us, does it not?"

"Indubitably," Matt assured him. "And it does not have beneficent intentions."

"Yet how can a tree do harm?" Yverne asked.

Matt skipped the visions of trees falling on houses and twiggy fingers grabbing somebody by the throat. "This is a magic forest, remember—raised by sorcery, activated by malice. What couldn't a tree do, in there?"

Yverne apparently had a more graphic imagination than he did, to judge by the way she shuddered.

"That's what I thought." Matt turned away to his right. "Let's just see if we can go around it, shall we?"

They saw. They saw all that morning, hiking on and on, the forest to their left, the hills to their right. After the first half hour, Matt stopped and said, "You're very noble and all that, milady, but it looks as if this could go on for a while. You ride Narlh, okay?"

"Nay, I have enjoyed the walk!" she protested.

"Maybe so far—but I don't want to wait till you're looking droopy. It's tiring enough just riding."

"But the poor beast . . ."

"Aw, you scarcely weigh anything," Narlh scoffed. "Wouldn't make me any more tired than a feather—and I'm carrying plenty of those."

"But 'tis not right that I should ride whilst you walk!"

"It is your privilege, as a lady," Fadecourt assured her, "and ours, as gentlemen. Be of good cheer, Lady Yverne—we have paced long miles already, and a few more will trouble us not at all. You, however, are unused to the exercise—nor are your shoes fitted to it."

"No point in waiting until your slippers are in rags," Matt agreed.

"Well—I am not booted," Yverne admitted, and it only took a little more cajoling to persuade her to ride again.

It was a good thing she did, because the hike went on, and on, and on. Finally, when they called a halt around midday, Yverne's shoulders were slumping as she slid off Narlh's back. The dracogriff wasn't looking too chipper himself; his scales had dulled, and his eyes had turned sullen. Fadecourt was still holding his head high, but you could tell he was working at it.

As for Matt, he was fuming. "Confound it! Will this blasted forest never come to an end?"

"All things end at last, Lord Matthew." Fadecourt sighed. "This, too, shall pass."

"I'm concerned with whether or not *we're* going to pass *it*." Matt glared at the gloomy wood. "I could swear I'm looking at the same evil tree for the fourth time! You know, the one that was staring at me?"

"Aye," Fadecourt said, weariness dragging at each syllable, "Yet that cannot be. It must be some oak that resembles it."

But Matt was suddenly taut again, with a realization that brought him something like horror. "It could be possible though, you know. Once you allow magic, the range of possibilities increases dramatically." He waved a hand at them. "You folks go ahead and start lunch. Let me see what I can cook up here."

Yverne looked up from opening the saddlebags. "But you, too, must rest!"

"I won't be long."

He wasn't. It didn't take that long to scuff around the long grass until he found an inch-thick stick, about a foot and a half long. He drew his dagger and cut a notch below the two little knots at its top, then jabbed it into the ground and came back to his companions with a vindictive smile.

Yverne held out bread and cheese with a frown. "What virtue is there in setting out a stake?"

"Yeah," Narlh concurred. "Tryin' to set a booby trap for anybody comin' after us?"

"No—I didn't even sharpen the top." Matt folded up tailor-fashion and accepted the slab of bread and cheese.

"Then what purpose will it serve?" Fadecourt asked.

"Let's just say that I hope like fury I don't see it again."

It took a long time. It took four hours, and Matt was beginning to think he was wrong, and it had all been his imagination, and the forest really was that large. It took so long that the sun was declining toward the horizon with a thought of reclining, and Fadecourt was sighing. "I can only admire your tenacity, Lord Matthew, and your zeal—but if we do not make camp soon, the darkness will catch us unaware."

"As long as it's only the darkness that catches us," Matt said grimly. "No, Fadecourt. We have to know what we're up against, before . . ."

Then he saw it.

He stopped dead, and Yverne lifted her tired gaze, frowning, wondering why he had halted; but just as she was about to ask, Matt sprinted ahead to something in the grass. He yanked it up, bellowing, "Damn it!"

Yverne turned ghastly pale, and Fadecourt stood ramrod stiff. Even Narlh scowled and muttered to himself.

Matt stumped back to them, holding out the stick and shaking it. "Do you see this? Do you see it?"

"Aye," Fadecourt said, his face frozen. "'Tis the stick you notched and planted."

"Planted, yeah! And it's grown into a regular nightmare! You know what this proves, don't you?"

"Yeah," Narlh said. "Some sorcerer moved it ahead of us."

"Sorcerer, yes—ahead, no! It stayed put—we did the moving! We came in a full circle! We've been tramping around in the same path all day!"

"But how can that be?" Yverne protested. "We have kept the sun behind us in the morning, and before us after noon!"

"And the wood on our left hand," Fadecourt added. "Can it be a circular wood?"

"Why not? It's a product of sorcery!"

"But the sun!" Fadecourt protested.

Matt nodded. "That proves it—that's the clincher. Gordogrosso twisted space on us, isolating us and those trees from the rest of the universe in a closed loop."

"Twist space?" Yverne gasped, eyes wide, and Fadecourt frowned. "Space is all about us—it is naught but air! How can one twist it?"

Matt started to answer, then scanned their faces and decided it wasn't the time for a lecture on math and physics. "Magic," he explained. "We've known we're up against sorcery—only Gordogrosso's a bit more of a heavyweight than I thought. Believe me, it's possible—here. And he did it." His face suddenly contorted with rage, and he whirled, hurling the stick from him. "Damn that stick!"

Yverne blanched. Fadecourt's face hardened to granite. "Well, then, we have wasted a day, and I doubt not the king has used the time well, to bring his army that much closer to us. Yet it is done, and there's naught we can do to counter it—or is there?"

"No," Matt agreed. "Nothing, until morning—or at least, there's no point in trying. If I come up with a spell that gets us out of here before night, I'll just give King Gordogrosso all the time he needs to come up with something worse. We'd better just find dinner and bed down."

"And make a defense line," the cyclops said grimly. "We shall need a strong one, surely."

Matt stared at him in surprise. Then he said, "Why yes, of course. Any special reason?"

But Fadecourt had already turned away, casting about the meadowland in search of a campsite—not that there seemed to be much to choose from. It was perilously close to rudeness, saved only by the fact that Fadecourt had managed to turn away before Matt got his mouth in gear—but it jolted the wizard nonetheless. He turned to Yverne, but she had already slid down off Narlh's shoulders and was walking away, too, dipping down now and then to pick up kindling wood. In desperation, he turned to Narlh. "How come I'm *persona non grata* all of a sudden?"

"Whadda ya expect, Wizard?" the dracogriff growled. "You just put us all in danger and set yourself up on the side of evil."

Matt stared.

Narlh nodded.

"I must have done it while I wasn't looking, then," Matt said. "What did I do?"

"You cursed the stick," Narlh explained.

"Cursed it?"

"Yeah—when you sent it to Hell."

"But I didn't . . . Oh." Matt's eyes widened. "You mean . . . when I said, 'Damn that stick'?"

Narlh winced at the repetition. "Yeah, yeah! Did ya have to say it again? Look—if you damn something, you send it to Hell—right? You set the worst of curses upon that helpless piece of wood."

"But I didn't mean it that way! It was just a figure of speech!"

Narlh winced. "What you say, can really happen here. And if you heap so much torture on such a poor little innocent object, you've done a lotta wrong."

"But it isn't even alive!"

"Doesn't matter. What the words said is evil—and that means you gave the sorcerer a hole in our defenses, by siding with Hell, no matter how small the issue was."

Matt stared at him, shocked.

Narlh cocked his head to the side, frowning. "So how come you didn't know all about this? You're a wizard, ain't you?"

"Yes," Matt said, "but I still haven't managed to shift my *Weltanschauung*, my worldview, along with my shift in worlds. You're right—I really should have thought of that."

Narlh started to ask, but Matt suddenly whirled and ran toward the forest, plowing to a halt and casting about frantically. He found the stick and yanked it up out of the grass, cast around again until he'd found three rocks, slapped them together into a rough hearth, then yanked up grass from all around it and pulled out flint and steel. He struck a spark and breathed on it as the grasses crisped around it, breathed the spark into flame, blew gently on it until the stick caught fire, and blew harder and harder until the flames surrounded it. Then he sat back on his heels with a sigh and looked up to see Yverne gazing down at him—and she was looking rather bitter.

Matt spread his hands. "Look—no more stick, no more curse."

She stared at him as though he'd lost his wits. "Can you truly think so—and you, a lord of wizardry?"

Matt just stared at her as the flames died down and guttered out, leaving only a small heap of ash. Then he said, "Okay—what basic, elementary fact have I overlooked this time?"

"The stuff of life," she said, "or rather, that life has no stuff. These sticks and rocks about us are but illusions, as are we ourselves; the real world is the spirit's."

Matt stared, horrified. Slowly, he said, "And in that real spirit world, I've condemned this stick to hellfire eternal?"

"You have," she confirmed. "What use is making the stick itself to vanish?"

He had the odd, irrational feeling that she was hoping he would explain some secret of wizardry to her, whereby his cursing the stick would be erased; but he had none to give, and after a moment, the light in her eyes died, her mouth twisted with bitterness again, and she turned away. Matt stared down at the pitiful heap of ashes before him, feeling foolish and, strangely, very, very guilty.

But it was just a stick!

Finally, he hauled himself to his feet and turned to look around and see what his companions had done while he was chasing the wild goose.

The first thing he saw was the dozen sharpened stakes on top of the hillock, leaning outward in an impromptu chevaux-de-frise. They made a neat circle around the top of a little hillock—a hillock that Matt hadn't even known was there. He wouldn't ever have, either, if Fadecourt hadn't been busy finding sticks and sharpening them, setting them up in a stockade. The cyclops was still at the task, setting up another sharp point to close the ring. Matt stared at him in silent tribute, shaking his head with a shamed smile.

If there was anything resembling a defense to be found or built, Fadecourt would do both. Matt pushed himself into motion, heading toward his companion. As he came up, he asked, "Anything I can do to help?"

"Aye," Fadecourt said, his attention still on the stake he was setting. "Seek out boulders and roll them back."

Matt accepted the unstated rebuke and turned away to go rock hunting.

Narlh was already on the job, bringing foot-thick rocks back to the hillock—except that he wasn't rolling them, of course, he was just picking them up in his jaws and carrying them back. He spat out the current one and called out, "This is stupid—I can haul 'em a lot faster'n you, Wizard. But it slows me down having to look for 'em. You just hunt 'em out, okay? And wave to me when y' find 'em."

So Matt did—and the dracogriff was right, it did go faster that way. As the sun was setting, they all settled down inside a ring of stone two boulders high, with a stack of eight-foot tree limbs beside them to sharpen and add to the stockade.

The atmosphere had thawed enough for conversation—sinner and klutz though he might be, Matt was on their side. He groused at Fadecourt, "Where'd you learn so much about the military, anyway?"

Since he intended it as a rhetorical question, he didn't really notice that the cyclops didn't answer.

Alisande neared the western border with an army at her back, and the peasant mothers ran home and hid their daughters, out of long habit. They had heard that the queen had already executed two men for rape, but soldiers will be soldiers.

The queen came to the border with an army at her back, yes, but the only unit she really trusted was D'Art's. And Sauvignon's, of course—at least, she trusted his intentions and his fighting ability; the marquis had been jailed with his father, after racking up quite a score on the tournament circuit.

But how he would fare in battle—ah, that was another matter. Due to the consequences of his loyalty, he had been forced to sit out the last war, unable to rally to Alisande's banner.

He had rallied now, well enough, with the gleam of fervor in his eye, and a look of awed worship whenever he glanced at his queen. Alisande glanced back to her right; he was there, like a shield on her shoulder, eyes only for his sovereign.

But not for the woman Alisande.

Regrettable, in its way, for he was a handsome youth, only a few years older than Alisande—clean-favored, with a strong jaw and flashing blue eyes. She reflected, not for the first time, that a pedestal can be an uncomfortable location. Not to mention its being an exposed position.

With a shock, she realized the course of her thoughts and deflected them, thrusting them from her angrily. The man was another woman's husband, after all!

Besides, she herself was betrothed.

Yet he was the son of a duke . . .

If only her Matthew were as well born as Sauvignon! Her Matthew, who regarded her not with awe, but only admiration— admiration, and a healthy lust.

Again, she thrust the thought from her; it was apt to weaken her with the womanly emotions it raised. She lifted her eyes unto the hills and beheld the borderland, with its lofty spires and rocky crags. A dragon drifted between the peaks, no doubt eyeing them with suspicion. She smiled and raised a hand in greeting, remembering Matthew's dragon friend Stegoman, who had aided them so strongly in battle, and en route to it.

Was there nothing that did not remind her of Matthew?

The dragon tipped its wings, rocking from side to side, and wheeled away, back into the mountains. "We are espied, Majesty," Sauvignon said in his clear, rich tenor.

It sent thrills up her spine, as Matthew's voice once had. But she kept her face impassive and returned, "Espied by friends, my Lord Marquis—for any who fight for their freedom must needs be enemies of Ibile, and Ibile's enemies are our friends."

"May they, then, seek out word of the enemy for us?" His tone was hopeful.

"They may," Alisande answered. "But look you, milord, these are not our minions to command, but allies to be asked."

"Brave and valiant allies," the young man murmured.

Alisande hoped he was right.

CHAPTER 13

The Burning Stake

Friends are friends, so the atmosphere couldn't stay chilly forever. On the other hand, it didn't have to become warm and cozy, either. The conversation gleamed with a veneer of great politeness throughout the meal. Matt could understand it—after all, he was the one who had made the crass, unbelievably basic mistake that had endangered them all. So, under the circumstances, he was more than glad to volunteer for the first watch. He was even gladder when his friends had rolled up in their blankets and left him to his vigil. The coals glowed on their blanket-wrapped forms, and the sound of deep, even breathing filled the air, punctuated by the occasional snore from Fadecourt.

Peace began to fill Matt's soul, or at least calmness; he felt his spirit filling with the elation of the star-filled canopy above him. The stillness of the night was soothing, only the sounds of nature about him, proceeding with their even rhythm. Even the shadowed, looming wall of the forest, bulking dark against the sky, seemed only the vandalism of a petulant child.

Narlh, however, was a little more suspicious of that tranquility, and its effects on Matt—especially as he saw the wizard's gaze drift to the wand lying beside him. When Matt picked it up and started gazing at it, the dracogriff decided it was time for action. He cleared his throat and growled, "You sure you want to take the first watch?"

Fadecourt looked up at the sound of the dracogriff's voice, instantly alert. Even Yverne lifted her head—under the circumstances, she wasn't sleeping too soundly, either.

"Yeah, sure I'm sure." Matt waved Narlh away without looking; his eyes were on the three-foot stick across his knees.

Narlh gave him a doubtful glance, but curled back up on his side of the fire. Yverne and Fadecourt, however, were not quite so sanguine. She looked up from her pine-bough bed to exchange a glance with him where he lay on the grass.

"Does he know the wielding of a wand?" Yverne asked. "For surely, if he does not, he could bring down disaster on all our heads."

"He is a wizard of experience," Fadecourt answered, "yet I share your misgivings." He turned to Matt and called out, "Ho, Lord Matthew! Dost'a know aught of magic wands?"

"Something," Matt answered, his eyes still on the stick. "Where I come from, magicians wave them around as part of the spell." He didn't mention that the magicians in question were illusionists, or that the wands were only there to call the audience's attention away from what the magician was really doing. "And I've read stories in which the magicians made 'mystic passes' with them—I assume that meant gestures that somehow reinforced the spell."

Fadecourt and Yverne exchanged a glance that said their misgivings had been confirmed. "'Tis not that, Lord Matthew," the lady said, turning back to him. "'Tis simply that, when the wizard casts a spell at someone, he points the wand at that person, and the spell is made far stronger."

Matt stared, his eyes losing focus, as he tried to remember what he'd seen during the magic fight. "That's right—the sorcerer didn't gesture with the wand. He just held it straight up until the last few syllables of the spell, then snapped it down as if he were a fisherman casting."

"Nay." Yverne frowned. "'Tis a wand, not a net."

"I meant an angler, not a commercial fish-harvester." Matt looked up, frowning. "You sure there's no chance this thing is dedicated to evil?"

Fadecourt spread his hands. "You are the wizard, not we. Yet surely, if it were, you would feel its malice in your hands."

Matt nodded slowly. "That's true, and I don't really feel anything in it, except maybe a residue of nastiness. But I should be able to clear that out with a magical cleansing spell."

"Take it away from us when you do, I pray you," Fadecourt said hastily.

"Don't worry, I'm not about to do anything with it until I have a fairly good idea of how it works." Matt shook his head. "But I don't see how it could make a spell stronger. I mean, once I conjured up a horde of insects, and they came from all four quarters of the sky. How could I have pointed the wand at them when they came from everywhere?"

Yverne was staring. "You truly summoned a plague of locusts?"

"Bugs, anyway." Matt squirmed, uncomfortable with the awe in her eyes. "Another time, I had to alter the weather a little, summon up a storm—and, of course, I had to control it. How could a wand help with that? I mean, a storm covers the whole sky, so a wand . . ."

"I have no idea," she said, shaken. "I have told you all that I can— yet methinks 'twas no need, if you are so puissant a wizard as that. By your leave, I'll retire." And she beat a hasty retreat back to her brush pile.

Fadecourt stayed long enough to shake his head. "And I had dared to counsel you! Your pardon, Lord Wizard."

"Oh, no, I appreciate your help! I mean, it's not as though I had spent a lifetime studying magic, you know. I had to pick it up quickly, and I'm sure there are still a lot of holes in my knowledge."

"I cannot patch them, then," the cyclops said. "Great or little, your knowledge of magic far exceeds my own. Nay, in future I'll stick to my boulders. Good even, Lord Matthew." And he turned away to find himself a nice soft patch of grass.

Matt stared after him, frowning, feeling somehow guilty. He certainly hadn't meant to hurt their feelings, or to make them feel small. He was just being honest—but of course, admitting that he didn't really know what he was doing wasn't exactly going to inspire confidence in people who were depending on him. Besides, though he hadn't been studying magic his whole life, he had been studying the controls for it, without knowing it—literature. He had become a student, though somewhat reluctantly, in elementary school—and Miss Grind, in junior high, had practically killed his love for poetry by forcing his class to read syrupy sentiments by minor versifiers and telling her students they were great. But Mr. Luce and Miss Soleil, in high school, had restored his wonder at the old songs, and a couple of his college professors had helped him to understand the new ones. The rest, at least, he had suffered in silence; their subject matter redeemed their teaching. His whole advantage, against the sorcerers in Merovence, had come from his knowing great poetry that they hadn't known.

Well, no, not *just* from that. To be fair, a lot of his advantage had come from being able to analyze the workings of magic methodically—being able to ask, "How does that work?" and figure out an answer.

And how had he done his figuring? Well, by the scientific method, really—observation, formulation of hypothesis, experimentation, revision, and conclusion. And where had he learned that? From that wonderful ninth-grade science teacher, and from the other science courses he'd been forced to take in high school and college. No, in a manner of speaking, he'd have to say that he'd been studying the background material for Merovence's magic longer than he had known—which was why he'd been able to learn it so quickly here.

So apply it all again. He'd figured out how magic worked in Merovence with nothing but his own observations to help him. Later on, he'd refined that knowledge with a lot of helpful hints people had given him—but he'd figured out his first purposeful spell on his own.

If he could have done it then, he could do it now. Okay—apply the scientific method to a fantastic object. Figure out how the magic wand worked . . .

On the other side of the fire, Narlh eyed Matt warily. He could tell from the way the wizard was staring at the smooth stick that he wasn't going to be paying any attention to anything else all evening. Silently, and without Matthew noticing, Narlh uncurled and started prowling. So the wizard would take first watch? Big deal. So Narlh would watch the wizard—and anything else that came up.

His back being guarded without his knowing it, Matt studied the wand, trying to apply the scientific method to magic. After all, it was a method for solving problems, any problems that produced symptoms, which could show the way to a possible solution, which could in turn be checked by experiment.

Okay. First: observation.

Well, Matt had observed that the wand was used, and he had seen and felt the result when it was pointed at him—but the consequences weren't noticeably different from those of any other spells he'd experienced. Of course, they were presumably stronger than they would have been without the wand—but maybe it had just been amplifying the magic of a very weak sorcerer.

Amplifier? No, certainly a stick of wood couldn't function as an amplifier.

But the idea did catch at Matt's attention, at least enough to make an analogy between magic and electronics—and he moved into the next step of the scientific method: hypothesizing. After all, electromagnetism was a field force, and from what Matt felt when he worked a spell, so was magic. Here in Ibile, the feeling of some sort of force gathering all about him was almost suffocating. If the analogy held, the field force could be channeled into a directional force.

Was that what the wand did?

Yes, of course! It was the "antenna" for the "transmission" of magic—and a spell converted the field force into a form that could be "modulated," formed, by a human mind! That modulated force could be radiated in all directions, which was what Matt had been doing—"broadcasting" magical energy. But the wand made the transmission directional, like a parabolic dish concentrating electromagnetic microwaves into a beam. Or like those sharp points of static electricity he once saw in the college laboratory, in his one required lab science course. If that was right, then the wand certainly wouldn't have been useful for summoning a horde of insects, controlling the weather, or anything in which the magic needed to affect everything in sight, in all directions.

Was that why some magicians used gestures, "mystic passes"—for the more general spells? Maybe the sawing of the air did do some good, after all—Matt had imagined it was just sort of an aid to concentration, or a way of boosting self-belief in the magic-worker's own power. But words were symbols, and it was those symbols that modulated, manipulated, the magical field. As Matt had recently proved, just thinking the symbols was enough, if you concentrated on making things happen through them—but for most people, himself included, it was easier to concentrate when you spoke aloud, which was why he had paced his room muttering to himself when he studied for exams. And why, come to think of it, magicians could write books of spells without making natural cataclysms erupt while they were writing—by deliberately *not* speaking the verses aloud, they'd been choosing to have the spells be ineffective. He'd noticed himself that a poem would concentrate a magical field about him, but that it couldn't discharge unless he put some sort of imperative at the end of the verse. If his analogy to electronics held, the verse accumulated and modulated that field, as a power amplifier increased the strength of a signal and a transmitter modulated it—but the completed radio wave couldn't go anywhere if you didn't route it into the antenna. The imperative at the end of the verse was like pressing the "transmit" button on a CB transceiver. The imperative, the command, was a matter of willing the spell to effect its results.

But if Matt had been broadcasting spells like a spark-gap transmitter, no *wonder* every wizard and sorcerer within range had suddenly known there was a strange magician in his territory! They'd picked him up, loud and clear.

Which was probably why the Ibilian sorcerers used wands—so that they could keep the king from knowing what they were doing. Of course, it also made spells more powerful, by making them more directional—so as Matt used the wand, it would direct the discharge of magic into a much smaller area, and there wouldn't be any spill-over for King Gordogrosso to pick up.

The wand could let Matt work magic without letting the king and his noblemen know Matt was there. Also, by concentrating a field into a beam, it should make the spells much more powerful. Of course, this would only work for a spell that was supposed to happen in a very small area. It wouldn't do any good for fighting a whole army, as Matt had once infected a whole host of besiegers with sal-monella, or for anything else that was supposed to apply to every-thing in the vicinity—but most spells were directed at specific people or things, anyway. With the wand, Matt wouldn't have worried that pushing the rock off Narlh's tail might alert the local magical gen-darmes.

If the wand worked as Matt was guessing.

Hypothesizing, rather—he wasn't guessing blind; he had some data to build on.

Okay. The hypothesis was complete—but it was based on an anal-ogy that might not really fit the actual situation. If the two forces only seemed to be analogous, but weren't really so, then the hypoth-esis would be wrong.

Only one way to find out—test it. Experiment—the third step in the scientific method.

What to try?

Matt looked about him and spied a boulder that Fadecourt had brought over for the fire ring, then found to be too large and tossed away. It was about two feet in diameter, and the cyclops had only tossed, not pitched, so it was only about twenty feet outside Matt's guarding circle. He stared at it and recited a quick rock-moving verse.

> "Roll down, roll down the meadow!
> You must roll o'er the meadow.
> Roll out and o'er the meadow,
> Whether you be young or old."

He felt the familiar gathering of forces, thickened, oppressive, and pushed back against them with sheer willpower—but not very hard;

just a little harder than they pressed in. He only wanted the rock to move a little bit, not become a perpetual motion machine, as the one he'd pushed off Narlh's wing had.

The rock stirred, then moved a little to the right, rolled back, moved a little farther to the left, rolled back and a little farther to the right—and, rocking back and forth, finally boosted itself up over its own shallow bowl, past the rim, and lumped itself over and over for about two feet, then came to rest. This time, there was no slope to keep it going. Matt nodded—all had proceeded as he had expected. So much for the control; now for the experiment. He introduced the variable—the wand. A moment of whimsy seized him, and he decided really to introduce the variable. "Rock," he muttered, "this is the wand. Wand, this is the rock."

The wand bobbed, and the stone wobbled.

Matt felt his hair try to stand on end. There was more power here than he'd realized! He summoned composure, pointed the stick at the stone, and recited the exact same verse again.

The boulder jumped into the air, landed, and jumped again—but only half as high—and went bouncing away toward the forest. It really was rolling, too—but the rolling was happening mostly in the air.

Matt's heart soared. Hypothesis validated! Now, if he tried a dozen or a hundred times and got the same results on every occasion, he could include it in the theory of magic he was developing. By necessity.

Enough gloating. He couldn't take the chance that the boulder might keep on rolling forever—that was what he'd been trying to avoid when he performed the control experiment. Matt pointed the wand in the direction of the rolling rock and tried to remember the verse he'd used to stop the stone that had gone rolling down the mountainside.

Before he could get it out, he heard the crash of snapping brush, a howl of pain, and several loud baritone voices cursing.

He'd hurt somebody! Quickly, he snapped out,

> "Sisyphus, you've gone too far.
> Stop your heaving where you are!
> Then rock, stop rolling! Stand you still,
> And so your destiny fulfill!"

The crashing stopped, and the cursing went on. It finally occurred to Matt to wonder who'd been skulking in his underbrush.

"Up!" Narlh shouted. "Enemies to the northwest! And they might not be alone!"

Fadecourt was on his feet before the dracogriff finished, blinking as he looked about him, crouched, arms spread to fight. Yverne was lifting her head, blinking sleep out of her eyes.

Matt suddenly remembered that he was supposed to be the sentry. He leaped to his feet, shouting, "Fadecourt, up! Fear! Foes! Fight!"

"I am awake," the cyclops snapped. "Yet where is the foe?"

"In the trees." Narlh hissed, wings spreading dark against the night, and Yverne rose with a single, sinuous motion that was so graceful Matt caught his breath for a moment, gazing, before he turned to follow Fadecourt toward the chevaux-de-frise, drawing his sword. As an afterthought, he called back softly, "Yverne! Watch the back, the other side of the circle! You never know, they might try to outflank us!"

Hooves filled the night with drumming, and boots rolled under them. Then a war cry cut loose, and a score of footmen dashed out of the trees and hit the barricade. Matt quailed inside, but his body was already running toward the attackers, because Fadecourt was smashing into the front rank as they struggled between the pointed stakes, and Matt was hanged if he'd let the cyclops show him up. Besides, Narlh was right behind him, so he drew his dagger to make it look good and yelled back. Leaping forward he struck a halberd spinning from a soldier's hand. It flipped up into the night, and Matt's heart jammed into his throat, hoping it wouldn't hit Yverne. He risked a quick look back and saw he'd almost been right—it had spun straight toward her! But the frail, vulnerable damsel stepped aside adroitly and caught the halberd by the middle of its shaft. Then it went on spinning, but by her intention—she brandished it over her head, whirling it about two-handed, and charged into the fray with a scream that chilled Matt's blood.

Fadecourt struck another pike out of a soldier's hand, and the man tried to shrink back—but that was very hard to do, sideways, and Fadecourt had set the stakes too close together for a head-on advance. As a result, he had time to turn and clobber the hand of the next pikeman, who was trying to sidle through the stake next door. But the men on either side were almost through, and Matt ran at the left-hand one with a yell that would have done credit to a Georgia rebel, while Narlh advanced on the right-hand one. All he had to do was advance; the man took one look, paled, and tried to pull back. But of course, the pressure of the men behind was too great, and the disarmed ones were being forced, bit by bit, through the fence of stakes—largely because, behind them all, the fully armored and thoroughly protected knights were shouting, "Advance! Smite them down! Or you shall feel my sword in your back!" And, "Charge them and risk death—for if you do not, I'll give you certain demise!"

Matt felt a surge of class resentment, even as he grabbed up a discarded sword, blocked the next pike, and chopped through the shaft. How gung ho would those knights be without their armor and horses, he wondered?

It was an intriguing notion. He jumped back into the clear—but before he could frame the verse, he saw a sight that took his breath away. Yverne was sparring with a pikeman who had managed to squeeze through the barricade. He leaped to help her—but even as he did, she blocked the soldier's jab, pushing his blade down, caught him in the jaw with the butt of her own pike, then jabbed him hard under the sternum and managed to get a foot on his pike so that it pulled loose from his hands as he fell back.

Matt skidded to a stop, with the vague notion that his help wasn't needed. He wondered where Yverne had picked up such skill with a weapon, but it was only a fleeting thought—he had to get back to the battle! Let's see, what had he been about to do?

Oh yes, cast a spell! On the knights. He called out:

> "His horse is slain, and all on foot he fights,
>   Seeking his foes in the throat of death."

The two knights suddenly shot downward, disappearing behind their men with a double crash that told Matt his effort had been successful. The soldiers crowded back from their fallen leaders, and Matt could see them struggling to get up. Their squires hurried in and tried to haul them up, bawling to the soldiers to help.

They would get the knights back on their feet, given enough time—which Matt didn't intend to allow. He added,

> "This tight-fitting cuirass
>   Is but a useless mass,
>   It's made of steel
>   And weighs a deal.
>   A man is but an ass
>   Who fights in a cuirass—
>   So off goes that cuirass!"

He heard two howls of shocked surprise quite clearly over the din of the fight, as the two knights suddenly found themselves devoid of breastplates, protected only by the thick padding of their gambesons. Matt grinned wickedly. Somehow, he wasn't hearing the knights threatening their men any more—and a few soldiers were developing gleams in their eyes, lowering their pikes.

Matt didn't stay to watch. He ran back to the barricade, blocked a pike but found it was a halberd that cut down at his foot. He hopped back, but the blade caught his leg, and pain seared through. He cried out, but muffled it quickly, shifting his weight as he chopped through the shaft and riposted with a thrust toward the halberdier. The man leaped back with alacrity, and Matt was grimly pleased to note that there wasn't any great push to shove him forward.

Then a halberdier on his right knocked the sword out of his hand.

Matt leaped back from the fight—he knew better than to try to pick up the sword. A quick glance showed him Fadecourt with a captured pike, beating back soldier after soldier, Narlh catching soldiers in his jaws and tossing them away, and Yverne, bleeding from two cuts but fighting with the deftness of an expert and a very pale face.

The sight of her blood made Matt's plasma boil. He caught up a fallen halberd and jumped back into the fray just as a pikeman wriggled through the chevaux-de-frise. Matt slammed a chop at him—but the pikeman blocked the blow and slammed the butt of his pike into Matt's knee. Pain exploded as the knee folded, and Matt sank down before his enemy, whose point was spearing right toward him . . .

A pike butt whistled around and clipped the pikeman under the chin. The man fell back, and Fadecourt leaped up to stab down. The man screamed, then sprawled loose, and the cyclops jumped back to his own sector, crying, "Desist, Lord Matthew! You are not accustomed to the halberd! Devote yourself to spells for our defense!"

Matt staggered to his feet, trying to ignore the pain in knee and shin. He stepped back from the battle, using the halberd as a staff to support his injured leg. His face burned with shame—at having a woman outdo him with a weapon, but also at his failure to aid his friends by fighting with his strongest weapon—magic.

And he'd better get with it—it was very odd that no junior sorcerers had started magical support for the attackers yet. If he moved fast, maybe he could forestall them . . .

With a meteor.

"Go and catch a falling star,
Get with child a mandrake root . . ."

A roar split the night. Matt stared, mouth hanging open, last line unfinished, because a towering flame swept toward him. The ranks of attackers split with a huge shout to make room for it, and Matt found himself wondering, *Oh, no! Did I do that?*

Not with the verse about the meteor, at least—for as it came closer, Matt saw a twelve-foot tree trunk, blazing like a Yule log, stamping up on two legs made by a split in its bottom end. Two fiery knots toward its top glared down at him; a gash below them opened and bellowed, "You! Vile sorcerer! Most evil of magi! Never did I do you hurt! Innocent was I of any wrongdoing! Wherefore did you cast me into the fiery furnace?"

Matt was so startled he could only stare back at it and stutter.

The tree blundered into the barricade, and three stakes caught fire. It glared down at them, then sought out Matt again. "Will you now condemn these poor twigs, also, to the eternal flame? Will you damn them, as you damned me?"

"But—I didn't!" Matt bawled. "I've never seen you before in my life!"

"Of a certainty, you have," the flaming tree bellowed, "though the powers of Hell have magnified me so that I may be the instrument of your destruction! I was the twig you set into the earth as a marker, the poor, unoffending stick that you threw from you with a curse!"

Even through his panic, Matt recognized the reference to Gordogrosso. The sorcerer-king had magnified the little stick he had thrown away with a "Damn you!" and pulled it back from Hell to threaten Matt.

Wait a minute . . . The torture chamber for damned souls . . .

"You can't have been damned!" Matt cried. "You didn't have a soul!"

The tree froze in place, its fiery eyes widening in astonishment.

Matt pressed his point. "Hell is only for the souls of the wicked! And no other person can send you to Hell—only yourself, by refusing God's help! Did you ever refuse God?"

"Nay . . ." the tree admitted.

"And you didn't have a soul to send to Hell in the first place! Material things don't go to Hell—not flesh, or stone, or wood! Only souls!"

"If that is true," the tree said, "I cannot have been damned." Its flames began to shrink.

"Right!" Matt cried. "And if you weren't damned, you can't be on fire!"

"Aye . . . that is true . . ." The flames guttered out.

"In fact," Matt shouted, "you can't even be alive! Some idiot sorcerer just made you *think* you were, so he could give you the tortures of the damned!"

That did it. The last spark of light died from the tree's eyes, and it began to tilt.

"*Timber!*" Matt shouted, and the smoldering trunk came crashing to the ground.

But it left a hole in the defenses, three broken stakes.

On the other hand, those stakes were burning, and the soldiers were staring at the flames in horror and fascination.

Matt saw his chance. "Quick! Flee! Hide yourselves in the hills and repent! Or you, too, will fall into everlasting hellfire!"

The soldiers howled in despair, turned, and fled. They left two men, clad in the padded jackets of gambesons, waving swords at them and shouting frantically, "Hold! Do not believe this madman! Come back! What is the fury of Hell in the next world, against the rage of King Gordogrosso in this?"

Apparently, the men were suddenly much more aware of the next world's perils, because they didn't come back.

The one unarmored knight turned to the other. "I, at least, fear Gordogrosso more than God! I would rather die in battle than face the king!" And he turned to advance with determination toward the burning stakes.

Reluctantly, the second knight started to advance.

"Stop and think!" Matt held up a hand. "If you die serving Gordogrosso, you'll go right to Hell!"

The second knight hesitated.

"Fool!" the first knight cried. "Will you lose all the manor and lands the king has given you? Not I!" And, with a bellow, he charged, leaping the burning stake and whipping his sword down in a huge cut as he landed.

Fadecourt leaped back from the sword, then leaped in again as soon as it had passed. Before the knight could recover, the cyclops stabbed with the pike. The knight tried to block with the shield that wasn't there, and the pike scored his arm, leaving a gash of blood as its point transfixed his throat. Fadecourt yanked the spear out in some agitation. "'Tis too slow a death! I'll not leave thee to suffer, enemy or no!" And, as the knight's knees folded, the cyclops drew back the pike for the deathblow.

Yverne touched his arm. "His soul!"

Fadecourt froze. "Do you repent of all your sins?"

The knight managed a feeble nod.

"We can save him!" Matt cried. Then he saw how much blood had already pumped out onto the earth, and said, "No, we can't."

The pike flashed down through the heart and pinned the knight to the earth.

Fadecourt released the shaft and turned slowly to the other knight.

The knight stared at him, white showing all around his irises, gave a cry of despair, and lurched into a stumbling run.

Fadecourt skipped aside, only to trip on the dracogriff's tail.

The knight barreled straight on, heading right toward Yverne.

Matt howled and threw himself forward in a flying tackle, just the way he'd seen it done in the movies.

He slammed into his quarry right behind the knees, and the knight went sprawling. Matt's shoulder added its pain to balance that of his opposite leg. He tried to scramble up, but only managed to roll over onto his elbow—where he saw Yverne, standing over the man with a pike point poised over his face, crying, "You dastard! You bully, you false knight! How could you be so dishonorable as to strike at a poor, defenseless maid?"

"Yes," Matt agreed. "Totally despicable."

"*You* should hesitate to speak for shame, sir!" Yverne reproached him. "You, who do not scruple to strike the lowest blow!"

"So," Matt said, "did he."

Fadecourt resolved the argument by stepping forward and kicking the sword out of the knight's hand. "Your life is the lady's, sir. Beg her indulgence, or die."

"I yield me," the knight groaned. "Claim what forfeit you will."

Triumph gleamed in Yverne's eye, but she kept the spear poised. "Why, then, my forfeit is this—that you kneel to God and swear to lead a life of virtue, defending the weak and punishing the wicked, as a knight should!"

The knight groaned. "Mercy, lady! To seek to live virtuously in King Gordogrosso's Ibile is to seek one's own death!"

"Not to mention the loss of your house and land, of course?" Matt put in, as Narlh gave a disgusted snort.

"That also," the knight agreed morosely.

"You have but to choose," Yverne said sweetly. "A short life of virtue, or a long death in Hell."

"Maybe not," Matt said thoughtfully. "We're not all that far from the border—if you move fast, you might be able to make it into Merovence before King Gor—before the king catches up with you."

The knight shuddered. "You know not Gordogrosso's power."

"I know he doesn't dare do anything in Saint Moncaire's domain," Matt said sharply. "Get far enough into Alisande's territory, and the king can't touch you."

"Even in Ibile, there is some defense," Fadecourt advised. "Seek the sacraments of your faith, sir, and maintain your soul in a state of Grace, and you put yourself beyond the reach of the evil king."

"My soul, perhaps," the knight said mournfully. "Not my body."

"Even your body may be protected, by sacramentals—by the wearing of scapular and crucifix, by the carrying of holy water and rosary."

"It is, at least, a chance, sir," Yverne said with pity.

The knight lay immobile for a moment.

"Of course," Matt said, "you could let him repent, then kill him instantly."

"For shame, sir!" Yverne cried.

"Wouldst kill in cold blood!" Fadecourt demanded, shocked. "I gave the other his death wound in battle, Lord Matthew! The coup de grace only finished more quickly what had been wrought in hot blood!"

"I suppose so." Matt sighed. "It was just an idea."

"One well intended, I am certain, sir," the fallen knight said, "but I quail at the thought of the centuries in Purgatory awaiting one who has lived so vile a life as I have. Nay, I thank you all and will accept your kind offer. I will brave the king—and if I die in torment, at least it will be brief."

Matt had a vision of a medieval torture chamber, and what he had heard about making the pain last for days. But the knight was right, it was brief—compared to his probable sentence in the domain of the spiritually deficient.

"Kneel, then." Yverne withdrew the spear point.

The knight rolled up to his knees, joined his hands in prayer, and bent his head.

The companions waited.

After a short while, the knight raised his head. "I have made my peace with God, as well as I may. And I swear, by all that is holy, to try with all my heart to live a virtuous life henceforth, defending the weak and punishing the wicked. Now I must needs find a priest."

"Rise," Yverne said.

The knight stood, and Fadecourt clasped him by the hand, slapping his shoulder. "Welcome back to the world of the living in spirit, brother!"

"I thank you." The knight managed a smile. "Yet forgive my abruptness, but I must ride as soon as I may."

"Aye." Fadecourt stepped back. "Away with you, then!"

The knight looked about him, at something of a loss. "Wizard . . . if I may . . ."

"Oh, sure." Matt snapped his fingers.

> "I have many spells—what say they?
> Boot, saddle, to horse, and away!"

A sharp whinny split the night, and the knight's charger came trotting up. It pulled up beside its master and blew. The knight managed the ghost of a smile, patted the beast's neck, and mounted.

"Ah," Yverne breathed, "so there was hope for him, ere he met us."

Matt wasn't quite sure what she meant, unless it was that love for a horse was better than no love at all.

"I shall chance finding sanctuary, ere the minions of Satan find me," the knight said, turning his horse's head toward the west.

"Remember the sacramentals," Matt advised.

The knight gave him a sardonic smile. "And what such may I take from here, Lord Wizard?"

"Hymns," Matt said. "After all, the lyrics rhyme. There's a definite chance that singing holy songs will protect you, at least a little."

The man looked startled, then nodded slowly. "Aye, there is truth in what you say. At the least, it cannot hurt me. I thank you, Wizard."

"You're welcome. Uh, do you know any hymns?"

"One or two, from my childhood. Hail, Wizard, lady, cyclops! Hail, great beast! Hail, and farewell!" And he turned, riding off into the darkness, disappearing in the murk. But they could still hear him, chanting a Latin hymn in a loud, off-key baritone.

Fadecourt winced at the man's grating voice. "Nay, I doubt not he will be quite safe indeed."

"You can say that again," Matt agreed. "Who'd want to come anywhere nearer any singing like that than they had to?"

Privately, he suspected that the knight would renege on all his promises as soon as he was out of sight and return to his lord's castle—what difference did honor make, in Ibile?

But he hoped he was wrong.

CHAPTER 14

Negative Narcissus

When they started out the next morning, patched up and refreshed, they chatted happily with each other, in perfect accord. Matt decided that he must have made up for his lapse with the stick and restored his companions' faith in him.

The slope was angling downhill, and the land they had ridden yesterday was now discernible as a mountain behind them—but a mountain without the plateau that would have held the enchanted forest they had marched around and around. That forest had disappeared, and their path wound down in switchbacks through a maze of evergreens, dark and massive to either side of the path, but the roadway filled with light, due to the angle of descent. This forest had very little underbrush, and certainly no aura of evil; it filled their heads with the clean scent of pine and spruce.

But they came out of the forest about noon and, as they rode on after the midday meal, they began to see deciduous trees. They were stunted and gnarled, though; every other tree seemed to be smothered by a vine whose leaves were so fine they resembled fungus, and between the trunks, the underbrush was a waist-high tangle of thistles, thorns, and leprous-looking blossoms.

"Ugly-looking plant life they have around here," Matt noted.

Fadecourt nodded, looking around him with heavy brow, and his tension was almost palpable. "We have come down out of the borderland, Lord Matthew. We are in Ibile now."

Then he saw the flat-topped boulder ten yards down the hill and halted so suddenly that Matt almost bumped into him. Matt stared at the rock in surprise—and saw a lizard sunning itself. It was pointed away from them, so he couldn't really see much of its face, but he had certainly never before seen anything like the fleshy excrescence that bulged out of its head, ending in five points that glistened like polished horn. Matt stared—never before had he heard of a lizard with antlers!

Yverne gave a little moan, and Fadecourt rasped, "Be still! 'Tis a cockatrice—and woe upon us if the creature turns to show its face!"

Matt decided to keep the stare. The basilisk, or cockatrice, could turn them to stone just by looking at them. In fact, it couldn't *help* turning them to stone, and you couldn't blame it if it looked around every now and then to see what might be coming up behind it, in case it was threatened. Of course, it never was—at least, no longer than it took to spot the threat—though Matt supposed the occasional lizard had been lost to predators that could sneak up from behind.

Fadecourt waved them back, and as silently as possible, the companions did their best to slip behind the stunted trees available. But not quite quickly enough; a stick cracked under somebody's foot, and the little monster whipped about.

"Hide!" Fadecourt bellowed, and everybody leaped for the leaves. Then things became very quiet.

Finally, Matt whispered, "Everybody safe?"

"Yeah," Narlh grunted nearby. Matt heaved a sigh of relief. Then he heard a stifled sob from Yverne, and Fadecourt said roughly, "'Tis naught. I'm yet alive."

"What *happened*?" Matt bleated. A hiss answered him from up the road, and he throttled it down to a whisper as he peeked around his tree. "Fadecourt! What's . . ." Then he saw the cyclops and broke off.

"Oh, be still, Wizard!" The cyclops shook a stone fist at him. "I am not hurt! I can walk, I can fight!"

Matt swallowed and turned away. "I think the danger is clear and present. How far back do we have to go before we can find a detour?"

"We cannot." Fadecourt picked up a rock, left-handed. "This is the only road down from the heights. Stay hid till I have done." And he stepped out from behind the oak.

"Whoa!" Matt caught his shoulder. "Hold on there, boy! If that beastie spots you, we'll be taking you for granite!"

"And how can man die better?" Fadecourt challenged him. "Yet though I die, mayhap I'll clear the monster from the pathway first."

He started to go, realized Matt's hand was still there, and frowned back at him. "Unhand me, Lord Matthew."

"Don't be silly; without your hands, you wouldn't stand a chance. Let's try a better way."

The cyclops turned back, glowering—and just in time; behind him, Matt caught a glimpse of the lizard starting to turn. He yanked Fadecourt back behind the trunk. "Don't look now, but our igneous iguana just turned around to see what all the fuss was about."

Fadecourt paled, but he stuck to his guns. "You spoke of a way. What way is that?"

"Uh . . . well . . ." Matt's brain kicked into high gear as he started to improvise. "Something that would appeal to the essential vanity of the beastie."

Fadecourt kept his frown. "I had not heard that they were vain."

"Neither have I." But Matt's mind had fastened on the word *beastie* and wasn't letting go. "Look at it this way—if a perversion of nature like that ever really had to confront itself, it wouldn't be able to bear it." He wondered why Fadecourt stared, but plowed ahead. "So let's let him have a look." He raised his voice a little, and chanted:

> "Ah, would a power the giftie gie us
> To see ourselves as others see us!
> It would from many an error free us,
> And foolish notion!"

The air in front of the basilisk fogged up, coalescing and hardening into a gleaming disk.

Fadecourt stared. "What engine is that, Lord Matthew?"

"Why," Yverne said, "'tis a mirror."

The cockatrice stared, wide-eyed, at its own image—and, as it stared, its greenish-gray skin became steadily less green and more gray.

"Why don't it turn away?" Narlh wondered.

"Why, for that it cannot," Yverne said, with a smile of whimsy. "It is fascinated by its own image; look you—it is transfixed!"

The basilisk was almost completely gray now, and its eyes were filming over—but as much with a look of ecstasy as with silicon.

"Can it truly think it is beautiful?" Yverne wondered.

"Of course," Matt murmured. "Only advanced creatures can be self-critical."

The cockatrice trembled with a single, protracted shiver, and a crinkling sound filled the clearing. Then it stood, frozen, totally gray.

"Stoned," Matt breathed. "Frozen in ecstasy."

Then he raised his hand, palm flat, and moved it in a circle as though he were wiping a hole in the frost on an invisible window.

> "Let the power take away
> That which it has left astray.
> Recall the mirror-surfaced pane;
> Remove afar the silvered plane."

Yverne frowned. "Why did you banish the mirror, Lord Matthew?"

"Because," Matt said, "I didn't want to leave it hanging there."

"Could we not have taken it with us?"

"Well, yes—but it might have broken."

Yverne stared at him with wide, frightened eyes, and Narlh hissed. Fadecourt nodded. "Ah. Yes, we have no need of seven years' ill fortune."

"No, we don't." Matt frowned at the frozen monster.

"Do not pity it," Fadecourt rumbled. "It had no more than it would have done to us."

Matt shook his head. "It wouldn't have meant evil—it would only have been following its nature."

The cyclops looked up, frowning. "Why, how is that?"

"The instinct to look at any threat is inborn," Matt explained. "I've seen machines that could do anything just by reacting to what people do, according to the instructions of the, ah, 'wizards' who built them."

Fadecourt shuddered at the notion. "Dost'a mean these sorcerers made suits of armor live?"

"Not live, no, though you'd think it to look at them. They could even fight a warrior by automatically blocking his thrusts and cuts, so people think they were alive. But they weren't, not really—they were just following their programming." He stopped, seeing the blank, wary looks all about him, and gave it up with a sigh. "Never mind. Just take my word for it."

"Why, certes," Fadecourt said. "It is you who are the wizard."

"If you say so." Matt sighed. "But while we're on the subject, how about I turn that fist back into flesh for you?"

Fadecourt frowned, lifting the fist and gazing at it. Then he looked up at Matt with a wicked grin. "Nay, I think not—but I thank you. I have some notion it may prove of use."

"Well, it's your hand." Matt tried not to think too hard about what kind of "use" the cyclops had in mind. "Back to the immediate peril, then. Let's just make sure the spell worked." He caught up a stick and pitched it at the little monster. Fadecourt and Yverne gave yelps of dread, but the cockatrice only tipped over onto its side and lay frozen, legs holding their poses in the air.

"Yeah, it's safe," Narlh opined.

"Well, you're the reptile—at least partly." Matt looked up, frowning—the dracogriff had sounded shaken. "What's the matter—genus loyalty?"

"Loyalty, my tail! No way, Wizard! Why would I be loyal to a jinni? It's just . . . well . . ." Narlh took a breath. "Do you have any *idea* how dangerous those beasties are?"

"Well, I've heard something about them, yeah."

"Something about them, he says," the dracogriff muttered. "Why didn't you *tell* me you were that strong a wizard?"

Matt spread his hands, at a loss. "Hey—it's not that big a deal!"

Then he wondered why all four of his friends eyed him so strangely.

It made him feel a little odd, so Matt shook off the moment and stepped up to the basilisk, albeit gingerly. He stepped right in front of its face—and stayed fleshly. "All safe, folks."

The joint hiss of four pent-up breaths answered him, and the companions stepped forth. "Hey, Wizard," Narlh grunted. "Next time let one of us take the risk, huh?"

Matt frowned. "But it was my spell."

"And therefore, if the first to pass had turned to stone," Fadecourt explained, "only you could have restored him."

Yverne nodded. "Yet if you'd been frozen, Lord Matthew, how could the rest of us have passed the basilisk?"

"It makes sense," Matt grudged, "but I should take my share of the risks."

"I do not doubt you shall," Fadecourt said, with some asperity, "since there will be many you cannot avoid. Yet I must ask you, Lord Matthew, to avoid such chances as you can."

Matt grumped and turned away to lead them past the boulder.

They swung on down the winding path. After a while, Yverne stepped up beside Matt, giving him a look of concern. "Why are you so silent, Lord Matthew?"

"Is it *that* rare?" Matt asked, astonished.

Yverne managed a smile. "Why, no, I think not—yet you do seem troubled."

"Oh, that." Matt shrugged, trying to hide his reaction to her proximity. "Just trying to figure out the logic of this land, that's all. Before it figures out me."

"Logic?" Yverne frowned. "How can there be such, in a land of evil?"

"*Just* what I needed to hear! Sorry, milady, but I'm the kind who tries to work magic by good sense. How can I counter something I don't understand?"

"By virtue," she responded simply, "since there is none of that here."

"That almost makes sense. But . . . do you mind if I ask how come the supernatural creature I ran into, back in the mountains, wasn't necessarily evil, but the monster of the foothills seems to be a hybrid of foul and unnatural origins?"

"Foul I do not doubt—yet how was this cockatrice unnatural?" Yverne looked up at him, puzzled.

Matt looked down at her clear, innocent face and hesitated.

She saw his embarrassment and laughed. "Do not think to shock me by saying how two creatures may make two more, Lord Matthew. I am the daughter of a country lord; I have seen the couplings of spring."

"Well . . . this isn't exactly a coupling . . ." Matt took a deep breath and decided to risk it. "Let me tell you how to make a cockatrice. First, you take a rooster's egg . . ."

"Oh, my lord!" she cried, pursing her lips with amusement. "It is hens who lay eggs, not roosters!"

"Yeah, that's just the first unnatural thing about it. So you take this egg laid by a rooster, see, and I can just imagine what kind of spells of perversion it takes to produce that! And you put it where a toad can fertilize it, and you bury the fertilized egg in a manure pile, and some time later, by the light of a full moon, out comes a cockatrice!"

As he had feared, Yverne looked slightly green. Matt hurried to change the subject. "So you see why I'm curious to know why the monsters of the foothills are unnatural."

"'Tis well asked." Yverne bore up gamely. "I had thought naught of it, thinking it natural in creatures of evil—yet I had ne'er lived in a milieu of virtue."

"Mayhap I can make sense of it." Fadecourt stepped up on Matt's other side.

Matt turned to the cyclops in surprise. "Well, sure. I mean, I'd appreciate the information—but I'd think it was a little out of your line."

"It may be, yet it is a part of life for all who grow up in Ibile. Nay, more—'tis a condition of life, for not to know it may lead one to toy with fell and dangerous monsters who do not appear so terribly threatening, as this little monster did not. It is a condition of life, for not to know it may bring death."

Matt could imagine a bunch of rowdy village boys coming up to torment the basilisk by poking it with long sticks and jeering—and the basilisk freezing them out. "Great. So it's part of the basic equipment of life, and I don't have it."

"'Tis easily gained," Yverne said, "for 'tis only that the foothills we now wander are most certainly within Ibile, which has been corrupted by the rule of Evil. The mountains, though, are not wholly within the domain of Satan."

Matt frowned. "But I thought Ibile claimed territory halfway into the hills. In fact, I'm sure of it, because I came by way of a spell that was supposed to put me over the border."

Yverne nodded. "Yet Ibile's king cannot enforce his rule so near to Merovence—nor can your queen lay the border country under her sway. When all is said and done, the mountains belong to the mountain folk."

Matt lifted his head as understanding dawned. "Of course! They're the gray area, aren't they?"

Yverne frowned. "Gray stone, do you mean? But their slopes are well watered, for the most part, and quite green!"

"No, no! I mean the place where neither good nor evil has total power!"

"Ah! That is true—yet it is more true, praise Heaven, that Evil can never have total power; for there will always be some few souls with courage so great as to stand against it."

"True, true—and there will always be some people so warped and selfish as to dedicate themselves to Evil, even within a realm governed by those dedicated to Good. But what about the montagnards themselves? Who are *they* dedicated to?"

"Why, to one another, for all I hear of them, and therefore do they guard their independence with ferocious zeal, harrying any army so foolish as to come within their hills."

Matt frowned. "But if they're dedicated to one another, that means they're dedicated to Good."

Yverne nodded. "Aye, from all that I have heard of them. They are fierce toward those who wish them ill, yet are kindly to one another. They do demand a toll of any who seek to pass through their hills, yet do not ravage caravans nor despoil wayfarers."

"Probably smart enough to realize that no merchants means no tolls," Matt mused, "and that banditry would kill the trade."

Yverne frowned. "'Tis an odd notion, and one not entirely charitable, methinks."

"No, but probably accurate."

"I misdoubt it." The lady frowned. "For they are hospitable folk, look you, and have been known to succor travelers caught by storm within their domain."

Matt nodded. "Sound like good guys, all right—and not entirely unfamiliar, either; I've heard of people like them, in mountainous countries. But if they're good people, doesn't that make them part of Merovence, for all intents and purposes?"

Yverne smiled. "They do not harken to the commands of Merovence's queen."

"Well, no—but in the battle of Good and Evil we're concerned with, they're on the side of the angels." He had a brief and poignant vision of Alisande.

"'Tis true," Fadecourt agreed, "and even in countries where Good rules, Evil is continually at work, tempting souls to ruin. Therefore the forces of Evil and Good are at something of a balance within the mountains, and Evil cannot exercise so harsh a sway as to pervert the very nature of the animals within it."

"But in the foothills, Evil's rule is dominant, so foul things like cockatrices are made." Matt nodded. "Not that it's any fault of theirs, of course. But there's one problem with this whole explanation, milady."

"What is that, Lord Matthew?"

"The minor difficulty of which action belongs to which power. Could you trust a wizard who wasn't sure of the difference between good and evil?"

Yverne and Fadecourt stopped and stared at him, appalled.

Matt nodded. "I thought not."

"But who could mistake?" Yverne gasped.

"Many, lady," Fadecourt said, his face grim, "the young and innocent most especially, for bad things can be made to seem good. But, Wizard, our Lord hath said, 'By their fruits ye shall know them.' "

Matt nodded. "If it has evil results, then it's probably evil, yes. But how can you tell before it has done its damage?"

"There are signs," Fadecourt said, frowning.

"Yes, if you can learn them." Matt smiled bleakly and turned back to the road. "Well, on we go. Hopefully, we won't run into anything we don't already know about."

He was sunk into contemplation before his friends began to follow him. Fadecourt's definition certainly did make the issue simple. Now all Matt had to do was figure out what the signs of devotion to God were—well, he'd grown up with the usual list—and how to tell the real thing from the fake.

He sighed, settling into the march again. It shouldn't be too hard—after all, a con man was a con man, no matter what the culture.

"Not so many soldiers as all that," the peasant told her. "They have clerks stationed by the path from the pass, Majesty, and there are but a handful of soldiers to guard them."

"How large is that 'handful'?" Sauvignon demanded.

The peasant shrugged. "Ten awake and at arms, milord. Another ten refurbishing their weapons or asleep."

"Why, this will serve but to whet our appetites," Sauvignon said with disgust.

"Bide in patience, my lord," Alisande soothed. "There shall be more anon; for when King Gordogrosso knows our Lord Wizard is within his borders, he shall strike against Merovence with all his strength."

"So *that* is why we are here! How *could* the Lord Wizard desert us in so cavalier a fashion?"

Actually, Alisande had been wondering about that, too, though on a more personal level—and that, in spite of her very vivid memory of their parting. But all she said was, "He serves God, milord, as do we all, and must go where the Lord directs." She turned back to the peasant. "How shall we come through the mountains? Will not the montagnards resent our intrusion?"

"How can this man know?" Sauvignon protested. "He is not one of them!"

"Mayhap not." The peasant gave him a gap-toothed smile. "Yet my wife's cousin's aunt is wed to a montagnard, and 'tis his cousin's sons who have spied out the clerks and soldiers for ten miles along the foothills of Ibile."

Alisande hid a smile at Sauvignon's surprise. "The common folk have respect for the border, milord, but never overmuch."

"Borders are for nations," the peasant agreed, "but pathways are for kin."

CHAPTER 15

Pack of the Quarry

"Well, at least you can't say the scenery is boring."

"Wouldn't dream of it." Matt eyed the hills to left and right—and ahead. Behind them, mountains towered, blocking the sun; it was midmorning, but they were still moving through false dawn. "Was I complaining? At least we're walking on level ground, more or less."

"We have come out of the foothills," Fadecourt assured them. "It will not be long ere we see little but plowed fields, and must needs go through many towns."

"I'd prefer to go around them, if you don't mind." Matt eyed the nearby slopes with suspicion. "Even out here in the open, I'm constantly watching for Gordogrosso's lackeys."

"His lackeys are noblemen," Yverne pointed out. "Dost'a not mean 'the lackeys of his barons'?"

"Well, no, actually, I was kind of meaning what I said. Besides, how many of his barons were born aristocrats?"

Yverne flushed. "Most, though there were always a dozen or so whom he haled down, to make room for his low-born lackeys."

"Let that go on long enough, and there'll only be a handful whose ancestors go back before the sorcerers."

" 'Tis even so." Surprisingly, her eyes filled with tears. "Only a marcher baron is given his due here. And the parvenus are ever eager to seize what is not theirs."

Matt was horrified to realize she'd been talking personally. "Hey, now, I'm sorry! No offense intended. Don't worry, milady—we'll put the old houses back where they belong."

"Do not promise what you cannot assure," Fadecourt rumbled. "Only cadet branches of the old noble houses remain, and even they are so embittered that most have turned to evil ways, seeking to recoup their fortunes."

Matt looked up, appalled. "You mean even if I *do* manage to kick out Gordo—uh, the sorcerer-king, I won't be able to find enough good people to administer the countryside for me?"

"Even so," Fadecourt answered.

But Yverne countered, "You must take them where you find them, Lord Wizard. There be good folk among the commoners, and some may prove able."

That rocked Matt. "Uh, you'll pardon my saying it, milady, but—I'm a little surprised to hear a lady of the aristocracy lauding the abilities of commoners."

"Any who have kept their faith in God and kept being good," Yverne answered, "are noble in heart. Mayhap goodness is the only true nobility left in Ibile, since 'tis done in the face of such adversity."

Somehow, Matt had thought of Ibile as masses of good, poor people, laboring under the yoke of oppression and cruelty imposed by evil magic. He hadn't realized that the licentiousness of the aristocrats would make the common people think that there was no reason in their maintaining honest conduct toward one another, or living by any law other than the aristocrats' selfishness. He hadn't stopped to think how thoroughly the violation of morals could trickle down to permeate every level of society. He should have, of course—Gresham's law applied to any medium, not just to money, and people's media of exchange were only analogies for their real interactions.

They rounded a hill, and Matt found himself confronting the physical image of the rejected virtues he'd just been thinking about.

Where two slopes met, there was a little cave, a grotto, and in it was a statue. But its paint was peeling, and vines had grown over it, almost hiding all but the face and the left hand. Matt looked closely, but didn't recognize the features. "Who's that?"

Fadecourt looked up, surprised. " 'Tis he to whom you have prayed, Lord Wizard—Saint Iago. Dost'a say you have prayed to him, but never knew his likeness?"

Matt reddened. "I'm afraid not. Worse, I don't know anything about him."

Nearby were the remains of a small building, roof fallen in, stone walls breached, with soot stains over every place where there had been woodwork.

"Alas! That so sacred a shrine should come to this!" Yverne cried, tears in her eyes.

Matt looked at Fadecourt.

"This was once the most holy place of all, Lord Wizard," the cyclops said heavily, "for it stands in the place where Saint Iago did appear to Brother Chard, a simple mendicant monk. His brothers built this little chapter house, that they might live by the place, basking in its sanctity and tending its grounds. They held it safe 'gainst the sorcerer-kings for a hundred and fifty years. Then, alas, there came one traitor, one Vile by name, who became a novice, then a monk. He was somehow turned toward Evil, mayhap in hope of preferment by the king, and he made the monks a plan whereby, said he, they could defeat Gordogrosso. They were to go forth from this small cloister of theirs and come one by one into Orlequedrille, Gordogrosso's capital. There they were to surround the palace and pray with all their hearts to God, for the downfall of the king."

"And while they were out, the king's men fell on the shrine and desecrated it?"

"Aye; the chapter house they tore apart and burned within, as you have seen; and they smashed the beautiful mosaics in the grotto." Tears flowed freely down Yverne's cheeks.

"Yet the statue they could not destroy." Even through his anger, the awe in Fadecourt's voice was clear. "The soldiers could not enter the grotto; 'twas as though an unseen wall withheld them."

"A wall they could neither breach nor scale," Yverne whispered, " 'Twas even then a miracle."

"So the shrine itself remains." Matt frowned, brooding, gazing at the ivy-covered statue. "But what of the monks?"

"They were slain as they entered the town," Yverne said, "for the soldiers knew of their movements."

"Don't tell me they were fools enough to wear their monks' robes!"

"Nay; but a tonsure's not so easily hidden, when the guards at the gate demand that all men uncover," Fadecourt told him. "Then the king gave them trial, of course, and had his chancellor prove them guilty of lèse majesté."

"After they were safely dead."

"Aye, poor souls!" Yverne's cheeks were wet. "Yet their shrine still stands—neglected, for none dare come here; abandoned and in disrepair; but it stands, that the doers of evil deeds may know they have never fully won."

Matt sat frowning at the shrine.

Fadecourt noticed, and his voice was apprehensive. "Wizard? What would you do?"

"Just thinking that *we're* here," Matt said, "and no more likely to draw the wrath of any sentry-sorcerers by doing one more good deed. Come on, folks! Let's tidy up this grotto a little bit!" He strode away toward the statue.

Yverne and Fadecourt exchanged a glance of surprise and delight, then followed him. So did Narlh, muttering, "Something bad is gonna come of this. I just know it."

The statue's paint was faded and flaking, and Matt was tempted to scrape it all off, since it was stone underneath, but he resisted the temptation, contenting himself with clearing away the ivy and sweeping out the debris, while Yverne transplanted wildflowers and Narlh helped Fadecourt rebuild the low wall that had surrounded the grotto. They did some general cleaning and scrubbing, too, though there was no stream within the grotto, and they had to haul water from a nearby rivulet in makeshift buckets. It was midafternoon before they were done, but Matt stood back with a feeling of accomplishment and said, "There! That was time well spent."

Whether or not there had been a cave there originally was hard to tell from his angle, though Matt had seen from the inside that there was. But the monks had built an arch in front of it, of blocks smoothly fitted and extending at the front into a low stone rail. Along that rail, they had packed dirt into steps that ran the length of the wall, overgrown with grass, which Matt had mown with his dagger. It formed a prie-dieu, a kneeling bench for praying. Yverne's flowers adorned the base of the statue. There were also plants at two points up each side of the arch, in little earth-filled basins built for the purpose.

"I won't say it looks as good as new," Matt hedged, "but it doesn't look totally abandoned anymore."

"It does not, indeed," Fadecourt said. "Your pardon, Lord Wizard." And he went to kneel on the grass by the stone rail, beside Yverne, head bent in prayer.

"How about you?" Narlh demanded.

Matt stood for a second, thinking it over. Then he shook his head. "I never was much for devotion to the saints, I'm afraid. But I'll say a short prayer." He closed his eyes and bowed his head. When he lifted it again, Narlh snorted, "Short, all right."

"But to the point. Besides, if he cares at all, I think the work will do instead of the words."

"Maybe," Narlh allowed, "and I guess I'd rather have a man who did something without saying he would."

"Over the one who talked a lot, but never got around to doing it?"

"You've met 'em, too, huh?"

" 'Fraid so." Matt was watching Yverne as she rose and came back toward them. Fadecourt followed a few seconds later. "Back on the road?"

Yverne turned a radiant face toward him. "Aye, Lord Wizard. I think I shall fear naught that the sorcerer can do against us, now."

" 'Tis good not to fear," Fadecourt rumbled, "so long as one remembers to take care."

The sunset was long on this side of the mountains, but the land flattened out amazingly, and by the time it was dark, they still hadn't found a good camping place.

Matt signaled for a stop. "Well, when there's no place right, one spot's as good as another, isn't it?"

"I think not," Fadecourt said, frowning, "though there seems to be little choice. I prithee, make thy circle quickly, Wizard, for I mislike this open land."

"Yeah, and you didn't even grow up in the city." Matt started to swing his improvised pack off his shoulder.

But Yverne put out a hand to stop him. "Hist! What comes?"

They were instantly silent, taut, listening.

Faint with distance came a horrible grinding, gnashing sound. Even as they registered its existence, it grew louder. It sounded like giant teeth clashing against one another in anticipation of a feast.

"Whatever it is, it's coming fast." Matt looked worried.

"Coming fast? It approches like a hailstorm!" Fadecourt said.

Yverne turned pale. "I mislike that sound, Lord Wizard."

"Oh?" Matt looked up. "Ever heard it before?"

"Aye—as a child. A sorcerer of the king's came to reside at my father's castle for a short space—a reeve, he was, a common-born popinjay." Her eyes dewed at the memory of her father. "To awe my parent, he brought to life a gargoyle from our roof. It sounded much like this, as it moved its stony limbs and clashed its iron jaws."

Matt caught an echo of some more ominous event underscoring her words and wondered if the reeve's visit had eventually resulted in the siege that had just ended. But he had to file it away for a better moment. "If that's a gargoyle, then there's more than one."

"I doubt it not." Fadecourt was grim. "I have heard that King Gordogrosso has raised these beasts before, to track and shred enemies of whom he particularly wished to be rid."

"Congratulations, Wizard," Narlh growled. "You've been noticed."

"This time, I think I could do without the approbation. What are we standing around waiting for, people? Run!"

They turned and started back the way they'd come, but the gnashing and grinding grew louder behind them.

"To where . . . do we . . . run?" Fadecourt panted.

"You . . . tell me!" Matt wheezed. "You're the . . . military! Where . . . can we . . . hole up?"

"Nowhere," the cyclops answered, with instant certainty. "There's naught of . . . a stronghold, nor even . . . a good battle ground, between us and the grotto!"

"The grotto!" Matt cried. "You told me . . . nothing evil could . . . enter there! At least . . . it couldn't when . . . Gordogrosso's henchmen . . . tried to defile it!"

"Can it . . . hold 'gainst . . . them?" Fadecourt panted.

"It's the only chance . . . we've got! Shut up and . . . run!"

But Narlh slewed to a stop. "Here, you little guys will never make it! I can carry triple, for that far at least! Come on, up!"

Matt started to protest, but Fadecourt was already up and yanking Yverne aboard. Matt shut up and scrambled for a seat, grabbed at a fin, and held tight as the monster leaped forward into a run. Matt leaned into the wind and hoped.

The distance that had taken them six hours to traverse at a walk sped past them at Narlh's gargantuan pace. The wind howled by Matt's face, and he realized that he'd never seen the dracogriff run flat out before. Even so, the grinding and gnashing swelled behind them, faster than they could travel.

"This is too slow!" Narlh snapped. "Hang on—I hate it, but I'm gonna have to get off the ground."

They hung on for dear life as the dracogriff spread his wings and bounded into the air. He flapped mightily, straining upward, farther and farther, griping savagely every second, until, about fifty feet up, he caught a breeze and began to glide. Then he swooped eastward so fast that the clamor behind them actually began to fade a little—but not much. Peering over Fadecourt, Matt could see Yverne's back, rigid and trembling. He didn't doubt she had her eyes squeezed shut, but she hung on without a word of protest. Could he do any less?

Then the double hills rose up before them, and Yverne cried, " 'Tis yon! The grotto!"

Narlh folded his wings and stooped.

He hit the ground running, cupping his wings against the wind, then dug in with his claws and plowed to a stop. "Down! Those monsters will be here any minute!"

They didn't stay to argue.

Now that they were back on the ground, the sound swelled again—faster and faster. They bolted ahead of it, Fadecourt hanging back a little, Matt pacing himself to Yverne. The clamor clashed and clanged louder behind him, and he was very much tempted to shoot past the girl, but he held himself in until he saw her bolt through the gateway. Then he shot through, with Fadecourt right on his heels. Matt turned to look back, dreading the sight of their pursuers—and saw Narlh.

The dracogriff was facing into the wind, wings spread, running at an angle from them—but toward their pursuers.

And there they were, just coming into sight, moonlight glinting off granite faces and steel teeth.

"Narlh!" Matt shouted. "Are you out of your mind? Get in here!"

Narlh skidded to a stop, head lifted, staring. "Me? In a holy place like that?"

"You're good enough, you're good enough! After all, you helped clean it, didn't you?"

The dracogriff took one look over his shoulder, then bounded toward the shrine. As he squeezed through the gateway, he panted, "You sure there's room?"

"You'll have to curl up around the statue, I expect," Matt said, "but you should be able to make it."

Narlh did as he said, curving right around the statue, then left, as his head came out from behind. He lay down as he went, the roof being low, and looked up at the statue. " 'Scuse me, sir."

Matt turned back to the plain and saw the gargoyles waddling up toward them. They were a horrible sight—bits and pieces of recognizable beasts, legs from crocodiles, wings from bats, tails from snakes, human arms that were covered with fish scales—but with heads never seen on any living man or beast. And every single one was different; no two were remotely the same combination.

The heads were crested with growths that looked like feathers, fins, or wattles, and the faces were travesties of the human, just close enough to look really horrible. But every mouth was filled with glinting, pointed teeth. Matt looked at the moonlight winking off them and felt a chill shiver through him. Were those polished surfaces really steel?

"Close the door!" Narlh called.

"I can't," Matt answered. "There isn't any."

"There are no walls, either." Fadecourt braced himself for his last fight. "I implore thee, wizard—ready a spell, in case this shrine is no longer shielded by God."

"Well . . . I suppose that's wise." Matt tried to remember a shielding spell.

> "Though evil things surround us,
> May saving grace be round us.
> May nothing ill betide us,
> Good comfort stand beside us . . ."

He stopped, eyes wide. The air seemed to tingle about him; he could feel some sort of field pressing in on his skin. But it wasn't the turgid weight of evil magic that he was used to pushing against.

"Why do you stop?" Fadecourt cried.

"Because," Matt said, "somebody, or something, doesn't want me to go on."

"Who could have taken power here?" Yverne cried.

"Nobody," Matt said with total certainty. "You don't know how this feels, but believe me, if you did, you'd know nobody could even ruffle it."

Then the monsters struck the shrine.

They struck—and reared on up into the air, just as though they'd slammed into a wall. The ones in back climbed up on top of the ones in front, then went on climbing with their front legs. Their rear claws flailed at thin air, seeking to gain purchase on something, but not finding it. Then the third tier climbed on top of the second, and they had a little luck—they were able to bend forward, as though they were leaning over the curve of a domed roof. But they couldn't climb it—not that it mattered; the fourth row of monsters did that. They crawled up above Matt's head on thin air, claws scrabbling at the unseen roof—but unable to dent it. It was quite a sight, wall-to-wall living gargoyles, and up above, too. Their ugliness was bad enough, but the sheer, unrelieved malice in their eyes made Matt's spirit quail. Every now and again, a gargoyle looked down at him as though to say he was going to get his—and that the gargoyle would thoroughly enjoy every second of shredding his flesh.

Matt shrank back against the base of the statue next to Yverne and asked, yelling to make himself heard above the grinding and clashing, "What *are* they? Did Gordogrosso have them all carved out of granite and brought to life, just so he could use them for his own hunting dogs?"

But Yverne only shook her head and yelled back, "I know not."

"They are demons, of course," Fadecourt called. "I can only conjecture how 'tis the artists who did carve the ornaments for cathedral roofs did know of them—but be sure that they are demons, brought hot from Hell for this night's chasing."

That explained the malice, and the feeling of pure, unmitigated evil. If they hadn't been carved from stone, they seemed to have been made of it; their hides varied from slaty gray to charcoal black, and looked like igneous rock. Their limbs grated as they moved, clashing against one another as they slipped or fell back, then clawed their way back up—and those claws glinted with metal. Each clawing roused anger and was answered with a sudden slash of glittering teeth, but it was a case of the impervious object meeting the superhardened alloy.

Then one of the gargoyles discovered the wall.

His jaws, grinding against each other with the sound they had first heard miles away, ripped into the stones forming the arch over the grotto. The jaws bit through the stone and met, taking a neat, smoothly beveled chunk out of the wall. The creature spat out the stone and bit again—and froze, its mouth open. It fought to close its jaws, but couldn't, though there was nothing between them; it had come up against the field force surrounding the statue and could make no headway against it.

Slowly, one by one, the gargoyles fell back, and didn't bother climbing up again—they'd found it was no use. Instead, they prowled around the grotto, their stone limbs filling the little valley with clashing and grinding, their steel teeth gnashing in fury.

Tears streamed down Yverne's cheeks, but she said bravely, "Praise Heaven! We are safe here!"

"Aye." Fadecourt patted her hand. "They cannot come in."

"On the other hand," Matt said, "we can't go out."

"Have we need to?"

"Unless we want to spend the next several years here—I'd say so, yes."

"Surely they will tire and go away!" Yverne protested.

"They don't look like the type to bore easily," Matt said. "Not very intelligent, at a guess, but very, very determined. Besides, there's the question of how long we can wait."

"I have fasted before," Fadecourt informed him. "I can endure some days without food."

Yverne looked apprehensive, but she nodded.

"All well and good," Matt said slowly, "but let's say, now—water?"

They were all quiet.

"Aye," Fadecourt admitted. "Thirst will drive us out within a day or two."

"And there's nothing to drink," Matt said. "We found that out this afternoon, while we were patching the place up."

"But surely they will not linger past dawn," Yverne protested.

"Only one way to find out." Matt lay down on a patch of grass and rolled over, covering himself with his cloak and pillowing his head on his arm. "Wake me if anything goes right."

Narlh nuzzled him awake. Matt sat up with a start, looked about him in a panic, and remembered where he was. He relaxed with a sigh. "Thanks, O Vigilant One. Anything changed?"

"Yeah—the sky." Narlh nodded upward. "Dawn's coming—and your gargoyles are getting restless."

"Not mine," Matt muttered automatically—but he watched the gargoyles.

They were pacing about, snapping at one another, apparently quite agitated. As the first ray of sunlight struck the hillside above them, each of them began to dig. They went down into the ground very fast, of course, with steel claws and all that weight—down, and down, dirt gouting up about them though they stayed pretty much in place, reminding Matt of pigs wallowing into mud. In a few minutes, they had disappeared, their places marked only by mounds of dirt.

Yverne sat up, stifling a yawn and blinking about her. Then her eyes went wide. "They have gone!"

"No," Matt said, "only gone underground. They'll rise again at sunset, I'm sure."

"What will?" Fadecourt sat up, scowling. He saw the mounds of dirt, at least a hundred of them, and realized what they meant. "So. Our enemies await us without and withunder, do they not?"

"They do," Matt agreed. "The question is, will they dare come out if they know they'll be in sunlight?"

"We might try them," Fadecourt suggested. "How much is the knowledge worth to you—an arm, or a leg?"

Matt gazed at the dirt mounds, thinking it over.

"Mayhap the course of discretion is wiser," the cyclops suggested.

"Definitely. After all, I'm not eager to lose a member."

"There are other ways to test," Fadecourt pointed out. "Yet to be clear, we must wait till sunlight covers the ground outside of this shrine."

"I can wait."

He didn't have to wait long. The sun's rays soon covered the grass outside the shrine, what was left of it. Fadecourt nodded, satisfied, went back into the cave behind the grotto, and came back with a boulder. He bowled it toward the nearest dirt pile. Matt wondered whether it would be able to pass out of the gate.

It did, rolling a couple of feet away from a burrow. There was an explosion of dirt, a blinding flash of granite legs with a horrendous clashing. Steel teeth slashed, and the boulder was gone.

Abruptly, the gargoyle froze. Then, slowly, it turned toward the humans, giving them a look of such pure malevolence that Matt felt his heart trying to sink down into his boot tops.

"It knows we deceived it," Yverne whispered. "It would rend us limb from limb for that deception, if it could."

Narlh snorted behind them. "How many pieces can it tear you into? It was ready to do that last night."

But already, the monster's skin was dulling. It turned and dragged itself painfully back to its hole, where it wallowed down, sending up a cloud of soil that settled to hide it from the light.

"It can endure the sun," Fadecourt said, "though not for any great length of time."

"Long enough to tear us to shreds, though." Matt shook his head. "No, we're very effectively penned up here."

They were quiet, digesting the fact.

Then Yverne rose. "Well, we must proceed with the morning's duties, as best we may. By your leave, gentlemen." She turned and went away, behind the grotto, to the cave. Narlh lifted his head as she passed and gazed after her.

Matt knew the feeling. After seeing those gargoyles, he would never trust honest stone again.

"Well, Wizard," the dracogriff challenged, "how're you gonna get us out of this one?"

"I don't know," Matt confessed. "If these obscene, uh, works of art, really do come from Hell, any power I can wield probably won't be enough. It'd take a direct miracle, straight from Heaven."

"Is our plight so desperate that a saint might intervene?" Fadecourt asked.

Matt shook his head. "As I understand it, that takes direct, personal participation by a major devil. Subordinate demons like these aren't enough—they're no more than the evil ideas Satan lends his minions, to make people miserable." He wondered about the nature of that power. Since he could feel a sort of magical pressure around him when he was casting a spell, maybe Satan just gave his worshipers the ideas for verses; the magical power was always there, only needing to be shaped and formed.

It would be very chancy, he realized, working for Satan. You'd never know when that devastating power would hit you, as well as your chosen target. You could never be sure your boss wouldn't turn against you.

Yverne came back just in time to hear Narlh growl, "So what would happen if you prayed real hard, and a saint came to kick these monsters out?"

"That would just provide an opening for a devil to show up for a showdown. See, God leaves it to us to work out our own destinies, but He'll give us whatever spiritual help we need—and guidance, if we'll just shut up and listen to Him."

"That is Grace," Yverne murmured.

"Right. He'll even perform constant small miracles, if they'll help us improve our souls and not hurt anybody else's, and we really, sincerely, want them enough to help open the way—like an alcoholic going on the wagon, or an incurable illness going into spontaneous remission . . ."

" 'Spontaneous remission'?" Narlh frowned. "What is that?"

"What you call a miracle when you don't want to admit it's a miracle. And, of course, Hell is allowed its own low-key interference, except that it has to work through the human agents it cons into its service, not directly—and the result can be some really gruesome temptations to despair. But outright, open meddling isn't allowed—so no saint would show up without a devil to kick out."

"But a devil may appear, to interfere in human affairs?"

"It's been known to happen. Not very often, because the devils know that, against a saint who's a channel for God's power, they can't do anything—and the first thing the saint will do is banish them."

"But then," Yverne cried, "if a saint did come to aid us, and a devil came to oppose him, the saint would banish the devil!"

"Yes—but the saint won't break God's rules. We have free will, after all—that seems to be the whole purpose of human existence, as well as I can understand it, which may not be much: for us to choose to go to Heaven, and transform ourselves into something good enough to belong there. Outright interference is too much influence."

"Hey, wait a minute!" Narlh frowned. "You're trying to say that to get to Heaven, we have to choose *not* to have free will, to just do whatever Heaven wants!"

"Yes, but we use free will in making that choice."

"But . . ." Narlh tried to follow the loop of the paradox, got lost, and grumbled, "Too deep for me."

"Me, too—I need an Aqua-lung. Of course, the trick is trying to know what Heaven wants; a lot of people have done some very horrible things, believing they knew God's will and were just carrying it out. And, of course, each of the few who really *did* manage to become a medium for God always had the temptation not to and had to constantly be choosing His will instead of their own. I understand it does require a lot of self-sacrifice. Wouldn't know from my own experience, of course."

Yverne eyed him narrowly, and Matt hastened to explain, "Of course, I don't really understand any of this."

"There are three of us who do not, then," Fadecourt said, with a quick glance at Narlh. "Yet I take it that all of this makes you believe you can do naught 'gainst these engines of Hell."

Matt nodded. "Unless I can figure out a way to harness some sort of natural force. I used to have a scab demon who had taken a liking to me—no, no, my lady, I'm not a sorcerer in disguise! He wasn't part of the Hell crew; in fact, properly speaking, he wasn't even a demon. Humans named him that, because they didn't know what else to call him. He was the personification of a natural process called entropy, and people called him Maxwell's Demon."

"Who was Maxwell?" Narlh grunted.

"A scientist—uh, that was the equivalent of a wizard, where I came from—and he never met the demon, just imagined that it might exist. Which it didn't, back home. But when I came here, I took a chance and called him up—and sure enough, here, he *did* exist!"

"And his power was enough to break such as these?" Fadecourt asked, looking skeptical.

Matt nodded. "He could make anything go to wrack and ruin, if somebody asked him to in the right way. He could freeze these monsters back into ordinary stone, for example, then make them crumble away into powder."

"Why, then, call him up!" Yverne clapped her hands.

"I wish I could—but he went adventuring with a friend of mine, and I can't take him back without asking. Asking him, I mean—and I'd have to find him, first."

"Can you not conjure up some other such spirit?" Fadecourt asked.

Matt sat still for a minute, letting the idea soak in. Then he nodded. "Yes, I could—but we'd be taking a chance. Whatever I got might do as much damage to us as to our enemies—or might not be willing to do what we ask. It's a risk."

"Could it be worse than what awaits us yon?" Yverne nodded toward the mounds of dirt outside the gateway of the shrine.

Matt thought about steel claws and teeth—vanadium steel, to judge from the way that one monster had sheared through a stone— and shook his head. "I don't think so, no—and there would be a chance that I might be able to banish whatever I called up."

"There is a chance that you could not?" Fadecourt stared.

"Depending on what kind of monster I got—definitely."

"Then don't start up something you can't finish off," Narlh growled.

"That's what they told Frankenstein. No, don't ask—he was another, uh, wizard from back home, though not a very wise one. Still, the point's well taken. Anybody got any ideas as to what kind of spirit I could call up, that would be strong enough to get rid of these gargoyles, but not likely to turn against us?"

A very deep silence answered him.

"Well, so much for that idea." Matt sighed.

" 'Tis a question without an answer, Lord Wizard," Yverne said, looking miserable. "What spirit could be strong enough to aid us, yet not apt to wreak unholy mischief upon us?"

"Mischief!" Matt sat bolt upright.

Then he jumped to his feet, stepped over to Yverne, and gave her a big, loud kiss on the cheek. "Thank you, milady! I should have known I could depend on you!"

"What . . . what have I said?" she asked, eyes round.

"Mischief! Not malice, mischief! A spirit who loves to play pranks, but doesn't get nasty about it unless people deserve it—or turn out not to be able to take a joke."

"But," she protested, "would a spirit of mischief not be one also of evil?"

"Not necessarily. My parish priest, when I was a boy, had a very active sense of mischief—you know, jumping out of dark hallways shouting 'Boo!' and that sort of thing. Gave you the willies, if you were an altar boy going into a dark church on a Sunday morning—but it did teach me to be alert."

"With a priest, all well and good." Fadecourt frowned. "But with a spirit, there might be less of goodness to alloy the meanness."

"Well, it could subject us to some very undignified pranks, of course, but no real damage," Matt answered, "as long as we can take practical jokes in good part."

"What spirit is this?" Fadecourt asked with foreboding.

"I can't guarantee the form or the name." Matt tried to smile. "The worst I've heard him called, is Hobgoblin."

"I like not the sound of that," Fadecourt said darkly.

Yverne, however, clapped her hands and cried, "Hop o' My Thumb!"

"Oh." Matt turned to her. "You've heard of him?"

"Aye. 'Tis said the careful housewife will now and again find a six-pence in her shoe, and 'tis his work—but the lazy sloven will discover naught but black stones, or mayhap beetles." She sobered. "Not a pleasant jest."

"You do have to watch your step," Matt admitted. "He has a knack of taking advantage of human foibles, finds them very fertile ground for humor. Not that he's alone in that, of course."

But Fadecourt was still frowning. "How could such a spirit aid us 'gainst monsters such as these?"

"By having fun with them."

"Fun! With . . . such as these!?"

"Fun," Matt affirmed. "Get them chasing their tails, or something. Look, it's possible, isn't it?"

"Don't tell him no," Narlh advised Fadecourt. "Anything else he dreams up is likely to be worse."

"There is that," Fadecourt admitted, "and these gargoyles are as-suredly far worse than aught else we might bethink us of. Nay, Lord Wizard, call thy sprite."

"Okay. Just a minute, though—I have to try to remember the verse." Matt frowned, running through it silently, then looked up. "Okay. Here goes:

> "Unless I mistake his shape and making quite,
>   He is that merry wanderer of the night
>   Who might a fat and bean-fed horse beguile
>   Neighing in likeness of a filly foal.
>   Or slips he in a gossip's bowl
>   In likeness of a roasted crab.
>   Against her withered lips he bobs,
>   And on her withered dewlap, spills the ale.
>   The wisest aunt, telling the saddest tale,
>   Sometimes for three-foot stool mistaketh he.
>   Then slips he from her bum, down topples she,
>   And "Tailor!" cries, and falls into a cough.
>   Then all the choir
>   waxen in their mirth, and laugh,
>   And sneeze, and swear
>   A merrier hour was never wasted there.
>   Let him come near, if he
>   Will aid poor wanderers beset, such as we!"

He ended holding out his hands, as though pleading, which was not perhaps the wisest idea—for a glimmer appeared in his palm, progressing to a glitter, then a luster of twinkling that clustered and faded—leaving a miniature human being, leaning back cross-legged in Matt's palm, one ankle propped on the other bended knee, hands behind his head, and a wisp of timothy between his teeth. He wore a sort of furry kilt, a feather in his hair, and nothing more. And he was very small. If it hadn't been for the feather, Matt might have thought he was a nut.

Later on, he was to decide he would have been right.

"Those that Hobgoblin call me, and sweet Puck," the apparition rumbled, in a surprisingly deep voice,

> "I do their work,
>   and they shall have good luck.

"And who are ye?"

"Uh—a poor wizard, down on his luck." Matt tried to stop goggling, and failed.

"At whom do you stare, horse-face?"

The other three companions were staring, too, but Puck didn't seem to notice them.

"Uh—sorry." Matt managed to blink and forced a smile. The real, genuine Puck! He felt like asking for an autograph. "Just that you're, uh—amazing."

"Certes. Yet not what you did expect?" The manikin sat up, pulling the wisp out of his mouth and tossing it away. "Why, what did you think I am?"

"Uh—well, a little bigger, actually. At least a foot high."

"A foot? Nay, faugh! What use would such a size be? How then could I capture bees to ride, or steal their honey bags? How should I lie in a cowslip's bell?"

"But . . . I thought that was Ariel . . ."

"How foolish can you be? Cowslips come from earth, not air." The little man leaped up, standing with legs spread, arms akimbo. "And, too, you did speak with your friend of 'Hop o' My Thumb'—and if 'tis by that name they know me here, 'tis in that guise I'll appear!"

He was, Matt had to admit, fitting the name. He was about three-quarters of the size of Matt's thumb, and he certainly did look as though he was ready to hop with excess energy. In fact, Matt realized he'd better figure out a way to channel all that mischief fast, or it would be turned against him. "Uh—thanks for coming. We really could use the kind of help you can give."

"I, and only I!" Puck thrust out his chest and strutted. "Nay, I will gladly help you—if you have the wit to use my aid. For look you, you must be careful what you ask for."

" 'Cause I might get it, huh?" Matt muttered. "How about if I asked for . . . No, never mind. We don't have time for that, now."

"There is always time for a jest." Puck smiled, not altogether pleasantly. "What did you think of?"

"Well, I was just wondering what would happen if I asked you if my thoughts had wings . . . Help!" His mind had suddenly filled with a picture of flapping wings, all kinds of wings—bee's, bird's, bat's, bounder's . . . What was a bounder? "No, no! I was just wondering!"

Puck made a wrapping gesture with his hand, grinning with mischievous delight. "Well done! Oh, well done! You will be a most excellent subject for my jests! Nay, go on! Do ask for more!"

Matt had the uncomfortable feeling that he had just set himself up as the straight man in a permanent, ongoing vaudeville routine. "Well, actually, we called you to help us against some demons."

"Demons?" Puck's smile turned to gloating. "Why, ever do I rejoice in countering those great chunks of evil! Nay, if you can find them for me, unleash me!"

"You have fought demons before?" Yverne asked, wide-eyed.

Puck gave her a quick look of appraisal and grinned at what he saw. "For you, fair maid, I would fight devils incarnate!"

"That's exactly what we were hoping for, on a minor scale," Matt interrupted. "You see, we're trying to get a chance to fight an evil sorcerer, but he's trying to make sure we don't get close enough. Last night, he sicced a score or two of gargoyles on us."

"Gargoyles?" Puck looked up, startled. "Why, what had you to fear from stone? It cannot turn to smite you!"

"*Eppur si muove*," Matt quoted. "And these ones really did move. They waddled, mind you, not galloped—but they still moved a lot faster than I would have thought they could have. And they had steel teeth, which they were very eager to use."

"Ah, those demons whom your sculptors saw in visions dread and rendered in stone to hang up high above your head! 'Twould be reason enough never to go into a church. But how stood you against them?"

"We were lucky enough to find this shrine to Saint Iago. It's still consecrated, you see, and . . ."

He didn't finish. With an ear-splitting screech, Puck disappeared.

He reappeared a moment later, outside the gateway, mad and hopping. "You fool, you idiot, you blind ass! Have you no better wit than to bring one of the elvin kind into a Christian holy place? Did you wish to see me shrivel in agony?" He leveled a forefinger. "Let us see if your appearance can accord with your . . ."

Under the circumstances, Matt was very glad the nearest gargoyle chose that moment to explode from the ground in a cloud of dirt.

Puck heard the noise and whirled to see the monster leaping straight for him, claws widespread, steel teeth reaching. The elf disappeared in a flash of light, and as the gargoyle jarred to land, looking about, befuddled and enraged, Puck appeared again at the monster's tail. He grabbed with both hands and pinched.

Matt wouldn't have thought someone so small could pinch so hard.

The gargoyle roared and reared up, whipping about to snap up the miniscule being who dared affront it—but the being had hopped backward far enough for another gargoyle to explode from the earth. The first one got there just in time to clamp its jaws down on the second. With a bellow, the second turned to bite at the first and took a chunk of granite out of its flinty hide.

But Puck had jumped backward again, triggering a third eruption of gargoyle, then danced toward the first two, who were snapping and clawing at each other like a quarry gone mad. The third leaped, Puck disappeared, and the third slammed teeth-first into the tumble of two—both of whom leaped on the interloper. But a fourth was rumbling out of the ground, to see Puck seated on the third's tail. The fourth snapped up Puck—and took a chunk out of its neighbor. The third whirled to snap out, bringing the first two along.

"Oh, the brave elf!" Yverne cried. "He is lost!"

Matt must have gone insane for a second, because he plunged out through the gateway. Fadecourt and Narlh both shouted and dived to catch him, but before he could go more than one step, Puck reappeared on the outside of the snarling, roaring ball, just as it rolled back into the living mine field. Other gargoyles launched themselves from their improvised silos, thundering with blood lust, and Puck disappeared as they plunged into the sphere of disaster. As the ball rolled, more and more gargoyles came out to slay, and wound up trapped in the round of biting and revenging.

Puck appeared on top of Matt's head, dancing and pantomiming punches as he cried, "Slay him, Stoneface! Gouge at him, Granite! Bite at him, Basalt! Aye, hew, gobble, chew, gorge, gnaw, gulp, and bite through!"

"I think they're all in there." Narlh stared in disbelief.

"But," Fadecourt protested, "how can they hurt one another? They are all of stone!"

"Yes," Matt said, "but they all have steel teeth."

Puck disappeared from Matt's head, appeared above the churning battle, then reappeared atop Matt, saying, "All gargoyles are indeed within the fray, and they fray one another quite well. Aye, they have chopped and ground several of the smaller into pebbles already!"

Yverne shuddered. "Praise Heaven we were not caught by them!"

Puck winced. "Mercy, lady! And pray be mindful who has wrought this coil!"

"The ball's getting smaller," Matt pointed out. "I think they've chewed up the medium-size ones now."

Puck popped over above the whirling mass of stone again, then popped back to Matt's crown. "Only the largest and ugliest remain, and they are chewing into one another at a most excellent rate! Why, one would think they had ne'er been fed in their lives!"

The ball grew smaller and smaller, until finally, they could distinguish separate monsters again—but there were only two, with vastly distended bellies, each chewing on the other's tail, each bite taking up more and more. They roared and shrieked and bellowed with each bite, but one gobbled faster than the other, devouring its hind legs, abdomen, chest, and forelegs, then chewed up its head and spit out the teeth. But it couldn't stop; it kept going, past where its enemies' jaws had been fastened into its own flinty hide, chewing and grinding in a roaring rage, grating its own substance until it expired in gravel, leaving nothing but a set of steel teeth that rolled on the ground, gnashing and snapping.

Puck appeared above it, making shooing motions. Then he reappeared on Matt's head, saying, "Its erstwhile foe's teeth also remain. Shall we see their fond embrace?"

There wasn't much choice; he had started the one set of snapping teeth rolling in the right direction, and it kept on rolling until it bumped into the other set of animated dentures. Then they clashed and slashed and chopped at each other until both were shredded into scrap. Even the bits and pieces still jumped about, slamming into each other.

Puck hopped down to Matt's shoulder, set his arms akimbo, and demanded, "Now, what did you wish me to do with these monstrosities?"

"Uh . . ." Matt could only stare at the barren, churned-up ground before him, strewn with bits and fragments of stone that might just possibly have been recognizable as parts of monsters, if he had looked really closely—which he had no intention of doing.

"Well, put them out of their misery, Wizard!" the elf snapped. "Can you not give these bits of iron their quietus?"

Matt snapped out of it. "Yeah, sure!"

> "Double, double, toil, and trouble!
> Furnace heat, make steel scrap bubble!"

It wasn't much, but it served the purpose. The bits of steel turned red, then yellow, then white, and flowed together into a huge, quivering droplet. Matt could feel a blast of heat; then the bubble was melting its way down underground. Matt could have just let it keep going until it hit the molten nickel-iron core of the planet, of course, but he didn't relish the volcano that would result, so he quickly recited an advertising jingle for a deep-freeze company, and the steam stopped rising from the hole. Matt decided he'd wait for a little while, then kick the dirt in.

Puck was giving him an appraising look. "Well done, Wizard! You are no inept apprentice to this craft, I see!"

"Not as good as I should be." Matt swallowed.

"We must not leave the detritus of evil so close by the holy shrine." Fadecourt sounded numb, but he stepped out through the gateway anyway.

"No, wait!" Matt stopped him with a hand on his shoulder. "I don't trust that gravel. Let me see if I can't do this a little more efficiently."

Fadecourt stopped, looking up at him in inquiry, but Matt didn't notice. He frowned out at the mass of detritus, thinking over his verses.

> "Out of the pebble-strewn days
> Let us all seek smoother ways,
> May these fragments that once
>   were like sand on a shore
> Be gone, and trouble us all
> Nevermore!"

The mass of pebbles glimmered, wavered, and was gone.

Matt exhaled a sigh of relief.

"Where have they gone, Lord Wizard?" Yverne asked, eyes wide.

"Back where they came from, I hope—whether it be a rock quarry, or someplace more sinister." Then Matt managed to smile as he turned his head to look at the manikin on his shoulder—out of the corner of his eye was the best he could do—and was glad that it turned into a real smile of relief and gratitude. "Thank you with all my goodwill, Hop o' My Thumb! That, I certainly could not have done without you!"

"It was my pleasure." Puck grinned, eyes glinting with delight. "What game would you have me play next?"

Matt's smile vanished. "Well, uh—now that you mention it, that was the only problem facing us at the moment."

Puck's face clouded. "You dared summon me for only one easily solved chore?"

Matt suddenly became aware, all over again, of the spirit's ability to wreak massive havoc simply in the process of having a good time. "Well, uh—yes, actually. You see, it was something we couldn't handle alone, and . . ."

"And would I have the courtesy to quietly fade from sight, now that you no longer have need of me?" The elf's eyes narrowed. "I think not, Wizard! Know that we faerie-folk always claim what's owed us."

"Uh . . . well, yes, I know I owe you a lot of thanks, but . . ."

" 'Tis more than thanks," Puck said with a wolfish grin. "Know that, when you accept aid from one such as I, you do incur an obligation to us—and we husband our resources; we stay hard by you, seen or unseen, until you've done by us as we've done by you."

Matt groaned. "Meaning that, unless I get a chance to save you from as much grief as you've just spared us, that you're my permanent companion?"

"Till debt do us part—or its discharge, at least. Yet I, more than any other sprite, grow restless in boredom. You must find occupation for me, Wizard—and if you can find no better diversion for me, I shall have to find my pleasure in tormenting *you*!"

Matt swallowed heavily, frantically trying to think of a way out.

It was Yverne who found it. "Can you not be patient for a short while? For surely King Gordogrosso will find new terrors to set upon us, and right soon."

"Yes!" Matt agreed with vehemence. "Now that he's finally taking us seriously enough to notice us, we'll probably have one monster after another to fight. At least one a day!"

Puck pursed his lips around a smile, eyeing Matt and considering. " 'Tis a better offer than I've had this last hundred years . . ."

"Take it, I prithee!" Yverne begged. "We shall have need of you right soon, I doubt not—and we would be so very wearied of staying within this shrine, for dread of you."

That decided the issue; Puck's smile disappeared as he glanced up at the statue of the saint, then quickly glanced away. When he looked back, his impish grin had spread across his face again. "Well, since it is a beautiful damsel who doth ask it of me, and a virgin to boot, with all the powers of enchantment that brings . . ."

Matt tried not to look surprised. He had wondered if a grown woman could be a virgin in Ibile, but Puck had just settled the issue. Considering the elf's earthy connections, he didn't think Hop 'o My Thumb could be wrong about such a thing.

"I shall travel with you!" Puck said magnanimously, then quickly held up a palm, modestly closing his eyes. "Nay, do not thank me—I shall be glad to aid you. Only find work for me, or . . ." He gave Matt a keen look. "I shall find my own amusements."

Matt didn't have to ask who would be the butt of the elf's humor. But he made himself smile anyway, and beckoned his friends out of the shrine. He turned back to Puck with a smile of welcome, feeling as though he had just tucked a nuclear bomb into his pocket. He promised himself that he would never ask Puck for another favor— owing him *one* was bad enough.

CHAPTER 16

Goblins in Bondage

Matt checked to make sure his wand was stuck in his belt, then turned back to his companions. "Okay—sun's up. Let's . . ."

"*Shh!*" Narlh glowered at him, then turned back toward the shrine, bowing his head.

Matt's voice trailed off; he saw Yverne kneeling at the railing of the shrine, head bowed in prayer. Fadecourt came up silently and knelt on the other side of the gateway.

"What holds you?" Puck demanded, arms akimbo. "Let us be off! The night will come too soon, and with it, the spirits of evil!"

Narlh gave him a glare. "We're thanking the one who protected us from the monsters."

"Why, thanks are welcome, though the victory cost me little effort! But I hear you not."

"They're thanking Saint Iago," Matt explained. "We wouldn't have been alive to call you, if he hadn't kept the gargoyles out of his shrine."

But Puck had already shied away at the mention of the saint. "Wizard, please! Have a care for my ears!"

"He *should* have a care for his allies," Narlh snorted. "What's the matter, Wizard—think you're too good to give credit where it's due?"

Matt balked; praying at statues ran against his grain. In fact, praying to anything had kind of disgusted him, ever since he'd learned about the development of religion in his freshman college courses.

On the other hand, that attitude had softened a bit, since he'd been in Merovence . . .

"Kind of hard to take credit, under the circumstances, isn't it?" He sighed. "And calling it 'coincidence' is stretching things a bit—here. Sure, Narlh, I'll pitch in." He went back to the gateway.

Yverne and Fadecourt looked up in expectation from either side.

So this had to be a public spectacle, did it?

Of course—he was the leader.

Since when? He didn't remember standing for election.

Since he came to Ibile. The whole expedition was his idea. Admittedly, an idea hatched in a moment of very dubious inspiration, but his own, nonetheless. He took a deep breath, looked up at the tranquil face above him, then reminded himself that the statue wasn't the saint, but only a reminder of him. Deliberately, Matt turned his eyes up to the sky. "I thank you, Saint Iago, for your protection and aid. I thank you with all my heart and pray you'll ever be with me!"

The shrine was awfully quiet.

Then Narlh sniffed. "Kinda cheap, isn't he?"

Matt turned, frowning. "What do you mean? Saints don't want bribes."

"Of course not," Fadecourt said slowly, "but it might be polite to at least indicate willingness to return the favor."

Matt frowned at him while his meaning percolated in. Then he sighed and turned away, calling out, "Stand by me, Saint Iago, while I do all that I can to save Ibile! Only guide me, and protect me, and show me the way to God that you have already followed!"

And, of course, that meant he was even more tightly bound to do or die than he'd already been.

Matt set a hard pace that day—Narlh had to stretch his legs to keep up with his demands, and started grumbling even earlier than usual, about noon. Matt called a halt for lunch then, somewhat against his will. As they finished off the leftovers from two nights before, Fadecourt asked, "Wherefore your haste, Lord Wizard? Have a care for the damsel."

Matt looked up at Yverne, startled. "I'm sorry, milady. Since Narlh's giving us a ride, I thought—"

"Rightly." She cut him off with a weary smile. "And truly, you must be far more wearied than I."

Matt frowned, his brain clicking over. "But even a saddle can be tiring, right?"

"I am accustomed to riding," she assured him, "and we have matters of greater moment than comfort."

"Yes. Kind of what I was thinking, too." But Matt frowned, brooding. "I want to move as fast as I can, now that the King seems to have found us. Once he has us spotted and analyzed—"

"Any lies?" Narlh frowned. "Sure, I know he'll lie every chance he gets, but what's that got to do with you?"

"No, 'analyzed'—meaning he has challenged me, tested me, found out some idea of how much magic I can do and can't."

"You do mean he has taken your measure," Fadecourt interpreted.

"In a manner of speaking—and I'm hoping the spells he's knitting will be a bad fit. But now that he does have some idea of my magical strengths and weaknesses, and what kind of allies I have, he'll probably be doing everything he can to make things tough for us. So the longer we take getting to Orlequedrille, the more chances he has to eliminate us before we can do any damage—and the more time he has to prepare his defense."

Fadecourt almost choked on his cup of water. Wheezing, he looked up at Matt. "Wizard, what defense has he need of? Even if we came to his castle this instant, what could we do?"

"I don't know yet," Matt admitted, "but there must be something, or he wouldn't be trying to stop us."

"There is truth in that," Yverne agreed. "Yet he is quite likely to smite you simply because you are not evil—but even more likely to strike, because you have saved me from his minions. Worse, you now keep me safe from him. Nay, gentlemen, surely 'twould be the course of wisdom to—"

"We would not think of it," Fadecourt cut her off.

Matt nodded. "Don't *you* think of it, either, milady. Please."

"We're all together on this," Narlh growled. "Besides, he'd strike us out of sheer revenge, milady."

"That's decided, then," Matt said quickly, giving Yverne no chance to interrupt.

Puck appeared in the middle of their circle. "Not so quickly, mortal! I have not spoken yet!"

Matt eyed him askance. "You really feel the need to?"

Puck took a breath.

"On this topic, I mean!"

Puck deflated. "Nay. You cannot abandon the maiden."

Yverne dimpled.

Matt took it as a sign of acceptance. "Fine, then. I do wonder, though, why Gordogrosso isn't causing us any more trouble. I mean, now that he's found out where we are . . ."

"Speak his name, and he will hear you," Fadecourt corrected him. "Let us speak merely of 'the king.' "

Matt frowned. "What difference does it make? We know he's found us now, and he can track us with that magic mirror of his."

"In all likelihood," the cyclops said slowly. "Yet 'tis also to be marked, Lord Matthew, that there be rumors . . ."

Matt hated it when people didn't finish sentences. "Rumors of what?"

"That there do be places into which the king cannot see," Yverne explained.

Narlh nodded. "Nobody knows where they are, though."

"Interesting." Matt's gaze drifted as he considered the idea. "Logically, we should have been in one of them last night . . ."

"Well, true," Fadecourt admitted. "Evil magic could not probe into holy places—but belike the king saw all around the shrine."

Matt nodded. "True, true. I mean, if the gargoyles could be there, why not the king's eyes?" He straightened as the implications hit him. "Hey, wait a minute! What's to keep him from having spies, for the places his mirror can't see into?"

"Naught," Fadecourt said grimly, "and sorcerers are reputed to have many such."

"You mean, besides the men and women they've corrupted for the purpose?"

"Oh, assuredly." Puck grinned, apparently reveling in the problem. "There are spirits a-plenty who delight in such service—and many more who can be coerced in some manner."

"Like familiars, you mean?"

"Aye, though sorcerers' familiars are oft demons disguised, bound to serve the foolish mortals who trade worldly power for eternal torment. Yet there are many who are not of Hell, but who care not who they hurt, or who are malicious by nature."

Matt stared. "You don't mean elves would work for the king!"

"Nay, surely not!" Puck dismissed the notion with a toss of his head. "Yet there are kobolds, though they rarely come so far to the west, and they delight in pain and harm—and lamias, and basilisks, and ghouls . . ."

"I get the point." Matt nodded, frowning. "Goblins, too, and all manner of cobblies. Which means that our every move will be shadowed, unless I can figure out some way of chasing off any spies that come near us."

Or unless he found some way to use those spies for his benefit— some way to have them report where he was, when he wasn't really there. He began toying with notions of stocks, artificial images of him and his friends—and doppelgängers, and analogues, and flat-out copies . . .

His friends noticed his sudden silence and abstracted gaze. They exchanged glances, finished their lunches, packed up, and tapped him lightly on the shoulder. "Lord Wizard," Yverne said, "we must walk."

"Huh?" Matt snapped out of his reverie. "Oh! Sure. Sorry, I seem to have drifted off there . . ."

But he was no sooner on his feet and trudging westward, than he lapsed back into the daze of thought. His friends took the burden of conversation on themselves—and of keeping watch.

Toward evening, the road came parallel to a small river. It made sense—agricultural roads frequently followed the rivers, which had done the great service of cutting through the hills for the farmers. Here and there, though, the hills did indeed rise up—and as the sun was setting, they came to a high bluff, with the road rising up beside it, so that there was a steep hillside to the left, and a steeper hillside falling down to the water on their right.

Fadecourt stopped. "I like this not."

Matt jolted out of his daze. "Huh? Don't like what? . . . Oh."

"Be a great place for an ambush," Narlh rumbled.

"Aye," Fadecourt agreed. "The slope is too steep for bandits to run down without a great risk of falling—though they might rain arrows upon us."

"Bad enough."

"Aye—but what I truly am wary of is the chance of entrapment between a force before us and one behind."

Matt studied the road, then said, "We have to go through here some time, right?"

"Well," Narlh said, "we *could* climb the hillside before we get to the road. Or . . ."

Matt didn't make him finish the offer; he didn't particularly want to be in the air, if archers were going to be shooting at him. "We'd be sitting ducks on the hillside, too, wouldn't we?"

"Surely," Fadecourt agreed.

"How about flying ducks?" Narlh grunted.

Yverne turned a beaming smile on her mount. "'Tis sweet of you to offer! But I would as lief not be a target, afoot *or* aloft."

"Flying *out* of a jam, though," Matt said, "has definite possibilities. So, all in all, our best course of action is to keep going—but carefully."

"I fear so," Fadecourt growled.

"Then forward we go." Matt set off. "At least this way we'll find out whether or not the king really *is* watching us."

"There must be a better way to get news," Narlh grumbled, but he followed Matt down the road.

In trepidation, they came up to the crest of the hill. Matt's heart thudded so loudly that he was expecting an accompaniment as they passed the top and started down the other side, but no enemies sprang out at them. Still, he didn't breathe easily until they were all the way down, and fifty yards farther along the road. Then Matt relaxed with a sigh, wiping his brow. "Thank Heaven! Maybe the king can't see us, after—"

A horn sounded behind them.

Matt whirled about and saw a man in a robe standing at the crest of the hill road, gesticulating and, presumably, chanting. To either side of him stood men in plate armor, seeming inhuman and certainly impersonal behind their iron helms. As Matt watched, they kicked their horses into motion and started down the slope.

Then Fadecourt shouted, and Matt spun back to the front just in time to see a phalanx of pikemen spilling out of the woods with an armored knight at their head.

"You take the ones in front," Narlh growled to Fadecourt. "I'll cover our backsides."

The cyclops turned, catching up a rock and swinging it. Matt didn't dare take his eyes away from his opposite number, but the crash of stone against steel from behind him was very gratifying.

"Duck down, damsel," Narlh snapped. "You, too, Wizard—get behind me. I've got a tougher hide than you."

Matt nodded. "You take care of the knights—and remember, if you can make their armor hot enough, they'll peel out."

Even as he spoke, the knights began their charge down the hill. Matt took a deep breath and recited,

> "The fierce spirit painfully endured hardship
>   for a time,
> He who dwelt in darkness . . .
> The grim spirit was called Grendel,
>   a rover of the borders,
> One who held the moors, fen and fastness . . .
> There came gliding in the black night
>   the walker in darkness,

> From the moor under the mist-hills
> Grendel came walking,
> Wearing God's anger!"

Night thickened around them, and Matt took off, following the crashing Narlh was making. On his third step, he slammed into something hard and furry. A roar resounded around him, and a huge, clawed hand reached down through the darkness. Far above, two little red eyes gleamed. Matt howled, ducked around the giant shin, and ran.

Grendel apparently wasn't about to change course for so small an irritation, because the crashing of boulders being ground into pebbles was going away behind Matt, and he didn't think that was just because he was running so fast. A yell of horror confirmed it, followed by the rattle and clash of suits of armor being jumbled together. Matt slowed and looked back, but all he could see was a black cloud with a horse arcing above it and a sorcerer beyond, sawing the air frantically with his hands. The horse landed on its hooves, by some miracle, and streaked off in a panic—but the sorcerer had to stand his ground and keep trying. Matt didn't think he'd have much luck when he couldn't even tell what the monster was—especially since he didn't think the man knew Old English. Too bad the Dark Age bards hadn't left a few verses with a wider range of applications—but their interests had seemed to be rather narrow.

Wide enough for current purposes, however. Matt noticed that the crashing seemed to have stopped. So did the sorcerer—he was frozen with his arms half-raised, looking uncommonly as though he were surrendering to a Wild West sheriff. Then he whipped about and disappeared back into the pass. The black cloud drifted after him, leaving huge, clawed, vaguely anthropoid footprints.

Not that he cared about the sorcerer, but Matt couldn't leave a scourge like that to prowl the countryside. He tried to remember how the fight finished, decided to be a little more humane, and improvised a different ending:

> "Grendel must flee from there, mortally sick,
> Seek his joyless home in the fen-slopes.
> He knew the more surely
>   that his life's end had come,
> The full number of his days."

The black cloud kept moving up toward the pass—but as it moved it thinned, until, by the time it reached the top, it was almost gone. A vague outline hung in the air for a second, huge and gross,

like a monstrous parody of the human form—or was it reptilian?—
then was gone, so quickly that Matt wondered if he'd really seen it.
He sighed and turned away—there had been something heroic about
the monster, after all.

Fadecourt was glancing warily up toward the hilltop, then back to
the place where his targets had been. There was only a dust cloud
there now.

Matt looked at it, surprised. "What did you do—knock them all
the way back to the mountains?"

"Nay. They saw that black cloud you raised, and turned tail. They
fled, and I came near to fleeing after them."

"Near!" the dracogriff snorted. "If I'd had a clear field, I would've
been flying out of here so fast my backwash would have knocked you
over!"

Matt looked up at Narlh, frowning. "I thought you hated flying."

"Some things I'm scared of more, Wizard. You found one."

"And you did banish it, also." Fadecourt looked up at Matt, white
still showing around his eyes. "Nay, you have certainly cleared our
pathway! Have you disbanded them so quickly, then?"

" 'Dismembered' may be more like it," Matt answered. "You'll
pardon me if I don't go back to check."

"Aye, certes." Yverne looked out from behind Narlh's back, eyes
huge. "How have you routed them so quickly, Lord Matthew? And
what monstrous apparition was that which you did raise against
them?"

"That's an old story," Matt said, "and a reasonably long one. I'll
tell it to you, some time—but right now, I think we'd better get as far
away as we can before we run out of daylight and have to camp."

"Surely we may hearken as we speed!"

Matt glanced around and saw that even the dracogriff was looking
mildly interested. He relaxed and took a deep breath. "Well . . . okay.
Once, long ago and *very* far away, a hero named Hrothgar built him
a hall, hight Heorot . . ."

And they set off down the road, eyes growing larger and larger, as
they listened to the wondrous tale of the hero Beowulf.

Alisande crested the mountain pass, with her army glancing up nervously behind her. She couldn't blame them—there were a great
many boulders up there, poised as though balanced, ready to fall, and
she doubted that the presence of such stones was due simply to nature. Still, they had not had the slightest difficulty from the mountain folk—nor the slightest sign of them, either.

"May we not see the enemy from this height, Majesty?" Sauvignon shivered, in spite of the sable-lined cloak wrapped tightly about him. Most of the other horsemen were shivering, too, except for Alisande. She wondered why she felt no colder than on a brisk autumn day. Perhaps for the same reason that the infantry did; they were not shivering, though they had wound mufflers close around their faces. On the other hand, it could be because toiling up the slope had raised their body temperatures.

"We should," she agreed. "Mayhap the scouts . . ."

Running footsteps crunched in the snow, and a pair of scouts rounded a boulder and skidded to a halt in front of their queen. "Majesty," the first puffed, sketching a salute, "the Army of Evil is drawn up below us, on the plain!"

"Battle!" Sauvignon's eye gleamed; his basal temperature must have risen.

"We shall see them," Alisande decided. "Lead on."

They followed the sentries back around the boulder—and stopped, staring.

The mountainside sloped away below them, too steep for a horse, though a man could have had a wonderful time with a toboggan; and, far below them, a black line of men straggled across a bowl near the foot of the mountain, interspersed with the orange buttons of camp fires.

"Majesty," Sauvignon said, "they are not . . ."

"On a plain." Alisande nodded. "Indeed they are not, good Marquis. They have drawn a battle line across a lower valley, and they have taken the high ground."

"May we not simply pass . . ." Sauvignon saw the jagged rock field that filled the valley just to the south of the one Gordogrosso's army had taken, saw also the sheer cliff face that fell a thousand feet into the valley to the north, and interrupted himself. "Nay. Of course we cannot."

"There is no passage," Alisande agreed. "We are not through the pass yet, milord. Satan's general but holds its lower reaches."

"I see that there is a reason for the course of a road," Sauvignon sighed. "Even in these mountains."

Alisande let the soldiers rest for a day, on the plateau just above the valley held by the Ibilian army. They weren't about to let her men rest in peace, of course—not if they could help it; her pickets and outriders had a glorious time actually crossing swords with the enemy. She had to pick and choose among the volunteers for guard and scout duty, and cautioned them all not to judge their enemy by the little sortie parties they encountered—most of them were coming very unwillingly to battle.

"Yet will not all their mates come so unwillingly, Majesty?" one footman asked in surprise.

Alisande was caught. "Belike they will, footman," she answered. "Yet when they charge, or wade as one into the fray, the turmoil of the battle will seize them, and the presence of their comrades will shame them, so that they will fall to their work with a will, emboldened by the many who surround them."

"There will be evil spells to catch them up in the stir of the moment, Majesty, will there not?" Sauvignon rumbled.

"There will," she answered, pleased by his support, and turned to the footman again. "Therefore, be not overbold."

"As Your Majesty will have it," he answered with a bow, and went off to tell his mates that the Ibilians were craven.

"What shall we do with them, Sauvignon?" The queen sighed. "We cannot bid them lose heart!"

"Remind them that they encounter sorcery," the marquis answered.

"The very thing," Alisande murmured, for the words sent a chill down her own back. The man was not, she noticed, always the best of company.

The skirmishes stopped about noon, and her soldiers prowled the perimeter line growling, restless as wolves for the remainder of the day, frustrated by the lack of prey. But when the night came, they remembered the enemy's sorcery and drew in around the fires.

"They may send monsters against you," Sauvignon counseled. "Be of stout heart natheless, and strike with your pikes and swords. Whatever its form, no beast can do much if it's cut in two."

The soldiers took heart at the notion, and just in time, too, for the swarm of giant bats that pounced on the encampment would have daunted the most courageous heart. But Alisande shouted her challenge at them and threshed with her sword, and her troops followed her example. Leathery wings and fanged heads fell to the ground, and the few left whole flapped away into the night with cries of woe. Rattled, the soldiers pulled themselves together and watched the night, fingering their blades with apprehension.

"There is no virtue in this," Sauvignon pointed out. "They will greet the dawn with grainy eyes, and in the fight, their arms will weigh like lead."

"Which is the sorcerer's plan," Alisande answered. "Let some guard others, that the most may sleep. Set a quarter of them to the first watch."

She had to quarrel with Sauvignon about who should stay awake to command, but won by the simple expedient of commanding him to sleep. He went off to his tent, disgruntled, and she prowled the perimeter, with a word of encouragement here and a spot inspection there, boosting morale by her sheer presence.

So the men weren't completely unprepared when the dead wolves hit.

They were horrible things, some only scraps of hide over bones, some half-rotted corpses, some only skeletons, and the men at first pulled back with cries of superstitious terror. But Alisande waded in with the cry of "Poor things! Put them out from their misery!" and demonstrated amply that a dead wolf cut apart can't attack any more than a live one—though there was a head that dragged itself after her on two forepaws before she cut through its neck. And, once scattered, the bones did not pull themselves back together again. The sentries took heart and cut the hundred corpses to pieces. When nothing moved under the moon except people, Alisande congratulated them all, praising them to the skies, and watched them inflate visibly as she did. Then she turned away to wake Sauvignon, gratified to hear behind her, "He must be a fool, the Lord Wizard, to leave such a one as her!"

The glow was enough to make her gentle when she found Sauvignon with sword in hand. He confessed, guiltily, that he had awakened at the noise and come running out to get in on the skirmish. There was no point in scolding him—half the camp had done the same—so Alisande only thanked him, turned over the watch to him, and went into her own tent to lie down.

Not that she expected to sleep.

It was going to be a long night.

CHAPTER 17

The Guiding Ghost

Caught up in the epic, Matt scarcely noticed that the sun was dropping toward the west. He wrapped up the tale, though not in its original verse, and his companions exclaimed with delight. Even Narlh
gave an approving grunt. Then Fadecourt said, "Mayhap, now you've
told the tale, we should seek a site for—"

Yverne gave a little cry of alarm, quickly strangled. Fadecourt
whirled, and Matt looked up, straight ahead.

The ghost was there again, quite clear in the evening dusk. His
plump, antique tunic and robe even had a tinge of color—purple and
gold—and his round face no longer looked quite so threatening, with
the bald head and wide eyes, even if those eyes were empty hollows.
But there was a feeling of asking about him, almost of imploring.

"Avaunt!" Yverne called, her voice shaking.

"Don't worry, milady." Matt's eyes narrowed. "We'll get him out
of here soon enough.

> " 'Miss Bailey, then, since you and I
> Accounts must once for all close,
> I have a five-pound note in
> My regimental small clothes.
> 'Twill bribe the parson for your grave.'
> The ghost then vanished gaily,
> Crying 'Bless you, wicked Captain Smith!
> Remember poor Miss Bailey!' "

The ghost actually made a noise—a whisper of a moan, as its form dimmed and disappeared.

"Praise Heaven!" Yverne slumped. "And you, Lord Wizard."

"You were right the first time. Come on, let's go." Matt started forward again. "But why do you suppose he bothered showing up, when he knows I can banish him?"

A yap sounded.

Narlh shied. "What the blazes . . . ?"

A spectral dog had appeared by the side of the road, one whose face looked uncommonly familiar. It struck a point, tail making a straight line through its backbone and nose toward the south.

" 'Tis back, Wizard!" Fadecourt danced aside.

Puck appeared on Matt's shoulder, the gleam of battle in his eye. "Shall I, Lord Matthew?"

"No!" Matt yelped. "I owe you too much already! I'll handle this myself, thank you!

> "And then each ghost.
> With his lady toast,
> To their churchyard beds make flight,
> With a kiss, perhaps,
> On her lantern chaps,
> And a grisly grim good-night!"

The ghost dog gave a faint yelp and disappeared.

"Okay." Matt relaxed. "Now, why do you suppose . . . ?"

A will-o'-the-wisp formed ten feet in front of them.

It danced ahead, swerving off toward the south. An enchanting melody came from it, blending pipes, harps, and viols. Yverne's eyes glazed; she slid down off Narlh's back and began to move toward the light.

"No way!" The dracogriff swung his head around in a half circle, pushing her back. Yverne came to her senses with a start. "Oh! 'Tis quite compelling."

"Shall I now, Wizard?" Puck asked.

"Not until I run out of spells." Matt peered closely at the ball of light. It could have been his imagination, but he could have sworn he could see the ghost's features inside the glow . . .

> "Fade, little glow-ball, glimmer, glimmer!
> Fade like a candle, growing dimmer!
> Fade till your fire has lost its glow,
> And go, luminescent, go!"

The will-o'-the-wisp faded.

"It will be back anon," Puck informed Matt.

"Anon or a monk, I'll banish it again!" Matt turned back toward his friends. "If I should, that is."

Fadecourt stared at him, scandalized. "Wherefore might you not?"

But Yverne was nodding. "I ken your thought, Lord Matthew. What harm has this ghost done us, after all?"

"None, really." Matt nodded. "Except for scaring you, of course— and he might not have meant to do that."

"Aye," she said. "I was overwrought, or I might not have fled. Yet even so, he did bring me to you, where I found sanctuary and protection from mine enemies."

"Could be he had good intentions. And he *did* warn us off from that forest—which, if the trouble we had outside it is any indication, would have been an adventure we might not have survived."

Fadecourt nodded, a reflective look on his face. "And he did afright our enemies, when we were beset . . ."

"You guys trying to say the spook might be on our side?" Narlh growled.

"Seems possible."

Yverne gasped, looking over Matt's head.

"Don't tell me—I can guess." Matt turned slowly, to see the ghost drifting before him, looking distinctly hopeful. "Listening, were you?"

The ghost nodded brightly.

"You can hear, but you can't talk?"

The ghost shook his head, then nodded it again.

"Look," Matt said, "if you can moan, you can talk. Try again."

The ghost opened its mouth, slowly forming a word—but all Matt could hear was a vagrant sigh, like a breeze blowing past. He shook his head sadly. "No go. But I might be able to read your lips, if . . ."

He let it go. The ghost was clearly talking, but his mouth was only opening and closing, forming an O each time—one of the constraints of ghosts in this universe, apparently.

Matt sighed and shook his head. "Let's try sign language again."

"While you do," Fadecourt interrupted, "pardon us if we set up camp."

"Huh? Oh, sure, go right ahead." Matt sat down on a nearby stump, not really registering what Fadecourt had said. He had a new puzzle to work on, and everything else became unimportant. "Okay. Now—hold up one finger for every word you're trying to get across."

The ghost held up ten fingers, then closed his fists, opened them to all ten again—then again, and again, and again . . .

"Let's try for something a little shorter," Matt said.

An hour later, Fadecourt finally dragged him away to dinner. Matt had established that the ghost didn't know what "syllable" meant, nor "preposition" nor "article," and that the notion of an infinitive was enough to make him split. He had been able to get across the idea of "little words," but the ghost seemed to have radically different ideas as to what "little" meant. Matt tossed in his metaphorical towel, gave the ghost an apologetic smile as he took the bowl Yverne handed him, and turned his attention to dinner, deciding that maybe there was some point in learning grammar, after all.

But the ghost was persistent; it hung around all through Matt's watch, pantomiming and trying to make Matt understand—with absolutely no success, try as Matt might. He stuck around while Matt was asleep, too, apparently, because he was still there when they woke up.

"Your companion awaits," Fadecourt told him as he cracked partridge eggs onto a hot, flat stone. "Are not ghosts banished by daylight?"

Matt looked up; the ghost was only an outline, barely visible at all. "I guess the sun just outshines them."

"If they wish to stay at all." Puck pointed. "Seest you not that he is in pain?"

Matt looked as sharply as he could, then shook his head. "No. I can't see it that well. How come you can?"

Puck shrugged. "An affinity of spirits. Believe me, he doth suffer—not greatly, though constantly."

"What's he wanna stick around that badly for?" Narlh wondered.

"He wants to tell us something, that's for sure." Matt shook his head, seized with a sudden pang of sympathy. "I'm sorry, ghost. What we have here is a *real* failure to communicate."

The outline of the ghost's shoulders slumped, and slowly, what little they could see of it faded away.

"Poor guy." Matt sighed.

"Yet 'tis better than his suffering to no purpose," Yverne said.

"I suppose so." Matt sighed. "Well, time to stir up the coals. Any journey bread left?"

"We never had any," Narlh snorted.

"Remind me to find some wild wheat to grind." Matt sat down by the fire. "Well, I've had plain eggs before, but I've never been gladder of them."

Fadecourt handed him a bowl. "Dine well."

"Hope so." Matt took out his dagger and tried to spoon scrambled egg into his mouth, being very careful of the point.

"You do realize," Puck said, "that you do owe me for another favor."

Matt swallowed hard, then swung to face the manikin in the sun shaft. "*What* favor?"

"Telling you that the ghost was in pain."

Matt's lips formed a "no" as he gave the elf a dirty look. "I didn't ask for that."

"Asking matters not," Puck said with airy nonchalance. "The favor is all."

"Uh-uh." Matt shook his head. "Not kosher. I won't buy it."

"Bought or not, 'tis registered." Puck gave him a sly grin. "After all, who is't who does register what is owed me? Only me!"

Matt turned purple. "So who do you think *you* are? The arbiter of . . ."

He noticed that Puck had suddenly stiffened, looking past his shoulder. It could be a trick—he looked up at Yverne and Fadecourt. They, too, were staring past him.

"Wizard," Narlh rumbled.

Matt spun—and saw the ghost, as solid as he'd been the night before, smiling and beckoning. Beside him danced a spark, so bright that it hurt the eyes.

Then the spark disappeared, and the ghost instantly faded to ordinary translucence—but that foggy view was a huge improvement over his being a mere shell of his former self.

"What witchery is this?" Fadecourt asked—and Puck, for once, could only say, " 'Tis a spirit of another sort!"

And Matt knew which sort—and which spirit. "That was Max!"

Narlh frowned at him. "Who's Max?"

"Maxwell's Demon! The one I told you about, the Spirit of Entropy! He controls the organization of matter and energy!"

"What spell is this?" Puck said with disapproval.

"It's not a spell, it's science! Uh, wait a minute . . ." Matt thrust the issue behind him with an act of will. "Max channeled more energy into the ghost, then took off about his business!"

"Hold on!" Narlh frowned. "If he's such a buddy of yours, why'd he take off so fast?"

"Because he couldn't stay! I'm not his controller now, anymore—Sir Guy is!"

"But then," Yverne said, eyes round, "if the demon appeared . . ."

"Can Sir Guy be far behind?" Matt finished. "And if the ghost went to get Max, then he must know where Sir Guy is!" He spun to the ghost. "And *that's* what you've been trying to tell us!"

The ghost nodded eagerly, face glowing. "Yet this ghost has been so earnest to tell us that," Fadecourt said, "even to the point of suffering pain. Is there not, then, some urgency in his message?"

"Good point! Ghost! Is Sir Guy in trouble?"

The ghost nodded eagerly, positively beaming.

"Then lead on!" Matt kicked dirt over the coals, then turned to follow the ghost. "To Sir Guy!"

The ghost took off, drifting away in front of them, looking back to make sure they were following.

Matt's conscience nudged him. "Uh, look, folks—this knight is a friend of mine, but he's no business of yours. And if *he's* in trouble he can't handle, it's probably pretty bad. I really can't ask you to put your heads in the communal noose with me—"

"You insult me!" Fadecourt cried, offended. "Could I turn away from an ally in danger, even though I've never met him?"

"And the danger would be mine, without the company of you gentlemen," Yverne said.

"I'll take my chances," Narlh growled, "since you improve them."

That left only one—and he was leaning against a pebble, grinning from ear to ear. "Wizard—do you ask a favor?"

"All right, all right! I'm asking a favor! I'll pay you back when I get the chance!"

"Then ho! For a knight of trouble!" Puck disappeared, but Matt's wallet bulged ominously, and Puck's muffled voice cried, *"En avant!"*

" 'Tis sad to speak poorly of one so eager to aid," Fadecourt said, "but yon ghost is not the easiest of guides to follow."

"He's got to be around here somewhere." Matt frowned, scanning the way ahead from left to right. "Narlh—I don't suppose . . . that grandfather of a nose you have there . . ."

"Oh, I'm great at tracking, all right. But it has to leave a smell, Wizard."

"And ghosts don't usually have much in the way of body odor." Matt sighed. "I *know* he's around here someplace."

"How could he be so bright at breakfast and have faded so dimly by midmorning?" Yverne asked.

"It was Max," Matt explained. "He shifted extra energy into the ghost—you noticed how the sunlight seemed a little dimmer? But when Max left, that extra charge wore off pretty quickly—and Max wasn't there to recharge him."

"Recharge! Charge! Energy!" Narlh muttered. "Will you quit using wizard talk and just tell us what happened?"

Matt sighed, searching for the simple explanation. "The ghost got tired. That's all it boils down to."

Fadecourt nodded. "He has been growing dimmer and dimmer this hour past, till he was but a shimmer before us."

"And it's not too easy, following an outline." Matt turned to his friendly nemesis. "Puck, I don't suppose you could . . ."

"Most surely! Since you *ask.*" Puck pointed south by southeast. "Yon."

Matt looked, but saw nothing. "If you say so. But how are the rest of us supposed to see something to follow?"

"Dost you *ask?*"

Matt sighed. "Yes, I'm asking! Would you kindly do me the *favor,* Puck, of finding a way for the ghost to lead us?"

"Why, surely, Wizard! 'Tis simplicity itself!" Puck called out, "Ghost! Do not seek to show us your whole body! Put all your strength into one part only, and show us that!"

A very long few seconds ticked by. Matt was just about to charge Puck with failure, when the ghost's head glowed into sight. Matt stared, swallowing his words.

" 'Tis not so bright," Fadecourt rumbled, "but we can follow. Come, milady, milord."

"Yes." Matt nodded. "Follow the guiding light."

But that wasn't so easy. The charge Max had lent ran down even further.

By noon, there wasn't even enough left to keep a full head going. They found this out the hard way, when the ghost vanished.

Matt called a halt. "Ghost! We've lost you! We'd better stay where we are until you can come back for us."

They waited. Nothing happened.

"Do you wish me to say where he is?" Puck asked.

"Not if it counts as a favor," Matt grunted. "How many do I owe you so far?"

"Three favors," Puck noted.

"And working on number four?" Matt shook his head. "I'm not that desperate yet."

"How if we do not find him?" Fadecourt asked.

Matt shrugged. "We keep on going the way we're heading, I guess. So far, we seem to have been going south, and just a little east. If we keep that up . . ."

A hand appeared before them, palely glowing, but beckoning.

"He heard us!" Matt grinned. "Thanks, kindly ghost! Let's follow, folks."

They trudged off again. The hand disappeared, and for a minute a toothy grin flashed at them.

"Why does that seem familiar, somehow?" Matt wondered. "Glad he's feeling good about it, anyway."

Over hill, over dale they went—following whatever sort of road or trackway would take them south by southeast. The ghost managed to stretch out his ectoplasm by switching from one part of his body to another; at one point, they were following a pair of shoes, striding forward at a goodly clip. Then they came out into a patch of bright sunlight, and the shoes faded.

"Where'd he go?" Matt came to a halt, looking about him.

"Yon!" Fadecourt pointed.

Matt looked, and saw a trail of footprints appearing in the dust of the road. They took up the chase again.

By the time sunset was approaching, they were all weary and dragging, especially Narlh—but they kept on doggedly following what little of the ghost there was. At the moment, they were down to a beckoning finger that appeared every hundred yards or so.

"The positive side," Matt wheezed, "is that as twilight comes on, he gets brighter."

"The bad side," Narlh puffed, "is that there isn't very much of him to brighten."

"This whole journey must have been painful for him," Fadecourt noted.

Matt nodded. "The advantage of showing less and less of his body. Must be a brave ghost."

"A quality one does not oft associate with specters," Fadecourt noted.

Puck appeared on Matt's shoulder, giving Fadecourt a keen look, but apparently deciding there was no insult intended.

Matt finally dragged to a halt. "I'm sorry, ghost," he called out, "but I . . ."

A finger flashed into sight, waving upright; a pair of pursed lips appeared behind it.

Matt lowered his voice to a whisper. "I just can't go any farther. Besides, darkness is coming on, and we need to pitch camp."

The shushing lips turned back into a hand, beckoning frantically, the rest of the arm coming into view behind it. The ghost's whole body appeared in outline again, urgency in every curve.

"There is need to persevere," Fadecourt sighed. "Come, Lord Matthew. He would not urge us on if our goal were not close."

Matt had to admit the cyclops was right—and, truth to tell, they'd only come about twelve miles; they'd lost a lot of time trying to follow an almost-invisible guide. "All right." He sighed. "Lead on."

The shushing had made them all cautious, though; they stayed quiet, except for whispered, necessary comments. They went as silently as possible down a long hill, then through a narrow gorge, the walls of which towered high on either side. Matt was very nervous through the whole length of it, constantly trying to watch for signs of ambush—but apparently Gordogrosso wasn't expecting them here. Or maybe he had other, more urgent matters he had to louse up.

Finally, the gorge debouched into a shallow valley. Coming to the edge of the pass, they found themselves looking down on a verdant bowl, rose-colored by the sunset. In its center was a large, rambling castle, filling a wedge of land where two streams met to form a third, much larger, river. The castle's towers were tall, but two were broken at the tops; its once-proud walls were darkened with fires where siege engines had burned, and its battlements were missing whole sections of crenels, where catapult stones had smashed into the fortification.

Around it, just a little farther than a bow shot, were thousands of tents. Cooking fires now gleamed in the dusk, and the clatter and growl of a waking army was borne on the breeze.

" 'Tis a siege," Fadecourt murmured.

Narlh groaned. "Not another one!"

"This time," Matt hissed, "we're here in time to *do* something."

"Against *that*?" the dracogriff protested in an appalled whisper. "You see how *many* of 'em there are?"

"And of the king's own army." Fadecourt pointed. "I know those pennons; they are knights of his household. And the soldiers' livery is royal—mixed with those of his chiefest vassals."

"I came here to fight the king," Matt reminded them. "Of course, I can't ask you to—"

"Stuff it, will you?" Narlh growled. "We're getting tired of that song. We're with you, y' know that."

" 'Tis only a question of tactics," Fadecourt confirmed, "and it may be that confronting eight thousand knights and soldiers directly is not the wisest of courses. You will come to the king more quickly by going around his army."

"But we can't leave allies unaided," Matt argued, "and there have to be a lot of soldiers inside, too."

"All that means is that they'll go through their supplies faster!" Narlh snapped.

Fadecourt shook his head. "They have river water to drink, and so vasty a keep could hold provisions for a siege of a year and more."

" 'Could' has a kind of chancy sound to it . . ."

"Oh, I doubt not they were well enough supplied at the beginning of the siege." Fadecourt frowned down at the churned mud before the walls. "Yet from the condition of that camp, I would conjecture that beginning was many months agone."

"It does explain why the king hasn't been working a little harder at hunting us down, though." Matt scowled at the army. "How much of his force is tied up here, Fadecourt?"

"Most of it, at a guess. He would have a thousand or so to guard Orlequedrille, and another thousand to maintain his will over his barons, as we saw at the duke's castle. But nine-tenths of his army is here."

Matt nodded. "Must be a mighty important enemy in there, to rate so much force." He turned to the glowing ghost mouth. "The Black Knight *is* in there, isn't he? Sir Guy de Toutarien?"

The rest of the head became visible and nodded.

"You trying to tell us this friend of yours is bigger magic than we know?" Narlh growled.

"Only in war," Puck put in. "Yet in battle, he does indeed have some sort of magic—and it is mighty, very mighty."

The monster glared down at him. "What makes *you* the expert?"

"Why," the elf said, "this Black Knight is almost as much a part of the land as I."

"We cannot let so great a force for good be slain out of hand," Fadecourt rumbled. "But what can we *do*, wizard?"

"Not much, out here. Inside, who knows? Maybe a lot, maybe nothing . . . No, strike that. From what I'm seeing here, Sir Guy hasn't learned how to persuade Max to do his utmost—he didn't really have the basic concepts, you see, thought *entropy* was a magic word . . ."

"It is not?"

"Whatever. But if I get in there, at the very least I can show him how to manage Max—or do it myself. The problem is to get inside, where we can join forces." Matt turned to Puck. "All right, I'm asking for another favor. I need something to distract the soldiers, *really* distract them, while we sneak through their ranks and up to the castle. Think you can do it?"

"I?" Puck looked up, startled. "Unaided? Wizard, you know not what you ask!"

"Sure, I do. I'm asking for, oh, an itching powder. Guaranteed, surefire, likely to drive a man mad if he doesn't scratch—but totally harmless. Think you can make it?"

"I?" Puck's grin was as much disbelief as anything else. "I, make folk to itch? Can an elephant mash grapes? But what use would it be, Wizard?"

"Use?" Matt stared. "It'd get them so busy scratching, they couldn't stop us sneaking past them!"

"For a hundred men, certes. For a thousand, mayhap. For ten thousand? Surely not!" The elf looked at Matt with exasperation. "Canst not see, Wizard?"

"Nay," Fadecourt rumbled. " 'Tis not his function, but mine. He is a mighty wizard, but in the ways of war, he has no more vision than a babe—or than I have in things magical." He stepped up between them. "Among so many knights, Wizard, there will surely be at least a score who will suffer anything for duty."

"Hey, these are *evil* knights we're talking about—"

"They will sacrifice all, for advantage—and the chevalier who captures you, let alone the lady here, will gain great preference in the king's eyes. Nay, as we wend our way through that host, there will be one at least, and more likely a dozen, who will ignore that itch, though it drive them to the brink of insanity. For they will see that it must needs be a wizard's diversion—and will suffer gladly, to apprehend such strangers as they see going past to the castle." He turned to Puck for confirmation.

The elf nodded. "What you have need of, Wizard, is not a distraction alone, but the army to follow it to advantage—and to clear you a road to that drawbridge."

Matt threw up his hands. "Great. All I have to do is conjure up ten thousand *good* soldiers and knights, and I can get us in." He frowned at a sudden thought. "I might be able to manage a thousand and one—but no, they'd be Arabian, and they might not be feeling too kindly toward Europeans just now." He shook his head. "Same kind of problem with any other knights I might conjure up—how long would it take to explain to them what was going on and persuade them to join us? Because, see, I can't *make* soldiers out of nothing— that's creating, and only God can do that. All I can do is move people from the place where they are to here—and you'll understand that they'd be a little confused when they arrived."

"You do not need so many," Fadecourt protested. "We seek to pass through the army, not crush it. A hundred would suffice—if they were excellent warriors, and fired with a zeal for the good."

"And the just, and the beautiful?" Matt eyed him with skepticism. "And just where am I supposed to find so many excellent and selfless fighters, pray tell?"

He looked from one puzzled, abstracted face to another, feeling a streak of vindication—till he got to Puck, and saw the canary-feather grin on the elf's face. He sighed, feeling vindication slide away. "All right, Puck, I'll owe you—what is it, favor number five? Who's the superwarrior?"

"Who else but my namesake?" Puck spread his hands. "I am Robin Goodfellow, and he is . . ."

"Oh, no." Matt squeezed his eyes shut. "*He* didn't happen in *this* universe, too, did he?"

"Aye," Puck said, "and in every earth in which good folk are oppressed by wicked rulers."

Yverne looked from one to the other, at a loss, but Fadecourt was a little better versed in military lore. "Do you speak of Robin Hood?"

"You have said it!" Puck crowed, pointing at the cyclops. "The very one! Nay, Wizard, how can you deny the truth of it, when even your ally speaks it?"

Matt threw up his hands. "All right, so Robin Hood would be ideal! I can't deny it, if even half of the stunts he pulled against the Sheriff of Nottingham were true. But wouldn't it be a little inconvenient if I tried to bring him here? I mean, Robin Hood's back at the time of Richard Coeur de Lion—or long before, since Scott admitted error."

Puck shrugged. "You may as well say, 'long after' if you speak of the man who gave the slip so often to the foresters of Edward III."

"That's still 'the old days,' where we are today. Wouldn't he be a little dead by now?"

"Oh, nay!" Puck laughed. "Brave Robin die? It cannot be. Whene'er the people of England groan under the hand of a tyrant, Robin's spirit will inspire those who fight in opposition. Mind you, he was 'Brave Robin' when the Saxons strove against the Danes, and Robert Fitz-Ooth, and Willikin o' the Weald, and many names before even that."

Matt frowned. "You trying to tell me that Robin was always supernatural?"

"Nay, he began as a living man—but when his body should have aged, we elvin folk laid an enchantment on him, and a geas—that he defend the poor for all of England's days. He and his band will never die, though they move from one plane of existence to another."

Matt frowned. If "plane of existence" meant "alternate universe," it made sense—but how could Robin and his merry men move from one world to another?

How had *he* moved from one to another? He scolded himself; by this time, he should have recognized a quibble when he came to one.

"After all," Puck said, "I allied with bold Robin only ... umm, was it a century ago, or two? A band of evil men sought to imprison England under rails of steel, for snorting monsters to scurry o'er. I could not act 'gainst Cold Iron myself, so I found need to call on Robin. He and his men made short work of those iron dragons, I promise you."

Inside, Matt shuddered. The Industrial Revolution, brought to a halt by an outlaw band from the greenwood, with Puck's magic behind them? He found the notion very easy to believe. After all, as a scholar, he knew that the legend that had grown up around Jesse James owed far more to the Robin Hood ballads than it did to fact. "That's all very well, but how do we get him here?"

Puck shrugged. "Who but now spoke of moving folk from one place to another?"

Matt pressed his lips thin, biting down on words of exasperation. "Look. If I could send people between universes, I would have sent *myself* back where I came from, a long time ago."

Puck glanced at him keenly. "Would you indeed?"

There it was, that nasty knack other people had for making Matt confront himself. "All right, already! So as long as Alisande is here, I won't go back to my home 'plane of existence'!" With emphasis on the "plain," he had to admit—in his home universe, he'd been just one more scholar in a market overstocked with Ph.D.s. Here, he belonged. Maybe even if Alisande hadn't been here ...

"What's he talking about?" Narlh demanded. "Can you make people go back and forth between worlds, or something?"

"That's what it boils down to." Matt heaved a sigh. "But if I have to admit that, I have to admit that I really wanted to come to this universe, Puck. And the corollary is that you can't move anyone out of his own universe against his will. What're the chances that Robin would be willing to come?"

"Do you jest?" Puck demanded. "When there is, here, a ruler who not only is wicked in word and deed, but has fully dedicated himself to evil? A ruler who does encourage his soldiers and vassals to rapine, plunder, and murder of the common folk? A ruler who grinds all into squalor and hunger? Tell that to Robin, and see if you can prevent his coming!"

"I think the forces separating the universes would do that. Okay, so he'll want to come if I tell him what's going on. How do we get word to him?"

"Sing of him," Puck suggested. "That will show me the way to him, where he bides at a moment corresponding to this, and I shall go to him and tell to him the plight that we are in. Then do you summon him, and be ready."

"All right, let's see how much of the Robin Hood ballads I can remember . . ."

The companions grew silent while Matt pondered. Then he began to intone a low chant:

> "Once more the knights to battle go
>   With sword and spear and lance,
> Till once, once more the baleful foe
>   Will face new circumstance,
> For Robin and his Merry Men
>   Will turn the tide of chance."

"I have it!" Puck cried, and disappeared.

So much for step one. Matt took a deep breath, trying to ignore his trepidation, and waved his companions back as he recited,

> "In sommer time, when leaves grow greene,
>   And flowers are fresh and gay,
> Then Robin Hood he deckt his men
>   Each one in brave array.
>
> When they were in Lincoln greene,
>   Save Will Scarlet in red,
> They took their bows and arrows keen,
>   And to Ibile they sped."

The air along the trail thickened with more than dusk. Matt began to notice an earthy aroma, compounded of fallen leaves and late-flowering plants, of small animals and musky deer . . .

"He has come," Puck's voice said in his ear.

And he had. The thickening air coalesced, and a whole troop of bowmen filled the trackway. Feathered arrows lanced up from quivers, feathers adorned hats, hoods shielded faces. A few rows back, one lithe young man clothed in glaring red leaned upon a quarterstaff; farther on, a slender, handsome blond man had a bow on his back, but carried a lute before him. Near the front was a short, round man in a monk's robe. He might have had a tonsure, but Matt couldn't tell, because he was wearing a leather cap reinforced by steel cross-straps—and that staff he was carrying *could* have been a pilgrim's staff, but Matt suspected he knew how to use it as something else.

And in the front stood a woman as tall as Matt was, whose demure tan gown and brown bodice and kirtle couldn't hide the bulging muscles underneath.

Matt felt an eldritch prickling creep over his shoulders and up the back of his head. Could that be Maid Marian?

It had to be, because the man next to her exuded a magnetism, a charisma, that instantly drew Matt's attention and made him want to ask for orders on the spot. Somehow, he had instant, total faith in this man and knew that, with him leading, they couldn't possibly lose.

By twentieth-century standards, Robin Hood was a short, round-faced man with a mustache, maybe five-feet-four-inches tall—but he was broad-shouldered, deep-chested, and muscular, and the eyes in that round face were glowing with the joy of life and anticipation of battle. And his mild smile expanded into a reckless grin.

Behind him, the "giant" towering over the rest of the band wasn't much over six feet—Little John? Matt felt the prickle renew itself—but he still stood a head taller than the rest, most of whom were only five and a half feet high.

"Good e'en," said the man with the mustache. "Are you the wizard Matthew?"

"Uh—yes, I am." Could he actually be talking with Robin Hood? "These are my companions—Fadecourt, and the Lady Yverne—and don't let the big one fool you, he may look ferocious, but he's on our side, his name's Narlh ..." Matt realized he was running off at the mouth and stopped.

Robin bowed in response to Fadecourt's bow and Yverne's curtsy. Matt, meanwhile, was noticing that Marian had a face of stunning beauty, no matter what her physique ... He wrenched himself back to the matter at hand. "And I think you know Puck ..."

"Aye, but not by that name." Robin Hood winked at Robin Goodfellow. "He is a staunch ally, and a merry one."

"I'd have to agree, even if he does insist on having his favors paid back."

"Paid back?" Robin frowned, and might have said more if he hadn't noticed Puck's shushing motions. Instead, he said, "He tells me that you are sworn to overthrow a brutal monarch who does grind his people into the dirt."

Matt might have known Puck would state it in a very colorful style. "Yes, though I should have realized what I was getting myself into. And at the moment, most of the king's forces are besieging that castle down there. They have a good friend of mine, who's a very powerful fighter, penned up in there, and I think that we can break him out—but only if I'm on the inside with him."

Robin was nodding. "Much as Puck did say. And you do think that, with us to aid you, you can cut through that force?" He indicated the army in the valley below with a negligent toss of his head.

"Yes—if Puck does his part." Matt noticed that Maid Marian and Yverne were already chatting like old pals and wondered about it— but they did come from similar backgrounds ... "Does that seem, uh, a little unrealistic to you? I mean, altogether, we can't number more than a hundred or so ..."

"An hundred twenty-three, with you and your friends. It will suffice." Robin grinned.

"Suffice? Look, at a guess, there are ten thousand men down there ..."

"Only a thousand of whom will be anywhere near us—and the Goodfellow assures me that most of those will be mad with itching. Fear not, Lord Wizard—our bows are strung, and our quivers are full."

"Well, yes—but are you sure they won't be empty before you come to the drawbridge?"

Robin seemed to become more serious, but his eyes still gleamed with amusement. "Our quivers are ever full, no matter how many arrows we shoot." He clapped a hand on Matt's shoulder. "Be of good heart, Lord Wizard—we shall prevail." He looked straight into Matt's eyes, and somehow, Matt was totally certain they'd come through to the castle intact.

Then Robin turned away, and the conviction faded a bit. "Always full?" Matt muttered. "I thought magicians had a monopoly on magic in this universe!"

"Not on the magic that is inherent in the being," Puck countered. "Could yon dracogriff fly in your world? Could he even exist?"

"Well, no," Matt admitted, "not a hybrid between a bird and a reptile, no ..."

"Yet in this world, 'tis possible—but even in being, it is magical. Thus you may be sure that Robin and his men have quivers ever full, no matter how many arrows they may loose. After all, have you ever heard of their running out?"

"Now that you mention it . . ."

"Or of their fletching more arrows?"

"Not really. But what if a bowstring snaps?"

Puck dismissed the notion with a wave. "An unlikely thing—yet were it to hap, there would ever be fresh strings in their pouches."

"Fantastic!"

"Is it not? But then, do they not draw their strength from the fantasies of the common folk?"

"I don't know," Matt muttered. "Do they?"

Robin came back up to Matt. "We are ready, Lord Wizard."

Matt's stomach sank. To ignore it, he said, "Uh . . . Puck assures me you really do never run out of arrows, or bowstrings . . ."

" 'Tis even so." The glint of amusement showed in Robin Hood's eye again.

"How do you manage that? I mean, is there a spell you say just before action, or . . ."

Robin Hood cut him off with a shrug. "I ken not, Lord Wizard, though I doubt not your interest. Yet for me and mine—why ask? That is simply the way of it. Come now, to battle."

"Uh—right." Matt looked around. "I'm afraid I didn't come properly prepared for this expedition. Would you have an extra quarterstaff?"

"Do not heed him," Fadecourt said to Robin Hood, then turned to Matt. "And do not heed yourself. Do you think there will be no sorcerers there, who seek to undo Puck's spell? Do you think there will be no wicked magi, 'gainst whose spells we would be as children?"

"All right, all right." Matt sighed. "I'll stick to my last." He whipped the wand out of his belt. *En garde!* Away, 'gainst the Army of Evil!"

Dusk was fading into night as Puck, standing on a boulder, made a few gestures reminiscent of small life-forms with many legs, scuttling and climbing about, as he chanted something in a language Matt couldn't understand; it seemed to be mostly squeaking and squealing. But it was very effective; Matt could almost see invisible creepies crawling about, just beyond Puck's fingertips. Maybe he had a closer association with them than Matt knew.

The army below suddenly fell deathly silent. Then it erupted into a cacophony of yells and howls.

"Now!" Robin Hood sprang forward down the path.

Matt ran to keep up with him. "Can you really see where you're going?"

"This star-filled sky is bright, compared with the gloom of Sherwood's night! Have a care, Lord Wizard—the path is not quite even."

Matt stumbled and regained his balance, but that put him far enough behind so that he was caught up among his companions, in the middle of Robin Hood's company. Little John, Maid Marian, and Will Scarlet went merrily leaping ahead, down the hillside and into the army. Quarterstaves whirled, clearing a path for them to an accompaniment of yells and curses. Matt saw a soldier freeze in midscratch, then grab at his sword—and suddenly, an arrow was standing in his chest, and he was reeling backward. Then he was gone, and they were pounding past the place where he'd been, but Matt was trying to remind his stomach that its place was with him.

Then an enemy sorcerer rose up on horseback, waving his wand. Matt didn't wait to hear what the man was saying, or to see its results; he just called out,

> "Your very, very rapid, unintelligible patter
> Isn't likely to be heard,
> And if it is, it doesn't matter!"

Then he snapped his wand down, pointing straight at the sorcerer. The man reeled in his saddle and fell, out cold. The ranks closed and hid the fallen sorcerer—but ahead, two knights, groaning with the torture of the suppressed urge to scratch, stepped together to block the group's path, swords swinging high.

Maid Marian thrust her quarterstaff between one's ankles and twisted as she leaped aside. The man tumbled, flailing—and as he fell, she swung the staff, knocking his sword spinning away. Then her quarterstaff rose up and slammed down.

Matt winced.

The other knight was struggling with an arrow that had somehow appeared between his shoulder piece and his breastplate. Little John reached out with a quarterstaff and tipped him aside.

Then Matt saw Friar Tuck parry a sword cut from a madly scratching trooper, riposte—and freeze. The outlaw next to him ran an arrow into the trooper, while Tuck's lips moved. Matt couldn't hear what he was saying, but followed the direction of his gaze, and saw a sorcerer with a striped foolscap waving a wand in a spiral, roughly in Tuck's direction. Matt lifted his own wand, but before he could say anything, the sorcerer crumpled like tinfoil under a horse's hoof.

Tuck turned away, his lips thin, and slapped another trooper aside with the flat of his blade.

Then Narlh roared behind him, and Matt risked a quick glance. A knight ran hooting, clutching at the seat of his iron pants.

And Matt slammed into the back of the man in front of him.

It was Fadecourt, who reached up in time to keep Matt from tipping over. "Have a care! We've come to the moat!"

Matt looked up and saw a huge blackness rushing toward him with a roaring clatter of chain.

But they had to stand still while they waited for the drawbridge to descend, and a sorcerer's chant pierced the din. Suddenly, the knights and men-at-arms nearby were rushing them, a hundred pikes and a dozen human tanks with swords and shields, pikes stabbing, edges whirling to cut.

Robin Hood loosed six arrows, almost too fast for the eye to follow, and the six knights fell, with arrows sticking out of various joints. More arrows filled the air, and Puck was shrieking something arcane in Matt's ear. For his own part, he sang out,

> "Oh see, these ferocious men of war,
>   Who come running right into our arms!
>   Lay them low for our sons and our country!
>   To arms, my citizens!
>   Withold your pity's sense!
>   We march, we march, till impure blood
>   Shall water deep our fields!"

The sorcerer fell, and the men-at-arms and knights let out a howl as the itching hit them redoubled. But their racket was drowned out by the huge thud of the drawbridge striking earth.

"Across!" Robin yelled, and the merry men ran for the great gateway, thundering across the bridge. Matt was shocked to see that several of them carried wounded comrades—he hadn't realized they'd suffered casualties of their own.

A hundred throats howled like baying dogs, and Matt risked a quick look back. In spite of the itch, armored men were pelting toward the lowered drawbridge—but a hail of crossbow bolts rained down on them. Matt turned away and ran.

They were in the gatehouse, but still running—and the portcullis was down across its end! Matt whirled—betrayed! But the drawbridge was already up and rising fast. Torches burned along the stone tunnel, and Matt could see Robin Hood, grinning in elation, as were most of his men—except Tuck, who was sighing and beating his breast.

Suddenly, Matt was very much aware of glittering eyes behind the arrow slits in the wall, and was even more aware that those slits could rain arrows to skewer them all. Worse, Robin and his men would fire back—and their arrows never missed, not even so small a target as the murder holes. Matt had no wish to see his allies slaughter one another.

"Who are you, and why are you come?" a voice behind a murder hole asked.

"Friends!" Robin Hood shouted to the tunnel in general, but Matt was elbowing his way toward the slit from which the question had come. He had recognized the voice. "I am Matthew Mantrell, Lord Wizard of Merovence!" he cried. "I am come in aid of my comrades, Sir Guy de Toutarien, Max, and Stegoman!"

The portcullis rose up so fast Matt thought the law of gravity had been inverted—and the Black Knight stood there in a pool of torchlight, arms spread wide. "Sir Matthew, my friend and ally! Praise Heaven you are come!"

But Narlh shouldered past, every muscle stiff, eyes bulging, staring at the huge, scaly form beyond Sir Guy. Then he charged, bellowing, "You misbegotten son of a sea snake and a buzzard! You're dead, monster, you are bait!"

CHAPTER 18

Strange Allies

Narlh scrabbled roaring toward the dragon. Sir Guy shouted and jumped into the dracogriff's path, trying to block him, but Narlh hurdled him in a single bound and sailed toward the bigger reptile.

A blast of flame filled the air between them.

Narlh hit the ground, flattened himself against it until the fire had died, then sprang at its source. The dragon leaped back and snapped, "Invader! Interloper! Go, get thee gone! Come not near these good folk!"

"Pretty loud, for a bully! But I'm not a half-grown drakling any more, you pie-eyed prowler!" He pounced, but the dragon leaped high, and people fled to the walls of the courtyard, screaming.

"Oh, yeah? Well, I can fly, too!" Narlh launched himself up, teeth slashing.

"Do you dare, half heart? I bade you go when you did trespass before! I bid you go now, or I'll hurl you o'er the wall!"

"*Bade?*" Narlh shrieked, outraged. "You did a lot more than *bid*, snake-face! You gave me a royal roasting, that's what you did! Toast *this*, you bat-winged belly-crawler!" And he pounced on the dragon like a hawk on a mouse.

Or an alligator, rather. The dragon twisted away from beneath him, all but his tail—and the dracogriff seized the tip with a bite like a vise. The dragon bellowed in anger more than pain—but also in high octane, and the flame swept the wall, just above the heads of the screaming spectators. The fire cut off, and they fled for doorways.

"Separate them, my friend!" Sir Guy cried.

"Darn right I will!" Matt answered.

> "Stone walls do not a prison make,
> Nor iron bars a cage—
> But both will function well enough,
> Till these two calm their rage!
> Let grilles form up round both of them,
> Lest monsters do engage!"

Not the world's greatest verse, but it worked well enough—huge iron grids suddenly appeared around all six sides of both monsters, clashing shut and dropping them to the courtyard surface with a crash.

"Lemme outa here!" Narlh tore at the bars in frustration. "Whaddaya think you're doing, Wizard?"

"Trying to prevent two of my friends from hurting each other!"

Both monsters froze, staring at Matt. Then, in chorus, they roared, *"Friends?"*

"He's a bully and a homicidal maniac!" Narlh screeched.

"This abomination is an insult to all Dragondom, and a trespasser besides!" the dragon howled.

"It was my beast of a father who was the abomination, you half-crocked dile!" Narlh bellowed. "He seduced my mother and flew laughing away! Her, the most beautiful, innocent griffin that ever was! And you have the gall to *defend* him?"

The dragon froze. Then he said, in glacial tones, "No. And if 'tis true, he will die battling a dozen dragons. His is the right of defense, but ours is the privilege of enforcing our law. Only tell me his name, and I will hale him before the High Council, to answer for his misdeeds with tooth and flame."

"I don't *know* his name!" Narlh bleated in agony. "He didn't exactly leave us his pedigree and his coat of arms, y'know! All he left was *me*—and a ravaged soul!"

The dragon crouched, eyes smoldering. At last, he said, "His deed shames me, and all dragonkind. We will seek him out, we will tear him."

"Oh, yeah, sure! The only thing *you* tear is half-fledged wanderers with dreams in their heads!"

The dragon glowered at him, then said, "None may enter the realm of the Free save themselves alone—or their guests."

Matt decided it was time to jump in—literally. He landed between the two cages, holding up a palm toward the dracogriff. "Hold it, Narlh!"

The monster gulped, then coughed and gasped. "Don't *do* that, Wizard! You know what it's like to swallow a fireball?"

The dragon stared, then swung his head toward Matt. "He *is* thy friend, Matthew!"

"Yes," Matt said. "He has saved my life twice, at least."

Narlh stared, frozen. Then, slowly, he turned his head toward Matt, and there was bitterness and blame in every line of his face.

"Don't look at me like that!" Matt held up both hands, beseeching. "There's a reason for it—what Stegoman did to you! He wouldn't do it again for the life of him!"

"Oh?" Narlh's syllable dripped sarcasm. "I suppose a demon made him do it, huh?"

"Of a kind, yes—the demon rum, or its first cousin."

"Doing what?" Sir Guy stepped up, frowning from one beast to the other, his hand on his sword.

"Burned Narlh and chased him out of the air, so badly that he fell, and just barely survived," Matt said, his voice low. "Stegoman was on sentry duty at the border of Dragondom, Sir Guy—and he was drunk."

Narlh stared.

Then he said, *"Drunk?* A dragon, *drunk?* What'd he do, drink a brewery?"

"Nay." Stegoman's face set into rocky lines. "Mine own fumes. When I breathed flame, I became giddy and crazed. I was rent for that, monster—my wings were torn in many places; I was condemned to crawl upon the ground for hurting other dragons."

"Oh, sure, dragons! But who cares about a lowly dracogriff, huh?"

"None saw that," Stegoman confessed, "or I might have been taken from the air much sooner."

"Sure. Right. A model of justice, these dragons."

Stegoman's eyes narrowed. "Do not mock."

"Why *not?*" Narlh blasted. "Who're you trying to feed the big lie, lizard? So you were grounded, huh? Then *how'd your wings get healed?*"

"By Matthew," Stegoman said simply.

Narlh stared at him. Then, slowly, he turned toward Matt again. "You traitor."

"I hadn't even *met* you yet! Besides, Narlh, I cured his drunkenness, too! He can breathe enough flame to fire a steam engine for a hundred miles and not even be tipsy! That's why I know he wouldn't fry you now!"

" 'Tis true," Stegoman said. "I would summon other dragons and chase thee away from our borders, aye—yet not even that, if thou wert to tell me of thy complaint against one of our number."

"Sure," Narlh said. "Sure." But he didn't bellow this time.

Then he turned to Matt. "If you're such good buddies, how come he isn't traveling with you anymore?"

"Because," Stegoman said, "Matthew is a wedded man, and cannot go gadding about on a quest—and there's no place at court for a dragon."

"There will *always* be a place for you at Alisande's court!" Matt protested.

A hint of a smile showed at the corners of the saurian's mouth. "Bless thee for thy fond protestations, Matthew—yet even had I stayed, thou wouldst have had scant time for the company of a confirmed old bachelor like myself. Nay, a wife leaves a man little time for unwed friends."

Sir Guy frowned. "I would not say—"

"Nor would I," Matt cut in, "considering that I didn't marry her."

Stegoman stared. "Not *marry* . . ."

Sir Guy looked up, startled. "Why, how is this, Matthew?"

"Alisande has this thing about being nobly born." Matt shrugged the issue away. "I developed a certain desire for a higher station in life."

Sir Guy lifted his head slowly, looking more and more worried as he went.

"Desire, yeah." Narlh's jaw lolled open in a grin. "And a big mouth. Tell 'em about your little memory lapse, Wizard."

"Memory lapse?" Stegoman turned to Matt, frowning.

Matt felt his face grow hot. "I, uh . . . kind of bent the Third Commandment a little . . ."

"Bent?" Narlh hooted. "He bent it so far it snapped back!"

" 'Thou shalt not take the name of the Lord thy God in vain'?" Sir Guy turned very somber. "What did you call Him to witness, my friend?"

"I'll, uh, tell you later." Matt forced a sickly grin. "Suffice it to say that it resulted in my undertaking a quest remarkably similar to your own."

"And not entirely voluntarily." Finally, a smile broke through Sir Guy's cloudy mood. "Well, no matter how you are come, you are well come! I thank all the saints for your presence; now I can hope!"

"So can I," Narlh growled. "Hope these bars'll rust! If I have to wait that long to get at that overgrown salamander, it'll be worth it!"

"Salamander? Why, thou knowest not of what thou dost speak, foolish halfling!"

"Halfling?" Narlh leaped forward, slamming into the bars and bumping the whole cage forward a yard. "You take that back, you nettled newt! Or so help me, I'll haul my brass over there and toast you for a mallow!"

"Thy cage is iron, not brass," Stegoman snorted, "and thou hast but half a brain! Half a brain, half a dragon, half a griffin—why, thou art so many things thou art naught of any, least of all a dragon!"

"I've *had* it!" Narlh bellowed. He threw himself against the bars, bumping his cage closer and closer to Stegoman's. "You high-and-mighty hypocrite! You self-righteous, pompous excuse for a syllabub! You're the kind of flag-waving traitor who'd turn around and lead a hunter to a nest, to kill the hatchlings for their blood!"

"I? Never!" Stegoman roared, outraged—and Narlh had to duck the tip of his flame. "I, stoop to so vile a vengeance? To crawl beneath the lowest of the low? How durst thou accuse me of such! Blood must answer! Wizard, take away these bars, for I am hot for . . ." He suddenly froze.

Matt looked at the dragon's eyes and made a guess as to what was going on in his mind.

Narlh turned to him, narrow-eyed. "What'd you do to him?"

"Nothing," Matt said, low-voiced. "I think he's just realized how come you would think of such a vile insult."

"Aye." Stegoman gazed at the dracogriff out of hooded eyes. "Thou, too, hast known their horrors, hast thou not? Thou wast not the only egg hatched from thy brood, wast thou?"

Narlh, glared, outraged. Then he whipped his head around to Matt. "You told!"

Matt shook his head. "I didn't know. You never told *me*. You were here, you heard—I didn't say a word about it."

"Why else wouldst thou have thought of such scum?" Stegoman said. "Why else wouldst thou think that the nadir of life-forms is the hunter who doth seek out hatchlings to drain and sell their blood, even as they destroy those of dragons? Thou must needs have known them, must thou not?"

"Awright awready! So I ran, I flew, I fled! The fiend was towering up into the sky, from where I was! I was only two feet long! I chickened out, all right? I didn't even try to fight! Now you know! Y' happy now?" Then Narlh bowed his head, his voice choked, hushed.

"All of 'em! All my brothers and sisters, all five! And I didn't even raise a claw to defend 'em! Well, almost none." His head snapped up, glaring at Stegoman. "I did scratch his face for him! And my sister almost got away! But he . . ." He choked and turned his face aside.

"None can blame thee," Stegoman said quietly. "Thou didst fight whiles thou couldst, and fled when thou couldst not fight. Nay, I, too, fled, for the wight was far too huge for me."

Narlh looked up, startled. *"You . . . ?"*

"I was not born vast, no more than thou wert," Stegoman reminded him. "I, too, was hunted by these vile humans, who pander to the more depraved of the sorcerers." He turned to Matt. "Take off these bars, Wizard!"

"Hey, hold on!" Narlh bellowed. "If you let him out, you got to . . ." He stared as his cage faded away. "I didn't even hear you talk."

"You were kind of loud." Matt was beginning to understand a lot about his monstrous friend.

Stegoman waddled up toward Narlh. The dracogriff braced himself, but the dragon only said, "Come. We must discuss how we will clear the earth of these vile sorcerers, who buy our blood—how we will chase them, as their minions have chased us, and scour them from the land, thou and I."

Narlh stared at him for a few long minutes.

Then he nodded. "Yeah, sure. Awright." He turned his head a little away, eyeing Stegoman narrowly. "Truce?"

"Truce," Stegoman confirmed, "and peace, if thou wilt, for no greater reason than our common friendship with one of the few wizards who doth disdain to feed his power from others' lives. Nay, and if thou dost wish to seek justice for thy mother, I will myself escort you into Dragondom—when this coil is done, and Ibile is cleansed."

"Yeah. Yeah, sure." Narlh nodded, faster and faster. "Yeah, we'll get the wizard to work up the right verses, and tear 'em outa their lairs! . . . You really think we got a chance?"

"As to that . . ." Stegoman said, and led the other monster away, chatting quietly, plotting mayhem.

People began to look out of arrow slits and doorways, wondering if the quiet in the courtyard meant anything trustworthy.

Sir Guy blew out a shaky breath. "For an instant, I feared our keep would be tumbled from within! Yet I doubt me not we have strengthened our forces amazingly, by these two monsters' union." He forced a grin and finally managed to clasp Matt's hand, slapping him on the shoulder. "And you do strengthen us tenfold! How good of you to come, Matthew! Yet how did you know we stood in your need?"

"Mostly because I had a friendly ghost trying to lead me somewhere—and when Max showed up beside him for a minute, I knew he was showing me the way toward you." Matt grinned, massaging his hand and trying to ignore the sudden ache in his shoulder. "So how's the quest been? Doesn't look like a total bust."

"Well, we are alive," Sir Guy said, "and that's no small task, after three years' sojourn in this land of evil."

"It's well-nigh impossible! But that was always your kind of job. Was Max any help?"

Sir Guy opened his mouth, but the spark was there, dancing in the air between them and humming, "Not a whit! This great lout of a knight kens no more the use of my powers than he knows of the shape of the earth."

Sir Guy reddened. "The earth is flat, Demon, as all do know!"

"He will not believe 'tis round!" the spark keened in exasperation. "Nay, the best he can think to have me do is to kindle fires in siege engines—a task that he could achieve with an arrow and a bit of tow!"

Matt shook his head in commiseration. "Sounds like a rough three years for both of you." He'd never seen Sir Guy run out of patience before. "Maybe it's a good thing I came."

"Aye, if he will give me back into your direction again!"

"Done!" Sir Guy snapped, with as much relief as anger. "Go you again to your old master . . ."

"Friend!" Max snapped.

"Friend, then." Sir Guy eyed Matt as though he doubted the term. "Let *him* direct you—and I will cleave to the steel that is my heritage!"

"Shoemaker, stick to thy first." Matt held out a hand, and Max darted up his cuff. He turned back to Sir Guy. "Maybe I can be some help here, after all."

"First?" Sir Guy frowned. "Wherefore should a cobbler adhere to a first?"

"Think about it. In the meantime, though, let me compliment you on three years of amazingly good work." Matt surveyed the tents pitched against the walls, the overflowing stables, and the stalwart peasants who were just now getting back to their evening chores, almost certain the monsters were done fighting.

Sir Guy nodded. "I thank you. And, yes, this is a worthy accomplishment—to gather together these few of Ibile's four estates who as yet live free of corruption."

"All four?" Matt looked up, alert for implications. "Clergy, nobility, commoners, and serfs? You found a few priests still alive?"

"Some dozen, from a proud Archbishop, whom Stegoman and I succored from a siege of evil that would surely have been his death, to a humble trio of nuns—all that was left of their abbey—who did come to us in the guise of beggars, to seek shelter among us. Yet their prayers gave us more strength than they took, 'gainst evil sorcery."

"Nice gleaning," Matt said, amazed. "But how about the nobility? I thought Gord—uh, the king, had been busy kicking out any lords who looked to be virtuous."

"He did, but some few hacked and hewed their way free, and roamed the countryside, defending the poor where they could and eluding his sorcerers and knights as well as they might. One by one, they came to us, estranged and dispossessed, but alive, and still a mighty force in the land."

Matt remembered the link between the land of Merovence and its people, and how the land virtually repelled a usurper—or sickened under his rule. "Well, between them and the common folk, you have a fair amount of strength concentrated here."

"Aye, if we can endure."

"I'd guess you could hold out for years." Matt looked at the fortifications around him. "This castle looks pretty sturdy."

"It is, a valiant maiden. She has guarded this confluence of waterways for three hundred years, never taken. Twice has she withstood siege and emerged victorious—but never against a host so wicked and so powerful as Penaldehyde."

"Penaldehyde?" Matt frowned. "What kind of weapon is that?"

Sir Guy smiled without mirth. "A living weapon, Sir Matthew, and as mighty a one as resides in the king's arsenal. Nay, Penaldehyde is a sorcerer most truly steeped in wickedness, whom the king wields as the sword of his right hand."

"Oh." Matt frowned. "Gord—uh, the gross one's chief assistant?"

"Even so," Sir Guy confirmed. "And he is mighty in magic, and devious. We are hard pressed, Matthew."

"But alive." Matt raised a finger. "Considering the sink of debauchery this kingdom is in, I'd say you haven't done badly."

"Yet not so well as I had thought to do," Sir Guy said with a sardonic smile. "I had wished to ride into Ibile and cleanse it in a month, aided by such doughty companions as the marvelous Demon and Stegoman."

"Even with them in your arsenal, you were outgunned by evil. But how about my idea for having you and Max get along? He was supposed to provide you ideas that you could turn into orders."

"It fizzled like a match with no fuel." The spark was there suddenly, dancing between them in midair. "I had not known that this medieval muscleman knew little of molecules, and less of atoms. Indeed, he knows so little of operations at atomic and subatomic levels that the words mean nothing to him. He thinks that Schrödinger's Cat is a German house pet."

Sir Guy reddened, but said, " 'Tis true. I can comprehend not one word in five of his mystical phrases."

"Not mystical, you dolt! Mysticism is conjecture about matters not subject to testing! 'Tis of matters physical we speak, not metaphysical!"

"You sure about that?" Matt said. "I mean, considering quantum mechanics and general relativity . . ."

The spark ceased its usual Brownian movement and hung still in midair. Slowly, its voice hummed, "You may speak more truth than you know . . ."

"Or can understand," Matt finished. "How about you retire and consider the matter?"

"Well said." The spark of light winked out.

Sir Guy heaved a sigh. " 'Twas well for me that the ghost appeared."

Matt looked up, startled. "Medium-size guy? Hangdog expression? Gray clothes? Kinda dumpy? Head in his hand?"

"Ah," Sir Guy said, "you know him well."

"I do indeed," Matt said. "Had a bit of a communication problem, though. I take it you didn't?"

"Not greatly," Sir Guy said, puzzled. "I did encounter him not long after my advent into Ibile. Near close of day, he did appear—and I own, I was fearful, though I let it not be seen . . ."

That, Matt could believe—at least, the part about not showing it. He wasn't so sure Sir Guy had really been afraid. Ever.

"Yet it made no threat, but only seemed to wish that we follow—so we did, though ever-wary of traps and snares. The ghost did lead us to a shrine, overgrown and ruined, but intact. We made our devotions; then, upon our outgoing, we were beset by a band of gargoyles."

"You were?" Matt stared. "Must be a local condition, then. *Hm!* And we thought they were just for us!"

"In truth?" Sir Guy asked, horrified. "Ah, Matthew! I repent I did not battle with them! They must have lurked about the landscape, to your peril!"

"Don't worry about it. But how did *you* get out?"

"Ah. There, at least, I managed a thought that Max the Demon could twist to some purpose. I but asked him to turn the gargoyles once again to stone, and he did—though he informed me he could not make the condition endure without his presence. That sufficed, of course, because when he had quit their environs, so had Stegoman and I—and I had thought they would disappear, having been summoned only to fight us. My apologies."

"Accepted, and not needed. We finished them off."

"You . . . ?" Sir Guy stared and almost choked. He turned aside to cough, then managed a weak smile. "Nay, surely wizardry accomplished what force of arms could not! Yet how, Matthew? What magic did you work, that could overcome such embodiments of savage urges?"

"Oh, I didn't do it! I just found a new friend."

"A friend?" Sir Guy was instantly wary, eyes flicking to left and right. "What manner of being was this, who could counter such fell foes?"

"A goblin more fell than they." Puck was there suddenly, standing arms akimbo on Matt's shoulder, grin flashing. "I but set them to fighting each to each, and let them chew one another to powder, whiles the wizard did watch and ponder. Then he dispersed the last one, and all was peace."

"He's got an unusual twist of thought," Matt explained. "Puck, meet Sir Guy."

"Nay, *this* manner of spirit, I can comprehend!" Sir Guy grinned, holding out a forefinger. "Well met, good sprite!"

Puck clasped the forefinger. "I like the look of you, Sir Knight! Say, what mischief might you find for me?"

"He's good at mischief," Matt explained. "In fact, he's the embodiment of it."

"Why, I have as much a liking for a good jest as any," Sir Guy said.

Puck made a face. "Good jests have little of amusement in them, Sir Knight. 'Tis bad jests that do delight—when one does watch his enemy chasing after phantoms, belike, or being mired in the slough of his own cupidity."

"I own to enjoyment of seeing those who care naught for their fellow creatures suffering from the very ruses they used upon their victims. What would you say, Spirit, to making these soldiers of vileness execute the opposite of each command they're given?"

"So that, when their captain sounds the charge, they turn and flee in rout?" Puck's eyes lit with something like respect. He turned to Matt, nodding. "You may have here a mortal with more than half a mind!"

"That's a compliment," Matt explained quickly.

"Aye." Puck made a face. "This man who has called me up has too much of the proper prude in him. He kens not a true amusement."

"Prude?" Matt bleated. "Why, you half-pint harlequin—"

"Enough!" Sir Guy held up a palm. "One must never give insult to an ally, Matthew, as you well know."

"A pin in the chair, perhaps," Puck suggested.

"Or an unseen hand that pulls at his hair whenever he ceases to expect it," Sir Guy proposed.

Puck's grin widened. "Better and better! Here stands a man of true insight!"

Insight into ways of making other people look foolish. Matt shuddered; he had never suspected that side of Sir Guy's nature before. But, now that he thought of it, to a man of war, it probably was better than having to carve your enemy into scrimshaw. "You were telling me about the ghost. He *talks* to you?"

"Um? Oh!" Sir Guy came back to the subject from some vision of practical jokes that would have made Matt shudder. "Nay, he spoke not—but I had little difficulty comprehending the gist of his intent. Therefore, when he appeared before me this morn, and was clearly in a state of great excitement, I understood from his signs and gestures that doughty heroes were nearby and could be gathered into our number—but they could not see him well enough to comprehend."

"No, I couldn't." Matt frowned, unable to understand how Sir Guy could guess the ghost's meaning so easily, when Matt had been stumped.

Unable to understand. That was it—Sir Guy had the referents; he naturally thought the same way the ghost did. Which Matt did not. At all.

Odd. The ghost didn't *look* like a warrior . . . "So you decided to help him?"

"Aye. I had understood, from your talk and the Demon's, that seeing had something to do with Max's function; so I asked him to move brightness from the morning into the ghost . . ."

"A most distasteful ambiguity," Max hummed, hovering between them again. "He seems not even to know the word 'energy,' or to be able to understand it as anything other than a liveliness within his limbs."

Sir Guy glared at the spark, but Puck hooted with laughter. "What have we here? A will-o'-the-wisp that's scarcely hatched?"

"Hatched?" the Demon sang in indignation. "Why, what oaf is this, who mocks even at the powers of the universe!"

"*Hoo!* So you are the universe, are you, small spark? What is the sun, then, your child? The infant dwarfing ever the sire!"

"What foolishness!" Max snapped. "How could the sun be begotten of me, when I was there to oversee its birth?"

"A midwife to the sun?" Puck cried. "Nay, enough of such vainglorious boasting."

"Of course," Matt murmured. "That's *your* province."

"Speak with respect, weak mortal! Whiles I do dampen the enthusiasm of this humorless coal!" Puck gestured, and a small rain cloud appeared above the Demon. It contracted in an instant, intensive typhoon.

The drops struck the spark and exploded into steam.

Puck frowned. "Strange."

"What would you expect, foolish sprite?" the Demon seethed. "Know you not Boyle's law?"

"Why, it shall be *my* law that you shall boil!" Puck started another gesture, but Matt held up a hand. "Don't try to fine-tune it any, will you?" He had a nightmare vision of a duel between the Spirits of Entropy and Mischief. Strange—he would have thought the two would have gotten along famously.

Or notoriously . . .

In desperation, he guessed the end of Sir Guy's story. "So the ghost left with Max—and I saw them together, and knew he must be leading us to you." Finally, he had a referent for the ghost's motions.

"And thus you are come." Sir Guy grinned. "In good time, Matthew! Shall we chew this host up between us?"

"Say, rather, that you shall grind them 'gainst the grit of your grating wit!" Max keened. "Wizard, you know not what I have endured at his hands! Scarcely one task in a week, and that so simple it could have been done with stone and stick! This enforced idleness has brought me to seethe with impatience!"

"You were free to suggest any course of action you wished," Sir Guy snapped.

"I did, and you comprehended not! Why, Wizard, his grasp of science exceeds a child's—inversely! It rivals an infant's! His notion of experiment is to see how close he can bring the point of his lance to a target! He thinks a field force is an army's bivouac! That relativity is the tracing of his kindred! How could you desert me with such a one?"

"Easy, easy," Matt soothed. "Nobody said you *had* to stay with him."

"How could I have deserted him, in the face of such foes?"

"Easily," Puck said sourly. "You gave him no gain by your staying."

The Demon emitted a single, high-pitched note that stabbed right through Matt's eardrums and veered up higher. In a panic, he called, "Easy! Easy! Ease off, in fact! Damp your gain! His worldview doesn't encompass science, you know! In fact, he doesn't really have the concept of causality."

The Demon's note cut off in something that sounded remarkably like a gasp of horror. "You jest!"

"Who, *him*?" Puck said in scorn.

Matt reddened and gave the elf a glare as he told Max, "Not really. Cause-and-effect thinking is a relatively modern idea, you know."

"Modern! In what sense?"

"From the Renaissance on. Well, okay, the classical Greeks had it, and gave it to the Romans—but it died out for almost a thousand years, in anything more subtle than hammering a door with a battering ram to cause it to break. Then Europe relearned geometry, picked up algebra from the Muslims—and scientists like Copernicus and Kepler rediscovered the idea that you could reason back from effects to causes."

"Do you say this knight's teachers did not know enough to learn true science?"

"Not really, no. At this stage, Europe hasn't learned any mathematics beyond arithmetic, and they don't even have the idea of the zero—they're still using Roman numerals."

"What other form is there?" Sir Guy asked, intrigued.

Matt swallowed heavily. "Arabic."

"Saracens!"

"They're good mathematicians," Matt protested. Then he turned back to Max. "Before they can really start thinking scientifically, they'll need geometry. Then Copernicus will be able to realize that the orbits of the planets don't look the way they should if they were revolving around the earth. Kepler will take his idea and try to make it specific—but he'll need Tycho Brahe's observations. With those records, Kepler will find out that the motions of the planets don't fit the shapes of the perfect solids he's been thinking of—but they do fit ovals. Then Galileo will have to build his work on top of theirs, and Newton will have to learn Galileo's ideas and invent his own version of calculus before he'll be able to figure out the law of gravity. Knowledge is built up like a pyramid, you see—and so far, Europe has only laid the foundations."

"Not even that, if what you say about their worldview is true!"

"Oh, the idea of cause-and-effect is implicit in the Judaeo-Christian attitude toward history. It's beginning to assert itself—but at the moment, it's only aborning."

"Yet what else can there be?" the Demon cried. "When you eliminate causality, what's left?"

"Coincidence," Matt answered. "One event doesn't *cause* another—they just happen at the same time, more or less. The clouds are there, and so is the lightning and thunder. They go together, but they don't cause each other."

Puck raised an eyebrow. "At last, some sense!"

"Sense?!" the Demon bleated, but Sir Guy nodded. "Even so. If two armies come, there will be a battle. He who is more right, will win."

"Blasphemy!" the Demon keened. "If men think thus, there will never be peace!"

"Well, even in *my* world people aren't very good at seeing their own behavior in terms of cause and effect," Matt demurred.

"What fools these mortals be." Puck grinned. "Thy race is excellent, mortal—your lives are the very stuff of comedy!"

"We are such things as vaudeville was made of, huh? So you see, Max, even with the best medieval education available—which I'm sure Sir Guy has had; he knows how to read—he can't understand our physics as anything but a metaphor."

"How can physics be a metaphor?"

"Well, the Church thought that the sun revolving around the earth was proof that human life was the most important part of creation—after all, we were made in God's image. And they thought that building tall towers had to be a sign of arrogance, because God lived above the sky. They didn't quite realize that an apple falling to earth was like the human soul wishing to be closer to God—but they would have loved it."

"What nonsense! What has this to do with physics?"

Matt sighed. "Think of it as analogies. They see the world as being suspended between Heaven and Hell, and everything surrounding the earth was made solely for its benefit, because it's the most important part of creation."

"What nonsense! When you are only a small planet, far out on the tip of one arm of a quite-ordinary galaxy? Wherefore should your world be more important than any other?"

Now it was Sir Guy who muttered, "Blasphemy!"

"Because human beings live on it," Matt said simply.

"How primitive a notion!"

"I told you we have a long way to go. So to them, see, the world is an analogue of the Church, because it's the most important part of society . . ."

"By whose reckoning?"

"The scholars."

"And whence come these 'scholars'?"

"From the Church. And the sun is analogous to the king, because it controls the seasons."

Max hummed without words for a minute, then said, "The knight would thus understand entropy only as analogous to a lack of government."

"You've got it!"

"But then all my works, to him, would be . . ."

"Incomprehensible." Matt nodded. "Fortunately, European culture has a mental structure for dealing with things it doesn't understand—it calls them magic, and lets it go at that."

"Then they shall never approach true understanding of their world!"

"No," Puck said, "but they may understand one another—as well as human folk can be understood."

Matt threw up his hands. "What can I say? Chaucer understood people as well as anyone did, before we discovered biochemistry and neurology."

"Faugh!" Puck made a face. "These are but words. One might as well speak of the elf shot and the mad."

"See what I mean?"

"Aye, and 'tis unbearable! Wizard, you cannot leave me shackled to one whose skull holds such a vacuum!"

Sir Guy's scowl turned dangerous. "What is a 'vacuum'?"

"Something for making things pure—or cleaner, anyway," Matt

improvised. "I know how you feel, Max—I'm currently dogged with a companion who rubs me the wrong way, too."

"Be rid of him, then!"

Puck grinned. "Let him try!"

"See what I mean?" Matt sighed. "You don't suppose you could counteract him, do you?"

"This sprite?" Max hummed, drifting closer to Puck.

The elf scowled. "Do not even *consider* . . ."

His voice ran down the scale, and his movements slowed. His features began working themselves toward an expression of alarm, and one hand began to move in a strange, but very slow, gesture.

"No, Max!" Matt cried. "I didn't mean . . ."

"Leave the elf be!" Sir Guy loosened his broadsword in its scabbard.

But Puck's hand had completed the gesture, and suddenly an icicle appeared in the air—a glowing icicle, with the Demon trapped inside it.

Or maybe not trapped—the ice immediately began to melt. Puck's voice soared upscale, finishing the phrase. ". . . any spell against me! Nay, since you have, deal with this!" He pointed at the ice-coated spark with fingers stiffened into a sort of cylinder, and a jet of darkness sped from his hand to enfold the Demon, shrouding him in a small sphere of night so total as to be absolute.

Light flared within it, banishing the darkness, and the Demon sang, "Know that I have power over entropy, foolish elf! Do you dare beard me in my own realm?"

"Foolish indeed," Puck admitted, rolling one hand around another and tossing something invisible at the Demon. He suddenly grew a white beard, shooting down from the spark, longer and longer.

"What do you do?" Max screeched, just before he took off like a rocket.

Puck met Matt's accusing glare with a shrug. "Make him a bearded star, and Nature will hurl him back to the firmament, where he belongs."

The "bearded star" turned into a falling star, and the miniature meteorite spat, "As a comet resembles a meteor, foolish spirit, so can I return unto you! But know that, in embodying entropy, I am also the Spirit of Perversity!" And Puck suddenly grew long ears, his nose stretched out and thickened, and he stood before them wearing a miniature ass's head. He brayed in alarm.

"There will be no ending to this," Sir Guy confided to Matt, "unless we provide it."

Matt nodded. "Let's sort this out the way it should be."

"Aye," Sir Guy said. "Do you take the Demon in hand, whiles I speak with the elf."

One step ahead of Puck's gesture, Matt chanted,

> "See as thou wast wont to see,
> Be as thou wast wont to be!"

Puck's head suddenly reverted to normal—with a look of fury. "I asked not for aid, Wizard!"

"You have abetted mine enemy!" the spark keened. "Are you a traitor?"

"No, and he's not your enemy." Matt cupped a hand around the spark and, as he turned away, noticed that Sir Guy was doing some pretty fast talking with Puck. "We're both fighting the evil king, after all—"

" 'Tis no contest of mine!"

"Okay, then—you're free. I can't ask you to fight in a cause you don't believe in."

"Ask?" The spark hopped in astonishment. "But the Black Knight—"

"Fully relinquishes any claim he might have upon you," Matt said firmly. "You're free to go back to the void if you want to."

"But how boring! Wizard, imagine eternity with no tasks to accomplish, none save to supervise the smooth, even progress of entropy!"

"Well, of course, if you *want* to . . . Heaven knows I'd appreciate your help . . ."

" 'Tis done!" The spark snapped. "I am free of Toutarien and bonded to you—till *I* wish to sever the bond, at least!"

"You were always free to. But you must understand what you're getting yourself into."

"Dost truly think this kinglet you fight can do damage to *me*?" Max said in scorn.

"No—but Sir Guy is over there trying to talk Puck into staying with the team. Just annexed to Sir Guy, is all."

The spark danced in midair, humming to itself a while. Then it sang, "I can endure his company, if I need not speak to him save with the strongest of causes."

"Done." Matt nodded. "In fact, I recommend that if *he* talks to *you*, you don't answer."

"Oh, be assured that I shall!" The singing turned flat and harsh. "And long will he regret it!"

"Friends, remember," Matt cautioned, "or at least allies. But at the moment, it would be politic if you got out of sight."

"A point," the spark agreed, and vanished.

Matt noticed that his wallet warmed up at his belt, and felt reassured. He turned to Sir Guy. "Any luck?"

"He is my man," Puck answered, grinning, "and I shall ride on his shoulder. Think naught of such favors as you owe me, Wizard—I shall be too busy brewing mischief with this knight to concern myself with you."

"Very generous of you," Matt murmured. "Sir Guy, you sure you know what you're doing?"

"Aye." The Black Knight grinned. "And if you will excuse me, Sir Matthew, we have already begun to brew a coil for the army that sits without our gate." He turned away, holding Puck in a palm and chatting like an old friend.

Matt gazed after, heaving a sigh of relief, but having a hard time accepting it all.

"Why do you stand amazed, Lord Wizard? Are you so surprised at your own peacemaking?"

Matt looked up and was astonished to see Marian standing beside him. For a split second, he was lost in the dazzle of her beauty; then the memory of how she had dented heads with a quarterstaff came to mind, and he managed to pull back to a safe emotional distance. From that vantage point, he noticed that Robin was conducting his band to places around the great fire pit near an inner wall and detailing a few to join the guard on the walls. The net result was that, for the moment, Matt was alone with Marian.

It wasn't the world's most comfortable feeling. What do you say to a legend? Especially one who had turned out to be rather intimidating? "Uh . . . don't you get a bit lonely, being the only woman in the band?"

"Oh, but I am not." The smile dazzled him again. "There are Allan-a-Dale's wife, and Will Scarlet's leman, and the wives of most of the other men of the band, save those who are too young."

"Families?" Matt stared, amazed. "But . . . but . . . you're a military unit! A guerrilla band!"

"Guerrilla?" Maid Marian frowned, puzzled; then her face cleared. "Ah! 'Tis a Spanish word, is't not?"

"Why, yes. I think it means 'little war.' " Matt was surprised that the woman showed evidence of education; it hadn't been common for anyone in the Middle Ages.

But then, Marian was a gentlewoman, a lady—only a generation or two from minor aristocracy. "I, uh—don't see any other women around."

"Nay. They wait in Sherwood, with the older men and striplings, where they bide in safety. I have not yet a child, so I am free to come venturing."

At a guess, she and Robin were finally married—but it would be difficult to think of her as anything but "Maid" Marian. "I take it you won't have any difficulty going back to your home, uh, world."

"Returning, no. Coming . . ." Marion shrugged. "We must know where there's need of us, ere we can march. But once having traveled the route, 'tis easy enough to go back."

Matt hadn't realized Robin Hood was himself magical. He should have, of course. "Do you still, uh . . . serve King Richard, though in his absence?"

"Ah! You know our tale well, I see. Aye, we served the Lionheart long, and aided in gathering pennies from the poor for his ransom—and jewels from the wealthy. So we labored, and guarded his people, till he was finally returned to England and put down his usurping regent John."

So. Scott had written better than he knew. But why not? With an infinity of universes, anything Scott had imagined must have really happened, somewhere. "So you all would have been happy to retire, as long as Richard lived?"

A shadow crossed Marian's face. "Oh, he rewarded my Robin amply, with restoration of his family's estates and two others that were taken from men who leagued with John. But the sheriff of Nottingham he would not punish, claiming he had only been obedient to his lord, as he should."

"A little shortsighted of him."

"He was in so many things. Within a few months, we saw he truly held no love for England; he was already dunning his noblemen for more gold, to take him adventuring again. In a year's time he was gone from England, and his brother was regent again."

"I know." Matt shook his head. "Rights of succession aside, he still should have known better."

"He did not truly care." Marian's voice hardened. "And John set the sheriff once again to plaguing my Robin, with boundary disputes and taxes on every excuse—yet he could be no more to him than a nuisance. But he could throw Robin's men into prison on the slightest pretext, and he seized upon the first who poached, to put him to death."

"Robin didn't let him get away with that, did he?"

Marian shook her head. "He rode against the sheriff in force, and in armor, and wrested his man from the Nottingham gaol. Then did John pronounce him once again outlaw, in that he had moved against the king's law—and Robin and I were off to the greenwood once more, with all our household, and our estates confiscated. But Robin's old band came, one by one, to find him in the forest, and we set ourselves to plague the sheriff as in days of old. Then Richard died."

Matt nodded. "In a pointless fight, by a virtual accident—but he was good at getting into pointless fights."

"A parfit gentil knight—but a very poor king," Marian agreed. "England was naught but a treasure house to him. Yet by the time of his death, he had taken all the treasure and left us only the house. And John became king."

"And you decided to stay in the greenwood," Matt supplied.

"We have." Marian turned merry again. "We plagued John till he died. Robin carried word of each nobleman's discontent to his peers, so that all knew that few would side with John, if he sought to move against any one of them—and they made him sign a great charter acknowledging their rights. It was Robin's proudest moment."

"The Magna Carta," Matt murmured. "I'll bet it was. Not that John felt bound to honor it, though."

Marian waved the objection away, irritated. "John honored naught but force, no matter how often he saw the folly of his efforts to tyrannize his peers. But he died at last, and his heir would have restored Robin's estates."

Matt frowned. "Robin didn't accept?"

"Nay, for he saw the poor folk would prosper under Edward. Then the elvin folk offered him life till Doom's Trump should sound, and work to keep him busied all his days."

Matt shook his head. "Tough choice—family versus career."

"Ah, but the elves promised lasting life to all his band." Marian raised a finger. "Not one of us has died since, though we've been wounded sore, and have endured great pain till the elves could heal us. Yet all become fit again and are ever filled with zeal to protect the common folk."

"But I thought the elves left England in the Dymchurch Flit."

"What of it? There are other Englands—so many, in fact, that they are beyond counting. Nay, somewhere there will ever be a Sherwood, and elves and merry men to fill it."

Matt grinned. "Comforting to know—especially now."

"Aye, now." Sir Guy came up to them, wearing a jaunty grin and an elfin shoulder ornament. "Night approaches and, with it, the assault of sorcery. Will it please you to come watch their feints and spells? Then, on the morrow, we can plot their overthrow."

Matt's blood turned cold, but he nodded, tried to grin, and followed Sir Guy toward the battlements. Marian accompanied them—and, after five paces, Matt realized Robin Hood had joined her.

Now that the fuss of arrival was over, he had time to take a longer and more thorough look about him.

The place was a mess. The reek that had been nudging at his consciousness all along finally sank in—maybe it was the relatively clean air at the top of the stairs that made him realize how badly the courtyard stank. Over against the juncture of curtain wall and keep, he saw a maze of crosses, cobbled out of scraps of lumber and not even painted. Bodies lay wrapped in shrouds, piled up along the edges of the little cemetery—they had run out of burial room.

Looking at the faces of the sentries around him, Matt realized that what he had mistaken for grim purpose was at least partly malnutrition. They weren't starving, but they were very lean—like Sir Guy himself, Matt now realized; he hadn't just hardened from campaigning. There wasn't an ounce of fat on his bones. His cheeks were hollow with hunger as much as stress, and the circles under his eyes came from vitamin deficiency, not lack of sleep. Though there might have been something of that, too—and, as Matt watched him, he thought the Black Knight's gaiety was a bit forced. Now and then, for just a moment, a grim desperation showed through.

Matt shuddered at the implications. What manner of deviltry was he going to see tonight?

Looking down at the courtyard below, he realized that the masses against the walls were trash dumps. The peasants who moved so silently below were thin as whipcord under their smocks—and filthy. Not that body odor was terribly unusual in medieval society, but they had taken it to new heights here.

Of course. Water from the river or no, they were rationing. Everyone had enough to drink, but they portioned out the baths.

Matt resolved to speak to Sir Guy about it. Lack of sanitation could kill them just as quickly as poor nutrition.

But there wasn't a murmur of protest or of discontent. Matt looked at people stretched almost to the breaking point, and marveled at the grim purpose that kept them moving. He wondered at the events that had brought them here, and if there were a soul in the castle who didn't have a harrowing tale to tell of cruelty and viciousness. Lean as it was, beleaguered as it was, this castle must have seemed a sanctuary to those who had suffered from Gordogrosso—and his imitators.

"This is a dirty war," he muttered.

"Aye." Robin nodded beside him, hard-faced—and Matt was startled; he hadn't realized he had spoken aloud.

"It is indeed," Sir Guy agreed, "and no quarter is given, or asked for."

Matt shrugged. "That was always the way of it, with the army of a sorcerer."

Sir Guy shook his head. "These lice of Ibile are far worse than those forced soldiers we fought in Merovence, Sir Matthew. There, the greater number of the soldiers were impressed into service and would take any chance to escape their own ranks. Here, though, even the lowliest soldier is thoroughly and completely dedicated to evil, in the anticipation of the power and preferment his lord may grant him. There's not a one of our besiegers but wishes to be here, not a one that would not delight to see us expire in torment."

Matt turned to look out at the enemy, surrounding them for as far to each side as he could see, and half a mile deep. The sun had set, and the dusk was hurrying on toward night. A strange, growling sound, half mutter and half chant, was rising from the churning mass before him.

Suddenly, a crimson ball shot up from the circling army, arcing toward the castle. A half-dozen others followed it, all along the walls.

"It begins," Sir Guy said grimly.

Surprisingly, Alisande did sleep, though her slumber was interrupted. First had come the attack of the fire snakes, but they were gone by the time she came out of her tent; Sauvignon, prompted by the apprentice wizard they had brought along, had simply told the men to throw snowballs. There followed the plague of rats, to be scared off by the young wizard's quick summoning of a hundred terriers. Finally, near dawn, Alisande was up, feeling moderately rested, and she sent Sauvignon back to bed just before she had to greet the flaming skeletons that came stalking up over the lip of the plateau. The snowballs worked again, of course, and the bones stayed scattered, but it did take her a little while to overcome her footmen's terror enough to get them all to pitch in.

And their yelling woke the sleepers again. That was the bad part.

So, all in all, it was a rather creaky army that finally greeted the sun that morning. Alisande paced through the camp, eyeing her soldiers like a worried mother, and murmured to Sauvignon, "Perhaps we should bid them sleep this day, then watch through the night."

"They would then be weary in the morning," the young nobleman pointed out, and a grizzled veteran looked up to agree. " 'Tis true, Majesty. Lead us out against them, that we may send them packing. 'Tis the only road to a sound night's sleep for us, now."

"You have the right of it, Sergeant." Alisande sighed and turned to give the orders to pack up.

CHAPTER 19

The Siege Perilous

Matt nodded. "Your wizards are ready to quench those fireballs, aren't they?

"Our wizards all are dead," Sir Guy said, his voice flat. "The last of them, a monk, died yestereen when an evil spell overcame his ward, in a moment of distraction. 'Twas a foul thing, a liquid that burned—as are these, I doubt not. There was little enough left of him to stack up with the dead. Now we are left without benefit of clergy—for he was also our last priest, and though there are two nuns left us, they cannot consecrate the Host, nor say Mass."

"Best argument I ever heard for female ordination." Matt stared at the crimson globes, watching them arc closer, then realized he was hearing a voice chanting a low, sonorous Latin to his left. He looked up, startled—and saw Tuck, his hands folded in prayer, his eyes on the crimson globes.

"Praise Heaven!" Sir Guy cried. "You have brought a friar! But ward him, wizard—it was such a globe as one of these that burned our monk to death!"

Matt jolted out of his trance, his mind kicking into overdrive. A liquid that burned? An acid, or a base—or some magical thing that was neither! He readied an all-purpose spell against fire.

Tuck shouted the last phrase aloud, hands snapping out, spread wide—and Matt realized he'd been reciting the Dies Irae. What good could *that* do?

One of the globes veered toward them, then suddenly puckered

and gushed, like a bubble of water pricked, the surface tension that
was holding it suddenly gone. Liquid fire ran from it, cascading down
over the battlements.

Naphtha! Matt thought. It had to be a petroleum derivative—one
of the sorcerers had gotten hold of the formula for Greek fire. But
even as he was starting to chant the counterspell, he saw the fire arc
away, running over an invisible curve to course down the outer battlements. For a moment, it masked their sight; then it was gone.
Matt glanced quickly along the battlements and saw that the other
streams of fire had similarly been shed without hurting anyone. He
whirled to Tuck, incredulous.

"I asked Him to shield us," Tuck explained, "and He did."

"You're a wizard!" Matt pointed the accusing finger.

Tuck shrank in on himself, shaking his head. "Only a friar, Lord
Matthew—only a poor, humble sinner of a friar. Nay, I can pray, but
not conjure."

There was no time to debate the topic, for roaring filled the night.
Whirling, Matt sprang to the crenels and saw a semicircle of lions ad-
vancing on the castle. But what lions! Their manes were fire, and
their teeth glinted like daggers. Their tails were tipped with stings,
and their coats glowed with an unwholesome radioactive sheen.

"Hell lions!" Sir Guy cried. "We can do naught till they come
nigh—but we can be ready! Cold water, men of mine!"

"'Tis boiling, Sir Guy." A footman pointed at a huge cauldron, suspended over the holes beneath the outslung crenels.

"It'll do as well as anything," Matt assured him—and became
aware that Tuck was chanting again. He glanced at the friar, then
turned to see what would happen to the lions—and saw greenish-
blue streaks stabbing downward toward the battlements. "What in
Hell . . . ?"

"From it, rather!" Sir Guy snapped. "Firedrakes! Shield men! Ward
the friar!"

"Nay!" Tuck broke off his chant, lugging out a broadsword. "If
there are enemies to fight, then in the name of all that is right and
good, I—"

"You must wield magic!" Sir Guy cried, his voice hoarse with anx-
iety. "Others can wield sword and shield, friar, but only you and the
Lord Wizard can protect us from ill sorcery!"

Tuck's hand fell nerveless from his hilt. "You are right. In my pride
and lust for a fray, I would have cast away our chances. Nay,
then . . ." And he began to chant his Latin verse again.

But Matt hadn't been terribly aware of what had been going on; all his attention had been focused on the firedrakes—or rather, the grotesque parodies of firedrakes, their snouts wrinkled like prunes, their teeth dripping venom, their wings swept back in a delta shape, their tails like scorpions'. Matt glared at them and chanted a verse designed to change them into ducks—when suddenly, Stegoman swept into the sky with a roar like a jetliner taking off. Flame stabbed out fifteen feet ahead of him. Wherever it touched a firedrake, the creature exploded. Matt could only think of matter and antimatter, good colliding with evil—until he could also think of the enemy archers, and the evil enchantments that must be on some of their arrows. "Stegoman, no! You're a sitting duck!"

The dragon must have heard him, because he began to weave across the sky as if he were drunken again. Matt couldn't see the arrows and bolts of the enemy; he could only try to shield his friend . . .

And Narlh? Matt ducked a quick glance back at the other side of the castle and saw a much smaller jet of flame sweeping the skies there, weaving in imitation of Stegoman's broken-sky flying.

Two to protect! Matt shouted out,

> ". . . take arms against
> The slings and arrows of outrageous fortune . . .
> And by opposing, end them! They shall
> Be set at naught, so we importune!"

He couldn't see the results—except that his two flaming idiots stayed in the air. If either of them were to fall, he would have failed.

Then he heard a change in the roaring from below—a note of outrage. He leaped to the battlements and peered down.

The lions had made it halfway to the walls—the enemy soldiers had pulled well back, leaving each beast an avenue to prowl. But now, suddenly, they were confronted with huge, bulbous beasts twice their size, apparitions with four legs like sections of tree trunks, huge bodies, and heads with huge, clamshell mouths surmounted by snouts that aimed at the lions and sprayed, each body squeezing smaller as the fluid gushed out. The jets of water washed over the hell lions from nose to tail, exploding into steam—but taking the lions with them. Even as they sublimed into nothingness, though, each cat sprang at its pachyderm nemesis, and the two beasts annihilated each other in a blast of steam.

Matt took a quick glance back at the friar, who was watching the results of his work as avidly as Matt. So he knew nothing about wizardry—sure! Only enough to pair opposite elements against each other—the fire lions opposed by the hippopotami, the "water horses" of Africa.

But it was his turn for the next magic offensive. He was scanning the field, wary for monsters, when the infantrymen along the wall let up a shout. Ladder tips slammed against the walls, and enemy soldiers were scurrying up even as the ladders landed. The pikemen bellowed their war cry and lit into the attackers—even as a malvoisin materialized out of the darkness and began to spew armored and half-armored men onto the wall.

With a shout, Sir Guy leaped at the enemy knights—and Tuck gave in to temptation and hauled out his broadsword, howling with heathen glee as he pounced on the grinning, gloating invaders. They saw him coming, huge sword windmilling, and they lost their grins— even as pikes pushed their ladders away and back, crashing down with their loads of soldiers crushed into the earth. But the men-at-arms hewed away, chopping off heads and stabbing through breasts, kicking the wounded and dying off their walls without the slightest compunction. They had fought this siege too long to have anything of pity left.

All, that is, except Tuck. He staggered back against the tower wall, burying his face in his hands and moaning, "Lord forgive me! I have slain evil men unshriven of their sins!"

The soldiers stared, stricken, unable to cope with a priest overcome with remorse.

Matt, however, had a more realistic view of the clergy. He stepped up to clap Tuck on the shoulder. "If you had given them the chance, they would have used it to stab you through the liver! Christ never said to let your enemies kill the people you were protecting! Buck up, shepherd, and guard your flock!"

Tuck looked up, amazed, his guilt evaporating on the spot. "Why, 'tis even as you say! How unmanly of me, to give way to remorse unmerited!"

He was bleeding from at least three wounds, Matt noticed, but none of them looked serious. "Just resist the temptation for hand-to-hand combat, okay? It's only you and me, countering those enemy sorcerers!"

"Aye. Aye, even so." Tuck heaved at his sword belt, settling his huge belly more firmly in place, and turned toward the battlements.

"They come!" a sentry shouted. "They come still, by their hundreds!"

"Why, aim and loose, man!" one of the knights cried.

"We have so few arrows!"

Tuck looked up, then bawled, "Robin! Little John!"

"Robin guards the north wall, and Little John the south," the tall, red-clad man said, stepping forward. "You shall have to manage with me, friar!"

Tuck relaxed, smiling. "Then all is well, Will Scarlet! Come, send your twoscore archers to prickle these invaders."

"Up and loose!" Will Scarlet bawled, and he leaped up to a crenel to begin suiting action to word. Matt spared a quick glance at the ground below, watching charging enemy soldiers fall flat on their faces, twenty-five at a time—then suddenly realized that Tuck was chanting again. He scanned the sky quickly, aware that he'd slacked off on his own duties, turning in place for a 360-degree survey, since Tuck was looking downward. He had almost decided everything was clear, in fact had looked down at the courtyard to see Narlh and Stegoman having arrows pulled from their wings—then suddenly looked back up at the sky. Yes, it was! The moon was getting bigger!

Not the moon, he realized—it was high in the sky; could the night really be half over? This other crescent, then, must be something sorcerous—and now he saw three more, one coming from each point of the compass, swinging closer and closer—

Giant scimitars! He didn't need to know if anything was swinging them; he chanted,

> "There is hissing like the serpent's,
>   From the blade so widely feared,
> It whirls down through the darkness,
>   But is caught in unseen weird,
> And strikes a hidden, viewless shield
>   Its counter and its curse,
> Like a strong gong groaning as it shivers
>   blades to burst!"

Screams echoed all about him. He whirled to see a huge blade sweeping the battlements behind him—and its point was chopping straight at him! He yelped, leaped back, stumbled—and fell just far enough so that the blade swept over him.

Then it shivered, and all the battlements quivered with the shock of a sound wave so low that no one could hear it, from a gargantuan collision between the crescent and its invisible opposite. A vibration sprang up all along its length, shivering it into a million fragments that faded and disappeared before they even landed on the stone.

Men were groaning, limbs cut off; other men were helping them, slipping in the sheen of blood that slicked the stone in the scimitar's wake. Matt saw a few dead and cursed himself for his lack of vigilance—then realized that he was seeing it all through a red film. He pulled out a kerchief and wiped his forehead, and the sheen disappeared. He became aware of a dull ache, knew that it would hurt horribly tomorrow—but just kept wiping it for now, as he paced the battlements, trying to see what else to do.

A huge monster was roaring and thrashing about on the ground below, a giant stake driven through it, holding it to the ground.

Matt turned away before his stomach flipped. He didn't know how Tuck had managed that one, and he didn't want to.

Then he realized he was hearing the flapping of leathery wings.

Not unusual, considering the enemy—but outside the rules, if it was a genuine devil.

No, it wasn't. It was a horde of huge bats, stooping to claw at the soldiers' chests, needle teeth reaching for their necks. Below there was shouting, and ladders thudded against stone—but the defenders were screaming, flailing at the flying rats, trying to drive them off. They clung, though, and their teeth probed.

One slammed into Matt's chest. Fire erupted across his pectorals as claws dug in, and a foul snout reached for his jugular.

Matt jammed an arm in the way and felt the teeth sink in, but his throat was safe. He tried to ignore the pain, the shifting claws as the monster tried to work its way around his arm, and shouted,

> "Eye to eye, and head to head,
> (Woe betide thee, bat!)
> This shall end when one is dead.
> (Go and hide thee, bat!)
> Darts of wood, match each to each!
> Fly like arrows, hearts to reach!
> Impale the undead flying leech!
> (Never rise thee, bat!)"

Skewers suddenly filled the air, stabbing through the bats' chests and into their hearts. Jaws gaped wide in screams the men couldn't hear, and the flying vermin fell backward, losing their holds and crumpling in death. Matt kicked his attacker out of the way, mopping at two more wounds, but scanning the sky frantically. Will Scarlet and his twoscore were shooting down along the ladders, knocking over invading soldiers almost as fast as they could clamber onto the rungs, and the pikemen were dealing with the few who came near the tops. Tuck was chanting again, but Matt didn't even want to know what it was about.

Sir Guy reeled up beside him, leaning back against the wall and panting, "We must find some way to take the offensive."

"Name it!" Puck appeared on his shoulder. "Only bid me offend them, and I shall have them thinking their tales of woe and tails indeed!"

"A most excellent notion." Sir Guy grinned. "And whiles you are about it, see that those tails are pulled, and pinched, and stepped on at every turn."

"Turn?" Puck cried. "Why, let us have them turn and twine about their owners' legs!"

"Well thought! See to it!"

The elf disappeared, but the spark flared in his place. "Have you no new task for me?" the humming voice demanded.

Matt was fed up with the enemy—he was running very low on the milk of human compassion and he'd only been fighting for half a night! "Freeze their armor."

The Demon hummed in astonishment. "Freeze . . . ? But they will scream with the chill and tear off their plate! What gain then?"

"Plenty, if you freeze it so fast it shrinks!"

"That will choke off their circulation! Their limbs will swell! Their breastplates will crush their ribs! Their helmets—"

"Have you seen what they've been trying to do here? Just make it fast, and it'll be relatively merciful."

"They shall scarce know what hit them," the spark promised, and disappeared.

Sir Guy nodded. "It is merited."

A sudden shocked howling broke out below, and all around the castle. Puck appeared again. "'Tis done; like Rover, they chase their latter ends."

"In more ways than one," Matt muttered.

"What say?"

"What matter?" Sir Guy countered. "Can you befuddle their sorcerers, Robin?"

A slow grin spread across the elf's face. "Make them think one another are Matthew and the friar? Or that their commander's tent is the castle? Aye."

"Those," Sir Guy agreed, "but I had more in mind having their thoughts so mixed that, when they wish to summon a demon, they speak of a cabbage!"

"I know just the place," Puck crowed, "within their brains! Nay, they'll speak of chard when they wish a flame!" He was gone.

"You sure that won't get us in worse trouble than we're in?" Matt said nervously.

Carrots began to rain on the battlements.

"What sorcery is this?" Tuck called, amazed.

"Evil gone wrong," Sir Guy called back. "I fear the Puck cannot so far transform it as to make evil impulses yield good—yet he has tried valiantly."

"Masterstoke," Matt muttered. "Should have thought of it."

Geysers erupted all along the castle wall, heaving huge foaming lances of water against the stone. Where it struck, the char left by past fireballs disappeared.

"What now?" Tuck cried.

"Soap and water, I think," Matt called back. "I'll bet the enemy was trying for acid."

A sound of crunches, with screams quickly cut off, approached from the north, coming nearer and nearer. It peaked right opposite them, then stopped.

The dancing spark appeared again. "All who wore armor are dead—or have disrobed and now are clad only in gambesons. What next would you, Wizard?"

"A quantum black hole!" Matt looked up slowly, a grin spreading over his face.

"Are you daft?" the spark keened. "That was a notion guessed at, but proven false! There are none such!"

"You mean you can't make one?"

The spark was still for a second; then Max said, "'Twill not be easy, for 'tis truly matter organized quite highly—yet 'tis the product of entropy, and yields chaos within its event horizon. Aye, I can craft it."

"Then do—and drag it around the battlefield."

"'Twill throw them into turmoil!" Max sang. "Ah, I have missed you, Wizard!" And he blinked out.

"What wizardry is this?" Tuck called out.

"Only a little misplaced cosmology," Matt called back. He stepped over to the crenels to watch the show.

For a minute or two, nothing happened. Then a woeful shout went up as a spark of light danced through the army, pulling soldiers together into its wake to slam into the ones coming from the other side. They stumbled, they fell, they were dragged over the ground, but nothing could stop them. The soldiers nearest the wake were stretched and crushed unmercifully, as though by unseen hands. They grabbed at tent pegs and hitching posts, but the pegs and posts were wrenched out of the ground and came tumbling along with them—as did the tripods from the camp fires, and the kettles, and any loose armor or weapons, all jumbled together with a huge clash and clatter—but above it all rose the shouting and moaning of dread, that went on and on as other voices took it up. The line of devastation, a hundred feet wide, began to curve as it reached the outer edge of the besiegers' army, turning back to cut another swath. A sorcerer rose up to bar its way, wand swirling, and Matt hauled out his own wand, beginning to chant—but before he could finish, the sorcerer's head snapped back, as though he'd been flung away. At the same moment, his feet surged forward. Then, suddenly, his body split straight down the middle from top to toe. Matt had a momentary sight of it; then tumbling men and material blocked the sight from him.

He was very glad.

A huge cabbage appeared in front of the spark. It, too, was sliced neatly through.

"What was *that*?" Sir Guy asked, wide-eyed.

"An enemy sorcerer trying to put some kind of demon in Max's way," Matt answered. "True to Puck's word, he said 'cabbage' when he meant 'devil.' Artificial encoding error."

A huge asparagus towered up in Max's path. It fell a moment later, like a felled redwood.

"If naught else," Friar Tuck said, "we'll eat vegetable broth enough when this is done."

Two giant knights suddenly appeared, twenty feet tall, barring the path. A second later, they crashed together and were buried under an avalanche of tumbling men.

"There is a strong sorcerer near," Friar Tuck noted. "He did not completely miss his mark."

"Then we'd better give him a little more to worry about." Matt weighed the wand in his hand, shrugged, and whipped it overhand to point eastward.

> "When the wind is in the east,
> 'Tis neither good for man nor beast."

He flourished the wand overhand and snapped it down toward the north.

> "When the wind is in the north,
> The skilful fisher goes not forth."

Then he swung the wand to each of the other two points of the compass as he recited:

> "When the wind is in the south,
> It blows the bait in the fish's mouth.
> When the wind is in the west,
> Then 'tis at the very best."

Then, finally, he swung the wand around in a great circle, chanting,

> "When all winds blow in unison,
> Our foes do flee our benison!

"Bless them, Tuck!" he shouted.

A look of delight broke over the friar's face. "Why, certes! What could weaken a foe of evil, so much as a blessing?" He turned to face the camp, sketching the Sign of the Cross in the air, and began to chant in Latin, his face softening, turning wistful, almost fond. Matt realized that, no matter how much evil the enemy had done, there was still room in this huge friar's heart to forgive, to understand, for they were God's handiwork, and he believed to the core of his soul that they were redeemable.

Sir Guy frowned. "What use were these invocations?"

But Friar Tuck caught his shoulder, eyes alight, grinning. "Hark! Do you not hear?"

Sir Guy bent his head, listening carefully.

Faintly at first, then louder and louder, a whistling came toward them, building into a howl. Sleeves and robes began to stir, then to whip in the wind.

"Grab something solid!" Matt yelled, and the word was relayed all along the battlements. Knights and men-at-arms grabbed at crenels, arrow loops, doorways—and just in time, before the storm hit.

It was a hurricane. It was a whirlwind. It was a tornado, and the castle was in the center. The wind screamed around the walls, tearing at the stone and howling in frustration. It careened off looking for less-guarded targets—and found the enemy's camp. There, it roared in glee, plucking up tents and horses and men and juggling them with a fine disregard for class or dignity.

But only outside.

Along the ramparts, the wind whipped and tugged at clothes and men—but only in passing, only as an afterthought—and within the courtyard, there wasn't even a breeze, though men and women crouched in hiding, fearful of the tempest.

Matt let it run, fifteen minutes, an hour, while he and Friar Tuck took turns, one watching for attempts at retaliation while the other tried to explain things to Sir Guy. But there was no reaction—neither from the sorcerers, who were too busy trying to cope with both the black hole and the wind, nor from Sir Guy, who could only understand the effects of the magic and was beginning to be bored with the causes.

Then, finally, as the sky lightened with false dawn, Matt called out,

> "A rushing noise he had not heard of late,
> A rushing sound of wind, and stream, and
>   flame,
> In short, a roar of things extremely great,
> Which would have made aught save a saint
>   exclaim—
> And when the tumult dwindled to a calm,
> I left him practicing the Hundredth Psalm."

As suddenly as they had come, the four winds sped away. The moaning faded off into the distance, like an express train leaving. Trees on the horizon, just barely visible in the predawn light, whipped about crazily for a minute or two, then were still.

They listened. The only sound from outside the walls was a low and constant moaning. They stepped up to the crenels and the arrow slits to look out—and saw a scene of utter devastation, broken tents and overturned carts, dead and wounded in winnows showing Max's trail—and the remnants of the Army of Evil, just pulling themselves together as they set out toward the east in a ragged double column.

The shouts of victory began along Matt's wall and spread all around the battlements, then down into the courtyard. Men and women laughed and shouted for joy, hugging one another and dancing—and, palely seen in the dawn light, a ghost appeared atop the gate house, now brighter, now dimmer. From what they could tell when he was visible, he was dancing a jig.

"Wizard," said the Demon, suddenly appearing before him, "shall we attempt some other device to confound the enemy?"

"Uh, no," Matt said. "I think that'll be enough for the moment."

CHAPTER 20

Guerrillas in the Mist

Sir Guy kept sentries posted, and a complement of men-at-arms within the castle, in case the rout had really been a ruse. But he threw open the castle gates and lowered the drawbridge, and the peasants streamed out to bring in all the provisions the king's army had left behind—salted meat, hardtack, grain, and even some fresh meat and fruits that the officers and sorcerers had kept for themselves. Squadrons of soldiers fanned out to both sides of the looting party, keeping pace with them to guard against any sudden reappearance by the besiegers—but the foraging went smoothly.

Not that Matt was up to participating. His head hurt, his chest hurt, and his arm hurt. More accurately, it felt as if slow fire streaked his scalp and his arm, while he was having a double heart attack. He gritted his teeth against the pain. Unfortunately, this made it very hard to chant a healing spell.

Friar Tuck saw and, in spite of his own wounds, tottered over to lay a reassuring hand on Matt's shoulder—gently, of course. "Be of good heart, Lord Wizard," he gasped. "I'll have us hale and sound directly." He sat down beside Matt, muttering in Latin.

Matt's head stopped hurting.

He looked up at the rotund priest, amazed. Of course, it *could* be prayer—and in this universe, the power of prayer could be greater than antibiotics were in his home world, maybe much greater. But some-

how, Matt didn't think that was what the friar was doing. Knowingly
or not, Tuck was working magic—and Matt suspected it was knowingly. Unfortunately, he didn't know enough Latin to be sure.

Either way, his arm had stopped hurting, and his chest. He yanked
up his sleeve and watched as the wounds closed, then smoothed as
neatly as if they had never been there. Matt found himself wondering
if they had.

Then he bent his arm, and decided they'd been real. He'd have to
use that arm delicately for an hour or two—and take shallow breaths.

He glanced at Tuck. The color had returned to the friar's face, and
he was breathing more easily. "Praise Heaven!" He sighed. "We are
well again."

Matt glanced out over the courtyard and saw a few men picking
themselves up, looking amazed and making the Sign of the Cross.
Apparently Tuck's spell had been broadcast; Matt wondered how
many of the enemy's wounded the friar had healed, too. That wasn't
so good—they could have hundreds more enemies to fight, all over
again . . .

He leaped up, winced, and climbed up to the battlements—stiffly,
but without much more than a set of aches. He looked out over the
slope and saw all the enemy wounded still lying where they lay, calling out for help.

"I can only aid those who are in a state of Grace, or wish to be."

Matt turned around to see that Friar Tuck had come up behind
him. "I should think," he said slowly, "that they're in great shape to
realize the error of their ways."

"Some, no doubt—mayhap most, now that they are removed from
the influence of their army's sorcerer."

"Or now that he has removed himself from them," Matt demurred.

"Even so. But there be those in whom hatred for all things good
and Godly has grown so strong that they will not even now repent."

That struck a false note. Matt looked at him narrowly. "Not trying
to come up with excuses ahead of time, are you?"

"Never!" Tuck looked up at him in indignation.

"Sorry, I didn't really mean it," Matt said quickly. "Just habit. I
owe you an awful lot of thanks, Friar."

"Then aid me with these enemy wounded." Tuck turned away.
"Come with me; I must visit the sick."

Matt frowned, wondering why the friar wanted him along. Then he
remembered that he could heal the bodies as soon as Tuck had healed
the soul, and followed after.

They joined the soldiers who were collecting fallen weapons and stray arrows. They also gathered up the extra crossbow bolts and other munitions that had been stored away, plus any hardware the army had left in its flight. Then they filed back into the castle, much more slowly than they had gone out, for Friar Tuck checked every load to be sure that nothing under an evil spell was being brought back into the castle. A few items did indeed grate on him, apparently having been put to some rather gruesome uses; Tuck even drew away, repulsed, by one or two. The soldiers threw them back among their dead owners. The incident set Matt to thinking of Trojan horses, and being very glad Friar Tuck was there.

The checking would have been even slower if Puck hadn't been screening the peasants before they got to the friar. He rode unseen within Sir Guy's helmet, murmuring to him as he walked among the peasants and soldiers. Ostensibly, the Black Knight was keeping up morale that had never been higher, congratulating the defenders and thanking them for their loyalty and faithfulness.

Matt, however, had adamantly refused to help out. He knew his own limitations and had no illusions about the amount of goodness in his soul. He knew himself to be secretly vengeful, with a repressed streak of cruelty. It never occurred to him that Tuck might have had similar failings, kept in check only by stern self-control. Matt had not quite yet realized that morality is not an inborn trait and does not come naturally.

"We can't stay here, though," he told Sir Guy, when all the peasants and soldiers were back in, and the gates had been closed with the drawbridge up. "We're sitting ducks."

Sir Guy nodded. "It was needful to seek refuge within this castle when the Army of Evil was hot on our heels; but now that they are gone, we may sally forth once more and carry the battle to them."

Matt felt cold inside at the thought of deliberately confronting that army again—but he nodded anyway. "That's what we came here to do, isn't it? Besides, if we let our soldiers disperse and go back to their homes, they'll be overwhelmed by local sorcerers and their henchmen."

"In unity there is strength," Sir Guy agreed, "though there is no safety for good folk in this land—and none for evil folk, either, if they only knew it."

"Yes. It's just a question of how soon the wolves will turn on each other, isn't it?"

"Not whiles we do move, I fear. Nay, we must band together, no matter where we go. As an army, we have at least some chance of survival."

Matt didn't bother mentioning that, in the position they were in, survival depended on winning. It went without saying.

So they gave everyone a chance to catch up on eating and sleeping—though they still rationed the food, at Matt's insistence; he knew what gorging could do to people who'd been on a bare subsistence diet for so long. Between snoozes, the peasants packed food, and the soldiers packed weapons—Sir Guy made it very clear that personal possessions would have to stay behind.

So it was a long triple file that flowed out across the drawbridge, in the early morning light two days later—an inner file of peasants, many driving carts filled with provisions, with soldiers pacing them on either side. Robin and his band led the way, right behind Sir Guy and Matt.

"So why don't I get to carry the knight?" Narlh growled. "Too low-class, huh?"

"Now, Narlh, you know 'tis naught of the sort," Yverne soothed him. " 'Tis only that Sir Guy is accustomed to the dragon—and I most surely am not." She shuddered.

Narlh immediately softened. "Oh, all right, lady. Yeah, you need to ride just as much as any of the other women—and I wouldn't trust you to that big lunk of lizard. And I suppose the knight shouldn't do much walking, in all that tin he's wearing."

"It would overtax him sorely," Yverne agreed.

Matt reflected that they were in the right country for overtaxing.

The day was bright and clear when they set out—but it clouded up fast. About noon, with the clouds lowering about them, Matt began to feel a thickening in the air—not really the atmosphere, of course, but his own personal ambiance. He stepped over next to Stegoman and called upward toward the knight. "Sir Guy?"

"Aye, Lord Wizard?"

"I'm feeling magic thickening about me. Not much, yet, you understand, just the first traces."

The knight frowned and glanced back at Friar Tuck. The clergyman was marching along with a strained face. "Our holy man must sense it, too," Sir Guy said. "He is telling his beads."

Matt looked behind, startled. Sure enough, Friar Tuck had hauled out a rosary large enough to qualify as a minor weapon and was mumbling the old, simple prayers as he fingered the beads.

"What ill do our sorcerous enemies brew for us?" the Black Knight demanded.

Matt shook his head. "I don't know—too early to tell. But tell everybody to brace themselves for an attack."

"Whence could it come?" Sir Guy waved an arm at the wide plain all about them. The land stretched away to the horizon, golden with ripening grain—except for the swath of waste where the fleeing army had trampled it. They were marching down the middle of that swath, for it spread twenty yards on either side of the road, reminding Matt that they were marching toward their enemy—who might have pulled his men together by now. The notion didn't exactly improve Matt's state of mind.

Still, Sir Guy had a point. How could there be an ambush in the middle of a plain that made Kansas look hilly? Where would the ambushers hide?

The answer to his question came right after lunch. The army had rested and eaten, packed up the leftovers, and set forth again—but as they marched, the clouds lowered farther and farther, until they touched the earth. The feeling of magic was as thick as the humidity.

"Faugh!" Yverne's voice called from ahead. "What stench is this!"

" 'Tis truly appalling," Maid Marian's voice agreed from farther off. "What evil mist has risen about us?"

"It's the work of sorcerers, whatever it is," Matt called back.

"Are they nearby?" Sir Guy's voice demanded.

"I doubt it," Matt called back. "They're probably still with their army. They can hex us quite easily from there, I assure you—especially since they've already been over this bit of terrain, and we haven't."

"Anything could hide in this fog!" Sir Guy growled.

"You can say that again," Matt called back. "In fact, say anything! Just keep talking, or I won't be able to tell where you are."

"Halt!" the Black Knight cried, and Stegoman slowed and stopped. Matt fumbled toward them, felt a scaly hide under his hand, then saw the slab of Stegoman's side loom out of the mist—and, above, some dark object that must be Sir Guy. "We cannot march amid such blindness," the knight called down. "Hold to the dragon's tail, Lord Matthew, and bid another hold to you. Then, mayhap, we can wend our way to light and safety."

"Not too much wending," Matt cautioned. "We could get trapped going around in a circle forever."

"Thou hast the right of it," Stegoman agreed. "Nay, are we marching west still? Or have we turned already?"

"I'll find out," Narlh's voice said. "Lady, if you would climb down for a few minutes?"

"Surely." There was the slithering sound of cloth against scales. "But what mean you to do, good monster?"

"There's the wizard, over there. Say something, Wizard!"

"Right over here, Yverne," Matt called. "That's right, here—take my hand . . ."

Yverne caught his fingers and stepped close to him with a shudder. "I had thought myself lost, even in the space of two strides!"

"You could have been," Matt assured her. "But back to your first question—Narlh, what're you trying—"

Wings thundered as huge feet pounded away, then ceased.

"Alley!" Matt swore, not daring to use the first word in Ibile. "He's flying!"

"He shall lose himself!" Stegoman cried. "Knight, dismount—or ride high!"

"What do you mean to do!" Sir Guy cried—but he slid to the ground anyway, then was almost bowled over in the back-blast from Stegoman's wings as the dragon leaped into the sky.

"Watch out!" Narlh's voice thundered from overhead. "Where do you think you're going, you plate-nosed platypus?"

"To find thee!" Stegoman rumbled, his voice dwindling. "Nay, come down! Thou'lt be lost forever in this fog!"

"There's got to be a top to it, somewh— Ow! Get off my back!"

"I am not on it, thou dunderheaded drake! Thou hast e'en now collided with mine!"

"Yeah, and those fins hurt, too! What're *you* doing flying upside down?"

"Upside down?" Stegoman cried, outraged. "Why, thou half-brained half hawk, I am an upright dragon in every sense of the term! 'Tis thou who art inverted!"

"Look, lay off the fancy language and tell me why you're flying with your back to the earth!"

"I am not!" Stegoman howled. " 'Tis thou who dost roll as thou dost fly!"

"Well, sheer off, then! I'm going to find the top of this fog if it kills me!"

"Nay!" Stegoman cried in a panic. "We have need of thee! Thou art too good a monster to squander thy life so untimely!"

There was no answer, except for a high, long, fading screech, as of a falcon stooping.

"He has gone!" Stegoman's voice grew louder. "Nay, Sir Knight, call out to me, so that I may land not too far from thee!"

"Back, everyone!" Sir Guy called. "Back, but stay linked by touch! Give the dragon room to land!"

"I hear thee!" Stegoman's voice boomed out overhead. "Keep thy call sounding!"

"Come nigh!" Sir Guy called. "Come hither! We await you! Come, kindly dragon! Lower thy great bulk to us again, that we might—"

His voice was drowned out by a huge thundering of wing beats that abruptly stilled. Matt strained to see, worried that his friend might have crashed . . .

"I am landed," Stegoman's voice boomed out. "Come nigh me, friends!"

They all started to move, but Matt called, "Wait! We might miss you in the fog! Give us a light!"

Stegoman roared, and Matt saw a dim orange glow ahead and to his right. He slogged over to it, picking up Sir Guy on the way and pulling Yverne at full reach behind him. He was careful to note just how far he was angling away from his former direction of travel. Then he felt Stegoman's scales under his hand, and called out, "We're here!"

The roaring stopped, and he heard Yverne weeping softly behind him. Sir Guy said, "Nay, fear not, maiden. You know the dragon to be a good friend and true. His roar is fearsome, aye, but only for our enemies, not for us."

"You are a great comfort, Sir Knight!" Yverne said, and there was a quality to her voice that kindled jealousy within Matt. "I am assured. But what of our friend the dracogriff?"

"Dumb beast," Stegoman growled. "Flew away. Up high. Couldn't finda topsh ofa cloudzh, and izh shtill tryin'."

Matt looked up, alarmed. He tried to stall it, and called, "You need to turn around, Stegoman! We're going the other way."

"How y' know?" But Stegoman slewed around toward Matt, mumbling and looking surly.

Matt frowned. "How's that again?"

"I shaid, shtupid shorsherer who triezh to blind ush all sho he c'n steal our blood," Stegoman grumbled.

Matt felt a chill that had nothing to do with the weather. He would have recognized that slurring anywhere! Stegoman was drunk again.

But how? On what? Had Matt's cure for his hatchling trauma worn off somehow? Or been counteracted?

Or . . .

"Vile shtuff musht be shtraight from Hell," Stegoman muttered.

"Even so." Sir Guy frowned. "Is't not made by a demon, Sir Matthew?"

"You bet it is!" Now Matt recognized that vile smell—it was charred rum! "Uh, come on, Stegoman. We've got to get out of this fog, before we suffocate."

"Ohh, awright." The dragon lifted his head. "Uh . . . whish way izh out?"

"*That* way!" Matt pointed straight ahead with total conviction. "I was careful to keep facing the same way I had been as I angled over toward you! Just turn around and head that way! We'll be right on your tail!"

" 'Sh not long enough for all of you." Stegoman lumbered around, headed roughly the way Matt was pointing, and started waddling.

Matt laid a hand on the dragon's tail and stumbled after, yanking on Yverne's hand.

Sir Guy strode along beside him, leaning over to set his helmet near Matt's ear. "Lord Wizard—dare we trust ourselves to a drunken dragon?"

"I think so—he's always had a great sense of direction. But if you think it'll help, you could ask Puck. I mean, this fog is mischief of the first order—if anyone can understand it, it would be him."

"A good thought. Dost'a hear, Puck?"

A diminutive head poked out of the knight's helmet, clambering halfway up on forearms and elbows. It scowled at Matt, squint-eyed, and gave a careful, well-considered hiccup.

Matt felt his blood run cold.

"What dost'a wish, knight?" Puck slurred.

"Canst tell us which way to travel in this mist, Puck?" Sir Guy asked.

"Why, whishever way you wanna go!" Puck's eyes widened, and a slow smile spread across his face. "There izh fog! Id'n it purty? Haven't sheen it in sho long I misht it!"

Sir Guy turned a mournful gaze on Matt. "It would seem even our sprite is not immune."

Matt could only stare while little prickles ran up and down his spine. What kind of a spell did it take to make Puck succumb to the smell of the demon rum?

"Roashted crabzh!" Puck muttered. "Roashted crabsh, floatin' inna bowl!" His grip loosened, and he slid back inside Sir Guy's armor.

"Wizard," Yverne's voice said behind him, "can you not banish this unholy elixir?"

"Well, I can try, I suppose." Matt tried to remember the spell he had used to dispel a fog three years before.

"Western wind, come now to save us!
Restore the breezes you once gave us!"

He felt the magical forces strengthen about him, felt as though he was trying to push his way through a wall of molasses . . .

"Clear this fog that you've allowed!
Rid us of this reeking cloud!"

He was actually surprised when the fog began to lighten.

Surprised, with good reason—the magic field strengthened, in a way that gave him a peculiarly nasty feeling inside, a feeling that reached all the way down to his groin with a painful, sickening wrench. Then the fog thickened again.

"You had some small success, Wizard," Fadecourt noted.

"Small, yes. Then my opposite number, whoever he is, clamped down with a counterspell." Matt turned to Sir Guy. "Gor—uh, the king, that is, has some really powerful sorcerers, doesn't he?"

"He always said so." Sir Guy frowned off into the fog, his feet still moving in time to the dragon's waddling. "Yet an he had some who were so much more powerful than you, surely he would have sent them to the siege we but now broke."

"Yeah, you would think that, wouldn't you?" Matt frowned as though he was only puzzled, but inside, he was hollow with dread. He had a nasty, unpleasant notion that he was opposing the magic of the king himself. "Let's give it another try, though.

"When the moan of the breeze
Echoes through the trees
And the mist lies low on the plain,
From earth and stones
Come boulders' groans
As the heat rises from them again!
And away the fog goes
As the warm breeze blows
In tatters and shreds quite soon,
For the sun's rays quench their holiday,
The end of the night's high noon!"

It must have been his imagination, but he could have sworn a male chorus echoed those last two words. Certainly the chord of magic seemed strained all about him, and for a moment, the mist glowed about them as sun rays broke through the clouds above—then dimmed and vanished, as the evil magic strengthened about him. Matt shook his head. "Too strong for me—and I think it's several sorcerers working in concert, not just one."

"In concert!" Yverne sounded appalled. "Nay, surely it must be the king himself who leads them—for none other can compel sorcerers to meld their powers!"

"I was afraid of that," Matt grunted. "But we're not licked yet. We have one more weapon in our arsenal, anyway." He opened his pouch and saw the glow within. "How about it, Max?"

"Indeed, how?" the Demon sang. "How could I clear this fog for you, Wizard?"

"Precipitate it," Matt said. "Bind the droplets of water together into raindrops."

"And how shall I do that?"

Matt took a deep breath. He had forgotten just how explicit Max wanted his instructions to be. "Reduce the surface tension, so the water vapor will condense into bigger drops."

"No sooner said than done!" the Demon cried.

"Put your hoods up, everybody," Matt called. "Sir Guy, we'd better see about some rust remover."

The air began to clear a little, and Matt felt a few raindrops strike his head. But only a few; they stopped, and the fog thickened about them again.

" 'Tis too much for me," the Demon reported. "Some power resists; a greater force than mine seeks to maintain the surface tension."

Of course, Matt's shiver *could* have been from the weather. He could only think of a few sources of power that could surpass entropy, and only one of them had always tried to cloud men's sight and lead them astray in a world gone murky. "Try heating it! Accelerate the Brownian movement of the water molecules! Make it all evaporate!"

"I shall," Max agreed, and again the fog lightened for a few moments—but thickened again. Max began to jump about, agitated. "Again it thwarts me! Some agency that has greater control over than I has bound it into mist!"

"He exceeds your power, and that of all our allies," Sir Guy said heavily. "In truth, it must be the king himself whose power you encounter, Lord Matthew!"

"I'm afraid you're right." Matt muttered a quick prayer to Saint Iago, his own tap into a high-Power line, then turned back to his friends. "Not much we can do except forge ahead, no matter how slowly, and try to stay together. We'll call out to one another and home in on voices." He boosted his own volume. "Do you think that will work, Robin Hood?"

"We shall essay it," the outlaw leader called back. "Should our good friar join you in leading the way?"

"No—I think we'll be safer with one wizard in each half of the party . . ."

"I am not a wizard!" Tuck said quickly.

"Whatever. We'll all follow Stegoman. Sir Guy, deploy your forces."

"Sir Loring, lead the right flank!" the Black Knight called. "Sir Michael, the left! Sir Dai, lead the center in pursuit of me!"

The knights answered him with a chorus of "ayes." Matt wondered how the other noblemen and knights had come to acknowledge Sir Guy's leadership—not that he doubted it had been earned. They'd had two years to figure out how vital he was. It was no doubt a fascinating, not to say hair-raising story, and Matt intended to hear every word of it—some day, in front of a roaring fire inside a stout castle, without an enemy for miles around.

At the moment, though, he needed to try to get his forces through this mess. "Ready, then? Away!"

"Away, he shayzh!" Stegoman muttered. "Doezh he have to lead the way? Nay! Izh he the one who getsh blamed if we go ashtray? Nay!" But, griping and protesting, he lumbered into motion and began a slow, if constant, movement across the plain.

Matt felt Sir Guy's hand on his shoulder, so he knew his own immediate party was together, linked hand to hand. "Robin Hood! Are you near me?"

But his voice echoed strangely in the fog. "Aye, I am nigh!" Robin's voice called from behind him—then called again, off to his left, "Aye, I am nigh!"

Matt frowned. "You only needed to say it once." He was startled to hear his own voice completely echoed from behind—"Say it once!"

"I spoke but the one time, in truth!" Robin called, but he hadn't quite finished before the words sounded again from Matt's left, then a third time, from his right.

Matt felt the dread creeping higher. "The sorcerer is trying to confuse us by making our voices sound from different directions!"

"Sir Loring!" Sir Guy called. "Do you follow me?"

"You follow me," the voice repeated, from behind and left.

"Follow," it said again, from ahead and to the right.

"Aye, Sir Guy! I follow the sound of your words!" But Sir Loring's voice faded even as he called—then came back, more strongly, from Matt's far side.

"Sir Nigel!" There was a tinge of iron in Sir Guy's tone. "Guide on my voice, and touch hands with me!"

"Guide on my voice," the Black Knight's echo called from his left, and, "Touch hands with me," the same voice called from behind and to the right.

"I come, Sir Guy!" But Sir Nigel's voice faded away, too.

"Sir Dai! Do you march forward double-quick, and link hands with the cyclops!"

"March forward," Sir Guy's echo called from behind, then, "Link hands with the cyclops!" from off to the left.

"I come, Sir Guy!" But even as he called it, Sir Dai's voice faded off to the left—then sounded from the right.

"Robin Hood! Do you hear me?" Matt called in a panic.

"I hear!" Robin's voice called from behind. "I shall summon my men by my horn!" it said from the right.

The horn sounded, and a ragged cheer went up from the men of Sherwood, off to their right, swerving around to the front, then back to the left. Another horn blew from the north, then its echo sounded from the south, then again from the east.

"I just hope his men know which one is the real horn," Matt groaned. "Are your people still together, Robin Hood?"

But this time, only the echoes of his own voice answered him—and, in the distance and fading, the blare of a hunting horn. On the other side, knightly voices called to their men, growing more distant. Steel clanked as the army marched, and the whole plain was filled with its distant susurrus—but all far away, and going farther.

"He has fragmented our army!" Sir Guy groaned. "He has led us away from one another in the fog! Pray Heaven the men of each flank stay together."

"Do," Matt agreed. "Please do. As for us, let's find out who's here. I'm still feeling Stegoman's scales—and that must be your hand I'm holding, Sir Guy, because it's metal. Squeeze the hand you're holding, and tell its owner to say his or her name."

"I am Sir Guy," the knight called. "Say your name when I squeeze your hand!"

"Squeeze not overly hard," quavered a female voice. "I am Yverne. Nay, say your name as I squeeze your hand."

"I am Fadecourt," the cyclops' voice answered.

Matt waited.

No one called.

Finally, he said, "Who's holding your other hand, Fadecourt?"

"I feel no hand upon that arm, Lord Wizard."

"Down to our original group," Matt groaned, "plus yourself, Sir Guy. I see why you stayed in that castle."

"Even as you said, we could not remain there forever," the Black Knight reminded him. "To live is to place oneself at risk, Sir Matthew. We must make that risk as small as possible, and lay protections in case we are beset—yet still is there risk."

"I knew I needed a savings account." Matt sighed. "Well, there's nothing to be done about it now."

"You did not pray while peace lasted?"

"Well, sure, but . . ."

"Then you have a font of strength to draw on—the channel you established between your God and yourself. Go forward boldly, my friend."

"Yeah, sure," Matt muttered, and followed Stegoman, somewhat shaken by the Black Knight's combination of theology and military science.

" 'Boldly,' he shaizh," Stegoman muttered. "Channel, he talksh about. Pretty good, for a man who spendzh all hizh time making noizh with a shword." Then his voice trailed off into ramblings that didn't make much sense, aside from the occasional reference to a foul hatchling hunter and vampires who drained dragons' blood to strengthen their charms. Matt realized there was still a lot of Stegoman's biography he didn't know about. "Anybody have any idea where we are?"

"Aye," Puck's voice slurred. "We wander on a darkling plain, beset by ignorance and confusion."

"Thanks for a summary of the condition of humankind," Matt grunted, then stopped bolt still. "Stegoman! Hold on!"

"Wha' for?" But the dragon ground to a halt.

Matt took a few more steps to catch up, making sure his hand was firmly on the dragon's tail plates. "I just had an idea." He ignored Puck's gasp of amazement and recited,

> "Then to the rolling Heaven itself I cried,
> 'Asking what Lamp had Destiny to guide
> Her little Children stumbling in the Dark?'
> And, 'A blind understanding,' Heaven replied."

It worked. He actually did begin to understand where he was—and the fog began to thin.

"You have done it!" Yverne cried. "You have lifted the fog!"

"Don't celebrate too soon," Matt cautioned, but he was almost limp with relief himself, as he began to be able to see all of Stegoman's bulk, then to make out the dragon's head and even, in front of that, the road, with huge boulders lining each side, a grove of fir trees ahead on their right . . .

And an armored man half as wide as he was tall, with a huge broadsword and an evil grin. "Wise advice," the armored man gloated. "Do not celebrate at all."

"Duke Bruitfort!" Yverne screamed.

Suddenly there were soldiers everywhere, erupting from the rocks and racing up from behind. A squadron of knights came charging out of the clump of fir trees. Stegoman saw the men on horseback, gave a roar of drunken rage, and pounded off to slam into them . . .

Leaving the humans' flank exposed. The evil duke laughed and stepped into the gap, sword slashing. Sir Guy's blade flashed out, but it was Yverne who leaped on the enemy. Grabbing a halberd and twisting it out of a trooper's hands, she swung it about with a sweeping motion that bespoke years of training, and clipped the trooper smartly with the butt, then swung the axe head to chop the next soldier in the hip.

Sir Guy leaped in front of Matt, blocking the duke's blow and riposting in a huge, deadly, sweeping cut.

Fadecourt roared, leaped on a soldier, and threw him into the men behind. He grabbed up the fallen halberd, broke it over his knee, and waded into the soldiers, chopping with his left hand and whirling his right as a club.

A net sailed out of nowhere and settled down over him. The cyclops bellowed and chopped at it. He slashed through the mesh, but two men caught his arm, and a third stepped up to slam a cudgel against his skull. Fadecourt slumped.

Matt scarcely noticed; he had pulled out his wand and was wielding it as a club, ducking pike thrusts and cracking skulls. Then some sixth sense warned him just in time to spin around and see a weighted club swinging down toward his sinuses with a fully armored knight behind it. He was just realizing that he might not have used the wand in the most effective way possible, when the club connected, and he didn't get to see how they managed to disarm Sir Guy.

•   •   •

The line straggled across the hillside above them, and the slope that had seemed small and insignificant when it was far below seemed to be lofty and forbidding now. The soldiers who had been ants were now fearsome gargoyles, frowning down on them.

Alisande found the grizzled veteran and summoned him. "How say you now, Sergeant? Shall I lead you in a charge up this hill?"

"God forbid!" the sergeant cried. "Begging your Majesty's pardon—but I would rather save your Majesty's life!"

"I, too," Alisande agreed, "for I have not so many men that I can spend their lives like pennies. Yet how think you we are to progress, if we do not climb this hill?"

The sergeant frowned. "Wherefore does . . ." He cleared his throat, also his impatience, and pulled his mask of civility back on. "I am surprised that your Majesty asks."

Alisande nodded in agreement, smiling. "We may not fly up, but the gray goose shall. Go call up the archers."

A few minutes later, a flight of arrows arced up from the ranks of Merovence.

But at the tops of their arcs, they burst into bright flame. What fell on the men of Ibile was little more than ashes.

Alisande just stood staring up at the sky.

Finally, the sergeant said, "Right glad I am, that 'twas only the gray goose that rose up against that sorcerer."

"Aye," Sauvignon agreed. "Better that our goose should be cooked, than we ourselves."

The queen finally spoke. "I'll not say nay to that." She turned to Ortho the Frank, Matthew's apprentice sorcerer. "Good clerk, you may be a novice in wizardry, but you are a veteran of many battles. How say you? How shall we ward our arrows from this sorcerer?"

"Ay de mi!" Ortho sighed. "Would that I had retained the profession of arms."

"But you were a poet."

"And a swordsman, Majesty. 'Twas useful, when men spoke of my verses. Yet now I'll seek among the scraps of verse my master hath taught me and see if I can find one that is apt to the condition.

> "Oh, let the rain come down!
> Oh yes,
> Do let the rain come down!
> Oh yes, oh yes,

Do let the rain come down
Upon our clothyard arrows
'Til their fires do drown!"

A few minutes later, a second flight of arrows sprang up from the
Merovencian lines. At apogee, they burst into flames—and rain appeared out of nowhere.

The arrows flew on, surrounded by their own private drizzle, while
the flames hissed, sputtered, and died. But just before the darts hit
their target, their points shot downward, and they fell short, rattling
against one another.

"What can he have done?" Sauvignon cried.

A moan swept the enemy line as cloaks snapped in a sudden gust,
and hats went flying.

"A gust of wind." Ortho nodded. "Brief, but strong—a 'downdraft,'
as Lord Matthew would call it."

A sudden chill engulfed them, then swept past them, and they
shivered, but not at the temperature alone.

"When it struck the earth," Ortho went on, subdued, "it splashed
out, as water does in a pool. Its gust struck the men of Ibile—but
when it reached us, it was only a breeze."

"Yet one that breathed despair!" Sauvignon shuddered. "Whence
comes such a wind, that chills even the soul?"

"I shall find a remedy for it," Ortho said quickly, ignoring the
question. "You shall see, Majesty—with each flight, our shafts shall
come nearer the mark."

"They shoot!" the sergeant cried, and they looked up, startled, to
see arrows sailing down at them. Ortho, however, muttered a rhyme
about someone lighting someone else's fire, and added a reference to
a lady who was still carrying a torch for someone. He understood neither, but Matthew had insisted he memorize them—and he was vin-
dicated, for the line of arrows blazed. Well before they reached the
Merovencian lines, they had guttered and gone out. Alisande could
distinctly hear the tinkling of a rain of arrowheads—uphill.

"This Ibilian sorcerer is most instructive," Ortho mused. "Between his example, and the Lord Matthew's spells, I may yet begin to
think of myself as a wizard."

Strangely, Alisande found herself beginning to be optimistic.

CHAPTER 21

Rack and Rune

The first thought through Matt's head, when he came to, was wondering why he had. After all, if King Gordogrosso had finally decided he was a big enough nuisance to swat, why would the king settle for a capture instead of a quick, clean kill?

Somehow he didn't like the sounds of "quick" and "clean." He wished he hadn't thought of them in just that way. With trepidation, he opened his eyes.

He saw a round, grinning face with a bowl haircut and a gloating smile. "I am Reginald, the Duke Bruitfort."

Matt squeezed his eyes shut, then opened them just a crack, hoping the face would go away, but it didn't. In fact it laughed. That irked Matt, so, carefully he began to raise his head—and found he couldn't. He tried to move his arms, but they were fastened down somewhere above his head. His stomach shrank and tried to crawl away. Yes, that was why the man hadn't killed him. He liked to make his pleasures last.

The duke must have seen that in his eyes, because he laughed and reached out, pushing Matt's head to the side. Matt squeezed his eyes shut, but not fast enough—he'd seen the torturer with the hot iron, at work on a half-naked peasant. Finally, Matt realized he'd been hearing screaming for a while.

A blow rocked his head, and a gravelly voice grated, "Look!"

That made Matt mad. He squeezed his eyes shut, but managed to bite back the retort.

A hard thumb jabbed his forehead, pulling up an eyelid and poking the eye in the process. Matt yelped in spite of himself and saw that there was a woman strapped down beyond the peasant man, one who might have been pretty once, but was scarcely enchanting now as she strained against her bonds, screaming at the things the torturers were doing to her.

The duke, however, apparently liked the sight—his breathing rasped, hoarse. He shuddered and snapped, "Cease! Matters of state must be resolved! We shall finish with these two anon!" He said it in the tone usually reserved for an extra helping of dessert. Matt wondered about moral obesity. Anything to keep from thinking about what he was seeing.

Especially as the duke seized his chin and yanked, turning his head the other way. Matt saw Yverne, strapped down and stripped to the waist. It was a sight he'd been secretly yearning for, but not in the current setting. Especially since Sir Guy lay strapped down beyond her, also with his torso bared and his hands manacled above his head, with Fadecourt in a similar bind between them. The knight's eyes, though, were calm, in spite of the bruises that marred his face and had welted his chest. His gaze seemed to counsel Matt to courage and steadfast faith.

Then a hot iron came between them, and touched Yverne's upper arm. Only a touch; she screamed, and the duke waved the instrument away, chuckling. "Do you not find the sight stimulating, Wizard?"

"No," Matt said. "Not at all." It wasn't quite true; it was stimulating him to some very lurid thoughts about what he wanted to do to the duke.

"Indeed! Would you rather be the banquet guest, or the roast? Come, join me in this sport! Or I shall set my torturers to work on you." To prove it, he snapped his fingers, and pain seared through Matt's belly. He let out a howl before he managed to choke it off, and looked down, amazed, to see a red-hot iron lifting away from his skin.

"The next shall be lower." The duke grinned, and a thin trickle of saliva oozed from the corner of his mouth. "Lower, and lower yet. Therefore, join me in eliciting delightful, musical shrieks from this wench, and we shall work our way down together. Then up, and I shall raise you to chief among my sorcerers. You shall have power, vast power—over my estates, over half the kingdom! And, at last, over all of Ibile." His grin widened, sweat starting from his brow. "After that, who knows? You have cause for revenge on Merovence, have you not?"

Understanding hit Matt almost like a physical blow. "You're trying to usurp the throne!"

"Certes." The eyes narrowed, the grin hardened. "And I have need of strong magics to aid me."

It all made sense. If Matt joined the duke in his torturing, he would be corrupted—and doubly corrupted, since the people they'd be torturing would be his friends. Then he would indeed have devoted himself to evil and could be trusted to become a sorcerer who would labor diligently for his wicked lord. Matt managed to get his voice working again. "What is this? If you can become evil enough, you get to be king? It's a corruption competition?"

"That is the way of it in Ibile," the duke verified. "Succession is usurpation. It is accomplished by assassination, either before or after the taking of the throne."

Matt frowned. "But the king's got all the power! He's a puissant sorcerer—and he has Satan's power backing him up!"

"So it may seem. But know, foolish meddler, that Satan will aid any pretender who seeks the crown—for the result of that is civil war, and amid the strife and suffering it brings, many lose faith and curse God."

"And Satan gets their souls!"

"He is a collector of useless things. Thus the king may be aided by the powers of Hell, but so am I."

"Then Satan's assistance cancels out." Matt nodded. "It makes sense. The sooner you challenge the king, the sooner one of you will die—and Satan doesn't have to wait as long for your soul."

Anger flashed in Bruitfort's eyes, but he contained it. "Even so. 'Tis then a contest of strength, and the king must strive mightily to overcome me ere I am grown great enough to topple him." His grin broke through again. "In that, he has failed. I have countered his magics with my own sorcery, and that of my apprentices and journeymen. I have matched his armies and beaten them back—and steadily gained ground. Already I rule half of Ibile, and 'tis soon to be more."

A random thought occurred. "Of course, you could be fundamentally good, but just pretending to be evil long enough to get Satan's support."

Bruitfort threw back his head and laughed. "Think you the Prince of Lies is so easily deceived? Nay, I assure you! He knows true evil

when he sees it! He would not aid a man who was good-hearted in secret!"

"So whose soldiers did I see looting and raping in the villages—
yours, or the king's?"

"Mine." The duke's grin widened. "Thus I bind them to me—by
the promises of the pleasures of cruelty, and the wealth gained by
looting."

And, of course, the disregard for law that made such decadence
possible. "Which means the king's soldiers are no better than yours."

"Surely not. If he seeks to keep his throne, he must be all that I
am, and more—and instantly ruthless in quashing the first signs of
rebellion. In that, he failed—for he had need of great enough intelli-
gence to see when a contender was rising, but he did not see through
my deception, my grinning sycophant's pose, until it was too late,
and I had power enough to contend with him. For that, he shall die—
and in not too long a while, I think."

So that was why Matt had encountered so little trouble from
Gordogrosso—he was distracted by a domestic rebellion. The thought
sent insight. "It was Sir Guy's attack! That's what gave you your
chance!"

"Even so." The duke turned to Sir Guy with a mocking bow. "The
Black Knight struck down the overbearing lords who preyed upon
their peasants—and left holes in the fabric of evil behind him."

"Which you filled."

Bruitfort nodded. "He put down the vicious outlaws who sought to
prey upon the weak, and gained the allegiance of the poor. He struck
down the king's tax grinders, and weakened the royal power over the
villages. He gathered about him all the fools who worship goodness;
they came out from their hiding places to band together, and the
king, of a sudden, had to contend with a challenge to his rule that
could have been fatal."

"So he had to tie up most of his army, keeping Sir Guy and his fol-
lowers penned in that castle—and while they were tied up, you took
over the estates of the lords Sir Guy had ousted."

The Black Knight was staring, pale and drawn.

"Even so." The duke's grin widened like a shark's. "Let others
waste their time in strife; I waited, and bowed, and scraped, then
struck. Yet to counter the king, I must garner all the power I can, for
even maimed, his magical power is formidable. Therefore, join with
me, Wizard! Swell the strength of my evil challenge! Free Ibile from
the rule of this corrupt monarch!"

"And replace him with another who's even more corrupt?" Matt suggested. "One who's much more efficient about making people miserable?"

"You will thus gain power you scarce can dream of. Join in my delights, and there shall be earthly power for you second only to mine! The most beautiful lasses of the kingdom, used only once! Fine meats, fine raiment, fine wines! What say you, Wizard? Will you have wealth, luxury, and power? Or a slow, agonizing death?" He looked up and gestured, and pain ripped through the sole of Matt's foot. He howled in agony; the room disappeared behind a red film. It cleared slowly, tending to pulse in time to the diminished but throbbing pain in his foot, thinned enough to show the duke, eyes bulging, teeth bared in a grimace of mounting pleasure. "Choose," he panted. "Choose."

Matt chose.

> "The screw may twist and the rack may turn,
> And men may scream and men may burn,
> But England's pride will cast aside
> All men who for others' pain may yearn."

The duke shot back away, slamming into the solid stone wall. But he didn't fall; he stepped back, shaking his head, only dazed—and a nasty little whip with sharp bits of metal at the ends of its thongs scored Matt's chest. Matt shouted with the pain but remembered to keep bellowing:

> "The lash sweeps back to score with thirst
> The hand that wields it last and first!"

The thongs snapped back, and someone out of sight screamed. The thrill of victory shot through Matt, and he cried out,

> "Like a mirror on the wall,
> Let each new torture turn and maul,
> So he who seeks another's pain
> Shall feel it turn on him a—"

"*Silence him!*" the duke screamed.

A hard hand slapped down across Matt's mouth, which happened to be open. He bit.

The torturer screamed, but kept the hand there, and Matt started chewing in spite of the taste. Suddenly, the hand yanked away, and a wad of cloth jammed into Matt's mouth. It smelled foul and tasted worse.

The duke loomed over him, panting and wild-eyed. "Well tried, Wizard! But poorly struck! There are too many of us here, ready to stop you! You cannot prevail against us!"

Showed how much *he* knew. Matt glared at him, gargling a few dire noises through his gag, while his mind raced, trying to dredge up verses that would be effective even though unspoken.

"Know then," the duke panted, "that your familiars are taken, and slain."

Matt frowned. Familiars? What was the man talking about?

"Your animals, your beasts!" the duke snapped. "The dragon, and that obscene hybrid! We have taken them, and drained their blood."

Matt stared, every muscle rigid. Then morality gave way—there could be no protection for so vile a man. He had forfeited all right to the protections of others' compassion or conscience. Matt would make him burn to death from the inside out, while his nails grew inward and his inner ears rocked . . .

Calm flooded through him, almost as if some outer spirit had filled him with charity and restraint. The man was human, after all, and though it might be Matt's duty to remove him before he could hurt anyone else, he had no right to work justice upon him. Torture could wait until after his death, if he deserved it, which Matt didn't doubt for an instant—but it wasn't his job.

Well enough. Back to high-powered, unspoken verses.

"Their blood will enhance my power enormously." The duke's eyes narrowed; he was all business now, sadism put aside for the moment. "So would your magic, though I can work quite well without it, if I must. Yet there is another source of power more vital by far." And he turned to Yverne.

Matt's heart nearly stopped. Then, frantically, he began to recite as much of the verse as he had worked out in his mind.

The duke's eye gleamed as his gaze moved slowly over Yverne's form, but he was all business as he explained, "Your father's lands marched with mine, damsel, but also marched with Merovence. His lands ran along its border, through the mountains, for fifty miles. That distance is long enough to admit an army that could hamstring my forces from behind. I might take the capital only to find my own hard-won demesnes lost to the Bitch of Merovence."

Matt froze for a moment; then his eyes narrowed, and he changed a line of verse for the worse.

"He was my prisoner, as you know." The duke watched her face carefully for signs of reaction to the past tense. "He was a brave, though stupid, man—he withstood all my tortures and would not cede his lands to me. Now he is dead."

Yverne stared in horror.

"It is hard, I know," the duke said gently, fairly oozing sympathy. "Let the tears fall; grief must be vented."

It was; the tears flowed, though Yverne squeezed her eyes shut and bit her lip to stifle the sobs.

"Let it loose, let it loose," the duke soothed. "None here will blame you for wailing with remorse."

Remorse! For what?

"Oh, my father! My poor father!" Yverne gasped.

"Aye, aye, 'tis hard, 'tis hard," the duke commiserated. "Yet you must know, poor lass . . ."

Finally, the wail cut loose and wrenched into sobbing. The duke, tense as a tent rope, kept murmuring inanities, patting his captive's bound hand, completely ignoring the fact that it was he who had caused her misery.

The strategy seemed to be working. As her sobs slackened, his murmurs turned to advice. "You are but a weak woman, damsel, and a young one at that. Nay, surely you are not schooled and hardened to the governing of a dukedom. 'Twill be a burden on you, a horrible burden. You will bend under it, you will break. The administering of justice alone will torment you. Can you truly order a murderer hanged, and sleep well o'night?"

Yverne wailed.

"Let her be!" Fadecourt barked. "Can you not allow her to be alone in her misery?"

The duke looked up at him, eyes narrowed, and nodded to a torturer. A hand slapped a wad of cloth over Fadecourt's mouth and nose; another set the glowing iron to his upper arm. The cyclops' body bucked, but he stifled his scream.

Yverne, still weeping and faced away from Fadecourt, had not even noticed.

"Nay, certes you cannot take up the weight of such a task," the duke soothed. "Poor lass, I shall aid you! Only cede your lands to me, and I shall govern them for you, well and wisely!"

"Never!" Yverne's voice was raw with tears.

The duke's eyes sparked, but he said, " 'Never' is a great expanse of time, damsel. Your people suffer, even now, from the ravages of war. Can they wait your leisure to take up their governance?"

"Be mindful," Sir Guy said in a low voice that nonetheless seemed to fill the chamber, "mindful that he may lie. Your father may still be alive, damsel, yet so badly hurted as not to be able to govern. It may be your regency you cede to him, not—"

"Be still!" the duke snapped, and daggers stabbed Sir Guy's chest muscles. His jaw clenched against a howl of pain, and a beefy hand covered his lips.

But his words had done their work. Hope glowed in Yverne's eyes, and she said, "Never, vile duke! Torture me as you will, I shall never yield my father's poor peasants and rich lands unto your cruelty! Far better that I should suffer for them!"

"Then be assured that you will!" Bruitfort bellowed in sudden rage. "Your father truly is dead! He died at these hands, mine own, wielding the instruments of agony—but the fool refused to cede his lands! The same fate awaits you!"

Pale and trembling with rage, Yverne snapped, "I can do no less than to follow the example of so worthy a sire!"

"Then you shall have the opportunity!" the duke thundered. But he calmed just as quickly as he had flared, the anticipation of depraved pleasures filling his face with unholy glee. "The power you deny me, I shall rip from you! If I cannot have the fullness of power from your lands and people, I shall have it by debasing and corrupting you! Aye, ceding your people to me would have been the ultimate abasement—but I shall do nearly as well, by ripping your virginity from you and grinding you down by pain and degradation, till you beg me to have my will, if only I will lessen your agony!" Spittle drooled from the corner of his mouth again. "I shall break your soul and drink its strength with mine! Yet we shall begin this feast of torture with the hors d'oeuvre of the knight's pain; you shall join me in watching as I ply him with agony so exquisite that he, even he, shall regale me with his screams!"

Sir Guy threw off the hand that gagged him with a mighty heave and cried, "Even if he should wring wailing from me, damsel, pay it no heed!" Then the torturer backhanded him across the mouth, and it was Yverne who cried out, "Foul villain! Do you think to ruin a man so goodly?"

"Easily," the duke sneered. "Think you his God will save him? Nay, for He only works through human agents, and I can best any of those! If you wish to free him from the throes of excruciation, you may cry out, at any moment, that you cede your lands to me. Yet be assured that if you truly summon the fortitude to remain silent until the Black Knight is dead, you will take his place on the rack!"

Matt couldn't take it any longer. He thought with all the energy he could,

> Both back and side, go bare, go bare,
> Let chains and ropes go slack,
> Until each hemp or metal strand
> Detach, upon the ground lie back!

Yverne's bonds broke, and she leaped off the pallet, filled with sudden vigor, even as Sir Guy and Fadecourt sprang up, leaping upon the torturers and wrenching instruments from them, then striking them down.

The duke shouted something in a corrupted form of Latin that Matt couldn't quite make out; it had something to do with laying low his enemies and binding them fast. Fadecourt, Sir Guy, and Yverne fainted dead away, and as Matt felt the dark tide pressing in, he recited inside his head,

> Gaudeamus igitur, Iuvenesdum sumus!
> Gaudeamus igitur, Iuvenesdum sumus!
> Vivat amicus meam, Non habebit humus!

For good measure, he repeated in English:

> Therefore let us all rejoice,
>   While we're young and sprightly.
> Long live all these friends of mine,
>   May earth not clutch them tightly!

But the unspoken verse was much weaker than those spoken aloud. The dark tide did lessen, and Matt struggled against it long enough to hear the duke say, "Bind the knight again—and throw the cyclops and the trickster into our most foul dungeon cell, bound and gagged. We shall have our pleasure of them, when we are done with the maiden. Go, begone!"

"The wizard wakes!" a voice cried behind Matt.

Bruitfort spun, swinging a truncheon. It cracked down on Matt's skull, and the dark tide bore him away.

CHAPTER 22

About Fates

Matt landed hard, but Fadecourt bounced—partly because his head landed on Matt's belly. Matt said, "Oof!" and Fadecourt bellowed, "You loathsome villains!" as he leaped to his feet. "Nay, unbind mine hands, and I shall—"

The door slammed shut, laughter echoed away, and they were left in the dark.

"Toadies!" Fadecourt raged. "Vile excuses for humanity! Nay, do not tell me, I know—they but did as they were bid, and would have been made to suffer an they had not."

Matt gargled something through his gag.

"Yet an 'twere no more than that, they would not have grinned like japing apes, nor have taken such pleasure in so cruelly hurling us within! So do not tell me of their goodness."

Matt tried to make agreeing noises.

"How is that?" Fadecourt's voice became louder; he must have turned toward Matt. Without light, it was rather hard to see. "Ah. Thou canst tell me naught, canst thou? Nay, not with that gag . . . Faugh! Away, thou crawling ferleigh!" There was a small, meaty thud accompanied by an outraged squealing, then a splatting noise off in the dark.

"Begone! You, and you and you!" Fadecourt stamped with vigor.

Rats! Matt scrambled to his feet—as well as he could, with his hands tied behind him.

" 'Ware the roof!" Fadecourt cried. " 'Tis scarce high enough for one of my stature, and for you—"

Something cracked against the top of Matt's head, and he slumped back to the floor, senses reeling.

". . . it would be a danger," Fadecourt finished. "Ay de mi! My regrets, Lord Matthew! I should have thought . . ."

Matt gargled something very nasty as he rolled up to a groggy sitting position.

"I deserve no such malediction!" Fadecourt protested. "I was but tardy in my warning, not omitting entirely."

Matt mumbled as loudly as he could, beginning to feel a little frantic.

"What . . . ? Oh, the gag. Aye, I would loose it an I could, Lord Wizard—but they have bound my arms in some manner of leather casings, like to gloves without fingers. I cannot aid thee, unless I can . . ." His voice broke off into a straining groan that rose up the scale till it broke in a massive gasp. " 'Tis no use; they have manacled my wrists with a steel most excellent. Nay, I fear I cannot loosen your restraints, Lord Matthew."

Matt made a noise that he hoped sounded philosophical and set himself to working out an escape spell. The duke struck him as the musclebound sort who had taken up magic as if he were learning to use a new weapon, rather than trying to discover how and why it worked—sort of a consumer's view of sorcery, without bothering to look in the owner's manual. He probably hadn't bothered putting a containment spell on his dungeon, either; he was the type to trust in metal and rope.

> Blest be the tie that binds
> This cloth that I taste of,
> And falls from off my jaw
> So that the wad inside may move.

The knot started to loosen itself before he finished the second line. It must have been the word *blest*—nothing in Duke Bruitfort's castle wanted to receive a blessing. Matt worked his jaws, pushing with his tongue until the wad of cloth fell out. It had never felt so good to close his mouth. Still painful, but a definite improvement.

"I would I could help you," Fadecourt mourned.

Matt worked up some saliva, moistened his lips, and croaked, "You don't need to."

"What in Heaven's name . . . ?" Fadecourt cried, and Matt felt magical forces enwrap him. "*Shh!* Don't talk about anything holy! We don't want to attract attention!"

"You can talk! But how?"

"Magic." Matt dismissed the issue with an airy toss of the head that went unseen—and shot another wave of pain through his skull. "But I think we need our hands free, too, and I'd rather not use another spell if I can avoid it. Max?"

"Aye, Wizard?" The Demon was there before him, a spark amazingly bright in the total darkness. Matt's eyes had adjusted to the dimness; he could see Fadecourt clearly in Max's glow. "Well, you've taken care of one of our problems already. Think you could crystallize the metal in our manacles, too?"

"Can a cat make kittens?" Max scoffed. "Only hold your places a moment." He shot over to Fadecourt and sank behind his back.

"What does he?" the cyclops demanded.

"Magic," Matt explained again. "Just hold still."

The Demon rose back into sight. " 'Tis done."

Matt nodded. "Give a good yank, Fadecourt."

The cyclops grunted, his shoulders, chest, and upper arms all bulging. A metallic *crack* sounded, and he brought his freed wrists up in front of his single eye, staring in astonishment.

"Don't know your own strength, do you? Okay, Max—try mine."

"Even so." The Demon zipped around behind Matt. A moment later, he sang, "Pull!"

Matt yanked as hard as he could, and the manacles clanked, but didn't loosen. "How about dissipating the molecular bonds?"

"Well thought; this primitive iron is far from pure."

Suddenly, Matt's hands were free. He lifted his arms, staring at the clean wrists. "I didn't say to dissipate them all the way."

"You did not say to stop," Max pointed out.

"Wise. Well!" Matt rubbed his freed hands. "Let me see what I can do about those mittens, Fadecourt." He untied the thongs around Fadecourt's wrists. The cyclops groaned, and Matt was appalled at the darkness of the skin he revealed on the hand that was not stone.

"Now we can get down to some *real* mischief! Which reminds me—I wonder what happened to Puck?"

"I should think he pursued the better course of valor and decamped when the knight was captured."

"Makes sense—but that means he probably has a grudge against the duke and his men."

"Have you any fault to find with that?"

Matt shook his head. "Sounds fine. Which means we should be seeing him making trouble pretty soon now."

"Aye, but we'll not be told of it."

"Until it reaches disaster proportions, anyway." Matt rose to a crouch, prowling about the cell. "Wonder what happened to Stegoman? We sure could use his light right now . . . Hey!" He looked up, appalled at a thought. "You don't suppose they really managed to catch him, do you?"

Fadecourt shook his head with conviction. "I had thought of it as soon as the duke said it, but knew it was not so. Even drunken, the dragon would be a formidable enemy—and it was by force of arms they captured us, not by sorcery."

"Good thought." Matt nodded, relieved. "The sorcery was only to suck us into the trap—but this military duke preferred to do the actual take by force of arms. And Stegoman is at least as dangerous drunken as sober." He didn't mention the dragon's tendency to blast at random when he was intoxicated—when he was surrounded by enemies, it really didn't matter much.

"What do you seek?"

"This!" Matt lifted a stick of rotted wood. "Max, could you set this flaming? Then you won't have to hover just to give us light."

" 'Tis no trouble to me—but if you wish it, why not?" The Demon floated over to the stick, touched its end, and it flared.

"That's fine. Thanks." Matt lifted the stick, squinting against the sudden glare. "Who'd have thought to have found a piece of wood in a dump like this? I could have sworn they wouldn't even have had furniture. Just a shot in the dark, looking for it."

" 'Tis not a stick," Fadecourt pointed out. "You hold the leg bone of a man."

"*Iyuch!*" Matt nearly dropped the limb. "How come it burns so well?"

"Because it is so dry." Max's tone was tinged with contempt. "Still, I did have need of high temperature to kindle it."

Matt debated with himself and decided he needed light more than the previous owner needed a decent burial. He said a quick mental apology to the departed spirit, then looked around at the floor, trying not to notice the rest of the skeleton. He was just in time to see rat tails scurrying away from the light. He shuddered and knelt down with a sigh of relief, letting muscles knotted from crouching relax. He winced at the stab of pain. The muscles would stop hurting soon enough—but how about his feet?

"Call at need." Max winked out.

"Need," Matt croaked, "but not of *his* type of services. Fadecourt, I think we might see about tending a few wounds, here."

"Indeed," the cyclops agreed, "though your feet must hurt so badly, I marvel you can think at all."

"A wizard's gotta do what a wizard's gotta do," Matt groaned, and chanted,

> "Within each wounded heel and sole
> Starts the healing of the whole.
> Knit up the epidermis neat,
> So I won't fall into defeat."

The pain disappeared so suddenly that he groaned in relief.

"Are you not well?" the cyclops asked anxiously.

"Oh, yeah! Just fine. Give me ten minutes to work up my courage, and I'll even try standing on them."

"I rejoice to hear it." But Fadecourt still looked concerned. "Yet what of Narlh?"

Matt shook his head. "I don't think he ever came down—at least, not anywhere near us. Sure, the duke *might* have caught him—but so might any other sorcerer. I have a sneaking suspicion that he figured out he'd lost us and flew for the nearest clear air."

"In any event, the monsters have escaped him," Fadecourt agreed. "Had they not, the duke would have shown us their heads, to afright us."

Matt nodded. "It would be just like him. Even if we didn't scare, he'd have a blast watching our grief."

Fadecourt's jaw hardened. "If they could escape, may not we? Wizard, I implore you, find us a passage! Exert your powers to the utmost! Expend your greatest efforts! The damsel lies in torment! We must to her!"

"Well, it might be easier to bypass the walls than to tunnel through them." Matt frowned and tried the verse he had used to escape from the dungeon in which Alisande had been imprisoned.

> "I know a bank where the wild thyme blows,
> Where oxlips and the nodding violet grows . . ."

He had scarcely begun chanting before he began to feel inimical magical forces gathering about him.

He strained, sweat starting from his brow—but the web of force held him tight. He relaxed, shaking his head. "He *did* put an enclosure spell on this dungeon."

"Can you not break it?" Fadecourt asked anxiously.

"Let me try a little better verse.

> "And thus when they appeared at last,
> And all my bonds were cast aside,
> I ask'd not why, and reck'd not where,
> So it was far outside!"

Again, the magical field pressed around him, grating on his nerves, raising the hairs on the back of his neck—but there was a greater sense of tension, and he felt the strain physically. Byron's verse was working better than his adaptation of Shakespeare, but not better enough.

"Can you not shift us?"

Matt shook his head. "It's *very* heavily enchanted. This is no amateur job. Either the duke is a better sorcerer than he looks, or he's got a crackerjack working for him."

"What is a 'crackerjack'?"

"*I* am—or at least, I'm a jack who's trying to crack us out of here." Matt frowned and tried again.

> "Alas, my foe, you do us wrong,
> To bind us up so close to death.
> Yet we will match you, song for song,
> Until we draw a free man's breath,
> For dying in a prison strong
>
> Is not the destiny that waits,
> For good men who still seek and strive.
> For them shall open many gates
> If they keep faith, and onward drive
> Till they behold their hard-won fates!"

The magical web enwrapped him again, but not so tightly. His whole body was raked with tension, though, as his spell contended with the duke's.

Then something seemed to lance through to Matt, and the tension was gone with an almost-audible snap. Matt went limp, staring about, startled.

They were still in the cell. "Naught has occurred," Fadecourt said, severely disappointed. "The duke's spell must be too strong for you."

"But I could have *sworn* I broke it!" Matt protested. "I felt some outside force reach through to me! We ganged up on him—or his spell, anyway! We broke it!"

"We are still here," Fadecourt pointed out.

"Yeah, we sure are." Matt frowned, then looked up, eyes widening. "I didn't say anything about moving us out of here! I only said we'd keep trying!"

Someone cackled just outside the cell door.

Matt stared at Fadecourt, the hairs rising on the back of his neck. Fadecourt stared back.

"Either that's a hen with a very odd idea of the ideal roost," Matt said, "or we've got unexpected company."

Fadecourt glanced sidelong at the door. "There is light through the wicket."

Matt stared at the glow through the little, barred window, hearing the cackle again, then a gabble of low-voiced conversation. Almost against his will, he sidled across and looked out.

A small fire lit a small area—it couldn't be called a chamber, there weren't any walls. In fact, Matt could have sworn the hall outside his cell had only been two feet wide. Now it was broad enough so that the walls were lost in shadow.

Around the fire stood three old ladies—at least, Matt hoped they were ladies, because they seemed to be discussing his future—or was it his past?

"Have you more thread upon your spindle, Clotho?" the one with the yardstick asked.

"Aye," Clotho said. "It could make his life longer—or make another life, anew."

"What, two lives for one man?"

The middle sister shrugged. "It would be rare, yet I have known wizard folk to achieve it aforetime. Sorcerers, now, some have spun out their lives to unbelievably long spans . . ."

"Yet I have cut them off, natheless," the third lady muttered darkly, "cut them off at last—have I not, Lachesis?"

"That you have, sister Atropos—and I have shown you where their threads must end, in such fashion that they would have no hint of their end coming."

"Indeed you have, and well done, too, for such as would cheat Death."

Matt shuddered. These three hags didn't play around, did they?

"Yet a wizard who holds to the straight and straitened path has no such cheating done. And, too, this one is young."

"Who speaks?" Fadecourt hissed in Matt's ear.

"I'm not sure," Matt muttered back, "but I think it's the Norns."

"Nay, surely not! I hear Greek names!"

"Cut him now," the middle sister mused, "and Ibile will surely subside in slavery and misery. Merovence, too, may falter—for see! In my tapestry, the queen will waver 'twixt despair and faith, 'twixt the slough of despond and the iron of duty."

Well. At least Alisande would miss him. That much was good to know, anyway.

Atropos clacked her shears impatiently. "Have done! Whether all of Europe succumbs to the rule of the Prince of Evil is not our care! Ours is the destiny of human folk, not nations or races! 'Tis for God to concern Himself with them!"

"Yet are we not His tools?" Lachesis argued. "Nay, I must listen for His voice, sister."

"How about *my* voice?" Matt called out. He shook one of the window bars and demanded, "Only a few more years! Let me finish what I've started, at least!"

But if the women heard him, they gave no sign. "My care is for the tapestry." Lachesis held out her cloth, frowning at it with a critical eye. "If one forgets that each thread is a human life, and regards the design as a whole, it grows to a harmony of balance. Yet will the myriad threads that must surely spread out from his actions enhance that pattern, or weaken it?"

"Enhance!" Matt opined. "Definitely enhance!"

"'Tis for you to say, sister, not us," the spinner said. "Natheless, I would hazard the notion that the bright strands he will enliven will neatly balance the uncolored throng that have stemmed from the first usurper of Ibile."

"Can you not stop them, Wizard?" Fadecourt stood at his elbow, ashen-faced.

"Uhhhh . . ." Matt's mind raced furiously. "Not 'can,' Fadecourt— 'will.' The question is, can I justify lousing up the rest of the world just to save my own life?"

"If you do not act, you will die!" the cyclops cried. "Ibile will have lost its one chance to be free of the reign of the Devil, and you will have lost the hand of the queen!"

Matt stood, galvanized by the thought of annihilation—not just of himself, but of all the bright dreams he had ever had of precious private moments with Alisande: the lovemaking he had ached for, the children he had hoped to gather about them, his determination not to let the little princes and princesses be raised by nannies, the physical training he would give them in the guise of games, the love of learning he and Alisande would imbue in them by their conversations . . . He steeled his resolve, and recited:

> "The raging rocks
> And shivering shocks
> Did break the locks
> Of prison gates,
> And Phoebus' car
> Did shine from far,
> To make and mar
> The foolish Fates."

Sudden and savage, sunbeams lanced down from the solid rock ceiling as the lock on the door exploded. The shafts of light caressed the women's faces, but wherever they touched, a face flowed like wax. The three women screamed, a horrible ragged cry, and their fire-lit chamber shrank, as if receding, to a globe, then a globule, still shrinking until it finally winked out.

"I did not mean you should smite them so!" Fadecourt said, aghast.

"That makes us even; I didn't mean to." Matt pulled in a deep breath to try to still his inner quaking. "Talk about power! That man couldn't write poorly even when he tried!"

The cyclops eyed the broken lock, then reached out a forefinger to nudge the door. With a groan, it swung open. "You have indeed taken the first step to bringing us forth from this dungeon, Wizard. Yet how shall you take us up this stair?"

"The steps should be easy." Matt was acutely aware of the word *should*. "After all, bringing the Fates here broke the confinement spell. But just to be on the safe side, I think I'd better try to work up a stronger transportation spell."

"How shall you . . ."

"Quiet! I'm being creative." Matt frowned, running over verses from a couple of old, old songs. Then he chanted,

> "The autumn winds blow coldly through
> The castle of Bruitfort.
> Yet anguish in its deepest depths
> Is wrought in chamber darke.
> Alas, foul Duke! You do her wrong

Who never sought to hurt ye,
You make her suffer horribly,
So we'll be in your company!
To beard you is my delight,
So I now come for fiercest joy!
I come with all my heart and zeal,
And shall confront you instantly!"

He was barely aware of Fadecourt's hand, clamping onto his arm like a vise, and of the room suddenly rocking in a tilt; he was already preparing the next verse in his mind . . .

The room jolted straight, but it was the torture chamber they stood in, with Yverne and Sir Guy stretched seminaked on tables, and bulky semihumans standing over them with arcane metal instruments. One was screwing a blocky boot-shaped object onto Sir Guy's foot, and Yverne was screaming at the mere sight of it as the duke, spittle running down his chin, watched another torturer pushing her skirt up, dagger poised over the smooth skin of her thigh.

Her screaming drove Fadecourt crazy. He bellowed and leaped for a guardsman, wrenching his halberd away with one stroke and felling him with another, then whirling to attack the torturer.

But Matt's attention was all for the duke, who was just looking up at him in stupefaction.

"Then reach this lecher-duke a blow!
Strike with might and maul!
Force him to reel about and land
Out cold, against the wall!"

The duke jolted upright as if he'd been hit with an uppercut, then slumped to the ground. The guards and torturers stared, shocked.

Savage triumph boiled up in Matt, and he gave in to temptation long enough to pick up the nearest torturer and throw him against the wall. The other snapped out of his daze with a bellow and yanked a poker out of a brazier. As Matt turned back to him, the bigger man leaped, lashing out with the iron. Matt leaped, too, slamming a fist into his attacker's belly. The poker's shaft cracked across the back of Matt's shoulders, then fell from fingers gone limp, its glowing tip bruising Matt's shin on the way down. The pain, coupled with the ache across his back, was enough to make him shout with rage; he slammed the torturer back, away. The man tripped, stumbled, and fell against the brazier, knocking it over and falling across the fire. He screamed and rolled away, then lay rocking and moaning on the stone floor.

Not that Matt stayed to watch. He whirled and saw that Fadecourt had caught up a torturer's knife and was slitting the bonds on Yverne's wrists as he mumbled soothing inanities. Matt nodded and turned to Sir Guy, frantically unscrewing the boot.

"My thanks," the Black Knight grunted. " 'Ware the guards." Matt looked up, appalled that he'd forgotten—but saw Fadecourt hurling two guards away, even as Yverne caught up a fallen pike and leveled it at a torturer who skidded to a halt, wavering between danger and the reputation of cowardice.

A shout from the hall saved him; the door burst open, revealing a senior guard who bellowed, "To the walls! We are beset!" and turned to run away, not even registering what was happening in the torture chamber.

The guards leaped on the excuse and ran for the door. Matt whirled to look about him—and saw the duke, hauling himself up on the edge of one of the torture benches, giving Matt a look that pierced right through him, promising even greater mayhem. Matt was just readying a verse when Fadecourt stepped up with a cold iron and slammed it against the base of the duke's skull. The duke's eyes rolled up, and he folded back onto the floor.

Suddenly, the room was silent, with no one moving.

Then Matt yanked a dagger from the belt of an unconscious soldier and strode over to the fallen duke. He dropped to one knee, raising the dagger . . .

Fadecourt caught his wrist. "Nay, Lord Wizard! He is not shriven!"

Odd as it seemed, that gave Matt pause. To kill the man without giving him a chance to confess his sins would condemn him to eternal torment in Hell—and even Matt didn't think that the monster deserved to suffer for ever and ever, with absolutely no hope of ever getting out. For a few years, yes, maybe even for a few centuries—but he was human, after all.

Still, there were practical considerations. "If we don't kill him while we can, Fadecourt, he'll attack us again as soon as he can—and next time, he might win. We'll be caught between his army and Gord—the king's, unless we give up and get out of Ibile while we can. The sensible thing is to kill him now."

" 'Twould be in cold blood, Wizard. 'Tis not needful; you would not slay him to save your own life, or another's."

"Maybe not at the moment—but a fool could see I'm doing it to save our lives in the future."

"Then we will deal with him in the future," Sir Guy said calmly. "But to slay him now, when he is unconscious and not a present threat, would be murder, Sir Matthew. 'Twould be a mortal sin—and such a burden on your soul would make you vulnerable to the king. It would put you in his, and Satan's, power."

"It's not murder, it's an execution! Not revenge, justice! Can you honestly doubt he deserves it? How many people has he already killed—in cold blood?"

" 'Tis not for us to judge," the Black Knight reminded him. "That prerogative is God's alone. Nay, an you will have him tried by a jury of his peers, when all this war is over and done, well enough—but you may not set yourself up as his judge. That would be the sin of pride, added to the sin of murder."

"You would imperil us all, Wizard," Fadecourt rumbled, "and give up Ibile's one chance of salvation, through you and us."

Matt dropped the dagger with a noise of disgust. Satisfied, Fadecourt released his wrist. Then Matt caught up the dagger again, and the cyclops leaped for him with a cry of alarm.

But Matt rose to his feet and turned away to Sir Guy. Yverne was there before him, though, slipping her dagger between the knight's wrists and severing the bonds, then turning to cut through the thongs binding his ankles. Sir Guy sat up, rubbing his wrists and swearing softly at the pain of moving his shoulders, the stabs of blood being released to recirculate. "By Our Lady! By the blue of her gown! Ah, but I thank you, damsel! An I had lain there any longer, I would have frozen in that posture forever! And I thank you, Matthew and Fadecourt, for timely rescue."

"Without you, we'd be lost," Matt assured him. "But I wonder to what we all owe the guards' sudden exit?"

"Whatever it was, it was on our side, whether it knew us or not."

Matt stepped over to help his friend off the table, then gathered up Sir Guy's gambeson and armor and shoved it at him. "Hold that in one arm, and Yverne in the other."

"And this for you." Fadecourt handed Yverne the remnants of her dress. She quickly draped them to cover most of her torso and hips.

"How shall we come out from here, Wizard?" the cyclops demanded.

Just then, a diminutive figure popped in through the door and gave a cry of triumph. "I have found thee, then!"

"Puck!" Yverne cried, amazed.

"Sober, too," Matt noted. "When did you become clearheaded, sprite?"

"Phaugh! Minutes ago, only! The dragon and I threw off our attackers, but found you gone. We wandered in that damnable fog for hours, till it finally cleared. Then we circled aloft and saw the duke's castle! Instantly I betook myself to the dungeons and heard your chatter! Well, I did discover a bolt hole, first."

"A hidden tunnel?" Sir Guy's eyes lit. "Nay, take us there, good Robin! Have you found any other mischiefs we might work?"

"I have given the matter some thought," Puck said, turning and leading them out of the torture chamber—without ever having seen the unconscious duke, which Matt thought was a great pity. He might be troubled by a conscience, but Puck was not.

Unfortunately, the chance was past, and he couldn't very well call Puck's attention to the duke without virtually committing murder himself—so he followed the chattering elf, the lady, the knight, and the cyclops down the dimly lit hallway and through the section of wall that swung outward. It swung shut behind them, too, but Puck muttered a spell, and a will-o'-the-wisp appeared to light them up the damp stone steps, through a clammy tunnel with mitered walls, up to a dead-end sealed by rough and convex stone.

"There is the small matter of a boulder blocking the entrance," the elf pointed out

"What problem is that?" Fadecourt stepped up to the boulder, set his shoulder against it, and heaved—then stepped back, a look of surprise showing faintly by the light of the fox fire. "It will not move!"

"Considering your strength, it must be enchanted. Let me see." Matt shouldered past and set a hand on the stone.

Immediately, he felt a web of magical force enclosing his arm with the stone and the mouth of the tunnel—an unseen seal that bonded the boulder to the rocky cavity with all the force of a high-voltage electromagnet.

" 'Tis dur?" Puck asked, low-voiced.

"Very durable indeed." Matt took his hand away, suppressing a shudder. "But as the safecracker said, no locksmith can design a lock that another man can't figure out how to open. Let me see what I can do.

> "Ascend the knoll! May this rock roll
> And find its way up to a crest—
> Let gravity then take its toll
> Until it brings this rock to rest."

The rock began to vibrate, then to shake, and finally exploded out and away from them. Matt jumped into the doorway and crashed through the screen of brush that hid it, suddenly worried about innocent passersby.

He needn't have worried. He found himself looking down into a shallow, grassy bowl. The rock came to a stop about halfway up the other side, paused, and started rolling back down. Matt looked around quickly, saw the castle off to his left, and no soldiers nearby. He turned back to his companions, satisfied. "All clear, and no damage done. Let's hike."

They came out of the tunnel mouth, Yverne still holding the rags of her gown about her. Matt stopped her with a touch on her arm. "Hold on, milady. Let's do something about that."

"About what?" she asked, startled.

But Matt was droning,

> "Of pale blue gems the belt,
> About her throat, like drops of milk,
> Were glowing pearls she scarcely felt."

Yverne's dress shimmered, turning cloudy, then stilled, having turned into a dress exactly like the one Matt had described. "Oh!" she breathed, eyes wide with delight.

"I thought you had said magic should not be used for inconsequentialities, Wizard." Puck's lip twisted in a half sneer.

"Believe me, this was something that could have bogged down our whole party." Matt noted that Sir Guy had taken advantage of the pause to pull on his gambeson. He stepped over to help with the armor. Fadecourt took the other side, and the knight was steel-plated again in no time, managing to stifle his groans as the pressure rubbed on his new welts. Matt frowned; what was a spell or two more, with so much magic in the air?

> "If anything anyone lacks,
> He'll find it all ready in stacks.
> If sickly he's feeling,
> He'll find himself healing,
> By seventy Simmery Axe!"

"Say, 'Seventy Simmery Axe,' Sir Guy."

"Seventy Simmery Axe," the knight said, almost automatically. "What is its meaning, Wizard?"

"It's an address—house number seventy, on a street called Saint Mary's Axe."

"But Saint Mary would never have borne an axe!" Yverne protested.

" 'Tis enough that she is mentioned." Puck winced.

Matt hoped so—that invoking the Blessed Mother would counteract the spell's having been written for a fictitious sorcerer.

Apparently it did; Sir Guy looked up, eyes wide. "The pain is gone—and the wounds that caused it healed, I doubt not. Sir Matthew, you never cease to amaze me."

"Well, now that I know what it's like to wear armor, I can sympathize." Matt turned his back on the tunnel. "It's going to be a longer haul, with no obliging monsters to carry us—but I'd still like to get away from here as soon as possible."

"Aye, certes!" Yverne set off, taking the lead. "Come, milords, and allow me to show you the way; this is, at least, ground I have passed over some several times, in my childhood."

"Beware!" Fadecourt cried, pointing upward. They all turned to look.

A small, winged shape swooped toward them, growing larger and larger.

"Stegoman!" Matt yelped in glee. Then he had to dodge aside, as the buffeting of air from the dragon's wings almost knocked him over. He bounced back, running up to his old friend with a grin. "How'd you find us?"

"I have been circling about the castle since first I struck at it with boulders carried aloft, then torched the battlements and stooped upon the courtyard," the dragon informed him. "Nay, I had thought thou wouldst never have come out from that place. What kept thee?"

"Bad spells," Matt explained. "That duke is a more powerful sorcerer than he looks to be. But it helped a lot, having the guards suddenly forget about us."

"I had hoped some distraction would serve. Nay, I bethought me to ramp through their halls in search of thee, but they brought arrows enough to engender some caution."

"Wise, and timely." Matt made a stirrup of his hands and boosted Yverne up. "Mind carrying the lady?"

"The lady, and all of thee! Let us not dally, ere the duke and his sorcerers think to enchant us again!"

"Good point; certain parties persuaded me not to kill him, and he might come to, any moment." Matt swung aboard.

"Ah, thou didst beset him, then! But what daft soul bade thee leave him living?"

"Certain parties with more conscience than I have." Matt reached down to help pull Sir Guy up onto Stegoman's back. Fadecourt, of course, had already leaped up from the hind leg. "All in all, though, I think they've probably saved us at least as much as you and I have, considering the local rules. So definitely, let's leave them to stew in their own brew."

"Even so." The dragon spread his wings and sprang into the sky, beating furiously to gain altitude.

"You cannot do this terribly long," Yverne said, worried. "We are too great a load, even for one so mighty as thyself."

"Gramercy, damsel," the dragon puffed. "And, aye, I shall come to earth so soon as we are clear of this vile duke's domain. If 'twere not for the knight's armor, I would carry thee from here to Merovence; yet I would not have him leave it behind, I assure thee."

"Save your breath," Matt advised, eyeing the treetops below with apprehension. "Find us a good updraft, okay? Or shall I make one?"

"I shall manage," Stegoman assured him hastily.

"Hey, I'm not making as many mistakes as I was three years ago!"

"I rejoice to hear it."

"Mistakes?" Yverne looked back at Sir Guy, questioning.

"A tale for another time," he advised. "Hold fast, milady."

"Be mindful, they have not spent all their arrows!" Alisande said sternly to her little army. "If they shoot, bring up shields, and right quickly—the more so since they'll likely wait till we're at close range."

The infantry glanced uncertainly at one another, then let out a half-hearted cheer, which became stronger as others joined in.

A swordsman in the front ranks hefted his shield—heavy oak, with three layers of oxhide. "Fear not, good friends—our planks shall stop their shafts!"

"Indeed they shall, good hearts." Alisande smiled as she turned to face the enemy, lifting her own shield and drawing her sword. "For Merovence and Saint Moncaire!"

"Saint Moncaire and the queen!" the army roared with a single voice, and they started their long climb up the hundred yards of hill.

They didn't run—Alisande had pointed out that there was no purpose to it, until the last ten yards or so, when it would give them some momentum to help break through the Ibilian line. But her knights ranged beside her, on foot, as were they all—horses would be small help in an uphill charge—and she felt the excitement of battle thrill through her. She had to give voice to it; she called out the old, old battle song,

> "Ran! Tan! Terre et ciel!
> Terre et ciel, et sang vermeil!
> Ran! Tan! Earth and sky!
> Earth and sky, and fire and flood!
> Ran! Tan! Earth and sky!
> Scarlet streams of blood!"

Her whole army roared out the verse after her, and, chanting, they strode up toward the army of witchcraft.

CHAPTER 23

Well Wast Well-Wist

They landed fifty miles away, though Stegoman insisted he was good for twice that much. "No," Matt said firmly. "I want some energy reserves, not utter exhaustion. You can never tell what we're going to have to deal with when we land."

Stegoman grumbled something about lack of confidence, but glided down in a spiral. His wings roared as he hovered and slowly settled the last ten feet, griping every inch of the way about it being unnecessary.

"Then why are you panting?" Matt asked.

"The Demon could . . . lend me energy if . . . I had need of it . . . Wizard!"

"Yes, but you'd have to pay it back when the emergency was over," Matt pointed out. "Not even magic can get it for you free, Stegoman. Wholesale, maybe, but not free."

The dragon struck earth, flexing his legs to take up the shock, but it still jarred Matt's back teeth. He swung down to a scaled knee, calling, "Okay! Everybody off except the lady! Give the dragon a break before you break the dragon's giving."

Fadecourt was ahead of him, leaping nimbly from knee to grass, then looking back up at Yverne—and stiffening. "Wizard, 'ware!" He pointed at the sky. "What great bird is that who stoops upon us?"

"Down, damsel!" Stegoman snapped. "I must be free to rise in battle!"

"Wait a minute, no." Matt put out a hand to Stegoman's leg, and could almost feel the adrenaline rising. "I think I recognize that silhouette. At least, I haven't seen too many birds with four legs."

"Is't a dragon, then?" Still, Stegoman craned his neck back, looking up. "Nay, thou hast it aright—the beast hath a bird's tail and talons. Could it be that irresponsible excuse for a monster, come home at last?"

The winged form swelled amazingly fast, and Narlh struck earth a hundred yards behind. He galloped toward them, wings cupped, slowing, and skidded to a halt beside them. "*There* y' are! Wadda ya mean, taking off like that without waiting for me?"

"Waiting!" Stegoman cried. "Thou great lumbering lummox, wherefore didst thou fly from us and desert us?"

Narlh tossed his scaly snout, dismissing the point. "I kept looking and looking, but I couldn't find you in all that clammy gray stuff. By the time I found the edge where it was clearing, you guys were just getting hauled through the gates. I figured the best idea was to lay low and wait for a chance. Then, first thing I knew, here was the dragon, scorching the parapets, and I figured it was now or never, so I started dive-raking the gate tower. Got all the sentries cleared out, too, and I held it for an hour at least, but you never showed up! What took you so long, anyhow?"

"We found the back door," Matt explained. "But you helped more than you knew—all of a sudden, none of the guards had time to worry about us. When did you decide to let them have their walls back?"

"When the duke came staggering out of the keep—and *you* know how I feel about sorcerers. So I made a quick exit, thank you, and climbed up as high as I could to get out of range. Then I saw wings off to the east, and I figured it had to be the dragon, if I could see him that far away. Not as fast as he used to be, though."

"Nor wouldst thou be, if thou didst carry four, one in full armor!" Stegoman retorted.

"No matter how, I'm awfully glad to have you both back," Matt said quickly. "I'd like to get as far away from the duke as I can, and I don't think Stegoman could carry us all very far. Think you could take Fadecourt and Yverne together, Narlh?"

The dracogriff growled low in his throat and shook his wings. "Sure, nothing to it. But can scaly-face there carry you and the knight-in-armor both?"

"Scaly-face, indeed," Stegoman snapped. "And what hast thou for a visage, birdbrain?"

"Takes one to know one, right?"

"I prithee." Yverne stepped up to Narlh, nicely short-circuiting the insult match. "Wilt thou carry me, good beast?"

"Well, for *you*, lady . . ."

No one wins like the winsome, Matt decided. He turned away to Stegoman. "Mind trying again, old saur? Or do you need some rest?"

"Rest? Phaugh!" Stegoman lifted tired wings. "A dragon flies so long as there is need! Mount, knights!"

They did—and Matt noticed that Sir Guy wasn't looking as enthusiastic as he would have expected. He began to wonder if his courtesy to Yverne was just good manners, after all.

He had also noticed that she didn't seem to mind having both the knight and the cyclops being very solicitous of her. He began to revise his opinion of the damsel, then remembered how steadfast she had been in the torture chamber. After all, he had to admit she hadn't exactly been flirting with either man or cyclops—and there was nothing wrong with enjoying the situation, after all.

Was there?

They took off in a thunder of wings, and Stegoman growled, "Whither away, Wizard?"

"I hope that was a question, not a wish." Matt turned back to the knight. "Any idea how we can find Gor—the king's castle, Sir Guy?"

"Castle?" Sir Guy snapped out of a first-class brood. "Oh, aye! I have not seen it, but my allies have told me much of it. The royal castle is by the sea, on a small tongue of land that is surrounded on three sides by ocean."

"Sounds easy enough to recognize." Matt nodded. "Hear that, Stegoman?"

"Aye." The dragon sounded less than enthusiastic. "Thou shalt wish to be set down near to that, I conjecture?"

"As near as is safe, yes."

"If aught can be said to be safe, in Ibile," the dragon grumbled—but he arrowed ahead into the west, anyway.

The castle was there, all right, a huge triangle of curtain walls containing a trio of courtyards, a brooding old keep, and a whole town of support buildings. But there was a sulky, sullen feeling of having gone to seed, of having been darkened by centuries of soot. "Max," Matt said softly, "what's wrong with that place?"

The spark appeared beside him in midair, then hummed, "Precisely what you suspected, Wizard, or you'd not have summoned me. Entropy has taken it, and none has fought it off."

"But I don't see any visible signs of decay."

"Nor would you. The rot is not physical, but spiritual."

"Castles don't have souls!"

"Nay, but a house reflects its owners' spirits, Lord Wizard. The denizens of *that* house have let their souls subside in decay; 'tis why they are termed 'decadent.' This is only the outward sign of that corruption."

It did seem corrupt, now that Max had said the word—like the corpse of a great fortress, rotting unburied. Matt shuddered and turned to the practical aspect of the situation, which meant talking backward over his shoulder. "See any way to get in, Sir Guy?"

"Nay, Sir Matthew. 'Tis impregnable, unless it chooses to be otherwise."

Matt toyed with the notion of trying to get in by ruse and disguise, but discarded it quickly. "We'd better get out of the sky, then—I don't relish having their sentries see us and watch to find out where we go. Think you've seen all you need?"

"For what purpose?" Sir Guy shrugged. "I have seen its overall plan and can draw it for you from memory, now—yet how will that serve? We shall not take it, though we camp about its walls for ten years."

"Let's mull that over at leisure, shall we? Stegoman, find us a safe place for relaxing."

The dragon banked away toward the east. Matt scowled down at the ocean below, trying to figure out how to take a castle on a headland. Then he sat up straight, eyes widening. "Down there, on that island! What castle is that?"

It was much smaller, only a curtain wall, an outer bailey partitioned off from the inner bailey surrounding the keep, and four towers situated around its irregular, ellipsoid shape. It was dilapidated to the eye, though not to the inner eye, and surrounded by the long slopes of a hill, barren and blackened—almost, Matt would have thought, charred.

" 'Tis the Castillo Adamanto," Sir Guy answered. "I have heard of it—how it has restrained past kings from tyranny, by welcoming such barons as disagreed with the king. If enemies opposed those earlier monarchs from across so narrow a stretch of ocean, and were able to blockade them by sea whilst others might wall off their peninsula on the landward side, they might bid fair to starve the kings out—as the counts of that castle have done, ever and anon through these five hundred years. Always has the king had to come to terms with his barons, and his tyranny has never been absolute—till now."

"Oh? The sorcerer king managed to conquer it?"

"Nay—but his ships have penned it up. None may come there, now, and 'tis likely that the last of the counts is dead. Yet his spells endure, to sear invaders with fire if they approach his walls."

Could that explain the charred look to the hillsides? But how could the count keep a spell going after his death?

By embedding the command in a poem, naturally. Literature endured, after all. Matt nodded. "Well, we're not approaching by land, and we don't want to conquer—we just want a bed for the night, and shelter while we try to figure out what we can do about the king. This strikes me as the ideal location—if we can come in without getting fired. Do you suppose your cohort could find out?"

"The Puck? What say, goblin, can you tell?"

"Aye, that can I," Puck's voice said behind Matt, making the hairs on his neck stand on end. "What matters fire to a spirit mercurial? Nay, if flames come, I may change my form and burn *them* out!"

Matt didn't doubt that he could.

A breath of breeze fanned the back of his neck, and he saw the elf diving down toward the castle. He held his breath, but nothing happened.

"How long must we tarry?" Stegoman demanded.

"Till he tells us it's clear," Matt answered. "Sorry about the weight, old friend."

"'Tis not so bad as all that—there are updrafts here, and I but glide from the one to the other. Natheless, Matthew, I shall be glad of a chance to lay me down."

"Just wait till we're on the ground, okay?" A dot was shooting up toward them, swelling into a diminutive human form—and Puck landed on Sir Guy's shoulder. "There is naught, not so much as a spark."

"Let us attempt it, Matthew."

"As you say. Gently, Stegoman."

"Indeed. I've no wish to be crisped." The dragon began to circle lower, a little at a time, very warily.

He brought them in to a thundering descent that was vertical for the last fifty feet, stretching his hind toes down to touch the granite, then taking up his weight as he sank down to crouch on all fours, folding his wings. Narlh wasn't quite so graceful—he came in at a low angle and landed running fast, cupping his wings to brake and trying to dig in his claws to come to a stop. He almost had to leap off the other side and try again, but at the last moment, he skidded to a halt, slewing around and bringing himself up sharply against a merlon.

"Done with excellent grace," Stegoman said dryly. "In truth, thou hast scant need to fly, thou dost run so well."

"Oh, put it in a bucket and drop it in a well!" Narlh growled, coming back to them. "If you're such an expert, maybe you could teach me that neat vertical landing, huh?"

Stegoman eyed the dracogriff's feathered wings with doubt. "I will essay it, surely, an thou dost wish."

Fadecourt clambered down and helped a very pale Yverne to dismount.

"But you just don't think I'm up to it, huh?" Narlh bristled.

"I have no basis for judgment," Stegoman confessed. "Ne'er before have I seen a creature like to thee."

Narlh's head snapped up, stung, and Matt leaped in to pour balm on the wound before the bomb exploded. "Quite a compliment, to think you're unique—and you wouldn't deny that you are rare."

"Well . . . special, anyway," Narlh grumped.

"Unique," Matt confirmed. "Now, do you two guys want to try to squeeze down that stairway with the rest of us, or do you want to stay up here and hold a mutual gripe session?"

"I will come," Stegoman said quickly. "I mislike the look of that dark maw of a staircase. Nay, Matthew, thou mayest have need of my flame."

"I'll beg off, thank you." Narlh eyed the hole in the roof with loathing. "I have this thing about tight places. Besides, you're going to need a sentry up here, just in case."

Matt couldn't have agreed more, though he couldn't think what "in case" might be. "Great. Hope you get bored, though."

"I kinda think I've had enough interesting times to hold me," Narlh agreed.

"Okay. Off to the lower depths, folks." And Matt strode away toward the dark doorway at the base of the north tower, trying not to show the qualms he was feeling.

They filed through the door and turned the first curve of the spiral into darkness, and Matt said, "I think maybe a small flare, Stegoman."

But before the dragon could comply, light burst ahead of them, several steps down. Matt stared in surprise, instantly tensed to face an enemy—but the light was coming from a sconce on the wall. It was an empty sconce, though, one that should have held a torch, but didn't. Instead, it held a bluish flame.

"What enemy awaits us?" Sir Guy demanded.

"None—only an automatic lighting system." But Matt frowned at the sconce, knowing that bluish flame was familiar, wondering why, and where he'd seen it before.

"Let us go further," Stegoman rumbled, and Matt went on, under the sconce and down into the next curve of darkness.

Light flared in front of them again.

"Is't another unseen torch?" Yverne asked, voice not quite steady.

"Yes." Matt gazed at the flame in the sconce, musing, then decided it was nothing threatening. "It's just a very good system for lighting this stairway only when it's needed. Fadecourt, tell me when that first torch goes out."

"I will," the cyclops answered, and Matt went on down the spiral. Another sconce burst into flame before him.

"The light has gone from the wall behind me," Fadecourt reported.

Matt nodded. "Each torch comes on as we near it, then fades as we pass it. Very efficient spell—and one that also warns the inhabitants that we're here, no doubt."

"If there are any to heed it," Sir Guy pointed out.

"There must be. The flames have burst forth from the hillside, whene'er the king has attacked." But Fadecourt was frowning, too, uncertain.

With good reason. If the torches could be automatic, why not the castle's defenses? "We'll find out in a few minutes," Matt said. "Let's go."

They went on down the tower stair with no more discussion, moving as quietly as they could on the stone.

Finally, the stairway opened out, and the last torch showed them a broad chamber beyond. Matt stepped out into that great room and saw faded tapestries covering the walls, an elaborate carved chair on a distant dais, and a fireplace with roaring flames. Beside it, hands locked behind his back and gazing at the fire in contemplation, stood a short, plump man with baggy hose and a threadbare doublet, high forehead shading into a bare scalp fringed with long, gray hair that hung down about his shoulders. His face was wan and wrinkled, with a brooding, thoughtful look, lit from below by firelight.

He seemed unaware of their presence. If his spell on the tower stair had given warning, he had paid it no heed.

It seemed a little rude to call out, so Matt cleared his throat.

The old man spun toward the sound, eyes wide in horror. He gave a little cry and cowered back, hands upheld to ward them off, quavering, "Enemies! My friends, come! We are beset!"

Suddenly the air was thick with gauzy, translucent shapes with huge gray moth wings and stunted, gnarled, almost-human forms. Wispy beards adorned faces like oak burls, and clenched fists pounded the companions. One blow struck through and into Matt's head; he heard nothing, but a blinding pain shot through his skull. "Max! Disperse them!"

But Puck was already in action, shooting from one creature to another, countering blows with his own, tiny, upraised palm—and the force of the punch rebounded, knocking the moth-men awry. Max danced out to join him, singing in glee as he shot through and through the translucent forms; the moth-men began to keen with pain.

"Cold Iron!" Sir Guy roared, whipping out his sword and whirling it over his head. The spirits scattered, pulling back from his blade, but hovering just beyond its reach, and their keening took on the tone of anger.

"Behind us!" Fadecourt called, and Matt whipped about to see more moth-men closing in from the rear. "It's a trap after all!" he cried. "Gordogrosso set an ambush for us! I should've known!"

"Gordogrosso, do you say?" the old man cried in surprise. "Nay, desist, my friends! The enemy of my enemy is my ally!"

The moth-men pulled back, simmering with anger, and Puck shot toward them.

"Nay, hold, goblin!" Sir Guy called. "'Twould be pity of my life, if we were to slay friends!"

Puck hovered, trading glares with a moth-man, but held his station.

"Patch 'em up, Max," Matt called. "Wait a minute—no. Just stop hurting them. If they *are* friends, we'll heal them."

"You have the power to undo the harm you've done?" the old man asked, amazed.

"That much, I can do," Matt confirmed. "The question is, should I?"

The old man spread his hands. "That's to say, am I your friend? And to that, I can only reply that I have resisted the king's armies and magic all my life, as did my father before me, and his father before him."

"Are your moth-men that strong?"

The moth-men set up an angry buzzing, and the old man frowned. "Call them well-wists, for they wist of all wells and other depths beneath the earth. They do flit through rock and soil as birds do fly through air, and thus learn all the secrets of the hidden places beneath the ground."

"Oh." Matt lifted his head, understanding. "It's not just their power to hurt that gives them strength—it's their knowledge."

"Aye. 'Tis they showed my grandsire how to defend his castle with flame, in return for some service he had done them."

Matt was suddenly very interested in the nature of that service—but the old man was asking, "Are you not the king's henchmen, sent here to slay me and seize my castle?"

"Never!" Fadecourt snapped.

Yverne lifted her head, indignant at the insult. "I have suffered too much from this vile monarch who broke faith with my father, good sir."

"None of us would even think of siding with Gord—uh, the king," Matt explained, without apparently attracting their enemy's attention.

Or *had* they attracted his attention, but without risk? Certainly the castle seemed impregnable, even from magic. Matt felt more confident, but also felt the heavy weight of an obligation to be honest. "Myself, I'm out to assassinate the king." It sounded ugly, when he came right out and said it—but that was what he intended, after all, and if there were anything wrong about it, he'd better find out ahead of time. "Not that I usually advocate murder, you understand, but he deserves it if anybody does, and it's the only way to save the people of Ibile from him. I'd prefer to kill him in open battle, of course, but I don't think I'll get the chance."

"Nay, surely not." Finally, the old man smiled. "And if you are indeed his enemies, you are welcome in my castle. But how came you hither?"

"Looking for a hiding place from the king," Matt explained, "but one where we could keep watch on him and try to lay some plans about invading *his* castle. Our dragon friend—" He nodded over his shoulder at Stegoman. "—brought us to your roof, and we came down the stairs. You don't seem to keep many guards, sir."

"I am the Don de la Luce, and I keep no guards indeed, save these my friends, who will come at my call—yet I would not trouble them without need."

"Neither would I." Matt gave the indignant well-wists a guilty glance. "I hadn't meant to hurt friends—but I didn't know you were on my side."

The biggest well-wist buzzed angrily.

"He says that they did not know you were not assassins sent by the king," Don de la Luce interpreted. "They knew only that you were intruders, and as such, sought to protect me by driving you away."

"Yeah, I can understand how I must have looked from their point of view. Well, uh, I'm sorry, well-wists."

Another moth-man—or was it woman?—stepped up beside the biggest, buzzing in an indignant tone.

"She says you might show your contrition by healing them," the don explained.

"Oh, yeah! What's wrong with me? No, don't answer that! Yeah, I should have fixed them up in the first place." Matt turned away, frowning while he tried to dredge up the appropriate verse, then turned back to the well-wists, spreading his open palms to include them all, and chanting,

> "Where steel and fire have torn and singed,
> Gossamer strands shall mend and knit,
> Making whole what's torn and tattered.
> What friends unknown have broke and shattered,
> Shall meld and mend, and heal what's split,
> Now setting firm what came unhinged!"

As he spoke, the very air began to shimmer. The well-wists buzzed and sang, churning together in consternation, just beginning to become alarmed when the coruscation died. The creatures looked at one another, their tones turning into chimings and flutings of delight.

"They are healed indeed!" the Don de la Luce said, staring. "You are a wizard brave and doughty!"

For a moment, Matt thought he had said "knave and dotty," and was about to agree with him. Fortunately, he realized what the old don had said, just in time to change his comeback to, "Glad to be able to make amends. Have we hurt any guardian spirits on your stairway, too?"

"Nay; there is only a charm laid on it. In truth, I should have guessed that you were not malignant, for the stairwell is enchanted only against those with evil magic."

Matt shook his head. "For all you knew, we might have been king's sorcerers who had managed to disable your spell."

"True, though none such have ever been able to rise to such heights within this stronghold."

"Sounds like you could use a few human guards. Don't you have any flesh-and-blood retainers?"

"Nay, I dwell alone in this great old stone pile; all our soldiers and servants fled, in my grandfather's time, to serve the evil tyrant." He shook his head at the memory. "I was but newly come to manhood then, yet I remember well the ferocious battles of my boyhood, when my grandfather strove against the king with his knights and men-at-arms, keeping the shores of this isle secure by sword and steel, even as his wizards battled with the king and his sorcerers. But they died, the wizards—they died, and the people fled to the mainland, sick and weary of battle, and afeard of the king's sorcery. I hope they fared well, yet I misdoubt me of it." His mouth tightened. "Ah me! What may have happened to them! Some we knew of, for their tattered ghosts spoke to my grandfather of torture and degradations as they flew past on their way to Heaven or Purgatory, and not a one but did not wish he had stayed to fight and died a clean death. Oh, yes, oh, yes! 'Tis better far to die in battle, than to fail by inches, serving the king's pleasure! Yet there were none to battle by our sides, my father and my grandsire and myself, save my mother and her ladies, yes, but no bride for me, no, for the ladies had fled and gone, fled and gone." A tear trembled in his eye; he blinked it back.

"But I remembered, aye, the well-wists, and the tale my grandfather told, of the time of *his* grandfather, when the land was newly sunk in evil, oh, yes, and our most doughty ally sunk beneath the wave, the waves. Oh, 'twas then the well-wists came flocking, filling our castle with aimless anger, and folk would have fled their haunting had not my grandfather's grandfather seen 'twas fear that moved them, and not anger. He found they feared the sea, oh yes, and fled to find a roost for their mates, since the sea was claiming their caverns below, below. He showed them the caverns 'neath this castle, yes, and gave them all his dungeons, and at this they rejoiced, for they do not like the light, you know."

"No," Matt said. "I hadn't known that."

"Had you not? They do not, you know. They are creatures of the under-earth, who need no light, but see by the essence of each stone and grain of sand. Nay, the dungeons were their delight, and the caverns beneath—the dungeons that are now their home, and there they dwell, to keep me safe in my loneliness."

The solitude, Matt realized, had touched the poor dotard's brains.

How much of what he was telling was truth, and how much demented imaginings?

"Safe?" Yverne asked, pity underscoring her tone. "I can see that they are company for you—but how do they keep you safe?"

"Did I not tell you? Oh, I see—I did not, did not. But you, pretty child—who are you?" The old man advanced, hand reaching out to touch Yverne's.

She did not shrink. "I am the Lady Yverne, daughter of the Duke of Toumarre."

"Ah, yes! I knew them well, or knew of them, I should say, for never have I gone forth from this island."

That hit Matt with a jolt. To have spent his whole life on this miserable piece of rock! No wonder the poor old guy had never had a girlfriend.

But how could he have left? Sorcerers hemmed him in on all sides, waiting to smear him into paste and gobble his island and castle. Not much choice—though Matt wondered if he'd have the courage to keep living, in the old man's place.

"They were good men, your ancestors." The old man patted Yverne's hand reassuringly. "Or as good as they could be, when they had sworn allegiance to the king. Nay, they must needs then have given themselves over to the evilness of his reign—yet by all reports and all the tales my grandfather told of those days, they strove for goodness in spite of all. Oh, the king would have haled them down and slain them root and branch, had he dared—or so my grandfather said. Slain them, but he dared not, for only they knew how to keep the borderlands safe from the soldiers of Merovence, yes, the soldiers who were hot to bring down the sorcerer then, they were."

"He dared do it in the end," Yverne informed him. "I am the last of my line, unless my father still endures, languishing in his enemy's dungeon."

"Oh, poor child!" The old man's head lifted, eyes huge. "But he must still live, must he not? For the king cannot gain full power over those lands of yours, unless one of your line gives them to him, yes. Without that, oh, he may hold them, but the magic of them he will never master, no. And failing that power, the land itself will welcome the champions of Merovence. Oh, yes, it will."

Yverne turned to Matt and Sir Guy, eyes wide. "Is that how you came unharmed through my father's lands, then?"

"Are they of Merovence? Oh, delight! Delight! Then mayhap the king's last hour is at hand. Could we not hope it? Yes, of course we could." The old man released Yverne's hand and turned to the cyclops. "What is your house and station, sir?"

"Call me Fadecourt," the cyclops replied, "and my house and station are of no consequence, while the reign of evil endures—for I am of Ibile."

"I see, I see!" The old man nodded wisely. "And you wish to live a good and godly life. Indeed, of no consequence—save that they make you a staunch ally, yes! But you are not of Merovence?"

"Nay, though my companions are."

"They are, they are!" The don turned to Sir Guy. "Your name, Sir Knight?"

"Sir Guy de Toutarien, and I am honored by your hospitality, Milord de la Luce."

"It is given, it is gladly given! And I am honored by your company, yes. You are welcome, well come indeed."

"And my friend, of whose tongue you have already made acquaintance, is Matthew Mantrell, Lord Wizard of Merovence, and a knight of honor."

"The Lord Wizard!" The don turned to Matt, eyes wide. "I had never thought to find so eminent a magus so deep in Ibile. Though . . ." His eyebrows drew down in thought. "You have not the look of the Lord Wizard of whom I have heard."

"If you're talking about my predecessor, he was assassinated, along with his king," Matt answered. "I, uh, attached myself to his daughter, helped her out of a few rough scrapes and such, so when she got her throne back, she made me her Lord Wizard."

"He speaks too modestly," Sir Guy interposed. "It was he, more than any man, who haled the usurper Astaulf from the throne of Merovence, and overcame his sorcerer, Malingo."

"Yeah, with you and Stegoman and a loyal giant to back me up—not to mention a few thousand monastic knights and a lot of loyal footmen!"

"Yet 'twas you who brought them all to her, Sir Matthew, and you who—"

"Milords! Good knights!" The old don spread his hands. "Enough, I pray! I see that the Lord Wizard was indeed a mighty ally of the queen's—yet thinks himself less than he was."

"Well—I certainly am not the great cure-all they seem to think. The queen's beginning to realize that, too, now."

"Is she truly?" The old man gave him a keen look that Matt felt all the way to his liver and lights. "Nay, I think there is more than a matter of faith and allegiance in this. And I have heard something of this struggle, too, yes—heard of a wizard who waked a giant made of stone, who brought down the castle of a witch who had enchanted hundreds of youths and lasses, then fought off a besieging, sorcerous army, not once, but twice—"

"With a lot of clergy to back me up! Not to mention the knights and men-at-arms."

"I shall not, since you ask it. But I doubt not you merit your title, Lord Wizard—I see that you are dedicated in your loyalty."

He saw a bit more than Matt wanted him to, so it was time to change the subject. "Well, I'll have to consider the source—and from what I see, you must be no mean wizard yourself. After all, you're attended by a flock of well-wists and holding firm against a sorcerous army next door."

But the old man was shaking his head. "'Tis only cleverness and goodwill, Lord Wizard, and as much my grandfather's as mine. Nay, all I can claim is having befriended the well-wists, and my grandfather's grandfather did that for me."

"But you were the only one who did more than know they were there?"

Again, that glance that cut through to his marrow. "There is no wonder in that. I was a young man, restless and unused to solitude—and the well-wists' cavern was the only strange land in which I could wander, the only folk to whom I was other than the don's son. Their friendship given, they showed me the marvels of their domain—and when I saw the great store of black water, and how they could make it flame, I could not help but realize how the fire could repel the sorcerers."

"Couldn't help it, huh?"

"Could any man?"

"Many, I doubt not," Fadecourt rumbled, "myself included. What did you with this 'black water' you speak of?"

"I drew it off, with the aid of my well-wist friends—drew it off into a great wheel of pipes that we pushed through the earth to surround the castle. Then, when the enemy marched upon us, we let the black water flow, and it spilled out to soak through the ground all about. It killed the grass, aye, and the bushes, more's the pity—but when I did shoot fire-arrows down into it, a curtain of flame sprang up, and the sorcerers could not douse it. Oh, if they had known it was rock oil, I doubt not they would have found a way . . . but who would have thought it? Nay, not I myself, had I not learned of it from the well-wists. Yet I had, I had."

"Maybe." Matt frowned. "Or maybe when the sorcerers tried, the well-wists were able to counter their spells. This is within the domain of their powers, after all, and they're obviously magical beings."

The old don looked up, surprised, and smiled. "There, now, do you see? You may well be right—but I would never have thought of such by myself, never! Nay, I am no sorcerer, but only a clever man."

"'Tis the work of genius," Fadecourt assured him, "to see a defense 'gainst sorcery, where others saw naught but a lamp."

"A wick and a fuel." Matt nodded. "You've fought off the king's army several times, haven't you?"

"Oh, a dozen, yes, twelve, and a few more, for I am old, milords and lady, old."

Matt had a notion the old man was exaggerating again. "After all that burning, the soil is probably so calcined by heat that it's providing capillary action, and functioning as a sort of wick."

"A wizard! A wizard, surely!" De la Luce shook his head in admiration. "There, you see it? Never would I have thought to phrase it so!"

No, but he'd certainly had the concept, and the insight to apply it—and without any more background than having learned how an oil lamp worked. It took immense brainpower to make that kind of cognitive leap. Matt didn't doubt he was in the presence of a genius. He shook off the shiver the thought gave him and said, "Pushing the oil into the pipes must take some kind of power source. How do you do it? It can't be just gas pressure, if you're drawing it from a seepage pool."

"'Tis not, 'tis not. The well-wists aided me in making a pipe, and a way of pushing rock oil through it, as a lad shoots a bean through a straw. Will it please you come see it?"

He seemed pathetically eager to show off his handiwork, but it would have taken a giant octopus to hold Matt back. "Oh, you bet I would. Which way?"

The way was down. They passed the dungeon early on, and the lower dungeon a little later. That surprised Matt; he'd expected that the tour would be in the lower depths, but he had thought they'd bottom out fairly early. He was getting tired just walking downhill; he was beginning to dread the thought of going back up. To make things worse, the old man kept up an enthusiastic monologue every inch of the way, pointing out minerals they were passing through, for all the world like a paid tour guide—and one who really loved his subject, too, to the point of never having any idea that anyone else might not find it at all interesting. Matt grew tired of the virtues of limestone very quickly and was actively resenting the gloss on celebration of sedimentaries, when he heard the old man say something about shale. He pricked up his ears and really looked at the wall passing by him. Sure enough, it had a darker look; it was oil-bearing.

Then the old man turned off the stairway into a dark tunnel mouth. Matt had a very strong urge to keep on going, but the well-wists were crowding closely around them, and they weren't exactly eyeing him with favor, still seeming to harbor some resentment at his earlier conduct—so he followed.

They came out into a cavern, so hemispherical that it looked as if it had been formed by a bubble in the rock. One look at what it contained, and Matt had no doubt that was what it had been—a gas bubble. For the light of a thousand well-wists reflected a thick-looking dark liquid, gently rippling under the breath of semisubstantial wings, and Matt knew by the aroma that it wasn't water.

Yverne wrinkled her nose. "Phew! What is this fluid, Milord de la Luce?"

"'Tis the rock oil, milady—oil seeped from the rocks themselves. 'Tis as light as any lamp oil, but I would not set a wick to burning here."

Too right he wouldn't! If he tried, they'd probably all go up in a bang that would knock the huge old stone pile above them into pebbles. "Stegoman," Matt called, "don't come in."

"I cannot," the dragon's voice called from outside the tunnel. "The cave mouth is too small."

"That's just fine." Matt turned to the don. "Seepage, you say?"

"Aye. There is no spring—it seems to rise from a thousand cracks in the stone."

"All light stuff, then—kerosene, gasoline, light oil." Matt turned away. "It's an awe-inspiring sight, your lordship—but if you don't mind, I'd rather do my admiring from a distance. I'm already feeling a little light-headed."

"Aye—'tis not good to breathe in the presence of the pool for overlong." The old don ushered them out of the chamber.

As they came out, Sir Guy asked, "You channel this stuff to the land about your castle, then?"

"Aye. There is a pipe let into the wall of the pool, below its surface." De la Luce turned away down even more stairs. "Its own weight makes it sink down into the tube."

"But what brings it up?" Matt asked, following.

"Hark!" The old don held up a hand. "Do you hear?"

They were quiet, and heard, afar off, a hissing sound that rose and fell.

"The sea!" Fadecourt breathed.

"Aye. It moves my oil for me. Will you come?" De la Luce led the way down, and down again, and again.

Finally, the stairwell brightened with daylight. A few more steps, and they came into a low sea cave, perhaps ten feet high. Its floor was only a narrow ledge, alongside a twenty-foot-wide channel of seawater, five feet below them. "The tide is flowing," de la Luce observed. "At its height, it will be scant inches below this track."

But Matt was looking at something else. "How on earth did you get the idea for that?"

It was a huge paddle wheel, almost as high as the roof, its lower arc already immersed in the seawater. With each surge of the tide, the wheel turned, but the ebb didn't turn it back. The old man had rigged an escapement, in a world that hadn't invented anything more elaborate than the water clock.

"From a mill wheel, naught but a mill wheel." The old man smiled, obviously pleased by the praise. "Though I did need long hours of pondering upon it, ere I seized upon a means of holding the wheel against the backwash of the tide's surge, yes, and longer hours yet to dream of a means by which that device could be reversed, so that the wheel could give me power at both ebb and flow."

Matt shivered, more certain than ever that he was in the presence of a genius. To make clockwork is no big deal, when someone else has shown you how—but to invent it yourself is quite another matter. "How do you harness the power of the wheel, so that it raises the oil to the soil?"

"By a thickened disk of metal, pushing the fluid up through a pipe. There are holes at top and bottom, the one to let the oil in, the other to let it out. 'Tis simple enough, once 'tis seen."

Simple, sure—but he hadn't seen it. Except in his mind's eye . . .

The old man stepped closer to the paddle wheel, frowning and reaching out to touch a slab of wood. "'Tis cracked; I must replace it soon." He turned to Matt. "For it turns, day and night, to keep it fit, even though I've no need of its power, no, not more than a dozen times these fifty years. But I make it work once each year at least, yes, to be sure it will bring the oil when I want it."

"Wise precaution." Matt swallowed. "And still you're going to tell me that you're not a wizard."

"Certes! For surely, I am not!" the old man said in surprise, then smiled gently. "Be not deceived, Lord Wizard—there's naught of magic in this."

"Only in your mind," Matt muttered. He had a brief vision of an attack on the castle—enemy troops charging forward with scaling ladders, as the pump pushed hundreds of gallons of inflammable fluid into the ground around the castle, now charred as porous as pumice. Then a fire-arrow would come arcing up from the battlements, stabbing down into the earth—and a wall of flame would explode all about the assault troops. Matt winced at the imagined sound of their screams, and mentally cheered them on as they charged back into their own lines. Then he remembered what their officer-sorcerers would probably do to them, and forced the vision away. "No wonder it's been awhile since you had an assault."

"Aye." The old man nodded with a sad smile. "Why waste troops, when the king has simply to wait? For I have no heirs, no, nor anyone else dwelling with me here, save the well-wists—and the sorcerer could deal with them quickly enough had I not bade them flee when I die. Nay, they think I am alone here, all alone, though I thank Heaven I am not. There is a lovely lass who visits me, bless her—aye, and not once a year, but once a day and more!" He gave Matt a keen look with a knowing smile. "You shall think her to be but a vision of my fancy, and myself but a crazed old fool." The sorrow evaporated from his smile. "None will believe that she is real, as real as I myself—so mine enemies think that I must die the sooner for want of company. Well, let them learn their folly! I shall endure, thanks to her friendship—and, God willing, I will survive them all, to see the deliverance of Ibile, and the destruction of its sorcerers!"

"Amen to that," Fadecourt said fervently, and Sir Guy and Yverne echoed, "Amen."

For his own part, Matt agreed with the sentiments, but wasn't too sure about the means. He didn't doubt for a second that the "lovely lass" was every bit as imaginary as the old man's enemies doubtless said. Loneliness could do that to a person.

Yverne, however, took him at his word. "A lass who visits you? When all other folk have fled this island? Nay, whence could she come?"

"From the sea," the old don explained, "from the sea itself. Betimes she does in truth come up out of the sea, to converse awhile with me—but nothing more." The sad smile returned. "Nay, surely nothing more, though I had some hope of that when I was younger, a lad of forty or so—yet I aged, and she did not. She is my friend still, and anon takes me with her down under the waves to visit with her father, where they dwell forgotten in their watery palace. Ah, 'tis sad! 'Tis sad!"

Yverne looked up at Matt in alarm, but he shook his head. There was nothing he could do; the poor don was sunk in illusion. Sure, Matt might be able to banish the delusion with the appropriate spell—in fact, one was nudging at his mind right now—but would he really be doing the old man a favor? None of his business, for sure.

But Yverne looked so forlorn.

Then she mustered a brave smile as she turned back to the old man. "Is she a beauty, then, this lass of yours?"

"The queen of beauty to me," he said, then surprised Matt by adding, "though I doubt if others would find her fair, for her skin shimmers with scales ever so delicately wrought, and her hair is green, as are her eyes. Yet she is no mermaid, no, for she walks upon feet as delicate as shells, and her lips are coral."

Matt made one try at dispelling the illusion, though it earned him a glare from Yverne. "How could she come in, milord? She can't very well come knock on your raised drawbridge."

"Heaven forfend ! Nay, she comes in yonder." He pointed back to the cavern they had just left. "Where the seawater rises, so rises she, riding upon the waves, then comes from the water and comes up to warm herself at my hearth, and warm my old heart with gladsome talk. Merry is she, and ever full of cheer, and her laugh is the chiming of silver bells."

"Through the sea door?" Matt stared. "And she climbs all those stairs, once a day?!"

The old man's mouth tightened, and he gave a single curt nod. "Be assured she does! This is no delusion, Lord Wizard, but only honest fact!"

"She must love you more than you think, then," Matt sighed, "to be willing to go up all those stairs. No way around it, though, is there?"

The old don gave a ghost of a smile, his good humor reviving. "Nay. As we have come down, Lord Wizard, so we must rise up."

For a moment, Matt was tempted to try a transportation spell—but there was always the chance that it might go wrong, and besides, he was going to need every ounce of magical energy he had. He started climbing.

•   •   •

The don bustled around, finding them some cold meat and bread—which, he claimed, the well-wists gave him. He also opened a bottle of wine which the sea-maid supposedly brought, and Matt could almost believe it—it certainly had an odd flavor. Then the don excused himself and bustled away, with an air of repressed anticipation that Matt didn't trust. He tried to relax, assuring himself that the old man was trustworthy—but he stayed on his guard in spite of himself.

"At last, a moment of tranquility!" Yverne sighed—and with surprise, Matt realized that she was right; since their escape from the duke's dungeon, they hadn't had a moment to relax.

Then she turned to Matt, and those limpid blue eyes suddenly held his gaze, unwinking. "Now, Lord Wizard, you must tell me—how did you bring Fadecourt and yourself forth from that dungeon cell?"

Matt stiffened, then forced himself to lean back and look casual. "Oh, just the ordinary escape spells."

"Aye, and they did not work," Fadecourt reminded him.

Matt spared him a quick glare. *Shut up, Fadecourt!* But the cyclops' mental telepathy wasn't working that day. "Surely you cannot have forgotten so quickly! You had need to attempt a more powerful verse, and it brought you not escape, but the three weird sisters."

"No, wait a minute," Matt was getting desperate now. "You've got the wrong story; the weird sisters belong in that play about the Scottish usurper . . ."

"Nay, they surely did come from the far north . . ."

"South. Definitely south. I keep telling you, they were the Fates, not the Norns."

"The Fates!" Yverne gasped, eyes huge—and Matt mentally cursed, because he really had no one to blame but himself; Fadecourt may have egged him on, but it was he himself who had let the fateful word slip. "Oh, they're not really so terrible as that. Wouldn't take any beauty prizes, mind you, but—"

"You summoned the Fates!" It was almost a scream. "The Fates themselves! Nay, surely they have now conspired against you!"

"Be of good heart, maiden." Fadecourt was patting her hand. "They did naught against him; nay, in truth, 'twas he overcame them."

"Surely not!" Yverne was about to cry. "You did not bait the Fates themselves!"

"That's right, I didn't," Matt said quickly. "I just recited a quick spell to protect us from them."

"But they shall have revenge! They shall not brook a mere mortal man to balk them!"

"Can't do any harm." Matt's reassurances were beginning to sound a little frantic. "I was planning on a short life, anyway. I positively shudder at the thought of growing up . . . I mean, old!"

There was a cackle from the far end of the great hall.

Every hair on Matt's head tried to stand on end, but he forced himself, slowly, to turn and look.

A globe of light shimmered in the gloom at the far end of the great hall, and within it stood the three old ladies, spinning, measuring, and, most especially, clacking scissors. Matt squinted, but he couldn't see through the shimmer clearly enough to notice any particularly devastating results from their last encounter. Whatever their screaming had signified, apparently it hadn't done any real damage. That beam of sunlight may have hurt—or had it just shocked them? Maybe even just startled.

"So! The upstart gives boast, sisters!" Clotho cried.

"Is't a boast to say he wishes a short life?" Lachesis demanded.

"Aye, since 'tis as much as to say he does not fear us!" Atropos snapped. "Come sisters! What shall we do with the braggart, eh?"

"Oh, now it comes!" Yverne cried.

"Why, take him at his word!" Clotho cackled. "If he wishes a short life, give him a long one!"

"Very long!" Atropos nodded sagely. "He shall wither in his age; his sight shall fail, his teeth shall fall out."

Clotho squinted at her web. "Nay, I cannot give him all of such infirmities, for I see he knows the counter to the most of them. Howsoe'er, a long life is by no means a peaceful one."

"Aye!" Atropos cried. "Fill his life with strife! If death is slow in coming, what matter? That does not preclude horrendous wounds in battle, maiming cuts, and dire mischances!"

"He shall beg for death," the youngest crooned. "He shall seek it! It shall become his most ardent quest!"

"A quest he must resolve himself!" Clotho cried in a fit of inspiration, her fingers flying. "He shall have to *earn* his death!"

"Alack!" Yverne cried. "How can they be so cruel?"

"Comes with the job." Matt's brave front was wearing thin.

"He shall attempt the impossible, he shall achieve the improbable!" Atropos shrieked. "And then, only then, when he has suffered to save his world, may he die!"

"Then he shall save Ibile?" Fadecourt cried.

"The saving of Ibile shall be the least of his labors," Clotho chanted, as if she had heard him. "He shall discover the ways in which the world is threatened to be engulfed by evil . . ."

"As it ever is," the youngest added. "He shall confront the most evil of men, he shall suffer at their hands! And when he has saved all of Europe, aye, and half of Asia, then may he die!"

Matt's skin crawled. She wasn't really siccing him with having to wait until Genghis Khan showed up, was she? That would be hundreds of years! Matt felt every instinct he had balking. "That's not for me to say! Shouldn't the people of Europe choose their own fate? Shouldn't the common folk of Ibile choose their own government?"

Now, finally, Clotho looked up, eyes boring into his—and, for a moment, the mist thinned; Matt saw a swath of smooth, flawless skin across her ravaged countenance. And, finally, she spoke directly to him. "Foolish mortal! How much choice have those people now?"

"Well . . . I suppose the sorcerers are pretty strict dictators . . ."

"The people are but slaves!" Clotho's lip curled in contempt. "The king and his sorcerous nobles dictate every step, every act their people make! And they are cruel, most horribly cruel, in their enforcement."

"The poor folk dare not even embrace one another in the solitude of their huts," the youngest said, "for fear the sorcerers might be watching in their crystals. Nay, 'tis the foulest, most oppressive tyranny ever known!"

Matt was about to ask them about Herod and Nero, until he remembered that he was talking to experts. If anyone knew, it was the Fates. He hid a shudder at the thought of just how bad the sorcerers must be. "But that doesn't give *me* the right to impose a government on them!"

"Can you free them, yet leave them in anarchy?" Clotho challenged. "Nay, then surely sorcerers will rise among them again! Yet be truthful, Wizard—had you not meant to take the throne for yourself?"

Sir Guy and Yverne looked at him, startled.

"Well . . . yeah," Matt admitted, "but I was going to give them a *good* government."

"With no tyranny nor oppression? No taxes, no torture?"

"Well . . . there have to be *some* taxes, or the government doesn't have any money to provide even the most basic social services. But torture? No! Definitely not! And I'd honor the basic human rights, even if I wouldn't tell them about them all at once."

"Then you, too, would steal their freedom!"

"Not at all! I'd start an educational campaign first thing—well, second, after I'd taken care of basic administration—and build it, slowly and gradually, until they understood the basics of government. Then, in about twenty years, I'd start a national assembly, and slowly turn it into a real parliament."

"Why so long?" Atropos demanded.

"To let a generation grow up learning self-government. That's absolutely essential."

Atropos nodded. "Aye. You must live a long life."

"But it's not up to me! It's up to them!"

"Even were you a tyrant," the youngest said, "you would give them more freedom than they now have. Do your best to rule justly, and you shall open their dungeon cell. Nay, Wizard, you must do your best."

"Shall he be king of Ibile, then?" Fadecourt's eyes were burning.

Clotho glanced at her web, then shook her head. "I have not yet determined that. There are many other strands to the weave, and the pattern has not yet emerged."

Emerged? Matt wondered who really controlled her loom.

"However," the Fate went on, "you shall be vital to giving them their freedom. Only do as you think right, and you will set their feet on the road to wise choice. They shall someday choose their own government, I promise you."

Matt wasn't entirely happy about that; it sounded too much like saying that people get the kind of government they deserve. "Why? Why does it have to be so slow? Why does it have to be me?"

"Because that is as we wish it!" Atropos snapped, her eyes glowing. "You are the man chosen by Fate, the man of destiny! Your own actions and choices led you to becoming our instrument, of your own free will! Do you say you do not like it? Pity! For it is what you chose!"

"Yes, in a moment of anger, in a fit of temper! Come on—there have to be other reasons, better ones!"

"Even so." The youngest smiled like a vixen. "There are, and many, and good ones—but we do not choose to tell you of them."

"Surely not!" Atropos said. "And seek not to know! Beware of hubris, youngling, of overweening pride! Do not seek to challenge the gods, and expect death!"

Which meant, Matt decided, that they weren't about to tell a young upstart like him.

"Not such a young upstart as yourself!"

Matt clamped down on his temper—mustn't let them know they were getting to him! Or did they already? Either way—they were egging him on, trying to make him do something rash again.

Indeed they were. All three leaned forward in expectation, their eyes glowing through the mist.

Matt forced himself to settle back, to relax. "No, of course I wouldn't do a thing like that. I'm not about to forget that I have to put on my pants one leg at a time, after all. I make too many mistakes for that."

Sir Guy frowned, not understanding, but not liking the tenor of the remark—and the three sisters relaxed with a sigh of disappointment. "Well enough, then," Atropos said, though she sounded as if she didn't mean it. "Wend your way through your life, weak and foolish one—but do not expect us to save you from the consequences of your own folly!"

The globe of light shrank abruptly, as if it were receding at an incredible rate, and winked out. The room was very silent, and the only motion was the flickering of their shadows on the wall, cast by firelight. Matt became uncomfortably aware that all his friends were staring at him.

So he pretended a nonchalance he certainly didn't feel. He turned away to the fire with a sigh that he hoped sounded like disappointment. "Too bad. I half hoped they were going to slip and tell me something *useful*."

CHAPTER 24

The Maid from the Sea

The old don came back into the room, nodding happily and murmuring to himself. "Oh, very pretty, yes, my little one, very pretty! Yet 'tis so pleasant to have guests, yes, and ones who wish to challenge the king! Ah, I am so concerned for them, little one, yes. Who knows what will become of them, when they approach . . ." He came within the range of firelight and broke off, seeing his guests. "Ah, my friends! Have you rested, then? Shall we converse?" Then he frowned, peering at them. "Yet something has discomfited you, has it not? Come, tell me! In mine own house! Nay, it cannot be! Only tell me what 'twas, and I will chastise it sorely, nay, even send it away, an I must! Was't a well-wist? Nay, tell me! I know they are slow to forgive, and you did pain them, though 'twas understandable, yes, quite understandable. Nay, tell me, and I'll remonstrate with them!"

"No, it wasn't the well-wists." Matt finally managed to get a word in edgewise. He could understand it—if he'd been alone with no one to talk to for twenty years, he'd probably run off at the mouth, too, when he had the chance. "Nothing you could have done anything about, milord—and nothing that concerns you, really. Our fault—no, mine, I suppose."

"Not concern me? How could it not concern me, when 'tis in mine own house? Nay, tell me, for . . ." He broke off, his eyes widening; then he began to tremble.

Matt spun about, staring off into the shadows where the old don was looking.

It was gathering substance, still a dim, gauzy cloud, but wavering and fluxing—and its outlines clarified as it pulsed and brightened.

"'Tis a ghost!" the old don shrieked. He staggered to the wall, pulled down a broadsword, and held it up as an improvised cross. "Shield me, my Lord, from vile and vicious specters who walk by night!"

The ghost's face, newly formed, quirked into a look of horror, thinning as it stared.

"No, my lord!" Matt was up and leaping in between the sword and the ghost. "He's not vile and vicious—he's a friend! And he doesn't walk by night—well, that, too, but he walks by day when he needs to. He just doesn't look his best."

"He will come by daylight?" The old don peered at the misty face across from him, craning to see around Matt's shoulder. "Then he cannot be completely a thing of evil."

"Hardly evil at all. He's been a big help—and he knows what we intend to do."

"Then if he seeks to help you, he must needs be on the side of Good." The old don nodded, his chin firming. "He is welcome, then—though I will confess 'tis the first time I've been host to a ghost. Yet though I may welcome him, he must make his own peace with the other nightwalkers; for there be other ghosts within this castle."

"What respectable castle would be without them? If you wouldn't mind, though, I think I'd better find out why he's here." Matt turned to the ghost. "Good to see you again, friend."

A smile appeared on the ghost's face, tentative at first, then a little more definite.

"You are our friend, I know now," Yverne put in. "Forgive my fright when first I saw you."

The ghost shook its head with a look of distress that as much as said the fault was all *his*. He pointed at his mouth, opening and closing it silently.

"Ah. You could not tell me, because you cannot speak." Yverne smiled, somehow at her most charming. "Then let me guess. Have you come to warn us of new enemies come against us?"

The ghost shook its head with a wisp of a smile.

"Probably just trying to find us. Our force got split up in a bad fog sent by a sorcerer-duke, and . . ."

"A sorcerer and a duke!" De la Luce shook his head. "How sadly sunk is Ibile, when even men of rank sink to evil magics!"

"'Fraid so. And I expect our friend, here, has been trying to round up the forces ever since . . . Say!" Matt looked up with sudden hope. "I, uh, hate to point this out, milord, but your castle would make an ideal staging ground for an attack on the king, and—"

"You wish to have your army rally here?" De la Luce answered with a wisp of a smile. "Well, wherefore not, after all? I am secure against attack, and even should the sorcerer batter down my walls— well, I have lived a long life, and will yield it gladly in the service of God and goodness."

"I hope it won't come to that . . ."

"It will not, if you act quickly. Yet be warned, young man—though you may gather your men here, how will you send them to the king's castle?"

"A point," Matt admitted. "I'll think of something. The early rounds will be magic against magic, after all, and that might be my opening salvo." But he doubted it—he shied at the notion of trusting men's lives to one of his spells. "Well, then, since you don't mind, let's see if I can get the idea across to our ectoplasmic messenger." He turned to the ghost.

"Can he understand you?" Fadecourt asked.

"Who cares? Whether he's reading thoughts or hearing us, he's getting the message." But Matt wished he hadn't mentioned mind reading—now he was wondering just which thoughts of his the ghost was tuning in to. He watched the misty face closely, but its look of intent attention didn't waver. Either it had very good self-control, which didn't seem to go with its genial disposition, or it *couldn't* hear thoughts—at least, not private ones. "Friend," Matt went on, "we need to get all our people back together. Think you can find them?"

The ghost broke into a smile, nodding vigorously.

"Great! Can you tell them where we are?"

The smile faltered; the ghost frowned. Then it shrugged and made shooing motions with its hands.

Matt nodded, satisfied. "You'll lead them or shoo them, but you'll get them here. Great. Especially since that means they'll be coming by night, when it's easier to get past Gor—the king's sentries."

The ghost frowned and shook its head.

"Oh. Not the supernatural ones?"

The ghost nodded.

"Well, Friar Tuck can shepherd Robin and his band past them—but it would be better if you could get them aboard boats, far enough away so the king isn't too much aware of it, and get them to row over here. Too tall an order?"

The ghost frowned in thought, then shook its head.

"Not too tall an order? You can get them to boat over here?"

The ghost nodded.

"Great! Bring them in . . . uh . . . Milord?" Matt turned to de la Luce.

"'Tis well planned," the old don assented. "The most secret point of embarkation is through a small ravine that runs far behind the king's castle, well out of sight of the sentries. Board them at the pier, where the fisher folk will turn their backs at the loan of their boats." His eyes twinkled. "Wherefore should they not? For it seems to me that you may find a score of boats there that belong to no one. Then have them row with feathered oars, and bring your friends in the sea gate, certes, where the tide comes in to turn my wheels. If 'twill do for my sea-maid, 'twill do for your friends."

"Well, they have to come in above the water—but there should be room, at low tide." Matt was beginning to get an eerie feeling about the way the old don talked so confidently of unlikely events—but he definitely wasn't about to ask where that score of boats was supposed to come from. He just hoped the ghost wouldn't count on their really being there. "Okay, ghost?"

The ghost nodded, grinned, and winked out. Matt exhaled sharply and turned to his friends. "End transmission. Now, Milord de la Luce—if we may impose on you a little further?"

"It is no imposition, but my pleasure." De la Luce frowned. "How may I aid?"

"We're going to need whate'er kind of supernatural aid we can get. Could you call up a few of your well-wist friends?"

"To ask them to aid?" The old don stared, then slowly smiled. "Aye, they might indeed ward you as they have me—if you can win them. Nay, surely I will call up such of them as may come." He raised his voice. "By mist and flight and gist and light! Come, friends of mine, and hear!"

Mist seemed to fill the center of the great hall, swirling and coalescing even as it appeared—and three well-wists stood before Matt, humming angrily.

"Yes, I know I offended you." Matt swallowed to fill the sudden emptiness in his belly. "But look at it from my side—we thought *you* were attacking *us*!"

The smallest well-wist quivered, and a deep rasping tone scored the air.

"Yes, I know, I know! We had no business being there. You had every right to think we were intruders—especially since we *were* intruders. We had just escaped from the dungeon of the Duke of Bruitfort, and we were looking for a safe place to hide. We thought this castle was deserted, because it was so close to the king's and didn't show any signs of having an army living in it."

Another tone rattled at him; the well-wist glared.

"You *are* an army, I know. But you don't leave any of the obvious signs of habitation—troops drilling in the bailey, horses stabled against the curtain wall, haystacks on one side and manure pile on the other. We didn't think we were invading." Matt took a deep breath. "So. I'm sorry. We didn't mean to hurt you."

The well-wists glowered at him, but their chord sounded more like a grumble than an explosion. Then the smallest stepped forward, still scowling, and opened its mouth. A rising tone skewed upward.

"Yes, well, I *am* going to ask a favor of you," Matt admitted.

"How can you tell what they say?" Fadecourt asked, in the hushed tones of wonder.

"Just good guessing." But privately, Matt wasn't so sure. He reminded himself that he was intrepid and wise, and pressed on. "It isn't anything out of the ordinary, actually—not for you, I mean. After all, you're guarding the castle anyway, aren't you?"

Cautious bleeps answered him.

"Right. Well, I'm just asking you to guard it a little farther away. I mean, if the king is locked up inside his castle, he can't get over here to attack your friend the don, can he?"

The well-wists stared, astounded, and their tones soared in delight.

This was much better. Matt hadn't really thought they'd become enthusiastic about the idea.

Then the smallest frowned and blatted a denial.

"Sure, I know he's powerful," Matt argued. "But I'm not talking about a frontal assault, alone—I'm just asking you to pitch in when the rest of our forces attack. If you can just flit around and confuse things, even, you'll be giving us a tremendous boost."

The well-wists exchanged glances, conducting a quick, private conversation that sounded like a symphony played at tripled speed. Then the smallest turned to the don, sounding an interrogatory tone.

"Yes, I wish this, too, my friends," the old don said. "But mind you, there is danger. The sorcerer-king has fell and puissant sorceries, and might hurt you sorely. Nay, he might slay you, dispersing your substance to the winds."

The well-wists looked at one another, buzzing in dark tones.

The old don nodded. "Aye, even so. He did despoil the land, filling the people with evil by his mere example and his cruelty, and they have tortured the animals and torn at the soil. The malice of the folk has filled the land, poisoning the source from which you sprang. Yet therein lies no reason to go blindly to the slaughter."

The smallest well-wist faced him squarely, emitting a series of angry chords with his companions.

"Why, as you will," de la Luce answered. "The death is not certain, no, and you may well prevail against his sorceries, with the aid of these good folk and their allies—how many did you number, Lord Wizard?"

"Maybe two hundred," Matt answered. "but two of those are wizards, and two more are a dragon and a dracogriff. Also, one of us has the strength of ten or so, and another is the Black Knight."

The smallest blatted back at him.

"Small enough, to challenge a king? Yes, I know—but we're going to try anyway." For himself, he didn't have much choice—and for Yverne and Fadecourt, it was better than going it alone. Sir Guy, of course, was Sir Guy, and ready for any challenge, no matter how overwhelming.

The smallest well-wist flapped its wings smartly and sang a high, clear tone.

"You are allies, then," Don de la Luce said, with a smile of satisfaction. "Gather your forces, Wizard. The well-wists will number amongst them."

The first allies to arrive were Robin Hood's band. Matt and his friends were waiting in the sea cave, shivering in the chill of the salt air and watching the water level drop with each outward rush of water. Then the chamber darkened, and they looked up to see a boat, crammed with men, filling the cave's mouth—and a wisp of a ghost drifting before them.

Fadecourt and Sir Guy let out a cheer. Matt and Yverne managed to join in while it was ringing.

So it was the old don who stooped and threw a rope at the prow of the dinghy. Maid Marian caught it and pulled them in to bump against the rock ledge. An outlaw caught the ring set in the stone at the stern and held them against the rock as Robin sprang out, followed by Little John and Will Scarlet. "Lord Matthew!" He clapped Matt on the shoulder with a grip that made the wizard wince and think about bone doctors. "'Tis right good to see you again! We had feared you lost, and were lurking about the duke's castle with a thought to breaking through, when we saw the dragon rise with you on his back. You are well, then? And the cyclops and the maiden?" He nodded to Sir Guy, apparently assuming that a steel suit was a sign of good health.

"Came through it almost unscathed." Matt found himself grinning; the man's enthusiasm was infectious, almost contagious. "We were worried about you, too."

"You need not have been." Marian was out of the boat and towering behind Robin. "None could best my lord and dear."

"I don't doubt it. Uh, Maid Marian, Robin Hood, this is our host, the Don de la Luce."

"My lord!" Robin seized his hand and began pumping. "How good of you to take us in!"

"Is it truly the Robin Hood of fable and legend?" Aristocrat or not, the don was staring round-eyed.

"The same, dragged hither by this good wizard to aid the poor against the proud and mighty." Robin was still pumping.

Matt reached out and disconnected their hands; Robin was closer to striking oil than he knew. "And therefore feeling responsible for you, which is why I was worried. Did you have a chance to look at the king's castle on your way?"

"Aye, and 'tis not a fair sight." Robin frowned and was about to go on when the old don interrupted.

"This has the sound of the start of a conference of war, and such should be held seated around a roaring fire with mulled wine, not tarrying on a rocky ledge whiles your men shiver with the chill and damp. Nay, Lord Wizard, conduct them up to my hall. You know the way by now."

"Yes, I do." Matt turned away, then turned back. "But you, milord! Surely you're not going to stay here in the damp!"

"Only for a brief while, I assure you," de la Luce answered. "My sea-maid will come soon, or not at all; 'tis nigh on the hour of the day when she approaches."

Matt gazed at him for a moment, then smiled. "Sure. See you soon, then, alone or in company. Speaking of companies, Robin, shall we go?"

"What maid is this?" Marian asked as they turned the first bend in the staircase.

"A delusion," Matt answered. "The poor old geezer has been alone most of his life, and his subconscious has manufactured a pretty girl who lives in a mysterious underwater castle and comes to visit him now and then."

"That has the sound of Ys," Marian said.

Robin asked, "Wherefore do you think it a waking dream?"

That halted Matt for a moment. To him, it had been pretty obvious. He checked back for signs, and said, "For one thing, she stays young while he gets older—and for another, she isn't a mermaid, but just somebody who can breathe either water or air, which is highly unlikely."

"In a world of magic?" Robin asked, with a grin, and Matt started to answer; but Marian touched his arm with a smile of sympathy. "Say no more till I've told you of Ys," she said, "but not here, I pray you. Let us speak of it above."

And they did, around the roaring fire the don had spoken of. There was a cask near the hearth now, no doubt courtesy of the well-wists, and the merry men dug flagons out of their packs.

Curled up on a few cushions, Marian looked surprisingly dainty, and Yverne was beginning to look a little jealous. "Ys," the maid said, pronouncing it *Eess*, "'twas a city to inspire awe, so legend says—a clustering of towers, with golden streets between, its palaces of jasper built, and jade, and ancient, oh! So ancient! Ys was old when Egypt was young, so legend says, yet vital still."

"Legend says many things," Robin murmured to Matt, "and adds the gloss that fact would scorn."

Well, Matt figured, he should know if anybody should. Nonetheless, he paid close attention to Marian's tale.

"Yet most wondrous of all," the maid said, "was its situation—for Ys stood below the level of the waves."

"How can that be?" Yverne asked. "The sea would have drowned it in an instant."

"Nay," Marian said, "for the sea was held out by a soaring wall, with massive gates. There ruled the king of Ys, over a court of constant mirth, his courtiers dazzling in their finery and glittering with jewelry—yet none shone so brightly as his only daughter."

Allan-a-Dale began to caress his harp, bringing a breath of melody to underscore the maid's words.

But Sir Guy frowned and said, "I have heard something of this demoiselle of Ys. I mind me that she was not kindhearted."

"Nay, quite otherwise," Marian said, "for she was mean of spirit, froward, shrewd, and cruel. Yet all deferred to her, for the sake of her royal father—and fear of her sorcery."

"Ah, then! She was a sorceress!"

Marian nodded. "A witch of great power—and one who could bend any man to her will. Yet therefore did she disdain all males, regarding them with ridicule and contempt—till she found one who was proof against her wiles, yet loved her for her beauty. Then at last did she become betrothed, and dallied with him a year and more—till love's sweet spell began to wane, and he came to some notion of her true and twisted nature."

"Then she broke him for her pleasure?" The minstrel wrung a discord from his harp.

"She would have, aye, and did brew potent magics against him—but he threw himself on her father's mercy, and the king spread his aegis over the poor wight, commanding his daughter to spare him. She withdrew from the palace, hate and rage commingling in her breast, for puissant though she was, she could not match her father's magic. Yet that night, whiles he slept, she cast a spell of deepened slumber over all the palace and stole back in, to pluck the keys to the city from her father's neck, and she opened the gates to let in the sea."

"Why, I cannot credit this!" Fadecourt scoffed. "Such a one would have valued her own safety and comfort above all else, and would have known that she would perish with her citizens!"

Marian shrugged. "She may have sought to bargain with the Sea King, may even have thought she had compelled his mercy with her spells. Yet if she did, her magic once more could not match a king's, for his sea horses destroyed her."

Matt frowned, trying to pick out the root of fact beneath this tree of legend. A port city, then, that had erected dikes to hold back a rising waterline, but was finally flooded by the sea it had depended on for its wealth—or buried by a tidal wave, more likely, considering the reference to the wall and the gates.

"So perished Ys," the maid murmured, and the harp rippled and was silent.

The merry men stirred, sighing, and began to talk to one another again.

Sir Guy asked, "Does our host, then, think this buried palace lies beneath his own?"

"So it would seem," Matt replied, "and if a legend like that is standard in this countryside, it's no wonder—it would be just the thing for a lonely old man to fasten his imagination to. But we can't depend on dreams to help us now."

"Nay, surely," Robin said with a grin, unaware of his own irony. "How shall we invest this castle, Lord Wizard? For surely, its walls must needs be proof against mine arrows."

"A trebuchet might make some mark upon its walls," Fadecourt offered.

"A mark," Sir Guy allowed, "but no break—scarcely a gouge. No, my friend, that castle has never been taken by force of arms, and never will be."

"Never, by force of arms?" Matt pricked up his ears. "That means it *has* been taken. The only question, is: How?"

"By treachery," Robin answered, "by a traitor opening its gates from within. Surely, Milord Wizard, we shall not stoop so low!"

"No," Matt said slowly, "but if one of *us* were able to get in and open the gates, that wouldn't be treachery."

"True," Robin allowed, "yet how shall we achieve that?"

"I might know a friend or two who could do it. Uh, Puck?"

"Aye, Wizard?" The other Robin popped his head out of a joint in Sir Guy's armor.

"A thought," the knight agreed. "Hobgoblin, can you penetrate the castle of the sorcerer-king?"

But Puck shook his head. "I have tested it already, knight, in such wise that none could detect. There are fell and puissant spells that guard that keep, and a miasma of old corruption throughout it. Elves have been slain there, slain wholesale. I have asked of the sprites of this land, and they tell me that, when the sorcerer took the castle, his second act was to annihilate every sprite that was not evil and would not serve his ends."

Yverne and Marian shuddered, along with most of the men. Matt managed to shelve the shudder and ask, "His *second* act? What was his first?"

"The slaying of the rightful king, and all his adherents."

"Pardon his innocence," Sir Guy told Puck. "He is a man of magic, after all, not of war."

"And you are a man of honor," the Puck pointed out.

"True, and therefore do I ken dishonor and shameful acts. I thank you, elf."

"At your bidding." Puck popped back in to Sir Guy's armor.

"Well, that lets one out." Matt sighed. "Max?"

"Aye, Wizard?" The arc spark danced before him, and the whole band drew away with gasps of horror.

"Don't worry, folks," Matt called out. "He's neither good nor bad in himself, and he's on our side."

"How foolish some mortals are, not to know!" the Demon scoffed. "What would you with me, Wizard?"

"Just some information. Do you think you could get into that castle, across the strait, and dry-rot the gates?"

"While rusting the portcullis? Nay. I had felt some strangeness there, and did go to investigate—but the place is wrapped about with some force that contains its corruption into some semblance of form. It is entropy bound, and anathema to me."

Interesting aspect of evil—chaos held together long enough to wreak disaster. Matt sighed. "Okay, thanks. I won't ask the next question—the answer's obvious."

"Should you not test it anyway?"

"Not by experiment, thank you. I only bet on sure things."

"Any number must play," the Demon droned.

"Not in *my* park. I'll call you when it's time for roulette."

"Baccarat," the Demon snapped, and disappeared.

Robin Hood frowned. "Wherefore would you back a rat?"

"Because he might be able to gnaw through the king's defenses." Matt leaned back in his chair, shaking his head. "I'm stonkered, Sir Guy. There may be a way into that castle, but if there is, I don't see it."

"Of course you may see!"

Everyone turned at the sound of Don de la Luce's voice coming from the archway that led down into the dungeons.

The old don stood in the pool of light from the torches that flanked the arch, holding the hand of a beautiful young woman, gazing down at her flawless features with a fatuous smile.

Matt stared. Her green gown had every appearance of being woven of living seaweed, leaves and fronds creating the look of a feathered cloak. Golden rings sparkled on her fingers and a golden coronet in her blonde hair—hair that was not really quite yellow, but faintly tinged with green. Her complexion was pale, but her lips were rubies, and her eyes the deepest green of the sea. She turned to gaze at them, those magical eyes wide and huge, her nose tip-tilted, her heart-shaped face composed and tranquil. Her lips curved with a smile. "They are, milord! Mortals, and not evil! I can feel their wonder! 'Tis a marvel!"

Matt felt an eerie tingling down his spine, and his skin prickled. He stood up carefully and turned to bow to the young lady. "Your servant, mademoiselle. Whom have I the pleasure of addressing?"

The girl clapped her hands and laughed with delight. "He is so impatient, this one! Milord, will you introduce us?"

"With pleasure." De la Luce beamed. "Lord Wizard, this is the Lady Sinelle, the maid of whom I told you. Lady Sinelle, this is Matthew, Lord Wizard of Merovence."

Matt looked up at the old man with a stab of panic. Was he out of his mind, disclosing Matt's real identity to someone who might not be sympathetic to their plot!

No. Of course he wouldn't. Matt forced himself to relax; the lady must be on their side.

Her eyes were round and huge as she looked about the hall. "Never have I beheld so many mortals, foregathered in one place! Though 'tis goodly to see this great hall no longer resounding with its emptiness. I had wondered, when you told me of it, my lord. Why do they come?"

The old don started to answer, but Matt beat him to it. "That's an issue that might be answered at some length—but only after you have met the rest of my friends." He took a quick glance, weighing who should be introduced first.

Fadecourt was still sitting dazed, holding the hand of a staring Yverne, both astounded to find that the old man had been speaking the truth. Sir Guy and Robin Hood, though, had recovered in an instant and rose, ready for anything—as usual.

"This is Robin Hood, the rightful Earl of Locksley, currently posing as a forest outlaw because he opposes tyrants," Matt said. "Milord Earl, the demoiselle . . . uh, Lady Sinelle."

"I am the demoiselle d'Ys, too," the lady said, pressing Robin's hand but withdrawing her own before he could kiss it. "Not she of legend, no, who brought disaster on my poor city, but her descendant. Yet she is dead, and the title has come down to me."

She turned to Sir Guy, and Matt said quickly, "Sir Guy de Toutarien, the Black Knight—the Lady Sinelle, demoiselle d'Ys." The lady inclined her head, but regarded Sir Guy with a smile of amusement. "A simple knight bachelor, you would have us believe? Surely, Sir Knight."

Sir Guy kissed her fingertips before she whisked them away, and regarded her with a steady gaze. "Methinks milady knows more than she speaks."

"As should any wise demoiselle," the lady returned, "or any prudent man, for that matter. My ancestress was not, though she thought she was—yet that was only vainglorious contempt of those around her, in another guise. It was for that pride that she drowned her island and city."

"Surely," Yverne protested, "so many folk did not die for one single woman's pride!"

"There were few enough good folk in Ys," the lady returned, "for my ancestress's influence had been wide-reaching and pervasive. Nay, my grandfather gathered those few good souls together within his castle, so that only they who merited the Sea King's wrath were drowned. We keep a merry court in our castle beneath the waves, where there is never want nor sorrow, for none of us need die, and my grandfather has taught the sea creatures to provide for us. This they do, in return for his protection. Tell your fellows, and beware—this cove is sacrosanct from all who fish or dive!"

"Even so," the don confirmed. "None will fish in my bay, nor in the strait between mine island and the mainland, for dire things have happened to they who have taken living creatures from these waters."

Matt didn't think he wanted to hear what. "You mean you haven't had any trouble with the current king?"

Sinelle made a moue. "Some irritation, when first he took the throne and sought to fish our waters for his supper—but a heavy sea capsized his sailors' boats, and a kraken cracked his ships. Since then, ever and anon we feel the power of his fell magics, like a bit of metal on the tooth, or a tone that grates upon the ear—but my great-father repels him with ease. Yet sea creatures flee to us in fear, and loathsome monsters prowl the waters without our cove, ever testing my great-father's warding spells. It is not in our power to smite this gross kinglet, yet if it were, we should not hesitate."

"Oh, really!" Matt looked a little more sharply at her. "That's our aim, too—and that's why we've gathered here. Don de la Luce is kind enough to grant us his hospitality, though he knows it increases his own danger—and the rest of these brave folk are as determined as I am, though we haven't the faintest idea how to get into the king's castle."

"Are you truly!" The lady stared, then smiled with delight. "Yet there are few enough of you."

"Only a hundred or so," Matt admitted, "but that's more people united against the king than you'll find anywhere else in Ibile."

"True, and well spoke." There was something a little more guarded about the lady now, a bit more wary. "Yet allies should meet and talk. Will you come to converse with my great-father?"

Matt stared, and stood frozen while panic rolled over him. Finally, he shook it off and croaked, "Under water? Uh, thank you very much, ma'am, but I don't breathe liquids too well."

"Nor do I," she assured him. "'Tis the Sea King's spell that withholds the water from my lungs and lets the air surround me—yet

I can extend that spell to anyone I wish, simply by touch." She held out her hand. "Will you come to meet the king of Ys?"

Matt stared, thoroughly aware of the corollary—that all she had to do was let go, and he would drown.

"Wizard, 'tis too great a risk!" Sir Guy exclaimed. "Without you, we are lost, and our cause is dead." He turned to Sinelle. "I shall go in his place, milady."

"You are not asked," she retorted, a merry glint in her eye, "in spite of your hidden station. Nay, Lord Knight, it must be leader to leader here—and valiant though you are, you have not come into your kingdom."

"That's okay, we'd be shot without him, too." Matt nerved himself up and took her hand. "But as you say, milady, this is something that *I* have to do." He raised his other hand to quiet Fadecourt's and Yverne's protests. "Never mind why. I got myself into this, and there's only one way out. My lady, will you walk?"

CHAPTER 25

The Castle of Ys

She did, as it turned out, though how she kept her feet on the ground with so much water pressure around her, Matt didn't know. For that matter, he didn't know what was keeping *him* down, but he chalked it up to magic. He had expected to swim, but he found that, as he stepped into the water in the cave, he sank like a stone. He shivered like an iceberg, too, but forced his way down into the water, took a deep breath, then took the plunge and was in over his head.

And, suddenly, he was surrounded by air. He looked around him, startled, and saw fronds of seaweed drift up past him. That's how he knew he was sinking—but where was the light coming from?

There—the mouth of the sea cave. Daylight filtered in through the murky water. He looked about for the demoiselle, saw her in front of him, beckoning, and followed her down the pathway.

For it *was* a pathway—very narrow, but very clearly laid out. It was covered with white gravel, and bordered by corals and sea anemones. Matt could see clearly for a foot or so on either side, before the murk of the sea took over—and he moved freely, without the resistance of water. The path, it seemed, was the bottom of a tunnel of air, winding down along the sea floor.

And down, and down, following the sea-maid. She had released his hand as soon as his feet had touched the gravel, and he had to hurry now to keep her in sight. There was no light here, other than what filtered down from above—and less and less of it came through as they went deeper and deeper. Matt was just beginning to wonder if he was going to lose sight of the maid, when a light burst forth from her upraised hand. Looking closely, he saw that the light came from a huge, fantastic seashell, shaped like a cornucopia. He felt a thrill of apprehension as he realized that the mollusk that had made that shell had been dead for millions of years.

At least, in *his* world.

They were hundreds of feet down, and the path wound its way among the hulks of sunken ships—the rocks surrounding de la Luce's castle must be treacherous. In fact, Matt suddenly realized, that's why de la Luce's keep was a tower, and was so much taller than the curtain wall—it had been a primitive lighthouse!

They rounded the bulk of a rotting trireme galley—just how long had this port been in use, anyway?—and there it was before them, in all its eldritch splendor.

The royal castle of Ys may not have been terribly spectacular in its day, but it was extremely impressive down here. A central keep thrust up from the center of a vast bowl, cylindrical, and surrounded by four more cylinders that grew out of it—but so slender that they seemed to be needles, with long lancing tips, instead of the towers they were. A low wall, perhaps twelve feet high, fenced in a wide courtyard all about the keep, decked with corals and other bright sea life, while the central keep glowed with the phosphorescence of the deep.

Matt caught his breath, then forced it out and reminded himself how unimpressive this stronghold would look on land. It didn't do much good, of course, because he *wasn't* on land—and within that circular wall, the absence of seaweed and the glow of the stone told him that a dome of air protected the castle and its environs. Whatever the magic, the sea did not enter the royal stronghold of drowned Ys, but formed a circle around the palace and its gardens.

And inside, true to legend, the ancient king still lived, preserved by the magic of the Sea King.

Matt followed the maid through the open gates.

Suddenly, the pressure of the water was gone, and he felt air all about him, saw trees and flowers nodding in the faint breaths of convection currents. He shuddered with the release of tension—he hadn't realized just how much stress he'd been under during that submarine passage. Then he realized that there were people around him, boys with switches loitering near herds of goats and sheep, men and women working in sheds along the insides of the walls, girls stitching embroidery under the trees. He looked again and realized that the men and women were painting, sculpting, fashioning musical instruments, and playing them.

Strains of music murmured all about him. A sudden, piercing longing struck him—to be able to spend his life working at his art!

Then he remembered that he was doing exactly that, more or less—only under greater pressure. His art just wasn't the tranquil sort that could be pursued in solitude. He sighed and followed the maid through the great leaves of the keep's portal.

There was a short passage of glowing, semiprecious stone that ended in two smaller doors of cavern wood with gilded highlights. Two courtiers loitered before them, long rapiers at their belts, exchanging gossip.

"No, good Arien, that is not Plato's meaning!"

"Meaning? Forsooth, Ferlain, 'tis his very words!"

"Nay, for you've translated the Greek very poorly! His true meaning is . . ."

Just idle gossip.

"Gentlemen," the lady murmured.

They looked up, startled, then drew themselves up. "Milady!" Then they saw Matt and stared, forgetting their poise.

Also their manners. "He is a guest," Sinelle reminded them, and they shook themselves out of their amazement. "Why, certes! Be welcome in the castle of Ys, O stranger!"

"We would speak with his Majesty," the demoiselle hinted.

"Certes, milady! He is within, debating the merits of the dulcimer and the lyre with the musical brethren!" His deprecating smile revealed the philosopher's old condescension toward the musician.

Sinelle tactfully forbore to mention it and gestured toward the doors. The courtiers drew them open.

The Great Hall glittered with a hundred candles, its walls damasked and tapestried, its floor gleaming malachite, its lofty ceiling painted with frescoes that Matt wished he had time to study—but the demoiselle was leading him toward a high dais topped by a gilded throne and flanked by two flaring lamps. At the top of the steps sat the king, wrinkled and silver-haired, but with a lively expression on his hawk-nosed face, and eyes that glinted beneath his golden crown. He interrupted the disputants with a polite smile and waved them away. They withdrew to the far side of the chamber, still arguing.

"My lord and ancestor," the maiden said, "this mortal is hight Matthew Mantrell, Lord Wizard of Merovence."

Matt bowed. When he straightened up, he saw a trace of humor in the old king's eyes—but the royal face didn't crack a smile, much less start talking.

This was going to get nowhere. Matt needed some kind of a conversational opener. "I am honored by your hospitality, your Majesty."

"It is gladly given," the majestic face proclaimed, in a voice of a grandeur to match its appearance. "I am intrigued by your presence, Lord Wizard."

"Oh?" Matt smiled, but was very wary inside. "Am I so rare a thing as that, your Majesty?"

"For a mortal to enter into Ys? Aye—yet that is explained by the presence of my great-daughter." He smiled fondly at the maid, who bowed her head in a gesture that managed to combine demureness with sauciness; then he turned back to Matt. "Therefore, 'tis not your presence in Ys that is remarkable in itself, but your presence in Castillo Adamanto, so near to the lair of the sorcerer-king."

"Oh, that?" Matt waved away the problem. "I spoke rashly, and in anger, Majesty—but I thereby bound myself to do all I could to unseat the sorcerer."

"Oathbound, though a wizard?" The king looked askance.

"I have this little problem with my temper," Matt confessed.

"More than a little, I should think." But the king's eye twinkled. "Do you always go about losing control of your words thus? Or is there one who can provoke you more easily than others?"

"All right, all right, so I was talking to the woman I love! Can you *blame* me for tackling a sorcerer?"

"For love's sake? Surely not, milord." The king chuckled. He exchanged a glance with the maid and said, "Yet I am rude in so questioning a guest. Come, examine me in my turn. Is there naught you would know about Ys?"

"Well, now that you mention it . . ." Matt glanced around at the courtiers, then back to the king. "The demoiselle does seem to be a little young to be your granddaughter . . ."

"Nay, my great-daughter—my daughter's daughter's daughter's daughter's . . . She is removed from me by some thirty generations, Lord Wizard."

Matt nodded. "I kinda thought it would be something like that. Was your daughter . . ." He broke off, chagrined.

"You think to make me grieve, in speaking of my child." The king shook his head with gentle sympathy. "Fear not, Lord Wizard. The years have flowed into centuries, the centuries into millennia, and the pain grows dim. I will not deny that it cannot be raised, but I am well consoled in my old age. Know, then, that the first demoiselle, my daughter, found a man to follow her."

"With her magic, she found many," Sinelle said with scorn—the quick judgment of the young, and quicker intolerance. "Every man that she desired, she enchanted—and felt only the greater contempt for them, in that they succumbed to her spells."

The old king nodded. "Yet at last, she met a nobleman's son, journeying with a merchant crew, who fell in love with her as soon as he saw her—and she with him, for that he loved her without the aid of her own artifice. With him she wedded, and did breed a babe—yet her true nature was ever there, no matter how well she hid it from him; I doubt not that, even as she carried the child, she planned the vile use which she intended."

"There was a spell of great power, which she could not attempt," said the demoiselle, in a hushed voice, "for it required the sacrifice of a babe, of the sorceress' own body—for know, Wizard, that it is the dedication to such wickedness that is the essence of evil magic, to exclusion of all else."

Matt could believe it; from his own experience of the magic "field," its manipulation was a matter of intent and will, expressed through symbols. He felt a chill at the thought of the kind of results the witch might have intended. "She sounds as if she deserved her reputation, all right. Was there anything that could have saved the baby?"

"Her father," the old king said, "for he learned of the wickedness his wife intended."

"His eyes were open at last to her corruption," Sinelle said with a shiver. "Knowledge that she intended such wickedness made the good man see her for what she was. 'Twas for the child's sake that he fled to my great-father, the king, and bore with him the babe—and for her sake that Ys was drowned."

"For in her wrath," the king said, "my daughter did raise up all manner of evil spirits from the sea, and hurled them 'gainst mine Ys—yet I had been ever steadfast in my devotion to the Sea King Poseidon, had ever done my best to govern well and wisely, and regularly made suitable offerings to his Oceanic Majesty. So while the sea pounded Ys elsewhere, the Sea King came to me, and we struck a bargain."

"Bargain?" Matt stared. "Why would a being who could control the whole sea, and everything in it, need to make a bargain with a mere mortal? Sure, being merciful I can understand, maybe even rewarding you for having been a good king . . ."

"In truth, I think he did even so—yet did wish to allow me to preserve some poor shreds of my pride." The king smiled. "Yet there was some need of it. For the Sea King hated my daughter's magic and wished all memory of it erased—but most especially all her implements of witchcraft destroyed, and all her books of spells. Some of those were warded 'gainst him, and the sea could not approach them. These, he proposed, I should destroy—for my daughter had not thought to ward them 'gainst mere mortal folk, sin that the door to her chambers was guarded by fierce spells and fell. For all that, she had left it unlocked in her anger, the whiles she went out to the tower's brim to summon her spirits—so I came in, and burned her books, and threw her alembics and crucibles upon the fire. Even as I did, I heard her scream in rage—but she could not turn aside from her work to punish me, for the fell spirits she had raised would have torn her asunder. In revenge, she turned them against my land—but the Sea King, for his part, had promised that my castle would remain inviolate, and he came to mine aid in that hour, defending me and mine from the avalanche of the waves. So as the surf pounded Ys to bits, all others of my people died . . ." His voice became somber, his darkened gaze drifting away from Matt. Sinelle laid her hand on his; he looked up, focused on her face, forced a smile, and turned back to Matt. "But this castle endured, sheltered by the vasty bubble that lends us breath. By some Sea King's magic, this air is ever renewed, and we who dwell here never die—so long as we do dwell here."

"But if you go out, you die?"

"We *may* die," Sinelle corrected, "if we go outside of the Sea King's realm; and protection cannot extend to us on land. Then will we age; then can we be slain."

"But if you don't, you're immortal?" Matt's brain swam at the thought—and at the magnitude of the cabin fever that could develop among these self-willed captives! No wonder the ones who stayed were the ones who valued tranquility and the life of the mind.

"In such fashion did my granddaughter grow," the king spoke up again, "dwelling beneath the water, and only knowing of the human realm above through my tales—for none of my courtiers chose to stay, of such few as had been near me when my daughter struck. Nay, as soon as Poseidon had turned against her the waves she had summoned, and she had drowned in her own evilness, my courtiers left me, by ones and twos, and finally in a body. But my granddaughter was my delight, and her father my boon companion—though he died at last, worn out with living. His daughter grew into a comely, good-hearted girl and found a husband among the folk on the shore, and brought him down to dwell with us in love. She birthed three children, who went above the waves to seek spouses, as her descendants have ever done. Yet one of my granddaughters chose to return to my palace here beneath the sea, and her children also followed the call of love to the land. One great-granddaughter brought her husband down here to me—and I have been fortunate, most fortunate, in that there has been at least one of each generation who has seen fit to join me here beneath the sea."

Matt marveled at the tale—then frowned at an inconsistency. "But weren't there ever any boys?"

"Aye, but they became restless, as boys will, and went out into the world to seek their fortunes—and their wives. A few wed happily, some never came back—but most lived the lonely life of the alien, for they were silkies and, as such, made rather ugly men, though they were very handsome seals. Some found seal wives, of course, and their daughters were silkie women, and their sons silkies still—but those who sought human women to wive were seldom happy with such matches and left their mates for their own kind."

"Their own kind?" Matt frowned. "You mean humans?"

"Nay—other silkies. There were some few others, and my grandsons heard word of them. They roamed the world, like seeking like—and found their silkie mates. Some came back to rear their families here, near my protection; some stayed with the folk they had found. Yet even of them, as often as not their children would seek me out when they came of age—and wed with my great-grandchildren. This isle above is peopled with several thousand of my descendants living all around the isle, though you will not see them—they hide in caves and rocks, for fear of the sorcerer-king and his hunters, who chase them with powerful spells to ward off mine. Here on the rock, he cannot touch them—but we do not wish to tempt him more than we must."

"They hide very well." Matt frowned. "I didn't see any of them—coming in. Of course, it was kind of dark . . ."

"And so are they. A few of them come down to visit with me, now and again—so I dwell here, in the midst of thousands of my descendants. I count myself richly rewarded for having led a blameless life."

A prickle kneaded Matt's back. He glanced sidelong at the courtiers. "Then all these lords and ladies . . ."

"Are my great-daughters and their mortal husbands, become exceeding long-lived here in Ys." The king nodded. "Aye, Lord Wizard, 'tis so. My youngest, though, has not yet found a landsman to her liking."

Matt glanced at her apprehensively, but before he could ask, the current demoiselle laughed like the clear chime of a running brook. "Nay, Lord Wizard, I am not enamored of you. In truth, by the reckoning of mine own people, I am yet too young to seek a husband. Be of peaceful mind; I have not yet met my one true love. I will own that romance does fascinate me, though, and I am intrigued by a man who would risk life itself to win his lady's hand."

Matt's mouth tightened with chagrin; then he forced it to smile. "Well, then, look your fill, lady, for I doubt you'll ever see such a fool again."

"Ah, but I will," she said, "whenever I look on the sons and daughters of men. You are rare, Lord Wizard, in that you will admit to your folly."

Matt frowned. "I have a notion you've just said something very profound, if I could understand it—but the fact of the matter is, I *have* sworn to oust the king of Ibile or die trying, and I have to figure out a way."

"Why," the king said, "take his castle."

Matt looked up at him, brooding. "Easily said, Majesty—but I've only two hundred fighters, and his castle is stout. We've figured out that the only way to make it is to get a sally party inside his walls and have them open the gate—but we're still trying to figure out how to get a few of our men inside."

"Why," the king of Ys said, "you may go through my domain."

Matt stared.

"I, too, wish this foul king gone," the king explained, "for the detritus of his noisome magics and his tortures fouls my waters, and his hunters slay my descendants. Nay, Lord Wizard, I am with you in this."

"I . . . I thank your Majesty . . ."

"Do not. You are the first in centuries to dare to challenge him. I honor you, milord."

"I thank you again." Matt ducked his head. "But how would going through Ys get us into Gordogrosso's castle?"

"I have told you that my people may go up to the land at will," the king explained. "That, too, was a part of my 'bargain' with the Sea King—that he would grant me a way to travel to the surface on the island, and a way to come up to land upon the mainland."

Matt lifted his head, feeling like a hunter when the fox has just come into sight. "And, uh . . . just where on the mainland did this passage come out?"

"Within an outcrop of rock atop a hill, that its entrance might be easily disguised; yet 'twas hidden too easily, for after a space of some thousand years, a king chose that hill for the building of his fortress, that it might ward the harbor mouth; and some two centuries agone, the sorcerer-king did hale down that king's descendants, to establish his ill rule there."

"You mean . . . you have a tunnel to the surface that comes out in Gord—uh, the king's cellar?"

"Even so."

Matt caught his breath. "I . . . don't suppose I could interest you in letting me bring . . ."

"Your army? Nay." The king smiled sadly. "That would, I think, strain the Sea King's bounty over much. This outlet for my people he did grant me, when he truly had no need to; and I am loathe to over-strain his kindness. He would, I think, be much wroth if you did bring an army through my domain and his cleared ways."

"Well, actually—I was thinking of a sally party. Say—twenty?"

"A score?" The king frowned, thinking it over, then shook his head. "Too many, I fear. Mayhap a dozen."

"Twelve it will be!" Matt fairly shouted. "I thank you, your Majesty! For the rest of my life, I'll thank you! For—"

"The rest of your life will be enough." The king smiled, amused. "I trust it will not be short. Godspeed, Lord Wizard. Gather your men."

CHAPTER 26

Passing Review

"People," he should have said—there was no way Maid Marian was going to be left behind. Matt would have liked to make it "beings," but he thought the king might draw the line at Stegoman and Narlh.

Of course, that meant he still had to explain it to them.

"You're opposite elements, you see," he said. "He's a king of water, and you're spirits of fire."

Stegoman exchanged a jaundiced glance with Narlh.

"Right, fire-breath," the dracogriff grunted. "He's making excuses."

"No, now, really! I mean, how would you feel if a water monster came into your nest and . . ."

"Lord Wizard." Sinelle touched his arm. "My great-father will not object to one of these beasts, if you truly wish it."

Matt stared.

"See, now?" Narlh grinned. "Should've asked, shouldn'cha?"

"Well . . . I just assumed . . ."

"Natheless, 'tis only the one of us," Stegoman snorted, "which I can comprehend readily enough. Nay, Wizard, say which it shall be."

Matt swallowed and turned back to look from monster to monster.

"I have more of fire in me," Stegoman allowed, "and am the stronger flier."

"Stronger?" Narlh yelped. "Look, lizard-brain—who's got the feathers here?"

The dragon turned, scowling. "Dost thou think to best a dragon in the far reaches of the air?"

"Hey, just because I don't enjoy it, doesn't mean . . ."

"Gentles, gentles!" Sinelle held up a hand, repressing a smile. "Did I not sense that the dragon did mean to be so gracious as to step aside and let the dracogriff have the place of honor?"

Narlh's head swiveled to stare at Stegoman.

The dragon shifted restlessly. "In truth, I had liefer go than stay. 'Twill be a glorious exploit, live or die, and—"

"Yeah, that's right!" Narlh snapped his beak for emphasis. "And I need the reputation more than you do!"

"And are not the dragon's equal in courtesy," Sinelle said sweetly.

"Hey, now, *wait* a minute! You can't say he's willing to be more self-sacrificing than I am! I'm just as humble as he is! And I'll prove it! Dragon, you can go jump in the pool! *I'll* stay with the siege!"

"I would not rob thee of so rich a courtesy," Stegoman began.

"Then do not." Sinelle snapped both hands wide in a gesture of finality. "Allow him the gallant gesture. Do you let him ride the high air, whiles you do accompany us beneath the sea."

Narlh stared, as if wondering if he'd been tricked out of something good, after all.

Matt wondered, too. Sinelle had managed it very deftly—he had to keep reminding himself that she was twice his age. And she had definitely wanted Stegoman on the submarine raid. He wondered why.

Not that he had time to think about it. Robin Hood touched his arm, saying, "Lord Wizard, we are in readiness. Do you pass in review, and say if anything lacks."

He was going to tell Robin Hood if everything was ready for a raid? He, the little boy who had read Howard Pyle with the reverence due the Bible?

But he was the resident wizard, and it was the magical side of things Robin was asking him to check, not the physical. Matt dutifully paced the line of recruits, merry men and peasants, knights and squires, all the defenders who had stood together against the siege of evil at the castle, about to become besiegers in their own turn.

They looked ready. Very. If there was any flaw, Matt certainly couldn't spot it.

Then the irony struck—Robin Hood asking him for a magical review, when he had a wizard of his own handy. Or did he realize it? Slowly, Matt turned to Friar Tuck. "Good Father, may I ask you to survey us all and say if you see any defect of spirit that might weaken us before the army of evil?"

Robin and Marian both looked startled, and Tuck fairly blushed. "I am only a meek and humble friar . . ."

Little John nearly choked on a smothered laugh.

"It's part of your office," Matt nudged.

Tuck stood still for a moment. Then he lifted his head with a sigh and stepped forward to scan the troops.

And, suddenly, there was a great deal of tension in the room. Either these men knew Tuck's powers, no matter how modestly he disguised them, or they were taken by surprise—for everyone in the room felt a sudden, searching pressure pass over them all.

It vanished as Tuck turned away, eyes unfocused, as if still in a trance.

"Is all well?" Matt asked softly.

"With them, aye," Tuck answered, as if from far away. "Lord Wizard, step aside with me."

The troops stared, and Matt felt a thrill of alarm pass through him—but Friar Tuck was stepping over into a small chamber that opened off the great hall, into a screened passage, and what could Matt do but follow?

There, the monk slipped his stole out of his pocket, kissed it, and slipped it around his neck. He folded his hands, bowing his head, and waited.

Matt realized it was time for confession.

Trouble was, he had no idea what to confess. Sure, he'd made a lot of mistakes since he'd come to Ibile, but he hadn't exactly been absent from the confessional, and surely his chat with the angel had counted as reconciliation. He hadn't committed any major sins since then, if you didn't count killing sorcerers and their henchmen in self-defense. "Father . . . I have no idea . . ."

"Why have you come to Ibile?" The friar's voice seemed wafted to him on a breeze from distant places.

Matt began to realize he was talking to more than just Friar Tuck. "Why, to unseat the usurper from the throne and restore goodness to Ibile." A sudden urge for truthfulness overwhelmed him. "Or, at least, to open the way to goodness. I don't know if I can do any restoring myself."

"In essence, that is good. But your motive may contaminate your purpose, Lord Wizard. Why? What is your personal desire in this? Have you come to be a king?"

"Well . . . yes," Matt admitted. "I had planned on taking the throne. What's wrong with that? I'm certainly better than the current inhabitant. On the other hand, that doesn't take much—"

"Yet it requires a great deal, to be a good king." The monk sighed. "You are not of the blood royal, Lord Wizard; you have not the qualities required of a prince."

Anger sprouted, but Matt recognized that Tuck was not entirely speaking for himself alone. Maybe he had no right to catechize Matt, but Whoever was speaking through him did. "You're saying that I am no more the rightful monarch than the current king."

"Even so. Ask of yourself, Wizard—'Why do I seek to rule? Is it for the good of the people, for the greater glory of God?' "

"No—it's so that I can qualify to marry Queen Alisande." The words were out almost before Matt realized he was saying them, and he stood there, appalled at what he had just heard.

Tuck made a sound like the air expiring from a concert organ and said, "You must not take the throne for your own personal purposes, Lord Wizard, no matter how worthy. It is of the people we speak, and what is best for them. Know, too, that the rightful heir to the throne of Ibile stands within this Great Hall hard by us."

That *was* hard—it jolted Matt like a short circuit. His head snapped up, and he stared at the monk—who was staring past Matt at something that he couldn't see. No, he didn't doubt for a moment that Tuck had spoken the truth. "The . . . real heir? Not Sir Guy de Toutarien!"

"Nay. 'Tis the maiden holds clear title."

Yverne? Matt stared. Sure, she was noble—but he couldn't quite see her as a reigning monarch. Alisande, she wasn't.

Then he stood stock still, letting that last thought filter down through all the layers of his consciousness. No, she wasn't Alisande, was she? Beautiful, gentle, kind—but not his Alisande.

The pang of loss was sudden and huge. "But Father! All my plans, all my pain—and I *still* can't marry the woman I love?"

"If it is best for the kingdom and the people, you will wed." But Tuck went on inexorably, "If it is not, you will not. You must chance that loss, wizard. For you to seek to win a throne is hubris."

Matt knew the term. The ancient Greeks had used it, for the overweening pride of a man who sought to rival the gods. In his own time and place, it had meant a man who had thought he was something he wasn't—who had sought to become something that was alien to his true nature. *Hubris*—overweening pride, stemming from lack of self-knowledge.

"Neither a throne, nor a queen," the monk droned. "If you are not born a king, you cannot become one—you can only usurp, which is a heinous sin as well as a heinous crime."

"Usurp . . . a wife?" Matt croaked.

"Even so. If she is yours, God will bring you together. If she is someone else's, or no man's, He will not."

The rage boiled up, and for a moment Matt was on the knife's edge, near the point of bellowing his frustration at Friar Tuck and telling them all where to go . . . But he caught himself at the last moment, held back the words, let the rage fill him and start to slacken . . .

And remorse rushed in to fill the void where the anger had been. Matt bowed his head, realizing how close he had come to being untrue to himself, and therefore to Alisande; how close he had come to making both their lives miserable, and those of hundreds of thousands of common people, too. For a moment, he had almost played into the hands of the lord of evil; but thanks to Tuck, he had sheered off at the last second.

That didn't mean he had to like the friar for it, though.

"Thanks, Father," he muttered. "I abjure the throne. I will unseat the sorcerer if I can, even as I've sworn—but I will seek to place the rightful monarch on the throne, not myself."

"It is well." Tuck sketched the Sign of the Cross in the air. "Go in peace, my son—and in hope, for she may yet be yours. I assure you, I shall search without rest, to seek a way to justify the marriage of a lord born a commoner, with a monarch reigning. But though you may be a consort, you shall never be a king."

"All I want is to be her husband," Matt muttered. "Put the titles on the shelf, Friar. I'll read them later."

The field was empty of foemen, except for the dead. There were no enemies wounded or dying—their own knights had slain them as they retreated.

"But wherefore?" Sauvignon's agony of soul was written in his face. "Why would they slay their own men?"

"Wherefore not?" the sergeant said dryly. "These were of no more use to the sorcerer, after all."

"But they might have escaped! They might have gone back to the sorcerer's army!"

"None go willingly to Gordogrosso's armies, I think," Alisande said slowly. "Belike they would choose to stay and fight for us, if they could surrender."

"Would they slay these men for treachery that they *might* commit?"

"They would," the sergeant confirmed. "Wherefore give strength to the enemy? Yet I think 'tis more than that, milord."

Sauvignon turned to him, scowling. "What should it be?"

But the sergeant only glanced at him, then glanced away.

"'Tis their souls, Marquis," Alisande said gently. "If they had not slain them, these men might have repented on their deathbeds and have cheated Hell of a few more souls."

Sauvignon only stared at her, then turned away. The sight of bloody entrails and torn limbs hadn't sickened him, but this did.

"Peace, milord," Ortho murmured. "'Tis not the speaking that matters, nor e'en the unvoiced words in the mind, but the thought itself, the upwelling of repentance in the single sharp surge that takes but a moment; and such could have come to each of these, in the moment of their deaths."

"And if it did not?" Sauvignon grated.

"If it did not, they have gone where they chose."

"But how if they did not so choose?" Sauvignon rounded on him. "How if many among them *would* have repented, if they'd known of their deaths—but did not, for the blow that laid them low came from behind! As, look you, it did, for most among them."

Ortho didn't bat an eyelash. "How if they would have repented, if they could have? Ah, my lord!" He heaved a sigh. "Were not most of these constrained to fight, whether they would or no? How many among them did already repent, and secretly asked forgiveness of God for not having courage enough to face the death by torture that would have come of saying no to the sorcerer's press-gang?"

Sauvignon stared at him for a moment, then said, "Well asked. How then?"

But, "I know not," was all Ortho could answer. "These are questions for a priest, my lord, not for a poor sexton whose soul was too wild to stay in cloister long enough to become so much as a deacon."

Sauvignon held his gaze, then nodded with gruff apology. "'Tis even so. I thank you for this much hope, at least." He turned to the queen. "Majesty, may we summon the chaplain?"

"We may, my lord, when he is done with the work of his office." Alisande gestured down-slope, and Sauvignon turned, surprised, to see the priest who had accompanied the expedition on his knees in the mud, his vial of blessed oil in his hand, marking the Sign of the Cross on each dead soldier, reciting the words of the last annointing in a quick mutter before he rose and went on to the next corpse.

"They may be damned," Alisande said, "but he, at least, finds room for doubt."

Sauvignon saw, and his eyes gleamed. He straightened, and she could almost see his spirit rise.

Ortho saw, too, and smiled. "The sorcerer may have dominion in this world, my lord, but not in the next."

"Why, then, let us reave him of even that!" Sauvignon clapped a hand to his sword hilt and looked up at Alisande with the lust for battle in his eyes. "Let us march, Majesty! Unleash us 'gainst the tyrant!"

Alisande decided that even the ugliest man might have a beautiful soul.

CHAPTER 27

Submarine Raid

They came back into the great hall, Friar Tuck folding his stole and putting it away, Matt trying to straighten his shoulders and put something resembling a smile on his face.

He didn't do too well, of course.

"Be of good heart, Wizard," Maid Marian murmured, stepping close. "She may yet be thine."

Matt looked up at her, startled. How had she known?

Marian smiled and gave him a gentle punch on the arm. "I have seen your face when you have spoken of the queen of Merovence— and you have told us why you have embarked on this quest. Nay, if a man is a-love, what else can make him so glum?"

Quite a few things that Matt could think of—but he couldn't knock it; the lady had read him rightly. The shock did help pull him out of himself, though. He straightened his shoulders and smiled at the stalwart woman. "Thank you, milady. Let's see about setting a siege now, shall we?"

"No," Robin Hood said. "This venture is mine, with my merry men. We must undertake the risk. You must wait until we have, at the least, begun to take up our positions before the castle, before you go below the waves. Only when the sorcerer is assured that we mean to front him outright, may we hope to surprise him from within."

"But while I'm submerging, you'll be dying! He'll haul out his mightiest spells and pulverize you!"

"We shall place our faith in Tuck, and God," Robin answered. "Be of good cheer, Wizard—and be quick. If you strike swiftly, most of us will live."

" 'Most' includes some dead bodies," Matt grumbled.

"How did you say?"

"Nothing—just grumbling."

"He is envious, in that he may not join you in the assault." Yverne laid a hand on Matt's arm. "Go, my lord Earl, and may you prevail."

Robin doffed his hat and gave her his most gallant bow, then turned on his heel and strode out of the tower room.

Marian stared after him, her eyes glistening. "He cannot die!"

"Right." Matt nodded. "He can't. He always rises again, doesn't he?"

"He ever has before . . ."

"Then he will again." Matt turned away to the window, trying to hide his feelings. "Come, ladies, gentlemen. Let's watch for our cue."

They looked on in trepidation, waiting, almost breathless, but there was nothing to see—their tower faced the mainland and the castle, and the fishermen were smuggling Robin Hood and his band around behind the forest on the point. They waited, the minutes trickling away until, finally, some spots of green separated themselves from the darker gray-green of the somber forest—Lincoln green, a dozen, a score, a hundred, filing out to take up stands before the castle. They were just a little too far from the walls for crossbow or mangonel to reach them—but not, Matt suspected, too far for Robin Hood's cloth-yard shafts to strike, driven by longbows.

They were scarcely in position before a fireball lofted from the castle wall and roared toward them.

Force of habit—Matt started to mutter a fire-quenching spell.

"Nay," Fadecourt rumbled at his elbow. "They shall have to hold off the sorcerer without your aid, Wizard. At the least, wait until you are sure your help is needed."

Matt held the final line on the tip of his tongue in an agony of suspense, aching to say it.

Suddenly, the fireball darkened and slowed. Its flames died, and it crashed into the sere grass of the dusty meadow, well short of Robin's lines.

Matt stared.

"What spell was that?" de la Luce asked.

"One I don't know." Matt didn't blame the old don—anything that could quench fire put de la Luce in danger. "Don't worry, milord—the one who put it out is on our side." Privately, he suspected Tuck had just prayed. Matt could only be glad his desires coincided with the Almighty's.

But then, Saint Iago had blessed this whole enterprise, hadn't he? Now it was *his* turn to help out.

"They come!" Fadecourt cried, pointing to a file of men trooping out of the forest.

Matt frowned. "So what's so great about that? Those are Sir Guy's people from the castle. We knew they were being ferried out right after Robin's band."

"They are not my stalwarts," Sir Guy said, peering keenly at the distant dots. "Nay, those are peasants' clothes, Lord Wizard, and peasants' weapons—scythes and flails. They have not the look of those who dwelt with us, and that knight at their head is not one of my friends; I know all their arms, but his are new."

"Another comes!" Yverne pointed off toward the north.

"And another!" Marian called from the southern window. "Yet these are stout burghers, from their look, with tradesmen and the city's poor behind them."

"None such labored with us at the castle." Sir Guy turned to join her, frowning out at the file of men marching up from the south.

"Where are they all coming from?" Matt asked, goggling.

"Why, from all about!" Fadecourt crowed. "Word of your stand has spread, Lord Wizard! These are those with old grievances 'gainst the sorcerer, and good folk who have the courage of their faith! From hither and yon, all about Ibile, have they come, needing but a man of courage to stand against the king! They will rise up in support of such a one, where they would have feared to come singly! Robin Hood and his band will not stand alone in this!"

"Talk about miracles," Matt said, his voice gone shaky. He turned away from the window. "Come on, folks. We've got to do our share in bailing them out."

As they came down into the Great Hall, Stegoman looked up, frowning. "Can none talk to this man o' gossamer? I speak, and he doth profess to fail in understanding."

Matt looked and saw the ghost, huddling in the darkened corner, staring at Stegoman with wide, frightened eyes.

"He can't hurt you, you know." Matt stepped over to the ghost. "You're ectoplasm, and he's protoplasm. No interaction."

But the ghost shook his head, eyes still on Stegoman.

Matt frowned. "What's the matter? Does he remind you of someone?" Then a hunch crunched, and he stared. "It was you! You're the one who spread the word to all the people with a shred of goodness left in them! You're the one who brought them out to join the siege!"

The ghost lowered his eyes, and Matt could have sworn he saw a faint tinge of rose to the ghost's translucency. Then the phantom looked up with a smile, gesturing and mouthing words.

"Not just you, but a lot of other ghosts you knew?" Matt nodded. "Makes sense. The specter network. But that's no reason to be afraid of a dragon."

"What, have other folk come forth in aid?" Stegoman waddled forward, scales clashing, and the ghost shrank back. "Nay, be of good heart, faded phantom. Be mindful, dragon folk, too, wish the foul sorcerer haled down, and all his ilk; there will be many fewer hatchling hunters abroad, I promise you! Nay, but send word to the Free Flyers, and I doubt not that a score or more will answer your call!"

"It'll be dangerous," Matt warned, "even for dragons."

"What matter danger to those of stout heart?" Stegoman thundered. "Go to them, ghost! Or send one of your number who fears them not! What—are there no dragons' spirits among your kind? Send word! Or I promise you, they will be wroth to have been cheated of the glory of this battle!"

"Well, we wouldn't want them to feel offended." Matt nodded to the ghost. "Can you call them?"

The ghost nodded, but he didn't look happy about it. His eyes flicked from Matt to Stegoman and back; then he flicked out.

Matt still found it unnerving, but put a happy face on it. "Great! We'll have an aerial arm."

"If the specter brings word to my kinsmen in time," Stegoman reminded him.

"Good point." Matt frowned. "How fast can a ghost travel, anyway?" Then the thought of another reason for speed chilled him. "The siege can't last long."

"Nay," Sir Guy agreed. "The sorcerer will destroy them ere the sun has set."

"Therefore, let us be quick, that they may live." Fadecourt turned to the demoiselle. "Pray lead us to the castle, milady."

They all turned to follow—and Matt jammed on the brakes. "Now, hold it, Lady Yverne! This is a bit too dangerous for your gentle self!"

But Yverne held her place, chin up and firm. "'Tis my own father that his henchman has slain or imprisoned, Lord Wizard. And, too, I have better reason to risk all with you than you know."

"Or than you can tell me?" Matt shook his head. "No, milady.

We'd all be breaking our necks trying to protect you, instead of getting that gate open."

"I shall defend myself, Lord Wizard! You need not be afeard for me!"

"Easily said," Sir Guy said gently, taking her hand, "but impossible to do. Nay, milady, I should have no thought for aught but your safety."

Fadecourt seemed to bristle, but Yverne looked into Sir Guy's eyes and started to melt.

So the demoiselle intervened. "She must come. Nay, gentles, do not object—there be cause, and good cause. You must all be together in this, or you will be sorely weakened."

Sir Guy and Fadecourt both turned on her, reddening, but Matt leaped into the breach before either of them could say anything. "Well, if we have to, we have to. Don't argue, gentlemen—we're guests, remember? And we mustn't disagree with our hostess, must we? No, of course not. Lead the way, milady."

And she did, down and down, deeper and deeper—but it was a route they had all traveled before. Only Stegoman had difficulty, squeezing around the corners, but again he turned out to be more flexible than they had thought he could be. He did start looking a bit nervous, though, and Matt cursed silently to himself. All he needed was to be caught in a tight spot with a claustrophobic dragon.

Then they were through, down to the rock pier that ran along the ocean inlet. The demoiselle leaped in with a cry of delight, but the rest of the party regarded it with doubt.

"This takes a little courage," Matt admitted, "especially for those of you in full plate armor." That only applied to Sir Guy. "Just take a deep breath and jump in—and don't worry about getting in over your head. That's when the air supply starts."

To demonstrate the point, he jumped in and hoped the others would follow. He was almost touching bottom before he heard and felt the jolts of the others splashing down. Then his feet touched sand; the demoiselle lightly touched his arm; the water rushed away from his face, then his body—and once again, he found himself walking, his clothes completely dry, down the anemone-bordered path, following the demoiselle. He looked behind him and saw Yverne, wide-eyed and wondering, with Sir Guy marching behind her, his visor open, his eyes flicking nervously from side to side. Maid Marian towered behind him, looking frazzled but delighted, and behind her, Stegoman lumbered, with Fadecourt astride his neck just behind the head. In fact, the row of fins along the dragon's back was hazy, seen through water; the fluid line came down about halfway along his back. Fear seized Matt for a moment, fright that the dragon might have broken the surface tension of the tunnel, and that tons of water might come cascading down on them—until he remembered that surface tension couldn't possibly hold that tunnel of air open by itself. If magic could make a tunnel, it could let that arch be interrupted and still hold out the water—and, sure enough, Stegoman's sinuous neck looped up above the tunnel roof, then back down into it, and his nose and eyes were close enough to the path for him to breathe. The dragon was looking a little wild-eyed, but he was holding steady.

Matt didn't blame him. He remembered how he had felt, the first time he had gone flying without an airplane—on Stegoman's very back, in fact. He wasn't especially eager to repeat the experience, considering the evasive maneuvers Stegoman had been running, trying to escape a fiery salamander—but he had survived. So would the dragon.

They came up to the jade palace, and the old king stood at the gate, watching them come. When he saw Stegoman's bulk looming up out of the darkness, he stared. "My great-daughter! A beast of fire, here within its element opposed?"

"The fire is within him, great-sire, just as we dwell within our bubble of air," the demoiselle returned. "He will offend the Sea King no more than we do—and it is vital that he ascend with them."

She held her ancestor's gaze with a strong, steady look of her own, and after a few moments, he nodded, looking grave. "Let him pass, then. But usher them quickly, demoiselle—through my precincts and up the passage. Let them not linger long in Ys."

Matt could only agree with the sentiments, though perhaps not for the same reason. He followed the demoiselle as she led the way around the palace, glimmering in its eldritch light. The party all stared, as they passed, at the spires and arches done in a style that had been forgotten before their own had arisen, gazing in wonder and awe.

"Ahead," Matt called softly, and they all snapped out of their trances and turned to look forward as the demoiselle passed out of the light of the castle precincts, into a huge maw of a dark and lightless tunnel.

Yverne and Fadecourt halted involuntarily, shivering at the miasma of evil that seemed to brush their spirits, even so far removed. The demoiselle must have been expecting the reaction, for she turned back and called softly to them, "Aye—'tis a blemish on the face of the earth, is it not? Even here beneath the sea, we sense its evilness. This pathway has not been trod for more than an hundred years, though I have ventured along it till I saw the castle's base. That far, I have gone, confident in the Sea King's power, that the sorcerer's sway cannot extend into Poseidon's domain—but I will not pass above his waters."

"We will, then." Matt nodded with grim certainty. "That's what we came for, isn't it? Although, come to think of it, anyone who wants to go back, go with my blessing—I wouldn't blame you for a second. Just because I have to march ahead is no reason the rest of you should."

They all turned to meet his eyes, and he almost flinched at the silent accusation they leveled at him. "All right, all right! No offense intended. Come on, let's go." He turned away to the demoiselle and nodded, before he had to listen to their rebukes.

The demoiselle led the way down a passage that grew steadily darker and darker. After a few hundred paces, only the sea anemones were giving light, and that only as colored dots that marked the borders of the path. Then their light grew dim and disappeared, and Matt realized with a shock, that something was killing off any creatures that lived beyond this point.

He hoped he wasn't included.

Light glowed suddenly, and he saw that Sinelle was holding up the gem that had nestled at her throat. It gave off light now, dim and chill, but far better than the darkness that had enshrouded them. She beckoned with the jewel. Matt nodded and pressed forward. His commandos came after him.

It couldn't have been more than about ten minutes of groping in that dimness, but it felt like a year. Matt slogged ahead, testing the ground with every step—then suddenly realized that the demoiselle had stopped. He looked up and saw a huge brass-bound door blocking their way.

"Yon is the dungeon of the sorcerer's castle," Sinelle said in a low voice, for there was something about this place that discouraged speech. "Farther I cannot go. I wish you well, my friends."

Matt swallowed through a throat gone suddenly thick, and nodded. "Thanks, milady. We're grateful for everything you've done. Hopefully, we'll be seeing you soon, to celebrate."

His companions muttered assent.

"I will rejoice," she said, trying to sound positive. "Fare ye well, good folk."

She stepped aside, and Matt reached out to grasp the huge ring set in the door. He twisted, and the latch mechanism groaned. Then he threw all his weight against the portal, and, slowly, it swung open.

The companions moved into the darkness. Marian murmured, "I am amazed it was not locked."

"Perchance the sorcerer does not even know it is here," Fadecourt said softly. "Wizard, can you bring us light?"

Matt shook his head in the darkness, then remembered nobody could see him. "I'd rather not use magic this close to the sorcerer—it'll let him know at once that we're here. Stegoman, can you manage some fire?"

A gout of flame roared out, showing them the blackened cones of old torches held in sconces against the walls. Matt reached up and plucked one down. "This will do—we can't keep the poor beast breathing fire all the time." He held its tip in Stegoman's flame until it caught, then raised it aloft. The dragon's flame shut off, and Matt stepped out into the middle of the chamber, holding up the torch.

Its light fell on the foot of a stairway that curved along the outside of the circular room, disappearing up into the darkness.

Matt swallowed and moved toward it. "Okay, friends. Here we go."

The way was long and tortuous. Matt had climbed enough steps so that his thighs began to ache, before it occurred to him to count—to break the monotony, if nothing else. But, of course, by then it was too late. It seemed to be a simple spiral staircase—but it was a very long one. Matt found himself beginning to wonder about architects inspired by the DNA molecule.

Then, suddenly, there were no more stairs; Matt slammed into a rock wall. Fortunately, he wasn't going very fast; unfortunately, Yverne, Marian, and Fadecourt slammed into him before he could tell them. "Dead end," he said, low-voiced in case something was listening in the darkness.

How paranoid can you get? Very—in a sorcerer's castle.

"If you'll back up just a touch, I'll see if there's a way out."

The pressure on his back eased up; he pulled his chin out of the wall and started groping around.

"'Tis here." Marian, at least, wasn't worried about who might hear them. "A hole in the wall—a masonry archway, from the feel of it."

Matt moved the torch around and saw the archway, ten feet away at the end of a landing carved into the rock. "Right. Well, at least there aren't any more steps." He marched through the archway.

They rattled. They buzzed. They came scurrying on little, chitinous feet, tails curved up over their backs, holding their stings ready to stab.

Matt leaped backward with an expletive deleted. "Scorpions! Get back, ladies!"

Yverne jumped back with a little scream, but drew her sword and began chopping at the little blighters.

"Nay, brave lady!" Sir Guy cried. "Let me essay it—this menace is mine!" He shouldered past; Marian gave an indignant cry as he elbowed her aside. But as his iron-shod feet began crushing sinister insects, she started cheering him on. "Aye, sir knight! Slay them, crush them! Let none survive to plague . . . Ah! Beware!"

A huge scorpion, stronger than the others, managed to leap atop Sir Guy's foot and scuttled up his leg, stinger probing for a weak spot in his armor.

"Watch out!" Matt shouted. "Behind the knee, he's—"

Maid Marian's quarterstaff swung, knocking the arthropod to the floor. Sir Guy's heel came down on it.

But other large scorpions had blundered into the same technique; a stream of insects was running up his legs, and some of their mates were getting past him, heading for softer prey.

"This is too slow!" Stegoman snapped. "Aside, ladies, knight! Let me reach unto them!"

Matt flattened himself against the wall. Marian knocked the last scorpion off Sir Guy and leaped aside. The dragon's huge head snaked through, knee-high, and a blast of fire lit the tunnel with a glare that seemed like that of the noontime sun. The air filled with cracklings and poppings. The companions turned to stamping out the few insects that escaped the fire.

Then Stegoman's blast winked out, and they blinked in the sudden dimness. Frantic to make sure, Matt leaned over, holding the torch close.

There was nothing left but powder.

"I thank you, stalwart friend," Sir Guy said. "I should have called upon you sooner."

"I would I could take the lead," the dragon growled, "but I misdoubt me an I could tell the way. Nay, Wizard, let us go on."

"Right." Matt stepped gingerly through the mass that had lately been angry insects, watching carefully for any more, but they seemed to have caught the whole nest. Either that, or the survivors had sense enough to hide.

Just past the last scorpion ashes, the tunnel narrowed—not enough to trap Stegoman, but enough to make Matt feel claustrophobic again. The hallway turned a little this way, then a little that way, ambling off into the bedrock as if it hadn't a care in the world. It seemed to have been laid out by some very careless workmen—or as if it were another form of life. Matt had a fleeting thought of the kinds of monsters that might have been able to make this tunnel at the Sea King's behest, and swallowed his heart down out of his throat. Then he pressed on, sorely wishing he could take Stegoman up on his offer and let him take the lead—just for the light, of course. The torch was burning down, and Matt didn't want it to get close to his fingertips. He knew that Sir Guy had collected the other, unlit, antique torches from their sconces below, and every so often, he'd found another one to add to his bundle, but still . . .

The torchlight flickered on something that glinted. Matt stopped. "Be wary, folks!" Then he inched forward, torch thrust ahead.

The glimmering light revealed two recesses, niches in the walls directly opposite each other, four feet deep, four feet wide, and four feet high. In each lay a skeleton with an empty jug beside it, rags of ancient cloth still lying about its hips.

Matt halted, apprehension creeping over him.

"The poor creatures!" Yverne cried. "Why were they caged here?"

"Punishment, I would say." Sir Guy scowled at the matched sets of bones. "I have seen this done aforetime—an unruly, disobedient one set with just such a cage in a wall, not high enough to stand in, or even to lie comfortably, and given little to eat or drink. 'Tis a punishment two-edged, for he is exposed to the jibes and mockeries of his fellows, even as they see him and are reminded of the reward for insolence."

"Yes," Matt said, "but prisoners like that are usually set free, aren't they?"

"They are only skeletons, Lord Wizard," Maid Marian said gently. "They cannot harm us now."

But Matt shook his head. "I'm getting a very bad feeling about this. If this were a public punishment, as Sir Guy said, there would have had to be a public to witness the punishment—wouldn't there? But there weren't any files of soldiers passing through here—this was a secret passage, not a thoroughfare."

"Dost say they are sentries?" Fadecourt demanded.

"Maybe worse." Matt pointed. "I don't trust the way they're set exactly across from each other, so that we have to pass between them."

"A trap, then?" Maid Marian asked.

"Could be. But I've run into things like this, back where I came from." Matt dropped to hands and knees; he was thinking of electric-eye photocells, with infrared light beams. "Down, everybody. Maybe we can put ourselves beneath their notice." And he crawled forward, wondering what he was going to do about Stegoman.

He needn't have worried. The skeletons screamed.

They sat bolt upright, fleshless jaws parting, emitting a clear, high tone that rasped right through Matt's head from one ear to the other. He was already clawing his way up the grid of bars before he realized that the screams had turned into a single, repeated word: "Master! Master!"

"Get 'em *out* of there!" he bellowed. "Shut 'em up!" Too late, he realized that the bars weren't there to keep the skeletons in—they were to keep intruders out, to keep them from getting to the bones and breaking them.

Fadecourt shouldered him aside, laying hold of the bars and wrenching them out of the stone. Matt reached for the skull . . .

And the bony hand reached down and came up with a sword.

The skeleton sprang out of its niche and swung, still screaming, "Maaaaster! Maaaaaster!"

Matt just barely managed to get his dagger out in time to block the swing. The skeleton whipped the sword around for an undercut . . .

And Maid Marian's quarterstaff cracked into its skull, knocking it against the wall. Then the staff knocked apart the bones of the hand; the sword clanged to the stone floor. The skull rolled against the stones, still screaming, while the headless skeleton leaped for her, its remaining hand clawing for her eyes.

The quarterstaff slammed into the rib cage, jarring the whole collection of bones back against the wall. Then Marian whirled and brought the tip of her staff down on the skull, cracking it open. The struggling bone dropped back to the floor, lifeless, and the screaming suddenly stopped.

But another scream still went on, then broke off. Matt turned to see Fadecourt rising from a jumble of bones, with a long line of blood across his chest.

"You are hurt!" Yverne cried.

The cyclops only looked down and wiped at the blood in irritation. "A scratch. We have greater matters to be concerned with."

"Darn right we have." Matt glanced ahead at the tunnel. Had he heard a faint sound? "Those things were calling for their master—and if these were the servants, I don't want to meet the boss."

It *was* a sound—a clicking, a clattering, growing louder.

"There is small choice." Fadecourt glared ahead at the sound. "We must retreat and give over our enterprise, or forge ahead and chance all."

"Maybe *you* have the choice, but I don't." Already, Matt could feel his geas pushing him onward. "I'm going as fast as I can. If their 'master' is coming for us, our best chance is to catch him before he expects us. Good luck!" He ran ahead, torchlight swaying. Behind him, his friends cried out, startled, and came running.

Matt rounded a curve and slammed into a jumble of bones.

The passage had widened into a small court, and it was filled with dancing skeletons, glowing coals in their eyes, rusty swords in their hands. Just looking at the weapons gave Matt lockjaw. He shied, daunted for a moment, then shouted, "Out of the way! Let Stegoman at 'em!" And he sprang aside, plastering himself back against the wall.

Marian leaped aside, too, but her style was with her quarterstaff whirling like a windmill, cracking bones and knocking skeletons apart. Fadecourt leaped over beside Matt and tore at the articulated bones, catching a femur to use for parrying sword blows, and Sir Guy stepped up beside Maid Marian, blocking and cutting, dispatching foe after foe. Yverne was slicing around her with one of the fallen skeletons' swords. Matt finally drew his own blade.

Then a roaring gout of fire surged past him, lighting up the chamber. Dry bones crackled and snapped, filling the whole passage with glaring flames. The jet of fire went out as Stegoman caught his breath, but the blaze kept on, though the skeletons still struggled toward the living people. Then the flame blasted again, and the few sets of bones that had still been standing keeled over, threshing even yet in a mindless homicidal impulse. The companions stepped forward, staves and swords ready to clear up the last few opponents . . .

And the whole cave darkened. Not into total night, but as if the chamber had suddenly filled with thick black smoke that dimmed the light and made every outline barely discernible. Stegoman's flame gouted out again, but it was reddened, growing more feeble, dimming as the darkness deepened, and Matt could feel the energy leaching out of him, weariness growing, weighing down his limbs like lead, while all about them, a giggling sound grew to a chuckle, then laughter, swelling and beating at their ears—and Matt suddenly understood how the skeletons had come to be there. The first usurping sorcerer had set a spirit to guard this place, a spirit who drank raw energy and was always hungry. Any living being stumbling into the midst of the monster staggered and swooned as the life energy was sucked out of it. Then the meat of its muscles oxidized, giving up more energy, and more, until even the marrow was gone.

But the monster could send energy back into the skeletons to send them against intruders.

"Wizard!" Yverne cried in despair. "Magic, or we are lost."

Not much choice, now. Matt had to risk alerting Gordogrosso to their raid, or atrophy. But there was one slender hope. A magical creature, just exercising its natural processes, might not attract attention, any more than this dark energy-drinking monster did. "Max! Get us out of this!"

"How, Wizard?" The bright spark danced before him, and the laughter halted. Then it redoubled, and the darkness thickened about the spark. But Max blazed brighter, and the darkness thinned and was gone, while the laughter suddenly transformed to a shriek.

"There!" Matt shouted. "Just what you did! Leach the energy out of that creature! Dry it up!"

The shriek turned to a snarl of rage, echoing all about them, and the darkness drew in to form a black ball in the middle of the passage, hiding Max from view—but the Demon's voice carried clearly to them. "Even as you say—though I am loathe to do it, to a creature so much akin to me. Still, it has no conscience, and knows only how to destroy. It shall be done."

The snarl soared back into a shriek again, and kept on rising and rising until it seemed as if it would shred Matt's brain—but the ball of darkness grew smaller and smaller, then thinner, till Max could be seen through it, growing brighter and brighter . . .

Then the monster was gone, with a final, echoing scream.

"It is finished," Max said.

Then suddenly, he began to vibrate, then to give off streamers of light-colored mist that radiated away from him and were gone.

"They are free now," the Demon said, "the souls he held imprisoned, the spirits of those skeletons you destroyed. So long as the bones endured to anchor the souls, the mortals were imprisoned here. But you have freed them."

"Us?" Matt gasped, astounded. "No way! It was you who zapped him, Max!"

"I?" the Demon vibrated with delight. "I can do naught, Wizard! I am only a force, a personification of a concept! I must be directed, commanded—and it is you who have loosed me. Nay, 'tis your doing; I am but your tool."

"If you say so." But Matt had his doubts. "Care to guide us the rest of the way?"

"I cannot. Summon me at need." And Max winked out.

Matt sighed in the sudden darkness. "Have any torches left, Sir Guy?"

"I have dropped them," came the knight's voice. "Let me see, now ... where ... No, that is a bone ... Here! Stegoman, if you will?"

Flame brightened the gloom, showing Sir Guy holding a torch in Stegoman's flame. Then the dragon's glow shut off, and torchlight flickered on the walls of the chamber. "Four left," the knight said.

"That ought to get us there—we can't have far to go now." Matt took the torch and turned away down the tunnel, trying to be careful about stepping over the bones.

The passage ran straight for about sixty feet, then took a sudden, right-angled turn. Matt slowed down, instinctively wary of a next step where he couldn't see ahead—but as he came around the corner, his torchlight flickered off oak planks and iron straps. "A door! We've made it through! Come on, folks!" And he leaped ahead, just as Fadecourt shouted, "'Ware!"

Matt's foot came down—and down, and down! He was falling, and he howled in fright—then jerked to a halt, slammed against a rock face.

He caught his breath, amazed to find he was still alive and not falling. Then he looked back up over his shoulder and saw Fadecourt, lying flat against the edge of the drop-off, one huge arm knotted and bulging with strain. "I saw," he grated. "Reach up and grasp the edge, Wizard. You must aid me in drawing you up."

"Yeah, right!" Matt reached up, as Fadecourt pulled, and caught the edge. Then he strained with every ounce of strength, and the cyclops yanked him up and over. Matt rolled away from the edge and sat up, wild-eyed and panting. "Thanks, Fadecourt. Guess I was right to invite you to join us."

"As I was, to ask." The cyclops squeezed Matt's shoulder. "Are you restored, Wizard? For we still must pass this pit."

Looking up, Matt saw that they stood on one side of a huge hole, filling the tunnel from wall to wall, and at least twenty feet across. Beyond it was about ten more feet of stone floor, then the door. "Somebody really didn't want visitors, did he?"

Then the smell hit him, and he gagged. The pit emitted a dank, fetid aroma, and far below, he heard suspicious rappings.

"Let us be gone, and quickly," Sir Guy said. "Whate'er dwells here, it may rise, and I have no wish to meet it by torchlight."

"Me neither." Even unseen, the thing was giving off vibrations that made the hair rise on the back of Matt's neck. "But I wouldn't try a broad jump."

"I would." Fadecourt stepped up to the edge.

The scrapings below became faster, more eager.

"I pray you, do not!" Yverne cried, reaching out to catch his arm. "We cannot bear the loss of you; 'tis not worth the risk."

Sir Guy didn't look all that sure about the last part, but he dutifully shook his head. "We must be all together to attack the sorcerer, good cyclops. We cannot spare your strength."

Fadecourt hesitated, flattered, then smiled up at Yverne and stepped back. She breathed a sigh of relief. "I thank you, good Fadecourt."

"At your pleasure," he murmured, and Sir Guy bristled.

The bulls were pawing the ground, and Matt definitely didn't need them to butt heads here. "Flying," he ventured.

Stegoman wagged his head from side to side. "I can barely squeeze through this passage, Matthew. Assuredly, I could not open my wings."

"Well, I might try . . . but no, I'd rather do this without magic." Matt glanced down to the pit, felt the emanations, and shuddered. Whatever was under there just might be able to cancel his spell in midflight. No, he didn't think he wanted to try levitation.

And the scrapings were coming closer.

"An arrow." Maid Marian took out her bow and strung it. "Can you lash a line to it?"

"Sure, if we had one!"

"'Tis bound to my waist." Marian pulled a rope end loose. Fadecourt caught the coil, took an arrow, and began to tie the one to the other. "But to what shall you affix the arrow?"

"The door," Marian said simply.

Fadecourt and Matt exchanged glances, both feeling like idiots for not having thought of the obvious.

"But who shall draw the rope across, and make it fast?" Yverne asked.

Maid Marian smiled, tying the light line to her arrow. "There is a ring upon the door, milady, and 'tis set into a plate—see you?"

Yverne looked and saw the huge iron circle set into the door in place of a knob. She frowned. "Aye. What of it?"

Marian aimed and loosed.

The arrow sped out over the pit, slammed into the metal plate with a clank like a boiler meeting a sledgehammer, and ricocheted down.

"Oh, well done!" Yverne clapped her hands. "But how shall you draw it back to us, to make it fast?"

"There is no need; 'tis a four-barbed head, and the shaft is iron." Marian drew back on the rope; the barbs of the arrowhead caught on the ring and held. She handed the line to Fadecourt. "Brace it well, cyclops." Then she took hold of the rope.

"Hey, no!" Matt cried. "Let one of the guys take the risk!"

"Wherefore?" Marian gave him a challenging glare. "'Tis my arrow, and my shot; 'tis my risk. Do not think to—"

With a roar, a huge gout of flame erupted from the pit, and the rope burned through.

Marian stared. So did Matt. Then he whispered. "That, too. Yeah."

"Back!" Stegoman thundered. "It comes! Stand back against the walls; leave me room!"

Nobody argued; they plastered themselves against the rock.

A head poked over the pit, a huge, blunt, questing snout with faceted eyes, under which were two huge clashing pincers. Behind them came a pair of crooked bowlegs—and another pair, and another. Up it came with a slither of scales, foot after foot, yard after yard, leg after leg.

Yverne screamed. Matt might have, too—he remembered all the little scorpions they had roasted back at the beginning of the tunnel. Their big brother had come for revenge.

It opened its jaws and blasted flame.

Stegoman roared, with a gout of fire that met the centipede's. Flame blasted against flame and splashed off the walls; the companions scrambled out of the way.

"He holds it!" Sir Guy cried. "Attack!"

Matt jolted out of his trance, whipped out his sword, and leaped forward, stabbing. His sword point skidded across the chitinous shell—then lodged between segments. Matt leaned on it with every ounce of his strength, and the blade went in.

The monster screamed and thrashed, four sword points skewering it, and the segments closed on the sword, twisting it out of Matt's grasp. He dove for the hilt, but it danced mockingly before him as the monster gyrated in pain, and it turned its snout back toward him ...

Fadecourt threw his huge strength against the body, holding a length of it still just long enough. Matt seized his sword and yanked it out, found another gap, and plunged it in again. So did Marian—she was on her third or fourth stab, and Sir Guy and Yverne weren't far behind. The monster shrieked and drew breath ...

Stegoman blasted, his flame catching the centipede broadside.

Its scream veered toward the supersonic; it whipped about, blasting a return at Stegoman. But the dragon held his flame steady, till the centipede's slackened—and slackened more and more, for the five companions were stabbing and stabbing. Matt tried to remember his freshman zoology class, figuring where a heart might be, and stabbed and wrenched, trying to avoid the green slime that welled between the segments, but not succeeding too well, remembering, with a sick, sinking feeling, that basic life-forms like this took an awfully long time to die ...

But breathing fire took a lot out of the worm. It gave a last, feeble puff of flame; then its legs folded, and its faceted eyes began to dull.

"It dies!" Sir Guy cried.

"Back!" Fadecourt bellowed. "It falls!"

For the first time, Matt realized that, no matter how much of the huge centipede had come out of the pit, there was more down below, and it was hanging loose from the side now, dead weight, the slackened claws having lost their hold on the niches in the rock. It slid backward faster and faster. The companions leaped aside just before the head whipped back over the edge of the pit and shot down out of sight.

They stood silent, staring down into the darkness, not quite believing the battle was over.

Then Matt felt a burning pain on his upper arm. "Yow!" He looked down and saw that the ichor had eaten through the cloth of his tunic. "It's acid! Everybody out of your clothes, quick!"

He scrambled out of his garments and shivered in the chill, glad that he had held to the habit of wearing underwear—in defiance of *this* world's custom. The ladies shed their dresses, standing almost as decently clad in their shifts, and Fadecourt and Sir Guy caught up the cloth to wipe the slime off skin and armor, respectively. Sir Guy inspected some mild etching and said, "I am nearly unscathed." He turned to Fadecourt. "And you, friend?"

Yverne saw the raw patches on the cyclops' skin and cried out.

"I will endure," he grated. "It is painful, but I am not hindered. Quickly, let us come out of this place! Then the wizard may mend me!"

"I may do so now." Marian took the belt off the remains of her gown and reached into a pouch. She took out a small jar, opened it, and began to rub the cream inside onto Fadecourt's burns. "'Tis an herbal compound I learned to craft, from a monk. 'Tis a sovereign remedy for small wounds of all kinds—does it aid you?"

"A blessing," Fadecourt said, with a huge sigh of relief. "I thank you, maid."

As she finished anointing him, Matt said, "I hate to rush things—but do you have another one of those iron arrows?"

"Aye." Marian took up her bow, drew a new arrow, and tied the remains of the rope to it. She drew and loosed, and in a very short while, Fadecourt was swinging hand over hand along the rope—having claimed that he owed it to her for the salve. Then Stegoman braced the other end of the line, and Matt and Marian between them figured out how to make a fireman's chair. They swung across one by one—and, when they were all standing on the far side, they looked back at Stegoman, with a sudden shock of realization.

"How," Matt said, "are we going to get the dragon over here?"

"I can leap with ease, if I have room enough to land," Stegoman answered. "But yon dozen paces is nowhere nearly enough. Ope the door, Wizard, and all of thee go through it; then I'll have room enough indeed, and shall be with thee straight."

On the word, Fadecourt turned and lashed a huge kick at the lock. Metal snapped, and the door slammed back.

There was darkness behind it. They stood in silence, waiting, until they heard distant voices calling.

"What sound was that?"

"The door, fool! Belike the warders bring another luckless soul to join us!"

"Or," a third, and nervous, voice said, "have they come to take one of us away to the gibbet?"

"'Tis the dungeon," Maid Marian breathed, "and no guards."

"Surely," Sir Guy agreed. "Wherefore would they ward a door that has not opened in hundreds of years?"

Matt frowned. "You'd think somebody would have remembered."

"Their guards were on this side of the door," Yverne pointed out. "If such a monster as this failed, what use would be human guards?"

She definitely had a point. Matt thrust the torch out and stuck his head behind it, inspecting for booby traps, then leaped through the door, just in case—but no nets fell, no barbs sprang out. "It's safe. Come on, friends."

They filed through. Then, with a whoosh, a huge thud, and a scrabbling of claws, Stegoman shot through the door and skidded to a halt, jolting against the far wall. Matt glanced at the floor; the dragon's claws had gouged grooves in the granite. "Glad you're on our side. Now—where do we go?"

"Yon." Fadecourt turned, pointing, then strode ahead.

He seemed very sure of himself. Matt wasn't about to argue—but he did wonder. He followed the cyclops while he wondered, though.

They followed a sloping floor up, where the rock was no longer quite so rough-hewn. They tried to walk as quietly as possible, but as they neared a door of planks, a low voice called through its small grate, "Who brings light in the darkness?"

They stopped, all looking at Matt. He swallowed and answered, "A friend. What are *you* doing here?"

"I performed pantomimes in village squares, and mocked the king," the voice answered dryly. "And you?"

"We have come to help those who deserve it." It was a justified gamble—Gordogrosso punished only goodness, not evil. Matt nodded to Fadecourt, who laid hold of the latch and shoved. There was a crack of breaking metal, and the door swung open.

There was a minute's silence.

Then a middle-aged man, with hair almost white, crept out of the cell, blinking in the torchlight. "You . . . you would not mock me?" Then he saw Stegoman; his eyes widened, and so did his mouth.

Maid Marian clasped a hand over his lips. "Softly, goodman—he, too, is a friend."

"I am not a-hungered," Stegoman rumbled. "Even if I were, I prefer my food clean."

The man looked indignant, so Marian removed her hand—and he growled, "I'll have you know I was most fastidious, till I was locked down here!"

"I understand," Matt sympathized. "They don't exactly provide running water." But a thought was hatching. "Think you can tell us who's down here for what?"

"Nothing easier," the actor said with confidence. "In the cell next to mine is a tax collector who let some poor folk, who could not pay, escape the whip. Next to him is a farmer, who sought to prevent the soldiers from taking his daughter. Farther on—"

"That's fine," Matt interrupted. "Tell us about them as we come to them. You go first."

The actor was only too glad to go, partly because Stegoman was bringing up the rear. He gave them a running commentary, and as they came to each door, Fadecourt bashed in the lock and let out the prisoner. Matt and Sir Guy herded them along in front, though Sir Guy gave Matt a questioning glance. Matt only gave a short shake of the head in answer.

It was very simple, really. He didn't want possible criminals coming behind his back—and he didn't mind letting them have first chance at the guards. He felt a little guilty at the idea that he was throwing the prisoners to the wolves, but he reminded himself that it was a better chance than they ever would have had otherwise—but the stab of conscience made him warn them, "Take up whatever weapons you can find. We're apt to have to do some fighting, if we want to get out of here."

The prisoners were only too glad to cooperate, wrenching table legs loose in the few well-appointed cells—the ones that contained more than moldering straw. Fadecourt took to yanking chains out of the walls in cells that had them; as they neared the door to the castle, half of the prisoners were armed with links.

There were also a lot of them—fifty or more, and others had begun clamoring for release, in the distance.

It gave Matt an idea. "Hold on! Don't hit that door—stand back!"

"Wherefore?" One of the prisoners glared at him as if suspecting treachery.

Matt couldn't blame him for a little suspicion. He explained quickly, "Your fellow prisoners are making a fair amount of noise. If there's a jailor on duty . . ."

"There is."

"He could be coming through that door any second."

The portal slammed open, and a hulking, barrel-shaped man, who would have given Quasimodo a beauty prize, came shambling through, with a squad of soldiers at his heels. "What clamor is this? What ails the fools? Have some . . ." Then he saw the prisoners, and his eyes went wide. The guards began to lower their pikes—

With a yell like a dam breaking, the prisoners swamped the guards. There were a few horrified yells and the dull, sick thud of steel against skulls; then the doorway was still, and the prisoners rose up, grinning.

Suddenly, Matt knew what was coming next, and tried to stop it. "Quietly, now! And slowly! We—"

They ignored him. Very loudly, they ignored him. With a shout of triumph, they ignored him and poured out through the dungeon door, howling for revenge—and freedom.

As they came out of the forest, relaxing and beginning to think the danger of ambush was over, the roof fell in.

Or at least Gordogrosso's soldiers did. They fell from overhanging branches and leaped out of the underbrush like living bushes, but ones with spear points. They made no sound, though, other than the scrape of metal and the clash of steel. They would have taken the queen and her men completely by surprise, if Sauvignon hadn't been watching, suspicious of magic.

He let loose a yell that could have waked the dead and whipped his sword out. Startled, Alisande looked up, saw a man leaping toward her, shouted, "Above!" and whipped out her blade as she kneed her horse aside.

Behind her, her men looked up, too, then let out a fearful shout as they crowded into clumps, trying to avoid the living projectiles.

So, of course, some of the enemy soldiers fell right atop the clumps.

Ugly cracking sounds came from their landings—before the broken ones' mates stabbed down with a bellow of anger. Other ambushers fell on the road, and the few that survived the fall were dazed and easy meat for Alisande's pikemen.

But the road before them filled in with mounted men, behind three ranks of foot soldiers.

"Retreat!" Alisande cried. "Back, in good order! We will come at these in another fashion!"

Emboldened, the enemy knights roared a command and rode slowly down the roadway behind the running ranks of their men.

Alisande set a good example by chopping down a few in the front rank even as she urged her horse backward. Behind her, grudgingly, her men gave way—save for a few who ducked around her to stab at the enemy. Still, foot by foot, the forces of Merovence retired, but thinned the ranks of their attackers as they went.

At the rear, Sauvignon bawled orders, and the more-alert footmen began to climb the trees.

Ten more paces, and the enemy army halted, seeing Merovencian soldiers perched up high among the branches. One or two of the climbers were hefting stones experimentally.

Ibilian men went scurrying up the trunks again, and the Army of Evil withdrew, slowly.

Alisande's footmen roared with delight and leaped in pursuit.

"Hold!" she bellowed. "That way lies death!"

Unconvinced but obedient, her men came to a surly halt.

"Retire to the edge of this wood," Alisande ordered, "for we cannot pass the night here."

"But, Majesty!" a sergeant protested, "we shall lose what we have gained!"

"'Tis better than losing our lives," the queen rejoined. "Take your men and go."

The Ibilians drew back out of sight—but Alisande had no doubt they were there, crouched and ready.

As her men came back into the little meadow before the woods, Sauvignon bawled orders to pitch camp. Reluctantly, they turned to obey. Everyone knew right where to go—to the buried embers of last night's fire.

"How shall we dislodge the enemy from these trees, Majesty?" Sauvignon asked.

"Why, by sending rangers above, to find and strike down at them," Alisande said wearily, "and all the footmen to follow them. Then, when we have taken the heights, may we bring the horses through."

"'Tis well." Sauvignon grinned beneath his visor. "Myself, I think I shall become a footman anon." And he turned to spread the good word.

Alisande watched him go and felt a pang of regret as she watched his athletic, mail-clad figure moving among the men. She turned away, murmuring, "Ah, Matthew! Wherefore could you not have been well born?"

It would be so easy if he were only here—or did it just seem that way? No, surely her Matthew could have wrought a spell that would have sent these hedge sorcerers packing, and would have made the Ibilian soldiers fall from their trees like ripe fruit before her army, ready for the gathering.

"Where are you now, my love?" she murmured, gazing off toward the woods and Orlequedrille. "Of what do you speak?"

Or to whom?

She felt a stab of panic at that—had he met another woman, one softer and more compliant? She had not forgotten how completely Matt had fallen victim to the charms of the lust-witch Sayeesa, nor how she had needed to hew her way in to rescue him. Even then, it was only his oath of fealty that had saved them all, not his love for her.

"What a fool I was," she swore, "not to make sure of him whiles I could! Ah my love, my love—an I find you again, be certain I shall wrap you quickly to an altar and a priest, ere you may make your escape from me again!"

But her heart sank at the very words. Did he truly think of his quest as an escape? Given his free choice, would he really choose her?

And would his choice be free? Would he, himself? Or did he, at this moment, languish in the dungeon of the sorcerer-king? Had he been put to the torture? Her heart began to race as she pictured him on the rack—though Heaven knew he deserved some pain, for abandoning her so!

But it was Heaven's doing after all, was it not? If Heaven had not wished him to sally forth against Ibile, surely his foolish oath would have had no effect.

Could Heaven strengthen him enough, against Ibile's sorcerers?

What blasphemy even to think it! If Heaven wished to scour the land of sorcery, assuredly it had the power . . .

But did the people wish it? The common folk, and the sorcerers who led them? For surely, God had given people the power to choose their own destinies, wisely or foolishly, and would not compel folk to choose well.

As Heaven would not constrain Matthew to choose wisely.

A stab of pure panic pierced her. Could her Matthew have wearied of virtue? Could he have fallen prey to the temptations of carnal pleasure and worldly power? For he was, surely, in a land where they who worked magic held dominion over all their fellows. Could Matthew have succumbed?

But no, he did not seek power . . .

Or did he?

All her old suspicions welled up again. Did Matthew want her because he loved her, or because he loved her power? Did he seek a love match, or a throne?

If only he had been well born, like Sauvignon!

Or, said the nasty voice of conscience, *like Duke Astaulf?*

Duke Astaulf, who had usurped her father's throne, then slain him. His soul toiled in Purgatory now, though it had wrought enough evil here on earth, in its time. Surely birth could yield as much ambition as its lack. Nay, more, for it had an easier channel for its striving.

Might Matthew, then, have sought the easier channel? Might he, perish the thought, have joined with the sorcerers in their government of evil?

"Heaven forbid!" Alisande whispered with a shudder, and drew her cloak more tightly around her as she sent up an earnest prayer that her love would still be free when she found him, still devoted to God, Good, and Merovence . . .

And to Alisande, of course. Pray Heaven he had not found another woman!

CHAPTER 28

Offensive Defenses

They burst out into the keep, a mob of filthy skeletons in tatters, wide-eyed and howling.

"After them!" Matt shouted. "There's still a chance!"

They charged up the dungeon stairs, nearly tripping in the dim light of the sconced torches, but by the time they reached the top step, it was too late. The huge oaken doors were broken; two mangled guards and a dying prisoner lay on the floor. The ground floor was an armory, and the prisoners were catching up weapons and turning on the guards like maniacs—which many of them probably were, by now. More guards came running, from the upper stories and from the courtyard.

"They blew it," Matt groaned. "What can we do for them now?"

"See that their sacrifice is not in vain." Sir Guy gripped his shoulder. "Use the diversion they have given you! Outside, Wizard! To the gate!"

Matt pulled himself together and stepped out into the armory. In the center of the huge room, guards were flailing at the riot of prisoners. Matt beckoned to his crew and sidled along the wall, heading for the main door.

They made it without a hitch, swinging around the side of the great portal—and coming face-to-face with a huge captain who was just running up with a dozen guards at his back. He put on the brakes and shouted, "Seize them!"

The soldiers dived for Matt and his people.

Maid Marian brought around her quarterstaff, the others raised their swords, and Fadecourt prowled forward, arms out to grab—but Matt shouted, "Hold, good guardsmen! Is't not enough that your king has scourged us forth with derision? Admittedly, our performance may not have been the most amusing—but are we to be pilloried for bad acting?"

He had an answer for that, but fortunately the captain didn't. He held up a hand to halt his troops, frowning. "What manner of vagabonds are you, then, who go armed in the king's castle?"

"Wandering players," Matt improvised, "and our weapons and armor are lath and buckram." He forced a laugh. "O worthy Captain! Would you believe that such poor folk as we could bear the weight of real armor?"

The captain glanced at Sir Guy, unsure—then his gaze lit on Fadecourt, and he relaxed. Matt didn't—he was waiting for the man to ask about Stegoman. He risked a glance back—and there was no sight of the dragon! Matt felt a moment of panic, afraid for his friend, then reminded himself that dragons can take care of themselves, and Stegoman probably had his reasons for hiding out.

Matt had to admit, it had been a good idea.

"'Tis bad enough to have been cuffed and kicked for our pains," he grumbled, "when we had hoped for silver, and expected copper at least—or dinner, if naught else!"

The captain grinned. "The king is hard to please." He looked up over their heads, frowning. "What noise is that?"

"Critics." Matt sighed. "A disappointed audience. What, are they still shouting after us?"

The captain didn't look all that sure, but one of his men volunteered, "They are naught, Captain. Let us cuff them on their way."

"Aye," another said. "Only a few blows with a truncheon, Captain!"

But an evil grin spread over the captain's face as he looked over the motley crew before him. His eyes sparked as he looked at Yverne and Marian in their shifts, but the hullabaloo inside deterred him, and he only said, "Nay. We shall escort them to the gate. Will it not be pleasant to see them step out?"

His men frowned—but one of them, a little brighter than the rest, suddenly got the idea. His lips spread into a very nasty grin, and he elbowed his fellow, who turned to him, frowning, caught his wink, and suddenly grinned with him.

"Ladies!" The captain gave them a mocking bow and stood aside. "Gentlemen! After you!"

They stepped forward, seeming very uncertain—and Matt knew their hearts were thudding just as his was. The gate? Perfect.

But why were the soldiers so happy to guide them?

Because they knew there was an army of archers outside! They expected the vagabonds to be turned into pincushions!

"That one, at least, is too good to waste," a soldier muttered to his mate as Yverne passed by, pale but resolute.

"Damn your eyes!" the captain barked, and the soldier started with horror. No wonder, considering what words could do here.

They almost made it; it almost went without a hitch. But, about twenty yards from the gate, a man in a dark blue robe sprinkled with zodiacal signs turned to see what was going on—and his eyes locked on Matt.

Matt could feel the sorcerer's magical field probing his own, clashing with his own, saw the man's mouth opening, heard him shout, "Seize them! Slay them! That one is a white wizard!"

The captain jerked to a halt, startled, but Fadecourt knew what to do. He slammed into the officer, bawling, and ran right over him as he fell, diving toward the sorcerer—who made a small motion with his hand as he chanted a quick rhyme, and Fadecourt's trajectory abruptly swerved to miss. Instead, he slammed headlong into the gate.

Almost headlong—he managed to flip over in midair, landed feet first, and bounced to the ground.

Maid Marian was there by that time, heaving at the bar—and Yverne was stepping up to the sorcerer with a seductive smile and saying, "Why do you worry over such nothings? Nay, have you no time for a vagabond lass?"

The sorcerer looked startled, then began an uncertain smile—and Yverne's little fist hooked up in an uppercut, slamming him back against the soldiers behind him.

But another sorcerer stood guard at the gate, and shouted, "Hold!" as he performed some elaborate gestures, ending with finger pointing stiffly at Marian and Fadecourt—who suddenly slowed, almost stopping, the huge bar in their hands.

Matt leaped up between them. The time for secrecy was over. He held up a hand like a traffic cop, shouting,

"Let the blow return unto the giver!
Turn and to its source deliver!"

It didn't quite make sense, but it was enough—Marian and Fadecourt staggered with sudden release as the sorcerer shot back against the wood of the gate. The cyclops and the maid heaved the bar up and out, and Matt shouted,

"Open locks,
Whoever knocks!"

The huge iron lock groaned as its innards turned; Fadecourt and Maid Marian threw their weight against the huge leaves, and the doors boomed open.

Sir Guy was fencing madly with sword and dagger, holding off three guardsmen who were frantically trying to hew their way to the portal, to close the doors. More guards came pounding, and Fadecourt and Marian turned to grapple with them. The maid's staff whirled like a flail, threshing a human crop, and Fadecourt picked up two soldiers at a time, hurling them back against their fellows. Yverne's sword was a blur, holding two soldiers at bay.

But two more minor sorcerers came running, their hands windmilling.

Matt decided to get the jump on them, and started reciting verses of his own—but he could see a veritable human wave building up inside the keep, about to fall on them . . .

Shouts of triumph pealed behind him, but he didn't dare to look until he saw the knights ride past him, men who had fought beside Sir Guy at the siege. Right behind them came a tide of Lincoln green, quarterstaves slamming out to break swords and pates, and a mob of commoners behind them with scythes and staves. Matt was caught up and borne by a human tide. He turned, bobbing in it like a cork, saw Robin's army streaming in through the gates, more soldiers thundering up behind him, and something towering against the sky, but he couldn't make out what it was before he was spun about to face front, as the human river slammed into the tidal wave of guards.

Then, for a few minutes, all was bellowing and screaming and confusion. Crossbow bolts hailed down from the walls, and attacking peasants fell, but so did defenders—the men of evil weren't worried about how many of their own they killed, as long as they wiped out the invaders. But Robin's merry men were already swarming up the stairs to the battlements, leaping on the crossbowmen and dispatching them with well-aimed blows of the quarterstaves. They didn't fire down into the courtyard—too much chance of hitting their own men—but they did blockade the stairs and hold them against the king's troops rushing up to charge them. Quarterstaff met pike in a furious, staccato concerto, and the king's soldiers fell like the spume of a river running into rapids.

The other half of the merry men were following Robin back into the keep, or trying to—guards kept getting in their way. Robin squared off against the big captain; there was a furious clanging of swords; then the captain was falling, and Robin was turning to help Little John against a band of five. His men echoed him; throughout the courtyard, pairs of foresters stood back-to-back, dispatching soldiers left and right. Blood stained the Lincoln green, and here and there a man fell—but very few.

The peasants bellowed with ferocious joy. They had weapons in their hands, and the hated king's livery in front of them; they were busy paying back old scores. Many of them died, but the frenzy was on them, and they scarcely seemed to notice.

"I can't believe it!" Matt stared, then had to turn quickly to parry and cut. But it was incredible—his troops were winning!

Then the king began to call up his reinforcements. With a bellow, a horrendous lion, with the face of a man and several sets of jaws, came stalking out of a tower, roaring. It set upon the peasants, chewing them up and tossing them aside. From the opposing tower, another lion stalked—only this one had wings, and a dragon's tail.

"A manticore and a chimera!" Robin drew his bow. "Aid me, Tuck!"

Friar Tuck gave a last blow of his sword, dispatched an opponent, and made the Sign of the Cross over him as he stepped back, sword down but buckler up, lips moving in a quick prayer for the soul of the fallen man. Then he looked up at the manticore, held up his hilt as a cross, and looked up to Heaven, saying something Matt couldn't hear—but Robin loosed, and his arrow slammed into the manticore's breast. It howled and leaped into the air, clawing and biting at the arrow—and fell back, dead.

Robin drew another arrow—but Matt's attention was diverted by a shout from the walls. Tentacles slapped over the battlements, drawing up after them huge, loathsome forms, half squid and half man, reaching out to catch and crush. The merry men and peasants chopped off arms with swords, but the monsters only hissed in fury and squeezed harder.

But other forms sprang up behind them, small, dark, and darting—and changing form even as they attacked, metamorphosing from seals into naked men who struck with spears taken from dead narwhals.

The squid-men hooted and turned to strike back at them, but the silkies danced back; this was an old and familiar game to them. Matt shouted with delight; the old king of Ys had sent his descendants against the abomination who fouled his waters. The merry men shouted, too, rallying and striking the monsters from behind.

Matt would have loved to watch them turn the squid-men into chowder, but he had to spare some attention for the guardsmen who were trying to carve out his liver. He was just getting them under control when a tearing snarl filled the sky, and defenders and attackers looked up in alarm, then stared in fright. Matt spared a quick glance and saw a host of gnarled dark forms scuttling across the sky, with a clattering of wings. For a moment, he thought he was in *The Wizard of Oz*, looking at winged monkeys—then he saw the faces and realized he'd done the monkeys a grave injustice. The faces were distorted visages out of nightmare—or off the roofs of the Cathedral of Notre Dame. They were more gargoyles come to life, but the flying kind this time, a hundred of them, swarming down at the defenders.

But a tawny streak split the sky, screaming as it dove into the herd of gargoyles, shrieking with rage, catching the monsters in its beak, raking them with its claws in a fury—Narlh, letting himself go without the slightest trace of inhibition, finally striking back at the force that had bled him for so long. But there were many of them, too many, and they pounced on the dracogriff from all sides. He went into a frenzy, snapping and biting all about him—but they were overwhelming him by sheer force of numbers. Matt started to form a spell to help him, but just then, two guards jumped him with whirling pikes, and he had to fall back and pay attention to fighting. When he had knocked them out of the way and cut off their spear heads, he looked back up to see the sky darkening, and felt a thrill of fear at the weather effects the king could call up—until he realized there was something glowing up there, off to the east, something that was growing larger very quickly, with a swarm of darker, huger shapes behind it. "Ghost!" Matt shouted in relief, then turned to parry a halberd, chop off its head, and swat the guard aside with a shield he grabbed up. When he looked up again, the ghost was swooping toward the top of the keep, but the dragons had dived into the battle with all claws out and flames roaring. The gargoyles shrieked as iron-hard scales shouldered them aside and glittering claws raked them from the skies. They fought back with ferocity, biting and clawing, and dragon blood misted the air—but the sorcerers were too busy to try to gather it up.

Ichor was raining, too, though, and gargoyles hurtled down like cannonballs. A shout went up, and guards and invaders danced aside as the skies cleared of enemies, the dragons swooping and roaring. Narlh screamed with delight, in his element at last, on the same side as the dragons.

Then the gargoyle ichor struck, and men howled as it spattered them and burned. With unvoiced accord, the soldiers and attackers both left off fighting and ran for cover.

"Come!" Sir Guy pulled Matt away toward the door of the keep. "This is not your place! Peasants and outlaws can hold only so long against evil magic—you must cut out the corrupted heart of this corpse!"

They turned, but they could scarcely push through the jam-up—with a caustic rain falling from the skies, every man was struggling to get indoors. They shouted and flailed, the king's guards trying to cut their way through, making a din that drowned out the battle above—until a huge roar boomed out, and men screamed and shouted and scrambled aside from the tongues of flame that slashed out at them. Matt stumbled to his feet, facing the door of the keep, and found it filled with a dragon. "Stegoman!" he yelled with relief—just before the merry men caught him up as they streamed through the doors to either side of the dragon, swirling him into the armory where the current broke up into eddies of merry men fighting Gordogrosso's guards.

Matt leaped aside, refusing to let himself be sidetracked. He ducked and dodged between fighting groups, heading for the broad main staircase, some strange compulsion pushing him on and up. There wasn't time! He had to hurry, not forget what the core of this battle was all about. On and upward he ran, up the stairs to find and fight the king. Guards leaped out to challenge him, huge men in rococo armor—but Robin Hood, Maid Marian, and Sir Guy dispatched them with a few cuts and parries each, finding the weak points in their armor that decorations hid. Fadecourt heaved the huge men up and tossed them crashing behind him, where Yverne jabbed between gorget and breastplate with her sword and ran on, her face set into stone, her eyes burning.

Then, suddenly, they were out of the stairwell and into the throne room. Matt stopped, suddenly awed by the huge space and the gloom that clustered above, hiding the dark ceiling—and quailing, for a moment, at the sight of the huge armored figure, a twelve-foot-high ogre with four arms and the ugliest face he could imagine, who bellowed laughter and shouted, "Fools! To think you can come against Gordogrosso the king, and live! Now die!"

Fireballs filled the air, hissing toward each of the companions. Matt shouted,

> "E'en the last ball of fire
> Is faded and done!
> All its blazing companions
> Have flamed out and gone!"

And the balls faded and disappeared before they could reach his friends.

The sorcerer snarled and gestured, shouting a rhyme in a language that seemed to slide around the consonants, hissing and clacking— and a forest of spears sprang up from the floor, shooting toward Matt and his friends.

But Matt was ready for that one. He shouted another verse:

> "Nine and twenty knights of fame,
> Lend your shields to this wide hall!
> That all these spears, with points of shame,
> Shall be deflected, and downward fall!"

A wall of shields suddenly blocked their sight of the throne room; the spears slammed into them and rattled back harmlessly. Then Matt called out,

> "Thanks, nine and twenty knights of fame!
> Take back your shields to whence they came!"

The shields disappeared—but the king was hissing another en- chantment, his fingers weaving sinuous patterns in the air. The spears turned into snakes, writhing toward the companions with fangs bared.

They all had swords; they all started chopping—except Fadecourt, who seized vipers by the handful and threw them back among their fellows. But Matt shouted,

> "At the hole where he came in,
> Red-Eye said to Wrinkle-Skin
> (Hear what little Red-Eye saith!)
> Snake, come out and dance with Death!"

The floor was suddenly filled with small furry bodies, dancing and red-eyed. The snakes turned from the humans to these much more dire threats, hissing and weaving, each faced with a mongoose.

Gordogrosso reddened and howled another spell. The air glittered and glimmered, forms becoming apparent, and Matt watched, waiting with apprehension—and wondered why the huge man didn't wade into physical battle while he was spell-casting.

Unless he wasn't really all that physical?

Then the glittering hardened into a thousand diamond points. Matt saw what was coming, and shouted,

> "The boss comes along, and he says, 'Keep still!
> And come down heavy on a diamond point drill!
> And drill ye Tarriers, drill!'"

The points shot toward the companions like buckshot—but a swarm of men was suddenly there, catching the diamonds out of the sky and slamming them into the stone with sledgehammers.

Gordogrosso barked a command, and the Tarriers disappeared—but so did the diamond points.

Matt managed to get a verse started while he was barking, though.

> "Now is an end to all confusion—
> Now is an end to all illusion!
> What truly is the king, we now shall see,
> For such as we are made of, such we be!"

The king screamed; his huge form grew cloudy and shrank, then was suddenly gone—and in its place was a little, gnarled, ancient figure, hunched over, with a huge nose and thin wisps of mustache. His chin receded so badly that it was scarcely there, and his eyes were glittering beads of malevolence.

"Why, how is this?" Yverne gasped.

"It was illusion," Matt snapped, "the ogre. This is what he *really* is."

"But so old . . ."

"Yes." Matt nodded, with grim certainty. "They were all illusions—Gordogrosso the Second, Third, and Fourth. There was only the one of them, all along—two hundred years old, and more. This is the original usurper we're looking at."

"Then he never was legitimate!"

"Vile creatures!" the ancient screamed. "Stinking traitors!" From out of his gorgeous brocade robes, he drew a shriveled hand that was almost a claw, wrapped around a glowing ring. "Let the hellfire have ye!"

He hurled the ring like a quoit, and as it sailed toward them, it grew larger and larger, settling about the six companions before they could run—and burst into flame.

Its searing heat hit like the belch of a blast furnace. The women screamed as their hair and dresses smoked, and a tongue of flame licked Sir Guy. He howled as the heat conducted through his armor. Fadecourt took a valiant chance; he leaped high, arcing over the tops of the flames toward the king—but a flare shot up and wrapped him in fire. He fell, bellowing in pain, rolling in agony and batting at the tongues.

"They will not die!" the old king cackled in vindictive glee. "'Tis hellfire!"

Inspiration struck, and Matt shouted out,

"The quality of mercy is not strained;
It droppeth as the gentle rain from Heaven
Upon the place beneath: it is twice blessed;
It blesseth him that gives and him that takes;
It is mightiest in the mightiest;
It becomes the throned monarch better than his crown;
It is enthroned in the hearts of kings,
It is an attribute to God himself!"

Moisture filled the huge chamber, condensing and falling in a soft but continuous rain. The fire hissed with the tongues of a thousand snakes, but slackened and died under the rain of mercy—and where the drops touched, charred flesh healed. The ladies cried out in relief, and Fadecourt rolled to his feet with a shuddering sigh.

The king screamed in fury and gestured.

Suddenly, the air was filled with offal.

But Matt had put up with enough. He whipped the wand from his belt and whirled it about his head, shouting a protective spell.

The garbage pelted toward them—and bounced back off the unseen wall of the wand's force.

"Max!" Matt shouted. "Make the monarch need new clothes! Unbind his bonds!"

"As you will, Wizard!" The Demon streaked toward the king, who howled in frustration and batted at the darting spark—but even as he did, his luminous brocade fell apart, leaving him naked. His wrinkled, emaciated body was elongated, with short bowlegs; his arms were much too short for him, ending in claw-hands. Sir Guy and Robin Hood laughed at his nakedness.

The king searched them out with a murderous glare and shouted a spell, directing its energy with both hands cupped toward them.

Sparks sprang up all about the companions, raw energy striking

Matt's wand-shield, coruscating in a million sparks—and growing smaller as the king droned on like a buzz saw in a high, shrill, nasal whine. Matt clamped his jaw and swung the wand more swiftly, putting every ounce of energy into holding the warding circle. It held, but he could feel the strain and knew he couldn't keep this up forever—and defense doesn't win wars. Worse, the king must have been preparing an even more dire spell, because there was suddenly a huge thumping sound, outside but growing closer, as of some huge monster looming toward them . . .

Then the wall caved in.

Blocks of stone shot out into the middle of the room, caroming off the walls and slamming into the floor. The king screamed and whirled, eyes wide, to face this new menace—and the shower of sparks ceased in his distraction.

A huge fist had slammed through the outer wall. It withdrew, and a vast face filled it, calling, "Wizard! I come!"

"Colmain!" Matt shouted, joy filling him at the sight of the ugly face of the giant who was bound to protect the Royal House of Merovence. "And the queen?"

"She comes." The huge face swam away, replaced by the huge hand—but spread flat this time, as a gangplank for the noble horse that sprang through the breach with a bright-haired figure in full armor astride, a blazing sword whirling about her.

The sorcerer screamed, and a hundred guardsmen were suddenly there, looking about them in confusion, then seeing the queen and turning their pikes toward her with a shout—but she howled back, hewing her way through them toward Gordogrosso. Behind her, ladders thumped against the hole, and soldiers started pouring into the throne room. Another knight swung up on the giant's palm and sprang through the hole, cutting his way quickly to Alisande's side. Then the other huge fist slammed through the wall, and stone blocks showered the guards; some fell, crushed, and the others retreated in terror.

It was long enough for Matt to recite the most devastating spell he could think of. He thundered the verse, wand leveled toward Gordogrosso, directing the spell. The ancient sorcerer spun to face him, eyes wide in horror as the magic bounded into his mind, restoring the conscience that he had so long ago expunged and giving him an instant and starkly truthful view of himself and his actions. "Nooooo!" the king screeched, falling to his knees with his fists knotted in his hair. "I cannot have been so vile a man! A pollution upon the earth! A desecration in creation! Ah, let me undo it! Give me the time back, the years that I have despoiled with my cruelty!"

"What magic is this?" Sir Guy cried, staring.

"The only real check on the worst parts of human nature," Matt said grimly. "It's called the 'moral impulse'!"

"I repent me!" the king shouted, tearing off his crown and hurling it from him. "I abjure the throne! I will divest me of all my ill-gotten gains! I will say where the true crown of Ibile is buried, that it may be bestowed upon a rightful king!"

The crown exploded.

It burst into dark, roiling smoke shot through with flames, a huge towering cloud that boiled up to the ceiling and churned in upon itself, with the flame at its heart hardening and forming into the shape of a vast, fiery rat.

"A demon!" Yverne shrieked.

"No, no, my master!" Gordogrosso howled. "I did not mean it, I but prattled without thought!"

But a huge, claw-tipped finger jabbed down at him out of the cloud, and the giant rat boomed, "You have failed! Enough, Gordogrosso! You swore to bring Hell on earth, and you have brought nought but nightmare!" A huge hand followed the finger, opening and wrapping itself around the huddled form of the king.

"No, master, no!" the king shrieked. "I will not repent, I will not do good! I swear it! I will be your faithful servant, as I have ever been! I will defile, I will forswear, I will betray!"

"You are forsworn already, and have betrayed me!" The huge snout opened, revealing a fiery maw lined with steel dagger-teeth. The clawed paw lifted the screaming king and pushed him, with deliberation, into the flaming mouth. Steel teeth clashed shut; the demon swallowed.

Then its whole form burst into flame, and it turned, bellowing, "What my servant has failed to do, I will effect! You, Wizard, shall die in the torment of flame—and you also, cyclops! You, maiden!"

Flaming claws reached for them.

Sir Guy shouted and darted in front of Yverne, but the vast paw knocked him aside as the demon snarled like nails on glass.

"No!" Matt leaped in front of Yverne and leveled the wand. "I don't know why you're picking her out, but you can't have her! Back off!"

The rat-demon bellowed, "So much the easier! Two in one catch!" and reached for them with wicked laughter.

"Never!" Alisande kicked her horse; it shied away, so she leaped to the ground, planting herself in front of Matt. "Avaunt thee!"

The demon's cackling filled the hall. "Richer and richer!" The huge paw scooped toward them, the other reaching out for Fadecourt . . .

Then the ghost appeared, a pale wraith in the light of the fire—but the being behind him was a blaze of light that burned white against the orange of the flames, and its voice was a trumpet blast. "Get thee gone, devil! Thou mayest have no place here! As the Almighty commanded thee, begone! Get back to thine own place, and burn!"

The demon shrieked, rearing back, its whole face contorted by rage—but the glowing figure snapped out an arm, forefinger pointing, and a searing beam of white light shot out, spearing the demon through the brain, then moving downward inexorably. The rat-devil screamed and disappeared in an explosion that deafened them all as it passed. Then it was gone, only a charred circle on the floor showing where it had stood.

They turned to look, but the glowing presence was gone, too.

The whole room was silent.

Then Yverne began to weep, softly, and Sir Guy gathered her in his arms.

"Gentlemen, uncover," Friar Tuck said into the hush. "We have been blessed with a visitation of spirit who dwells in the presence of God, a holy saint—the patron of this land."

"Saint Iago!" Alisande breathed.

Friar Tuck nodded. "Know that, in two supernatural entities of equal rank, the good one will ever be more powerful than the evil. The demon knew all was lost, but it had nothing further to lose by the attempt, so it manifested itself and sought to do, by its own force, what its agents had failed in yet again. But God has forbidden the spawn of Hell to interfere themselves in human matters—we mortals must be left to work out our destinies for ourselves, to choose salvation or damnation as we will. Therefore did God send one of His saints as a channel for His own Power, that Grace might stand against Evil—and, as it always must, Grace stood triumphant. For Good is stronger than Evil, and will always win in the end."

The people stood in silence, dazzled by what they had seen, exalted and humbled at the same time, and rejoicing that they had been there to see it.

CHAPTER 29

Masks and Matches

The air was split by a howl. Shocked, the crowd turned to see who had cried.

Fadecourt was up on the dais, hurling the cushions away from the throne, searching all about on his hands and knees, sifting through the dust that had been the king's robes, howling, "Where is it? Where? It cannot have been turned to powder with his robes! It cannot have burned with him—he was naked!" He leaped to his feet. "His workroom! It will be in his workroom!"

"His workroom was here," muttered a stunned guard. "He never moved from out of this chamber."

Matt looked up, startled; he'd have to check for warding spells.

"Then 'tis yon!" Fadecourt ran toward a tapestry, yanked it down. There was only blank wall, so he yanked down another, and another.

"Has he lost his wits?" Sir Guy said in a low voice.

"Assuredly, the sight of the demon has driven him mad," Maid Marian said. "Wizard, can you cure—"

"'Tis here!" Fadecourt tore down another tapestry with a cry of triumph, revealing a long workbench with towering shelves above it. He leaped up onto the table and began to yank at jar after jar, scanning the labels, then hurling them aside. Glass crashed, pottery shattered. Dark and noisome things littered the floor; stench filled the air.

"Wizard, stop him!" Robin Hood coughed. "He will poison us all!"

Matt hated to do it, but he thought up a spell to sedate the cyclops—it was just a matter of time before he broke a jar that held some really toxic charm . . .

Then Fadecourt held up a small jar with a cry of triumph. "I have found it! 'Tis mine again!"

They all stared, trying to make out what was in the jar, but all they could see was a murky fluid with a lump floating in it.

Fadecourt yanked the lid off and scooped out the lump. Yverne cried out, but before they could stop him, he had pressed it against his forehead.

"He is surely demented!" Sir Guy moaned—but Yverne gasped, staring.

For Fadecourt was growing.

Growing, and swelling—his huge muscles redistributing them-selves, the stone of his arm becoming living flesh, and his single eye moving over to leave room for the lump where Fadecourt had set it. As they stared, it came alive, gaining luster, and sank into his skin, the bone hollowing itself into a new socket—and two eyes stared out at them. Fadecourt cried out in pain, but also in triumph—and he stood before them, tall and straight, a normal human man, arms up-raised in thanks. The ghost hovered beside, smiling.

This man was still very muscular, though—and very handsome. Alisande and Yverne both blinked, then stood a little straighter, and Maid Marian purred, "What a fine figure of a man is this!"

"Not too fine, I trust?" Robin looked up sharply.

"None could ever compare to you, my lord," she answered, taking his arm. "But I rejoice to see the man returned to his natural form."

"But *is* it his natural form?" Matt frowned. "Let's have it, Fadecourt! What happened? And what does the ghost have to do with this?"

"Call me not Fadecourt, friend Matthew," the tall man said, still in the cyclops' voice. He grinned as he jumped down to the floor. "That is the name the sorcerer gave me, in mockery, when he stole my eye by his magic. Call me the name I was given at birth—Rinaldo del Beria."

"The prince!" Alisande cried. "The rightful heir to Ibile, dead these many years!"

"Nay, lady and Majesty, to whom I stand in debt." The prince turned and bowed to her. "I had gone into hiding, many years ago, when still a child—and those who loved me gave out news that I was dead, the better to protect me till I was grown. But the sorcerer set hounds upon me, single-minded sorcerers, who rested not till they had found me. Then his soldiers came to take me prisoner, though I slew a dozen of them—I was no child then, but a man grown, though very young—and haled me here, to the king's throne room, there to transform me into a shape that my countrymen would never honor as a king."

"Thanks be to Heaven he did not slay you!" Yverne cried.

"Thanks to Heaven, indeed—but he said he would gain magical strength by my living in humiliation, and spurned me from him with his foot. My eye he kept as a charm—and I thank Heaven again, that he had not yet seen fit to use it in a potion! All these years since, I have sought a means of overthrowing him—and thanks to yon knight and the Lord Wizard, I have found it!"

"Yet here is a pretty mess." Sir Guy had turned somber, but he said the words as one who has to do a duty he would rather shirk. "This lady is the daughter of the Duke of Toumarre, the only lord left who was not one of the sorcerer's pawns, and great-great-grandchild of the last king! She is the rightful heir!"

Alisande looked as if she were about to ask how Sir Guy knew, but she held her peace; nobody really doubted the Black Knight's word, or wondered about the source of his knowledge.

They all turned to stare at Yverne.

"'Tis true," she said. "'Twas not for my father's lands alone, that the sorcerer and the Duke Bruitfort wished to catch me."

"Bruitfort!" Alisande turned and beckoned to her knights. They parted, and two of their number hustled a man to the front and hurled him to the floor at the queen's feet.

"The duke!" Yverne gasped.

"Even so," Alisande said. "The wicked duke, none other, whose castle I invested whiles he lay unconscious, and his men rode willy-nilly in search of something that had evaded them."

Bruitfort looked up at them, drawn and forlorn, his massive shoulders slumped, his arms and legs loaded with chains. He looked about him, saw the final death of all his ambitions, and turned gray.

"Speak, sirrah!" Alisande commanded. "Is't true, what the maiden says? Did you seek her hand to assist you to the throne?"

The duke looked up, read the death notice in her face, and said, "Aye. Her claim is legitimate; she is the rightful heir. Thereby would I have gained the people's favor, as I sought to overthrow the sorcerer!"

"Wait a minute." Matt frowned. "Somebody else seems to have some doubts."

They all followed his gaze and saw the ghost, standing by the throne, shaking his head violently, looking appalled.

"He does not wish it—and, since he is party to the wisdom of the Afterworld, I should think he has good reason." Fadecourt, now Prince Rinaldo, turned back to Sir Guy. "I, too, am the great-great-grandchild of the former king, Sir Guy, and by the male line."

"She, too, is of the male line, and of the elder branch," Sir Guy said. "Milady, tell them your lineage."

Yverne looked at him with wide, frightened eyes—almost hurt, Matt thought—but she spoke. "Tomas, the last rightful king, had two sons. Of the elder am I descended, for he was my father's father's father's father's father."

"And I am descended from his younger son." Prince Rinaldo frowned. "From the elder sons of the younger son."

"But of the cadet branch nonetheless—and here's a stew!" Alisande looked from the one to other, frowning. "The lady is of the elder's line, but is herself a woman—and the male line holds strongest claim! While the prince is of the cadet branch, but is a man!"

"Their claims are equal." Sir Guy's mood seemed to be lightening. The ghost drifted forward, making hand signals, pantomiming.

"She." Matt frowned, following the pointing fingers. "He . . . *and* she?"

The ghost joined his two hands in front of him.

"He means that they should wed!" Alisande cried. "Aye, here's the way to unravel the coil! Two claims of equal strength, united—and Ibile's throne is secure! None could doubt that their offspring would be rightful heirs!"

Sir Guy turned away, looking thunderous.

Yverne glanced at him, then turned back to Alisande, wide-eyed. "By your leave, Majesty—I had liefer abdicate."

"Abdicate?" Alisande stared. So did Rinaldo—wounded.

"I will forswear my claim to the throne." Yverne lowered her eyes demurely. "I will forswear it for myself, and for all heirs of my body that I may bear."

"Why, how is this, lady?" Prince Rinaldo cried, woebegone. "You cannot wander homeless!"

"She cannot, nor can she take up again her father's estates, for her mere presence within Ibile will be a focus for discontent, and an impetus toward rebellion," Alisande said. "Lady, you must wed or be exiled."

"Then I shall be an exile," Yverne answered, without a moment's hesitation. "I shall retire to some hidden hermitage where none shall ever find me, provided . . ." She glanced up at Sir Guy's back.

"Provided?" Alisande prompted. "What is this proviso? Mind you, the idea itself is excellent—you would be removed from contention for the throne, but you, or your heirs, might be found if there were need. But what is your proviso?"

"That Sir Guy de Toutarien shall escort me to my place of exile," Yverne said, "and shall himself choose that hiding place, so that none other may ever know of it."

Sir Guy looked up in surprise.

Yverne met his eyes, then looked down and blushed.

Prince Rinaldo stood taken aback, amazed, elated—and crestfallen. "Milady, do not! 'Twould be hard, immensely hard on you, to be shut away from the world so, never to return to your home! You are too vibrant, too filed with joy of life, and take too much delight in company to endure such solitude! And will there not still be the promise of rebellion? For no one will believe that anyone would willingly give up a kingdom to become a hermit! I am your friend, at least, and would not see you miserable!"

"I will not be miserable," she said quietly, and glanced at Sir Guy.

He met her gaze, and his face fairly glowed. She blushed again and lowered her eyes once more, but he did not take his gaze from her face.

"What say you, Sir Knight?" Alisande demanded. "Will you escort the lady hence, far from Ibile, and find her a hermitage secure? Will you swear never to reveal it to any soul, living or dead?"

"I will," Sir Guy said, "and will ever keep faith with her!"

Rinaldo looked woebegone, and Matt's heart went out to him. To labor so long on the slenderest of hopes, to be exalted with victory one second, and cast down to despair the next!

"All wounds shall mend," Friar Tuck said gently, "those of this land—and those of its people. All wounds shall mend, and joy shall fill them once again."

"Mine, too?" Alisande turned slowly to Matt. "And yours, Lord Wizard? Nay, have you cast me so much into grief that your own is assuaged? Have you healed the hurt to your vanity by the wounds you have given my heart? Are you so loftly now, knowing that you have trod on a queen? Are you—"

"My lady, enough!" Matt stepped forward, hope budding in his heart. "You mean you *care*?"

"Care! Would I have fought my way across all of Ibile, aye, and grieved my soldiers and their wives, and all of Merovence belike, if I did not *care*? Would I have gnawed out my heart, hollowed my breast, stained my cheeks with rivers of . . . Oh!" She caught his arms in a fierce, iron-coated grip. "Matthew! I was so a-frighted that harm would come to you, that I would find your tattered corpse, that I would come too late . . . or that you might . . . might have . . ."

"I didn't." After all, she was a queen, and in public—but the last thing Matt would have wanted would have been to see her humiliated, even if they'd been in private. He looked long and deeply into her eyes and wished he would never have to look away. "I'm still here," he murmured. "I'll always be here—and I'm free of my rash oath now, free to take another. Only this time, I'll mean it."

She stared at him, her face paling. Then, abruptly, she let go of him and turned away, her face reddening.

But Matt understood, now, the pride of a queen. He smiled and couldn't take his eyes off her.

There was a huge hullabaloo from the hole in the wall.

Everybody spun about just in time to see three huge forms hurtle past and hear voices saying:

"Let me be, I tell you!"

"Nay! Thou art wounded sore!"

"Not as sore as your head! Look, I can fly—see?"

"He does not fall quite so fast, 'tis true . . ."

"He cannot lift. We must!"

The three forms pulled back into sight—two dragons with a dracogriff in the middle.

"I can land, at least!" Narlh squawked. "Let go—I can land!"

"Don't listen to him!" Matt called. "Bring him inside!"

The dracogriff was horribly burned. Wing feathers were scorched all along his left side, and large patches of his hide were missing. He squalled in sudden pain. "Easy, there! Y' didn't have to jam me against the stones, y'know!"

"I regret," Stegoman huffed. "'Tis so small a hole, do you see . . . Aside, small and soft ones! Our comrade is wounded; we must come unto the wizard who can cure him!"

"Aside!" Alisande called. "Stand aside! Let them pass!"

The soldiers crowded back, opening up an aisle from the stairwell—and two huge dragons limped into sight, Stegoman and a stranger. Between them, supported by their upraised wings, growling and protesting and complaining every inch of the way, limped Narlh.

"Look, I . . . I can make it on my own . . . all . . . all right? I . . . don't need any help, I . . . Ouch! Go easy, there!"

"Narlh!" Matt cried. "You're wounded!"

"A scratch," the dracogriff snapped. "A little burn. So what? Look, it's not as if I can't fly, y'know!"

"He cannot," Stegoman explained to Matt. "He has chased off the last of the gargoyles—in truth, I should say he fought half of them himself."

"He is a doughty fighter," the other dragon said in tones of awe, "and wondrous in his valor. He is a source of great pride to us, that the blood of dragons flows in his veins!"

"I just did what I had to," Narlh muttered, lowering his eyes.

"As do any of us! But thou didst fight, with never a thought for thine own safety—or life! Nay, thou shalt dwell in honor in Dragondom for as long as thou shalt wish, whenever thou dost wish! We shall be elevated by thy presence."

Narlh looked up at Matt, an incredulous joy in his eyes.

"The last was the most huge," Stegoman explained to Matt. "He was half again my bulk, and his wings were granite. He struck me with them, battered me, would have knocked me out of the sky—had not this berserker pounced upon him with a scream of fury, struck at him again and again, enduring his flailing attack and his flame whiles the dragon folk beset the gargoyle and tore him apart. I take my life from thee this day, Narlh! I will be mightily honored if thou wilt let me claim brotherhood with thee, among all Dragondom."

"Well . . . if you really *want* to . . ."

"Let's see to those wounds first," Matt said briskly.

"By your leave, Lord Wizard." Friar Tuck stepped forward. "I have some small skill at this. Good monsters, will you step aside with me?"

"Awright, awright!" Narlh grumbled. "Just make it fast!"

Matt grinned and turned back to his favorite view, Alisande's eyes. "Looks as if we came out of it all right, Majesty."

"Aye," she said, returning his gaze, full depth. "We have."

There was a sudden fanfare. Everyone looked around, startled—nobody had a trumpet to his lips. They looked at the throne . . .

And saw the ghost, standing beside the gilded chair, beckoning to Prince Rinaldo.

"Why, I know you now!" the prince cried. "Ever since I first saw you, I have known I had seen the resemblance to your face before!"

"Yeah—in a mirror." Matt looked from one to the other. Allowing for age and another fifty pounds, the family resemblance was unmistakable.

"'Tis Tomas!" Rinaldo cried. "'Tis the last rightful king!"

The ghost hung his head.

"Why do you stand ashamed! You have done naught to regret!"

The ghost looked up, tears streaming from his eyes, and Sir Guy, that repository of all the lore of this alternate Europe, said softly, "He has—though he has now, at long last, set it aright. For look you, Tomas IV was a kind king, a just king, a good king—but the legend speaks of him as unbearably clumsy. He was ever stumbling, spilling, lurching about—"

"Still kind of clumsy, about his materializations." Matt frowned. "Though lately he does seem to be getting them right, his timing could be better . . ."

"Regrettably," the Black Knight said, "his clumsiness extended to matters military, and therefore did he not trust in his own instincts. He took for a counselor the infamous Gordogrosso, who advised him to be less harsh in his soldiers' training, and to keep fewer men under arms. King Tomas hearkened to these false words, and when his army was weakened, the sorcerer brought in his own hellish troops to seize power. He cut off King Tomas' head and threw his body into the dungeons, that his humiliation might be complete—for the good king did not live long enough to be shut living in a cell."

"And he blamed himself for Ibile's fall to the powers of Evil, so he's been hanging around ever since, looking for a chance to kick out the sorcerer!" Matt cried.

The poor ghost nodded, then looked up, brightening.

"And we gave him that chance." Sir Guy clapped Matt on the shoulder. "Now he can lie in peace."

But, "No," Friar Tuck said, "not till he has had Christian burial."

"Why, that shall he have!" Prince Rinaldo cried. "It shall be my first act as king, the building of his tomb, and his poor remains shall have a solemn burial with the honors due a hero! You shall be free, Majesty, free to find your way to Heaven!"

The ghost turned a radiant smile upon his descendant.

CHAPTER 30

Leave it to Fates

The choir broke into song, and the Dies Irae rang through the lofty dome of the huge cathedral. The crowd standing before the altar separated as people stood back to make room, opening an aisle from the altar to the doors, and the Archbishop followed the pallbearers down the length of the nave with an altar boy swinging a censer before and two more carrying candles behind.

Matt glanced to each side as he carried his corner of the coffin, impressed all over again by the number of faces lining each side of the long center aisle. He had really been startled, two days ago, when so many had trooped into the huge church and begun scouring the dirt and graffiti from its pillars. Then he had looked again and realized that most of them were poor, dirt poor. Many were beggars; many more bore the marks of the king's justice: a missing finger or ear, or even a limb. For two hundred years, so many people had kept their faith in God! Even though they were crushed into the dirt for it. But there were more substantial citizens there, too, the burghers and master craftsmen, who had given aid and shelter to their less fortunate fellow parishioners; for all, all, had been driven to worship in seclusion and keep their faith secret for so many, many years.

But now the cathedral was clean again, and whitewashed, with new linens on the altar and a new carpet before it. A crucifix stood over the sanctuary again, albeit it was made of wood, and had been quickly carved; and priests followed the Archbishop down the aisle.

It was flabbergasting, how many priests had risked slow death by torture to keep ministering to their flocks, well hidden—but Friar Tuck had found out a dozen of them within twenty-four hours, and others had stepped forward. It was even more astounding that young men had chosen to become priests under such circumstances—though Alisande had told him that Merovence had sent its share of missionaries to the benighted land. Incredible, that men who could have dwelt securely and in comfort at home should be willing to condemn themselves to a life of fear and misery, should risk death and torture, all because they had felt a call from God!

Of course, Matt had done that, too—but he hadn't been watching his language.

They marched in solemn procession down the full length of the nave, then back up a side aisle to one of the many chapels that opened off the passageway behind the altar—a chapel that bore the catafalques of dead kings and queens.

One of these low tombs was open.

As the priests intoned the De Profundis, the pallbearers lowered the coffin into the empty tomb, then stood back as the masons spread mortar and hefted the huge stone cover back into place. The Archbishop said a final blessing, and the procession returned to the main altar, where the prelate blessed the congregation and sent them forth. Then he left the altar, and Matt and the other pallbearers—Sir Guy, Prince Rinaldo, Robin Hood, and three of the knights who had stood by Sir Guy—filed down the aisle to a chamber near the door.

There, though, they doffed their black cloaks and robes and put on clothes resplendent with scarlet and gold. Then Matt and Sir Guy turned to help Prince Rinaldo with his coronation robes.

He seemed somber, nervous. "I am not worthy of this honor, Lord Wizard."

"You are," Sir Guy said, with such total certainty that the prince looked up at him, astonished. "You have proved your worth in adversity, in suffering, in loyalty to a cause that seemed lost, and in striving when all seemed hopeless. You have been tried in the flames and found worthy."

Prince Rinaldo looked directly into his eyes and nodded slowly. "I thank you, my friend. I shall do all that I may, not to disappoint you."

"'Tis not myself to whom you must answer," the Black Knight said, "but to God, and your people."

Not quite true, Matt knew—but Prince Rinaldo didn't. He didn't know that Sir Guy was the descendant and legitimate heir of

Hardishane, the emperor who had brought all of Europe into his empire five hundred years before. If any living man knew who had the right to rule and who didn't, it was Sir Guy de Toutarien—for he had the right, but chose not to assert it. Instead, he had spent his life laboring unseen and unknown, to prevent the dominion of evil that would require his ancestor to wake and reestablish the Empire.

The choir's massed voice rang out again, but this time in a joyful hymn.

"Your people call," Sir Guy said.

Prince Rinaldo swallowed heavily and turned to the door.

Down the aisle they marched, with Sir Guy bearing the scepter and Matt carrying the true crown—found buried in the deepest dungeon and restored to its rightful place. Before them walked Alisande, garbed in gold and purple, her cloak bordered with ermine, every inch a queen.

The throne stood on the altar now, with the Archbishop behind it. Prince Rinaldo stepped up to it, but turned to his people, not yet sitting.

Alisande turned to face the crowd. "It is not the custom for one monarch to present another to his people," she cried, "but all King Tomas' noblemen are dead, and their descendants only newly come from obscurity to their estates. One alone of the old houses has remained in his demesne. Milord!"

The Don de la Luce, blinking and round-shouldered, stepped up to the altar and stood blinking at the huge crowd before him, bemused.

"You have abided in faith, though you suffered in loneliness," Alisande cried. "To you belongs the honor."

But the old don shook his head and held out his hand. Yverne stepped up and took it; then both turned to Alisande, with a curtsy and a bow, and stepped aside.

She looked from the one to the other, then back at the people. "They will have me speak for them. Look, then, upon the faithful lords who are left to you! Lords, look upon your people! O faithful of Ibile, who have kept troth with your God and your royal line through centuries of adversity, look now upon your king!"

She turned, one hand outspread, and the choir burst into song.

Rinaldo sat then, ramrod straight, hands gripping the throne, eyes on his people—as the Archbishop took the crown from Matt and lowered it onto the prince's head.

Then Yverne turned and knelt before the throne, took Rinaldo's hand, and swore fealty to him, acknowledging him as her suzerain.

• • •

The celebration was still going on, and the new king had to wave to the cheering throngs that lined the way as he rode with Sir Guy and Yverne to the great gates that guarded the town. At his signal, the porters opened the huge leaves. Then the king, who had been Fadecourt, took the maiden's hand. "I had liefer you stayed to rule with me, a queen of Ibile."

"I thank your Majesty." Yverne lowered her eyes. "I will ever be your true vassal and will come if you have need of me—but my destiny lies elsewhere."

"I had feared as much." King Rinaldo turned to clap Sir Guy on the shoulder. "I need not bid you ward her well—she could have no more stalwart a guardian. But I can bid you find a priest together, ere you have journeyed too far along your road." For a moment, Fadecourt's insouciance lit his eyes again. "Or I'll pry you out of your armor with my own hands!"

"I warrant your Majesty." Sir Guy inclined his head gravely.

"Farewell, comrade-at-arms!" Rinaldo clasped him by the shoulders. "I will miss your wise council, your good cheer!" He turned to Yverne. "Farewell, milady! Whom I shall never leave off missing."

"I pray," she said softly, "that there shall come a one who shall make you forget me."

He only gazed at her, as if to say it was impossible; but all he said aloud was, "Farewell, good friends both!"

Alisande nodded to her heralds, and the trumpets pealed. Sir Guy and Yverne rode forth beyond the gate, turned back to wave once, then rode away side by side.

Now Rinaldo turned to the two huge monsters who stood flanking the gate. "You need not go, lordly ones! Ever will there be welcome for you, in Orlequedrille!"

"I thank your Majesty," Stegoman rumbled, "but we must needs see the knight and his lady safely to the mountains, that none of the Free Folk seek to harm them as they pass through—and I must needs take this orphan back to his long home, that his people may honor him as ever they should have done."

"Orphan!" Narlh said indignantly. "So what are you, my papa?"

"And your mother, too, if ever thou hast need of our care," Stegoman returned, "though I would liefer be your brother."

"Yeah, I'd love it." But Narlh's eye glinted. "Gonna find someone to be my godfather?"

"I do not doubt that my sire will delight at the honor. You shall be acclaimed as the dragon you are, and all shall hail your name, for my kin have gone before us to the land of the Free Folk, to spread word of your glory."

Matt wondered about sibling rivalry.

Stegoman's jaw lolled open in a grin. "Come, god-sib! The road is long, and already the knight and lady have the long start! Majesty, farewell! And Majesty of Merovence—again, till I see thee once more, God be with thee!"

Then, wonder of wonders, both monsters managed something resembling a bow. They rose, turned, and went off after the couple on horseback, as the trumpets rang out once again. Alisande signaled, and the huge portals closed.

King Rinaldo turned back, blinking only twice, and saw Robin Hood and his band standing before him. "Will you, too, leave me?"

"Aye, when we weary of peace and soft living." Robin smiled. "Yet we will accept your hospitality some little while longer, till we see you secure with a loyal band of knights and men about you, and lords to keep your countryside secure."

Rinaldo clasped the outlaw on the shoulder. "Why, then, I shall have to see to the fomenting of rebellions! Maid, I thank you for your good intercession."

"Pooh, Majesty," Marian answered. "He would have thought of it himself, in time."

Rinaldo turned to Alisande. "You, though, I cannot importune. Your kingdom cannot endure too long without you."

"Even so," she agreed. "Another day, and I, too, must leave you."

"Ibile shall ever be friend to Merovence, while I live!" Rinaldo swore. "I cannot repay what you have done for me!"

"There shall come a chance," she said evenly. "For the nonce, you might speak to your comrade of the duties he owes his sovereign."

"Duties!" Matt squawked. "When have I ever been less than totally faithful to you? When?"

She favored him with her best glare. "Why, when you went dancing off to Ibile and left me to mourn!"

Matt's defenses melted. "Well. I'm glad to know you weren't celebrating."

"Celebrating! My love and my life! How could I ever be aught but grim, when you are not by me!"

Matt bowed his head, then looked up with a forced and weary smile. "It's not that I don't believe you . . ."

Alisande's face hardened. "A queen cannot lie!"

"Not about public matters, no . . ."

"Majesty," Prince Rinaldo said softly.

She froze, then turned to him slowly. "Aye, Majesty?"

"If you love him," one of her few peers in the whole world said, "why do you not marry him?"

She stared at him so long that Matt was afraid the silence would crack. But she finally answered, low-voiced, "You know well, sovereign Majesty, that we of royal blood may not marry as we choose. I cannot wed a man who was not born a lord."

"Not so," the king contradicted, with Fadecourt's old glint in his eye. "Your duty as queen is to marry so as to strengthen your kingdom—and to give your heirs noble blood, that will make them worthy monarchs."

She stared at him, paling—but she nodded slowly. "Even so. Thus much do we learn at our sires' knees."

"And Lord Matthew's magic strengthens Merovence," Rinaldo said. "Indeed, who should know that better than I, who was a gnarled cyclops, a creature of contempt, but who am now made a king, through his wizardry and your force of arms? And how should Merovence fare without his enchantments?"

Alisande seemed suddenly unsure; she glanced at Matt out of the corner of her eye.

"To wed him would be a diplomatic victory unparalleled," the king murmured, "for it would bind him to the service of Merovence for all his life."

Alisande bit her lip, suddenly vulnerable, suddenly very much a woman. "There is merit in what you say. But all of tradition, the weight of common law—"

Rinaldo saw her uncertainty. "Good friar!" he called.

Friar Tuck looked up, surprised. "Aye, Majesty?"

"This poor woman stands in need of such magic as her wizard cannot provide—the more so since he is the source of her quandary. Do you give her aid!"

"Why, that I will." Tuck joined his hands and raised his eyes to Heaven. "Father above, help this poor woman to know both her heart, and Your will! Send her some sign that will show us her fate!"

There was a clap of thunder, and everyone drew back in horror—for three women stood between the two monarchs suddenly, one spinning, another measuring, and a third standing with shears poised—but all three had young, beautiful faces now.

"What!" Clotho cried, staring at Matt. "Is it not enough that you have repaired the damage you did us! Must you torture us again? We shall not brook more of your impudence, I warn—"

"Sister." Atropos nudged with her elbow. "'Tis not he who seeks us, but the woman."

"What?" Clotho glanced up at Alisande and said, irritated, "Well, follow your heart, woman! Or has your crown squeezed out your brain?"

"Not her brain, but her heart," Lachesis pointed out. "She hesitates to follow the course of love, for fear it will not be the course of wisdom."

"Wisdom, forsooth!" Clotho scoffed. "Where can there be wisdom, when folk speak of wedding? None of you mortals can see the future! But this much shall I tell you, damsel—you shall wed this man, will you or nill you, though you may take years to settling on it! And when you have wed, you shall bear two children—a son and a daughter who, together, shall lead all of Europe into an age of peace, prosperity, and devotion."

Alisande sat stiff and said through numb lips, "She speaks truth. My sovereign's heart has felt it—and my woman's heart aches for it!" She whirled to Matt. "I shall wed you, Wizard, if you still wish it!"

"Wish it? I'd die for it!" Matt grabbed her and, forgetting about her royal dignity, kissed her right there in front of all the people.

They cheered.

Alisande was rigid for a few moments, then forgot about the people and melted into the kiss.

Prince Rinaldo finally smiled again.

They came out of the kiss, moving a little apart, staring at each other in surprise and wonder.

Then Matt whirled to Friar Tuck. "Good father! Marry us, quickly!"

"What, on the instant?" Tuck asked, his eyes round.

"Yes! Right now this instant! Before she changes her mind!"

ABOUT THE AUTHOR

"A wandering Catholic, aye,
A thing of texts and catches."

Early in life, Christopher Stasheff found a catch in almost every point of Catholic dogma except the main ones, and has been spiritually wandering ever since. He has a lot of doubts about the Church, but only questions about the Faith.

One day, he realized that most of the medieval fantasies he read seldom mentioned the Devil, and never God. He vehemently maintained that wasn't the way medieval Christians really saw the world—they saw God everywhere, in everything, and the Devil always lurking, looking for an opening—and that authors really ought to write their fantasies a little closer to reality. Then he realized that, being a fantasy author, he was stuck with writing his next story that way.

He spent his early childhood in Mount Vernon, New York, but spent the rest of his formative years in Ann Arbor, Michigan. He has always had difficulty distinguishing fantasy from reality and has tried to compromise by teaching college. He tends to prescript his life, but can't understand why other people never get their lines right. This causes a fair amount of misunderstanding with his wife and four children. He seeks refuge in fantasy worlds of his own making and hopes you enjoy them as much as he does.